"Against a richly historical and violent backdrop, McCarty deftly weaves a surprisingly moving love story that demands a skillful writer's touch. Her exquisite prose makes this a book readers will treasure."

—*RT Book Reviews*

"The characters leap off the pages and into your heart. With a stunning plot that has enough twists and turns in all the right places, McCarty has created yet another captivating story that is sure to please!"

—*Fresh Fiction*

"Passion and politics abound in this exceptionally well-researched romance that skillfully interweaves fiction with history and sheds new light on a particularly fascinating and violent time."

—*Library Journal*

"Readers who deplore 'wallpaper historicals' will appreciate not only the romance but McCarty's efforts to go beyond the superficialities of historical Scotland."

—*Publishers Weekly*

"Spectacularly entertaining. . . . McCarty is a master of blending fact and fiction."

—*Romance Junkies*

"One of those amazing books that captures your attention right from the get-go. . . . McCarty has written a tale fit for a king."

—*Coffee Time Romance*

"Thoroughly enjoyable. . . . Cleverly interwoven plot twists . . . kept me on my toes!"

—*The Romance Reviews*

OTHER BOOKS IN MONICA McCARTY'S
HIGHLAND GUARD SERIES

MONICA McCARTY

The Rock

Pocket Books

New York   London   Toronto   Sydney   New Delhi

Pocket Books
An Imprint of Simon & Schuster, Inc.
1230 Avenue of the Americas
New York, NY 10020

This book is a work of fiction. Any references to historical events, real people, or real places are used fictitiously. Other names, characters, places, and events are products of the author's imagination, and any resemblance to actual events or places or persons, living or dead, is entirely coincidental.

First Pocket Books paperback edition December 2015

POCKET and colophon are registered trademarks of Simon & Schuster, Inc.

For information about special discounts for bulk purchases, please contact Simon & Schuster Special Sales at 1-866-506-1949 or business@simonandschuster.com.

The Simon & Schuster Speakers Bureau can bring authors to your live event. For more information or to book an event, contact the Simon & Schuster Speakers Bureau at 1-866-248-3049 or visit our website at www.simonspeakers.com.

Interior design by Leydiana Rodríguez

Manufactured in the United States of America

10 9 8 7 6 5 4 3 2 1

ISBN 978-1-5011-0878-5
ISBN 978-1-5011-0880-8 (ebook)

For Jami.
Rain, sleet, or snow? The postal service has nothing on you! Thank you for being the first reader of every one of my books—even when life doesn't make it easy. You are the best.

THE HIGHLAND GUARD

TOR "CHIEF" MACLEOD: Team Leader and Expert Swordsman

ERIK "HAWK" MACSORLEY: Seafarer and Swimmer

LACHLAN "VIPER" MACRUAIRI: Stealth, Infiltration, and Extraction

ARTHUR "RANGER" CAMPBELL: Scouting and Reconnaissance

GREGOR "ARROW" MACGREGOR: Marksman and Archer

MAGNUS "SAINT" MACKAY: Survivalist and Weapon Forging

KENNETH "ICE" SUTHERLAND: Explosives and Versatility

EOIN "STRIKER" MACLEAN: Strategist in "Pirate" Warfare

EWEN "HUNTER" LAMONT: Tracker and Hunter of Men

ROBERT "RAIDER" BOYD: Physical Strength and Hand-to-Hand Combat

ALSO: HELEN "ANGEL" MACKAY (NÉE SUTHERLAND): Healer

FOREWORD

SINCE 1306, WHEN he first made his bid for the throne against a seemingly undefeatable foe, Robert the Bruce has been preparing for the decisive battle with England that will either legitimize his kingship and cement his place on Scotland's throne, or strip the crown from his head and bring back English overlordship to Scotland.

By the late fall of 1313, King Robert is secure enough on the throne to force the enemy's hand. He issues a proclamation that he will disinherit any Scottish nobles still loyal to the English who do not submit to him in a year's time. Edward II of England cannot ignore the threat. He issues his own proclamation in December 1313 for a call to muster at Berwick-upon-Tweed in June 1314 to march on Scotland.

The English are coming, and Bruce intends to be ready for them. In the crucial early months of 1314, the king wages a preemptive war by continuing the raids in England to fund the costly war, and taking back the remaining Scottish castles still in English hands. The taking back of two of these castles, Roxburgh and Edinburgh, leads to feats of military skill that will become legend, ensuring the hero status of Bruce's two famous lieutenants, James Douglas and Thomas Randolph.

But they will not do it alone. The elite warriors of the Highland Guard and a man of much more humble birth will prove instrumental in the final push toward the most important battle yet to come.

PROLOGUE

Douglas Castle, South Lanarkshire, Scotland, June 1, 1296

THOMAS MACGOWAN—WEE THOM as everyone in the village called him (his father being Big Thom)—looked at the top of the tower and forgot to breathe. He nearly stumbled, too, which would have been a disaster, as his da had entrusted him with the very important task of carrying the laird's sword. Considering the hours his father had spent sharpening the blade until it could "slice a hair in two," and polishing it until "he could see every speck of soot on his wee laddie's face," had he dropped it in the mud, his bum would have stung for a week!

He wouldn't have minded too much though. Big Thom was the best blacksmith for miles around, and Thommy (it was what his mother called him—a lad of nearly nine sure as the Devil shouldn't be called "wee") took fierce pride in his father's work. Big Thom MacGowan wasn't just an *ordinary* village smith, he was Lord William "the Hardy" Douglas's *personal* smith and armorer.

But as Thommy stared up at the tower ramparts, he could almost excuse his near mishap. For what had caused his breath to stop and his limbs to forget their purpose was a glimpse of something extraordinary. A rare, exquisite beauty of the like the little boy who had spent most of his days surrounded by the fire and soot of his father's forge had never imagined. It was as if he were seeing a brilliant jewel for the first time when all he'd known were lumps of ore. He didn't need to know who it was to know that he was seeing something special. The way the light caught her white-blond hair blowing in the breeze, the snowy perfection of her tiny face, the shimmering gold gown. It dazzled the eyes. *She* dazzled the eyes.

"Is she a princess?" Thommy asked in reverent tones when he could finally remember how to speak.

His father gave a hearty guffaw and cuffed him on the back of the head fondly. "To you she might as well be, laddie. 'Tis the laird's wee lassie, Lady Elizabeth. Don't you remember . . . ?" He shook his head. "You must have been too young when the family left for Berwick Castle four years ago—she was little more than a babe then. But now that the laird has been released from Edward's prison"—he spit on the ground as he did every time the English king's name was mentioned—"she and her brothers have returned with the laird and Lady Eleanor to live here."

Thommy knew that Sir William had been keeper of Berwick Castle when King Edward had attacked the city and slaughtered thousands of Scots. For his defiance in holding the castle against him, King Edward had thrown the laird in prison. But he'd been freed on signing the king's "ragman rolls" of allegiance that all the Scottish lords had been forced to put their names to.

At the thought of such a beautiful creature in their midst, Thommy's eyes must have widened.

His father might be the biggest man in the village, with heavy muscles as hard as rock from clobbering steel into shape for a living, but he wasn't thickheaded. He still had a smile on his face, but his dark blue eyes had narrowed just enough for Thommy to take the warning. "Stay away from her, lad. The wee lass is not for the likes of you. Your mother may have been the daughter of a knight, but you are the son of a smith—about as far from noble as the roof of that tower. You may like to climb the rocks around here, but you'll never be able to climb that high."

His father laughed at his own jest and pushed Thommy on ahead.

But Thommy wasn't so sure his father was right. He was pretty good at climbing.

Midsummer's Day

"Why are you crying?"

The little girl's voice startled him. Thommy looked up and blinked, shielding his eyes with his arm, as if a ray of sunshine had just slipped out from behind dark clouds.

It was the little princess from the tower a few weeks ago—Lady Elizabeth.

"I'm not crying!" He wiped his eyes furiously with the back of his hand, shame crawling up his cheeks in a hot flush.

She held his gaze for one long heartbeat. Her eyes were big and round and startlingly blue. Up close her features were even more perfect than he'd realized, small and delicate set in an adorable heart-shaped face. Two chunky plaits of hair at her temples had been pulled back in a crown around her head and tied with a long pink ribbon that matched her gown. He'd never seen a gown of pink before. The material was strange, too. It wasn't scratchy like wool but soft and shimmery. He wanted to reach out and touch it, but his hands probably had soot and dirt on them.

There was no one to remind him to wash them anymore.

The resulting wave of sorrow made him scowl at her, trying to make her go away. Why was he even noticing blue eyes and pink gowns? His mother was gone and never coming back.

He had to force back a fresh blast of heat burning behind his eyes. He'd never been so humiliated in his life. Almost-nine-year-old lads didn't cry, and to be caught doing so by a lass—*any* lass, but especially a fine one like Lady Elizabeth—made him want to crawl under a rock and die.

She ignored his warning, however, and sat beside him.

He was sitting on the bank of the river that wound its way through the village, well away from—and what he thought was out of sight—the Midsummer's Day festivities. But the dull sound of merriment could be heard in the distance.

"Why did the fish swim across the river?"

He was so startled by the question it took him a moment to respond. "I don't know."

She smiled, revealing a big gap in the space where her two front teeth should have been. "It couldn't *beach* the sea."

She barely got the last word out before she startled giggling. He didn't think it was very funny, but he couldn't help smiling when he saw how much she enjoyed it.

When her giggling finally died down, they sat in surprisingly comfortable silence for a few minutes. He didn't know much about little girls, but it seemed unusual that one could be so quiet. A few of his friends had little sisters and they were always bothering them with their chatter.

As it was summer, Thommy wasn't wearing shoes, and

he dug his heel back and forth in the dirt as they watched the swiftly moving current. He only stopped when she started to copy him, and he realized her fine leather slippers were getting muddy.

"How old are you?" he asked.

"Six. How old are you?"

His chest puffed out. "Almost nine."

Her nose wrinkled. It was a tiny nose, so there were only one or two, but they were kind of cute. "When is your saint's day?" she asked.

"The twenty-third of November."

She grinned, and he was embarrassed again. It was still a full five months away.

She was quiet again for a while, before she asked, "Don't you like the fair?"

Hearing the gentle probing of the question, he stiffened. His mouth turned in a scowl. He didn't want to talk about it. He was about to tell her to go away and leave him be— lady or not—when he looked over at her face and all the anger seeped out of him. She didn't mean to pry; she was just trying to be nice.

He picked up a small, flat rock from the ground and threw it into the river. It skipped twice before sinking into the water. "My mother died Sunday last."

He could feel her eyes on him, but he didn't look up, not wanting to see her compassion. "You must miss her a lot."

He nodded, his throat squeezing hot again. He missed her terribly—the beautiful, smiling woman who'd loved her husband and son with such abandon. But that was no excuse to bawl like a baby.

She must have guessed the direction of his thoughts. He felt a gentle touch on his arm, as if a butterfly had landed and spread its wings. The sensation enveloped him with a strange warmth. For a moment it reminded him of the way he felt when his mother hugged him.

"I never knew my mother, and I still miss her."

He frowned. "You didn't know her?"

She shook her head, her flaxen hair floating around her shoulders like a veil of spun silver and gold. "She died giving birth to me."

"My mother died giving birth, too." He paused. "To my new brother."

She must have heard something in his voice. "He didn't mean to hurt her," she said softly.

Thommy sucked in a startled gasp. He stared at her in horror, realizing what he'd said.

"My brother blamed me, too, when I was little." Those big blue eyes pinned him. "But he forgave me."

"There was nothing to forgive, it wasn't your fault." The response was automatic, but Thommy realized as he said it that he meant it. It was no more her fault than it had been his two-week-old brother's.

Someone shouted her name, and she made a face, crinkling up her nose again and pursing her pouty mouth. "That's my nurse. I better go. It was nice to meet you . . ."

"Thom," he filled in. "But everyone calls me Thommy." Somehow it was very important that this lass never think of him as "wee."

"I'm Elizabeth," she said. "But you can call me Ella, since we're such good friends now."

He nodded, trying to hide his smile. She was sweet and all, but almost-nine-year-old lads weren't "friends" with six-year-old lasses—especially ones who looked like princesses.

She jumped to her feet so quickly she would have slipped in the mud had he not caught her arm, steadying her. "Careful," he said. "You'll fall and hurt yourself."

She laughed as if that were the funniest thing she'd ever heard and ran off to find her nurse.

He watched her go and realized that for the first time since his grief-stricken father had told him the news of his mother's death, Thommy felt as if the dark cloud surrounding him might have lifted just a little.

One month later

Thommy was about to tell Joanna to hurry up—again— they were going to be late to join the others, when he heard her voice. "Hi, Thommy."

He looked over to see Lady Elizabeth standing beside him. He'd noticed her arrival in church with the rest of her family, including the black-haired lad of about his own age who was hastening none too happily through the crowd toward them.

"Hi," he said uncertainly, aware that some of the other villagers who were milling around the churchyard following the Sunday services were looking at them—probably wondering why the little lady was talking to the smithy's son.

"I'm Ella," she said to Joanna, who was staring at her with a similar look to the one he'd had on his face the first time he'd seen her.

"J-J-o-anna Dicson," she finally managed, and then remembering added hastily, "My lady."

"Just Ella. You are the marshall's daughter?"

Joanna nodded mutely.

The dark-haired lad with the stormy expression came up behind her. "What are you doing, Ella? You can't run off like that."

She sighed, with a short movement of her eyes that in a few years Thommy assumed would be a full roll. "This is my brother, Jamie." She turned to the lad who might have even been an inch or two taller than Thommy (who was already as tall as lads two or three years older than he). "I was just saying hello to Thommy and," she turned her head, "Joanna."

Thommy glanced toward Jo and frowned. What was wrong with her? She was staring at the young lord as if he were one of those knights from the silly stories she was always going on about. His frown deepened, realizing that the young lord was staring right back at her with a silly look on his face, too.

Thommy stepped in front of her protectively. Joanna was a pain at times—like today when he was supposed to be joining the other lads to swim and she'd asked to come along right in front of her mother. But since his mother had died, her mother was always doing nice things for him, and he couldn't say no.

Jamie returned the frown, seeing his movement. He turned back to his sister. "How did you meet?"

Thommy tensed.

Ella turned to him and smiled. "At the fair last month. Thommy saved me from slipping in the mud."

Thommy released the breath he didn't even realize he'd been holding. The only thing worse than having Lady Elizabeth see him crying might be her telling other people about it. Their eyes met in understanding. She'd kept his secret, and now they had a bond.

Jamie shook his head and ruffled her hair fondly. "What else is new, Ella? You need to stop being in such a hurry all the time; one of these days someone isn't going to be around to catch you, and you're going to get hurt."

Now Thommy understood the reason for Ella's laughter at his warning last time. Apparently her slipping wasn't an unusual occurrence.

Ignoring her brother, she asked, "Where are you going?"

"To the falls at Arnesalloch to go swimming with some of the other lads in the village."

"I asked if he would take me along," Joanna volunteered.

"Jamie is supposed to help teach me to ride my new pony," Ella countered.

The two boys exchanged looks of commiseration. Apparently Thommy wasn't the only one having to watch over a younger sibling—or in Jo's case an almost sibling. He'd known her as long as he could remember, and since she pestered him most of the time, he suspected that was about like having a sister.

"Would you like to come?" Ella asked. "You could bring your horses and we could all ride together."

There was an awkward silence eventually filled by Jo. "We don't have horses. Thommy and I don't know how to ride."

Ella looked perplexed. "You don't?" She looked accusingly at her brother. "I thought you said all knights needed to know how to ride a horse."

Jamie shook his head. "I did. Thommy isn't going to be a knight. He's going to be a smithy like his father."

Thommy was surprised that the young lord knew who he was.

"You mean you don't have to practice all day with a wooden sword like Jamie does?"

Thom shook his head. "Sometimes I get to watch my da work on them though—steel ones," he clarified.

"I'll be getting a steel one soon," Jamie boasted, with an eye to Joanna.

"Maybe you'll make one for Jamie?" Ella asked him.

Thommy shrugged, not wanting to confess that all he did right now was carry the charcoal and pump the bellows. "Maybe." He took Joanna's arm, knowing he was going to have to drag her away. "Come on, Jo. We should probably go."

She resisted, and before he could stop her she asked the two Douglases, "Do you want to come along?"

"Sure," Ella said so quickly he knew she must have been waiting for the invitation. She turned to her brother, who wasn't looking quite as certain. "We can go riding tomorrow. It's such a hot day." She turned back to Joanna. "I don't know how to swim, but Jamie does."

"I don't know either," Joanna said.

"I could teach you sometime," Jamie offered.

Ella looked at her brother as if he'd just grown a second head. "How come when I ask you to teach me, you always say lasses don't need to know how to swim?"

Thommy tried not to laugh at the boy's red, I'm-going-to-throttle-you-later expression. He sure was glad he didn't have a sister.

The girls, however, were oblivious to Jamie's discomfort. Joanna, at a year older than Ella, had already perfected the eye roll, which she executed in his direction. "Thommy says the same thing when I ask him to teach me to climb," Joanna said to Ella. "He climbs the rocks up near Sandford with the other lads from the village. But he's the only one who goes up the Devil's slide."

"Really?" Ella's eyes widened, looking at him as if he were some kind of hero from a bard's tale.

Maybe having a sister wouldn't be bad *all* the time—not if Jo was going to talk about him like that.

Jo nodded, and then looked at Jamie. "Do you know how to climb, too?"

"Of course," Jamie said, as if surprised that there was even a question.

Thommy was amazed that Jamie didn't split the seams of his fine doublet with the way his chest and shoulders seemed to puff up.

Ella gave her brother a funny look and opened her mouth as if she were going to argue, when Jamie cut her off. "Do you want to go or not, Ella?"

The little girl let out a cheer of delight and linked her arm with Jo's. As if they'd known each other forever, they skipped off ahead, not giving Jamie a chance to change his mind.

The two boys took one look at each other, shook their heads in tandem as if to say "lasses," and followed.

As it turned out, before the day was over, the two girls weren't the only ones who were fast friends.

The boys swam in the burn for a couple of hours while Jo and Ella sat on the edge with their toes in the water, when one of the other boys from the village—Iain, the constable's son—suggested they play a game of hide-and-find.

The dense forest of big, domed oak trees, downy birch, and hazel trees, with the thick bracken and mossy under-wood, was ideal, providing plenty of places to hide. It had been a warm spring, otherwise the ground would be a car-pet of faerie flowers. The blueish purple flowers that were shaped like a bell had been his mother's favorite.

Thommy had played it many times before, but he explained the rules to Jamie. All the boys except for one would hide. The one who didn't hide—the finder—would have to cover his eyes and count to a hundred before trying to find them. The rest of the boys couldn't move once the hundred count was up.

Jamie, apparently confident in his tracking abilities, volunteered to be the "finder." It was then that the trouble started, when Ella—who apparently wasn't used to being excluded—objected to the no-lasses rule. Although it really wasn't a rule because up until that point they hadn't needed one: all the village lasses had understood that they weren't included.

"But that's not fair," Ella said with a surprisingly mulish look on her cherub's face. "I'm smaller than all of you, I can hide the best."

The boys looked at each other as if she were daft. Everyone knew lasses didn't best lads. They instinctively looked to Jamie to do something. Normally, they would look to Thommy, but under the circumstances he was happy to defer his role as leader.

Jamie tried reasoning with her, but when that didn't work, he grew frustrated and just told her that was the rule, and if she didn't want to follow it, they would go home.

That stopped her. Ella slammed her mouth shut, pursed her lips together as if sucking on a lemon, and plopped down angrily on a rock with her small arms crossed in front of her. The wee lass apparently had a stubborn streak.

The other boys looked relieved, and Jamie tried to act as if her agreement had been expected, but Thommy thought he detected a whiff of relief.

Jo, who could normally be counted on to be reasonable but had been surprisingly vocal in her support of her new friend, shot Jamie a disappointed look (his star apparently having dimmed), and sat down beside Ella to wait.

At least that's what they were supposed to do, but when

Thommy and Jamie came to collect them after the game was done (Jamie had been correct in his estimation of his tracking skills), the girls were gone. Apparently stubborn *and* willful, he amended.

At first they were more annoyed than worried. The other lads had gone home, so he and Jamie split up, Jamie yelling threats to his sister, while Thommy yelled some of his own to Jo.

Thommy found Jo after a few minutes. She'd picked a good hiding place under a fallen tree covered in a veil of moss, but she'd neglected to ensure her skirts were tucked completely out of view.

It took far longer to find Ella. Actually, they didn't find her. Jamie finally had the smart idea to shout out that she'd won, she could come out now, when a moment later they heard a soft cry in response.

Realizing where it was coming from, Thommy felt his heart tumble to the ground. Dread quickly rose up to take its place.

The light was already fading as he gazed up into the branches of the massive old oak tree to see the tiny lass perched on a branch about fifty feet above him. Lord have mercy, how in Christendom had she climbed up so high?

His stomach churned like he'd just drunk a glass of soured milk, thinking about what would happen if she fell.

"God's blood, Ella, what are you doing up there?" Jamie said. "Come down before you break your neck."

Thommy thought he heard a sniffle. "I can't. I'm stuck."

"What do you mean you're stuck?" Jamie said. "Just climb down the same way you went up."

"I don't remember how."

She started to cry and Thommy couldn't take it anymore. "I'll get her," he said.

Jamie shook his head. "I'll go. She's my sister." A fact he didn't sound very happy about at the moment.

Jo looked terrified. "Are you sure? It's getting dark, and Thommy's the best climber in the village."

Thommy winced. He was old enough—and proud enough himself—to understand that Jamie would never back down now. Unintentionally Jo had just thrown down a gauntlet. Jamie was the young lord; it was inconceivable that he could be outdone by a village lad—especially in front of a lass he wanted to impress.

Jamie removed his velvet doublet and started up the tree. Thommy and Jo were quiet as they watched the lad navigate the lower maze of branches. It was so dark in the canopy of leaves that Thommy could barely see, when Jamie glanced down and stopped about halfway up.

"What happened?" Joanna said, her eyes round and filled with worry. "Why did he stop? Why isn't he moving?"

"I don't know," Thommy lied. He didn't tell her that Jamie had probably looked down and gotten scared. Lads didn't like girls knowing things like that. Tossing off his own doublet—made of scratchy wool—he started up the tree after them.

He reached Jamie first. The other boy's face was pale and his lips bloodless from being clenched so tightly. He seemed to be frozen in place. Some people didn't like being high up. The future Lord of Douglas must be one of them.

Ella was still quite a ways above him, but she must have seen Jamie stop and was asking him what was wrong and why he wasn't moving. His nonresponsiveness was making her increasingly upset.

"He's fine," Thommy shouted up to her. "He's stuck, that's all."

Jamie met his gaze. Thommy could see his fear warring with his pride.

"I should have told you not to look down," Thommy said. "I'll wager you haven't been up this high before?"

Jamie managed to shake his head.

"Next time, I'll take you up slower so you can get used to it."

Jamie managed a scoff, and Thommy suspected he wouldn't be climbing a tree again for some time.

"What's happening up there?" Jo yelled from below.

The girl's voice seemed to do something to Jamie. Some of his fear vanished, and the gaze that met Thommy's was braced—almost as if he expected Thommy to try to humiliate him.

"Nothing," Thommy shouted back down. "His tunic is stuck on a branch, that's all."

The other boy visibly relaxed. He gave him a nod of thanks, and Thommy knew that another bond had been formed that day. Secrets had a way of doing that.

He was able to talk Jamie down the first few branches, instructing him first to turn and face the tree, and then to slowly and carefully ease himself down to the next branch, with Thommy there to provide him guidance where necessary.

When Jamie reached a place close enough to jump, Thommy scrambled back up the branches to where Ella waited.

"Are you all right?" he asked.

She nodded. He could tell she was scared, but like her brother she was trying not to show it. What concerned him more, however, were her shimmering eyes and trembling lower lip. Ah, blast it, she better not start crying!

"What was that joke you told me last time? About the fish and the river?"

The beginnings of a smile appeared on the edge of her mouth. "You mean about the beach?"

He nodded. "Do you have any others?"

The tremble was gone—thank goodness—replaced by a full-fledged gappy grin. "You mean you like them? Jamie won't let me tell them anymore. He says they're all dumb 'wee bairn' jokes."

Thommy leaned close and whispered, even though there was no need, "You can tell them to me. I don't mind. But first, I need you to scoot a little closer so I can help you off that branch."

She did as he asked without thinking, but her dress caught on one of the broken branches. She reached out, leaning all her weight on the thin branch to try to unsnag it. He tried to warn her, but it was too late.

The branch didn't break, but the cracking sound and sudden movement as if it might startled her. She lost her balance.

Thommy's heart shot to his throat and jammed. He may have cried out, but only the "nay!" was intelligible.

It happened so fast, yet he saw it in slow-moving time. She fell back, and he lunged. Somehow he managed to catch her around the waist and catch hold of the branch above him at the same time. But now he had a screaming, terrified little girl latched to his side, unbalancing him on the less-than-solid branch on which he was precariously balanced.

For one terrified heartbeat he thought they were both going to plummet to the ground, but he dug his fingers into the bark until his arm burned and, after a stomach-in-his-throat few seconds, managed to steady them both.

He could feel the frantic beat of her heart against his as he stood there for a moment letting his own slow.

Her eyes didn't blink as they stared into his. He'd never been this close to a lass before. Did they all smell clean and fresh as a patch of wildflowers after a spring rain?

Jo and Jamie must have seen enough from below, as he was suddenly aware of their shouting.

"We're fine," he yelled back, in a far calmer voice than he felt. "Ella is going to hold on real tight, and we'll be down in a minute." To her, he asked, "Can you do that?"

She nodded mutely, still too stunned to do anything else.

"Good. I need you to wrap your arms around my neck and keep your legs wrapped around my waist so I can use my hands."

She looked uncertain for a moment, but then brightened. "My father sometimes carries me around on his back like that."

Thommy smiled back at her. His da had done the same when he was a wee one. "Aye, just like that, except you'll be on my front, not my back."

She retracted the kitten claws digging into his side long enough for him to help maneuver her into position.

"You're strong," she said. "Jamie says I'm too big to carry now."

He'd been thinking the same thing (despite the heavy loads of charcoal he carried every morning for the forge), but the admiration in her eyes gave him a burst of strength. "Aw, a wee lassie like you? You don't weigh much more than my da's hammer. Now, what about those jokes you were going to tell me?"

For the next few minutes as he wound his way back down the maze of moss-covered limbs to the ground, he was barraged by a stream of silly jests from a seemingly bottomless well. They weren't all that funny, but he made sure to chuckle at the appropriate time.

When he finally hopped down from the last branch, every muscle in his body was shaking with exhaustion. But he'd done it. The lass was safe.

"That was fun! Can we do it again?"

Thommy tried not to groan, while Jamie started yelling and cursing something fierce, the way Thommy's da did when he burned himself.

His arms tightened around her in an involuntary squeeze of relief before he started to hand her off to Jamie, who looked as if he didn't know whether to shake her or hug her to death.

But she held on to him long enough to press a small kiss to his cheek and whisper in his ear, "Jamie was wrong, you are a knight, and when I get old I'm going to marry you."

He was so startled by the proclamation he didn't know what to say. He should have laughed—it was as ridiculous as some of those jokes she'd told him. Even if he wasn't only almost nine and she six, she lived in a castle and wore gold circlets in her hair. He lived in a two-room wattle-and-daub cottage with a thatched roof that they shared with the livestock for warmth and didn't own a good pair of shoes for the winter.

But he didn't laugh. Instead he felt something in his chest squeeze. Something that felt a lot like longing for something he knew he could never have. But for one moment he allowed himself to wonder if such a thing were possible.

It was a mistake, as his father would hammer into his head many times in the years that followed. But Thommy never forgot those carelessly uttered words spoken by a little princess that made him feel like the greatest knight in Christendom. Words that made a boy who had no right to dream.

1

Douglas, South Lanarkshire, February 1311

THOM (NO ONE called him "wee" anymore) had waited long enough. He struck one last blow with the hammer before carefully setting aside the hot blade.

Wiping the sweat and grit from his brow with the back of his hand, he pulled the protective leather apron over his head and hung it on a peg near the door.

"Where are you going?" his father asked, looking up from his own piece of hot metal—in his case a severely dented helm. The Englishman who'd once worn it must be suffering a foul headache. If he was still around to be suffering, that is.

"To the river to wash," Thom replied.

His father frowned, the dark features made darker by the layers of grime that came from toiling near the fires all day. Every day. For forty years.

Though no longer the tallest man in the village (Thom had surpassed his father in height almost ten years ago), Big Thom was still the most muscular, although a few more years of Thom wielding the hammer might force his father to cede that title as well. Physically the men were much alike, but in every other way they were opposites.

"There is still plenty of time before the evening meal," his father pointed out. "Captain de Wilton is anxious for his sword."

Thom gritted his teeth. Although the villagers in Douglas had no choice but to accept the English occupation of their castle—with the current Lord of Douglas a much hunted "rebel"—it didn't mean he had to jump to their bidding. "The captain can wait if he wants the work done properly."

"But his silver cannot. Those tools aren't going to buy themselves."

Though there was no censure in his tone, Thom knew what his father was thinking. They wouldn't need the coin so badly if Thom wasn't being so stubborn. He was sitting—or more accurately sleeping—on enough silver to replace every tool in the forge and expand to take on a handful of apprentices if they wanted them. But that was his father's dream, not his. His mother had left him the small fortune, and Thom wasn't ready to relinquish it—or the opportunity that went along with it.

They wouldn't need coin at all if the current Lord of Douglas wasn't so busy making a name for himself with all his "black" deeds that he actually gave thought to those who were left in his wake and bore the brunt of English retaliation. Thom tried to push back the wave of bitterness and anger that came from thinking of his former friend, but it had become as reflexive as swinging his hammer.

The last time Sir James "the Black" Douglas had attempted to rid his Hall of Englishmen—about a year ago when he'd tricked the then-keeper, Lord Thirlwall, from the safety of the castle into an ambush but failed to take the castle—the remaining garrison had retaliated against the villagers, whom they accused of aiding the rebels.

"War is good for business," his father liked to say. Except when it wasn't. Big Thom MacGowan, who'd never been shy about his loyalty to the Douglas lords, had paid for that loyalty with a nearly destroyed forge and the loss of some of his most expensive tools. Tools that were probably in some English forge right now.

Fortunately the garrison and commander who'd replaced Thirlwall, De Wilton, seemed a more fair-minded man. He didn't blame the villagers for the actions of their rebel laird, and he and his men were frequent customers of the village smith, or as the wooden sign not-so-imaginatively proclaimed it, The Forge. His father might not like the English, but he was happy to take their silver, especially at his special English rates.

"I'll finish it soon enough," Thom said. "And Johnny is almost done with the mail, aren't you lad?"

His fourteen-year-old brother nodded. "A few more rivets and it will be as good as new." He grinned, his teeth a flash of white in his blackened face. "*Better* than new."

Thom grinned back at him. "I don't doubt it."

Although more like their father in his even-keeled, contented temperament, Johnny possessed the same instinctive skill with the iron as Thom. Big Thom liked to say his lads were born to it, which made Johnny beam and grated on Thom like emery under his plaid. The instinctive skills such as knowing just when to pull the metal out, where to strike it with a hammer, and how to make it strong enough to do its job without being so hard that it shattered or broke that made his father so proud felt like a chain wrapped around Thom's neck.

It would have been far easier if he'd never showed any talent for the work. If he'd shattered one too many blades by cooling the metal too quickly or striking it in the wrong place while hardening. If he were less precise in detail, couldn't fit a handle to save his life, a poorer judge of temperature, off on his proportions . . . anything.

His father didn't understand how someone with Thom's

"God-given talent" wasn't content. Skill like theirs was meant to be used.

Which was part of the problem with Johnny. Johnny was too good with the hammer to haul coal and operate the bellows, the tasks normally given to a young apprentice. With Big Thom handling most of the day-to-day smithing work, from repairing cast iron pots to shoeing horses, and Thom with more sword work than he could handle, they were turning away jobs as it was. Big Thom wanted Johnny at the forge, which meant they needed someone to do the apprentice work. But Thom couldn't bring himself to give up the one chance he had to change his destiny. His mother had wanted to give him a choice.

Thom opened the door and—ironically—coughed at the breath of fresh air. His lungs were so accustomed to the black smoke it was as if the purity somehow offended them. Daylight at this time of the year didn't last long, and night was already falling. The mist, however, was not. The stars would be out tonight in full force. That was what he was counting on.

He wasn't all that surprised to hear the door open behind him. "Son, wait a minute."

Thom turned, seeing the features so like his own aged by time, hardship, and loss. He knew his father had a woman in town he sometimes saw, but no one had ever replaced Thom's mother in his father's heart. Not that you'd ever hear his father rail or complain about the injustice fate had handed him. Like everything else, Big Thom had taken his wife's death with unquestioning, stoic acceptance.

Thom never accepted anything. It was his curse, and the source of his discontent. He envied his father and brother sometimes. Life was simpler when you didn't question. When you didn't want more than what birth so capriciously allotted.

He met his father's worried gaze.

"Don't go, son."

"I'll finish the sword—"

"I know she's back."

The words fell with the weight of an anvil between them. Thom stiffened, his jaw clamping down like a steel wall, an implicit warning that beyond there be dragons. The subject was not one he wanted to discuss with his father—ever. It was a subject upon which they would never agree.

But his formidable father wasn't one to back down from dark looks—or dragons. "I know Lady Elizabeth is back, and you are going to try to see her tonight. But don't go, Thommy. No good will come of it. Leave the lass be."

"You don't know what you are talking about." His father had never understood about him and Ella—or Jamie for that matter, when they were still friends. From the first time he'd come home after rescuing Ella from that tree, his father had tried to discourage his friendship with the Douglases, warning him not to get too close. But the four of them had been inseparable before Ella had been sent away to France for her protection at the start of the war—and Jamie had discovered Thom's secret. He'd lost the girl he loved and his best friend in one day.

Thom tried to turn away, but his father took hold of his arm. "I know more than you think. I know she's been back for the better part of a fortnight. I know she's staying at Park Castle with her stepmother and younger brothers. I know that she could have come to see you, if she wanted, but she hasn't. I know you've loved her since she was a little lass, but she's not a little lass anymore. She's a lady. A noble. The sister of our laird. She's not for you. She's never been for you, and there is nothing you can do to change that. I wish it were different, but that's the way it is."

"So I should just give up, is that it? Accept it?" Thom shook him off. "That isn't me, that's . . ." *You.*

He stopped before the word was out, but it was too late. He saw the flinch reverberate through his father's big frame. His father, who was one of the toughest men in the village, who'd broken up more fights in the alehouse because no one was fool enough to strike him, could be hurt by his son's unthinking words.

"I'm sorry," Thom said, raking his fingers through his sweat-soaked hair. "Don't listen to me. I've no right to take my foul mood out on you. I just wish you'd try to understand."

"I do, Thommy, more than you know. I was in your place once. But the daughter of a household knight is a far cry from the daughter of one of Scotland's leading nobles and sister of one of Robert the Bruce's chief lieutenants. The lass has spent the better part of the last five years in France; can you honestly see her happy with the life you could give her?"

His father's words struck too close to the mark, raising fears Thom didn't want to give voice to. "Ella isn't like that. You know her."

His father's eyes leveled on him somberly. "I knew a chattering magpie of a ten-year-old lass who I had to ban from the forge so you could get some work done, and I knew the sweet, teenage lass you used to sneak out to go visit at night." He paused at Thom's look of shock. "Aye, I knew about that. Just as I knew that if I tried to stop you, you would only find another way. The lass looked at you like a brother, I didn't think there would be any harm. But I was wrong. The Douglases put ideas in your head. They made you think this wasn't good enough." Thom started to protest, but his father put up his hand to stop him. "Maybe not in words, but by bringing you into their world. A world in which you don't belong. Not even your mother's coin will raise you high enough for a Douglas—whatever you try to make of yourself. You've a God-given gift, son. With your skill you could be making swords for a king one day; don't waste it by chasing a foolish dream."

Thom tightened his jaw. It wasn't foolish. The bond between him and Ella was special—different.

Acceptance. Fate. He didn't want to hear it. "So I can stay here and chase your dream instead?"

Thom regretted the words as soon as they left his mouth. But it was too late to retrieve them.

His father stilled, his expression as tight as steel hardened right to the shattering point. After a pained pause, he stepped back. "Perhaps you are right. I've no right to interfere. You're a man now. Three and twenty is old enough to make your own decisions. I'll not try to hold you here if you wish to leave. But make sure you are doing so for the right reasons. Leave because you don't like being a smith, not because you think it will give you a chance with Lady Elizabeth." He paused and held Thom's gaze. "I know how you feel about her, lad, but if she feels the same way, why hasn't she come to see you?"

It was a good question, and one Thom would have answered tonight.

The old stone peel tower of Park Castle wasn't as easy to climb as Douglas Castle. Or maybe it was just that Thom was out of practice. It had been nearly five years since he'd scaled the walls of the tower house of Douglas Castle to meet Ella.

Their rooftop meetings had started not long after his father barred Ella from the forge, where she would sometimes (often) "drop by" with some excuse to watch him finish his work. His father was right. The lass could chatter for hours. But Thom had never minded. He'd listened to her stories and her silly jokes and even cleaning up had sped by.

Knowing how disappointed she was, and missing her company more than he'd expected, one night he'd decided to surprise her. She'd mentioned that sometimes when she couldn't sleep, she climbed up to the roof and sat on the battlements, looking at the stars. He had to climb the tower five nights in a row, but on the sixth she finally emerged.

She'd been shocked, excited, and amazed. Not just at his ability to climb the keep, but also that he could do so while evading the castle watch. It hadn't been all that difficult—although he certainly didn't tell her that (even back then he wanted her admiration)—people didn't look where they weren't expecting to see anything. All he had to do was watch the guardsmen on patrol, figure out their pattern, and stick to the shadows. The castle itself, although "enceinte," and fortified by a stone wall, was of wood frame construction, giving him a virtual ladder to climb.

For the next handful of years, a few times a month on the nights the mist permitted the stars to shine, Thom would wait in one of the outbuildings for the castle to quiet and then climb the tower where Ella would be waiting for him. They'd talk for hours—actually, Ella would do most of the talking, except when he'd point out the constellations and tell her the old stories his mother had passed on to him before she'd died. He didn't know how many times he'd had to retell the one about Perseus and Andromeda, but the lass never grew tired of it.

Those nights on the tower were where their friendship had turned to something more—at least for him.

The meetings had been their secret, until Jamie discovered them right before he'd marched off to join Bruce. Or so Thom had thought. He still couldn't believe his father had known this whole time and never said anything.

Thom's arm muscles strained as he reached for a gap in the rock big enough to grab on to in the rough surface of the stone wall. He made sure his grip was solid before moving his right foot and then his left up another couple of feet. Finally, with the next handhold he was able to reach the edge of the crenellated parapet wall and lift himself over and onto the battlements.

Christ, that had been harder than he'd anticipated. His arms were burning as he took a moment to look around and catch his breath. It hadn't looked that difficult, but the jagged stone walls of Park Castle didn't provide as many foot- and handholds as the wooden framework of Douglas Castle. Although the tower was small and no more than thirty feet high, he might not have been able to climb it at all had it not been neglected for years, with much of the lime-rendered harling—meant to even the surface and protect the stone from weather—cracked and worn away.

Park Castle had been built as a watchtower years ago by the church, but was purchased some years back by the English knight Lady Eleanor Douglas had married after the death of the old laird. William the Hardy had died in the Tower of London about two years after Thom's mother for rebelling against King Edward again. Ella had been forced to leave Douglas Castle for a couple of years then as well. It had been a difficult time for her, one that she didn't like to talk about.

With the English and Sir Robert Clifford in possession of the old Douglas lands, Park Castle now served as home to Lady Eleanor (recently widowed for the third time), her stepdaughter, Elizabeth, and Elizabeth's two half brothers, Archie and Hugh.

He looked around. The pitched wooden roof and surrounding battlement were deserted. Thom tried not to be disappointed. It was early yet. Ella usually waited until well after everyone went to sleep, making it easier to sneak up to the garret to access the small door.

Despite the clear night, it was cold, and Thom was grateful for the extra plaid he'd tossed into his sack as he sat to wait. He'd been right. The stars were out tonight. Coupled with the nearly full moon, a soft glow had been cast across the quiet countryside. It seemed so peaceful it was hard to believe they were in the midst of a long, brutal war.

The village of Douglas had seen more than its share of conflict, and as long as the English occupied its castle, Thom knew it would see more. If James Douglas had to destroy the entire town, he would to rid Douglasdale of the English for Robert the Bruce. Thom wanted the English gone, too, but Jamie's vengeance went too far. His former friend had changed.

Had Ella?

Thom didn't want to think so, but why hadn't she come to see him? When she'd left, he'd been so certain that she'd begun to feel the same way as he. *"Will you wear my ribbon around your sleeve when you are a knight in a tourney, Thommy?"* or, *"I know you hate it, but how will we go to France when we are older if you don't learn to speak French?"* She'd been thinking about a future with him, even going as far as telling him one of the rare times he lost his temper with her that if he were her husband, she'd put spiderwort in his soup (which was known for its *digestive* effect), and give him cause for his black mood, if he ever snapped at her like that again. He'd been chastened and enchanted. His little princess had some fire.

If only Jamie hadn't sent her away, damn it.

Time passed slowly while Thom waited. After a few hours, he was forced to concede that she wasn't coming. He stood and started to stuff the plaid back into his sack. He was a fool. His father was right. Five years was a long time. She'd probably forgotten—

The door opened, and his heart dropped.

He glanced up as she stepped over the threshold, a beam of moonlight catching her in its hold and taking his breath along with it.

Jesus.

He might have jolted. The glimpse he'd caught of her with her stepmother, as she'd ridden through the village a couple of weeks ago, had not prepared him for the vision before him now. Long, shimmery waves of flaxen hair tumbled around her shoulders in a silky veil down her back. Her features were small and even, perfectly positioned in an oval canvas of snowy white. Her mouth was red, her cheeks pink, and her chin delicately pointed. Dark arched brows and long feathery lashes framed round, wide-set eyes the unusual blue of peacock feathers. She was gowned in an ice-blue dressing robe lined with white fur, the thick gold braid belt around her waist emphasizing its trimness as well as the softly rounded curves above and below. Her breasts were firm and generous, her hips slender, and her legs long.

Ella had always been beautiful, even as a child. But it had become so commonplace to him that he stopped thinking about it. The last time he'd seen her at a just-turned-sixteen, she'd still possessed the vestiges of the girl who'd traipsed all over the countryside with him and Jo. But the woman standing before him didn't look like she'd ever traipsed anywhere—she floated. She didn't look real; she looked like a figment from a faerie tale or an ice princess from the lands of the Northmen. Refined, sophisticated, and utterly untouchable. She looked nothing like the girl he remembered.

Thom didn't second-guess himself very often, but he did so now.

It was only when he looked down on her wrist and saw the faint edge of brass that he felt some of his confidence return. She still wore the bracelet he'd given her right before she'd been sent away. She hadn't forgotten him.

2

THOM WAS GRATEFUL to be hidden in the shadow of the roof, as it gave him a moment to recover from the shock. But his voice still came out as a question when he spoke. "Ella?"

She turned at the sound. For a moment the icily perfect facade cracked, and he glimpsed the expression that he remembered, the broad smile and twinkle of girlish delight that had always lit her eyes whenever she first saw him.

"Thommy!" she exclaimed, the single word uttered in the familiar sweet voice filled with happiness.

He felt a rush of relief that was quickly doused when her expression changed to one of distress. She bit her lip.

Something he'd seen her do countless times before, but now the sight of those tiny white teeth digging into the plump pouty lower lip provoked a very different reaction in him.

"You shouldn't be here."

He stepped out of the shadows. "Why not?"

Her eyes widened as he came toward her. "Good gracious, Thommy, what happened to you?"

He frowned. "What do you mean?"

She took a few steps back, her hands fluttering nervously. "You . . . you," she sputtered accusingly. "You're huge! You must be as tall as your father."

"Taller," he pointed out, stopping in front of her, feeling a little bit like a horse at market as her eyes looked him up and down.

"And your shoulders . . ." She let her voice drop off, as if unable to find the right word. Her eyes lifted to his. "What have you been doing this whole time? Lifting all those rocks you like to climb?"

Thommy frowned back at her, not sure how to react. What had she expected? That he would be the same stripling lad she'd left behind five years ago?

Suddenly it hit him. Hadn't he been having the same thoughts a few minutes ago about her?

Maybe they both had changed. But in appearance—not in what mattered. Inside he was the same. Was she?

One side of his mouth lifted. "I've grown up, El. I'm not an eighteen-year-old lad anymore."

He'd wanted her to see that, but it seemed he need not have worried. She'd noticed. Although right now she didn't appear very happy about it.

"Surely you didn't think I'd look the same?" he asked.

She stared at him with that same frown on her face

that she'd had when he'd accidentally ruined a Christmas surprise she'd had for him by showing up early one night on the roof. She'd been halfway through setting up a special picnic of his favorite sweets on a plaid, replete with a candle and wernage. The sweetened wine tasted like syrup, but he'd choked down a glass to please her.

Finally the frown fell, and she seemed to compose herself—the nervous fluttering stopped. "Which is why you shouldn't be here. We aren't children anymore."

Something in her tone bothered him. It was as if she was trying to put distance between them—as if she was trying to forget.

"Yet here you are, too," he said.

She looked up at him, unable to deny the observation.

"Why haven't you been to see me, El?"

His tone was questioning, not accusing, yet she blushed guiltily as if it were. She dropped her gaze. "I intended to, of course. I've wanted to see both you and Jo; it's just that we've been so busy since we arrived. The castle is in poor condition and you know my stepmother."

He did. Lady Eleanor had been a wealthy heiress most of her life, and she liked to surround herself with the best of everything. It had become even more pronounced in the years following the old laird's death, after she'd had most of her possessions stripped by Edward for being the wife of a traitor. Unlike the Douglases, however, Lady Eleanor was able to successfully petition for their return a few years later. It was Jamie's dispossession and his inability to get his lands returned that had set him on the road to Scone five years ago where he'd joined Robert the Bruce on the way to his coronation.

But from the way Ella was avoiding his gaze, Thom knew it was more than Lady Eleanor wishing to bring the castle up to her high standards at work. Ella had always been a horrible liar.

"I thought you might have forgotten your promise," he said softly, his deep voice blending into the dark night.

The heat that rose to her cheeks told him she hadn't. The memory of that day hung between them. She'd run away from the castle the morning Jamie told her he was sending her to France and had gone straight to Thommy in the forge. She'd been crying and near hysterical as she'd launched herself against his chest and held on to him the same way she'd done in the tree all those years before. She wouldn't do it, she told him, she wouldn't go.

The horror of her words had been the only thing that had prevented Thom from embarrassing himself. At eighteen the feel of her in his arms had stirred his body in ways that he couldn't control. He'd been instantly hard and hotter than he'd ever been at the forge, and in danger of exploding just from the pressure of her against him. But "go" had chilled him.

In between sobs, he'd learned that Ella was being sent to France for her protection during Bruce's rebellion. She didn't want to leave her home and friends again. She didn't want to leave *him*. But Jamie—with the agreement of Lady Eleanor—would not be gainsaid.

After the falling-out between him and Jamie the night before, Thom wasn't surprised. It was the speed of Jamie's reaction that came as a shock. Jamie was taking no chances in allowing whatever it was between Thom and Ella to progress. In a strange way it had heartened him: Jamie had seen it, too.

Knowing there was nothing he could do, Thom had held her in his arms, smoothing her hair and trying to comfort her while his heart was being torn apart. It had been one of the hundreds of times he'd reminded himself not to touch her, not to press his mouth to hers, when she'd stood there looking up at him with tears glistening in her lashes and made him promise that he would never forget her. That he would be here when she returned and nothing would change. She knew about the money his mother had left him, and feared he would do something "stupid" like run off and "get yourself killed" in the war.

He'd promised, and she in turn had sworn she would return as soon as she could. He would take her and Jo to the Crags of Craigneith to see the cave just like they'd planned. She'd been recovered enough by that point to jest that maybe he would overcome his aversion to horses by then and they could ride rather than walk. He'd grumbled good-naturedly, used to her teasing about his lack of regard for the "infernal beasts"—a feeling that seemed to be mutual.

He'd never imagined it would be nearly five years.

Ella shook her head, a wistful smile turning her soft red lips. "I didn't forget, but it's been a long time. I wasn't sure you would remember." She gave him a sidelong look from under her lashes, her smile turning teasing. "I thought maybe you'd be married by now with a couple of bairns."

The lighthearted words made his chest pinch. "How could you think that?"

Her perfectly etched brows furrowed. "You are three and twenty. It's only natural to suppose that one of those village lasses who was always trying to get your attention might have caught it by now." She laughed, and the sound eviscerated him like a blade honed at the stone for hours. It was the same way she'd teased him when they were younger, utterly oblivious that for him there was only one woman whose attention he craved.

Did the thought of another woman "catching" him still mean nothing to her? Did it cause her not the slightest twinge of jealousy? For almost five years he'd lived in ago-nized fear of hearing she was betrothed or married. Yet the same thought on her part seemed to cause her not one smidgen of distress.

He'd been so sure that she'd felt the same way as he. That she was just too young to realize her feelings. But she was twenty now—almost one and twenty—and no longer a girl of sixteen. There were no more excuses. Either she felt what had always been between them as he did or she did not.

He could wait no longer. He took a step toward her, his gaze boring into her. His voice held a hint of the frustra-tion burgeoning inside him. "I am not interested in any of the village lasses."

She took a step back—an unconscious evasion—and frowned. "What's the matter with you, Thommy? Why are you so cross with me? I'm sorry I didn't come see you, but surely you realize that things can't be as they were. Jamie is rumored—"

He took her arm, practically growling in frustration, hurt, and anger. "I've heard enough about your damned brother."

She shook her head. "You sound just like him. What happened between you two that night? You were the best of friends."

"Were," he repeated angrily. "Until I overstepped my bounds."

"You presume too much. We are not friends, I am your laird."

She frowned. "I don't understand."

For the first time in his life, Thom felt like shaking her. As if he could force her to see what was before her eyes. *Him.* Where he'd always been. Loyal friend, frequent res-cuer, and would-be lover—for the rest of his life, if she'd have him.

"You are always there when I need you, Thommy." How many times had she said that over the years? Didn't she know why?

"Don't you?" he demanded angrily. "Can you not see what Jamie did? Can you not guess why your exalted brother was so determined to separate us?"

Eyes wide, she blinked up at him wordlessly. Cluelessly.

Thom couldn't believe it. For five years he'd been waiting for this day. For five years he'd faithfully waited for a woman who still had no idea how he felt. Could she really be that blind? How could she not see what was right in front of her?

He released her, frustration teeming through every muscle and vein of his body. He didn't trust himself to keep touching her and not pull her into his arms and show her exactly what he meant. Would that shock her? What would Lady Elizabeth Douglas think if her childhood friend took her in his arms and showed her a man's desire?

Instead he told her. "Jamie saw how I felt about you and realized what was happening between us."

She tilted her head questioningly. "What was happening between us? We were friends. The very dearest of friends. Like we'd always been."

Friends. She had no idea how deeply she'd just twisted her dagger.

"Is that really all it was to you?" he demanded. "Did you feel nothing else for me? Did you not imagine a future between us?"

Those big, beautiful eyes stared at him with confusion and incomprehension. When something finally sparked in her eyes, he felt the first flicker of hope. Hope that was doused the very next moment.

"You mean those games we used to pretend when we

were children?" She smiled, as if the memory was a fond one. "Of course, marriage between us is impossible . . ." Her voice drifted off. She gasped, her eyes filling with horror as understanding finally dawned. Her hand covered her mouth. "Oh God, Thommy, you didn't think *you* and *I* could *really* . . . It was a game. I was only a girl, I didn't know any better."

He flinched, as if the words were a whip upon his heart, shredding it apart. *Didn't know any better.* He knew she spoke unthinkingly and wasn't trying to hurt him, but that's what made it worse. The fact that there could be nothing between them was so obvious, he was the only one stupid enough not to see it. Caring for him in that way had never occurred to her because it was out of the realm of possibility. *He* was out of the realm of possibility.

The feelings—the *friendship*—between them did not change what anyone who was not a child or a lovesick fool would know: the blacksmith's son was so far beneath the Lord of Douglas's daughter as to be unworthy of consideration.

But of course he *had* thought. That was the problem. For five years he'd thought the tender looks, the heartfelt smiles, and all those hours of talking meant something. He'd thought the connection between them—the feeling as if she was the other part of his soul—was too powerful to deny. He'd thought that because he was the first one she ran to, that because no one understood him better than she did, it would always be that way. He'd thought what they had was so special it defied normal rules and boundaries like birth and station. He'd thought she saw beyond all that and saw *him* for who he was.

And never had he felt like such a fool. His father had tried to stop him. Why hadn't he listened?

Thom's fists clenched at his sides as he fought the

maelstrom of emotion lashing around inside him. But it was too hot, his pain too raw. It filled his chest with a savage heat, wrapping around his throat and squeezing higher. He cursed the pressure building behind his eyes. Cursed the weakness of emotion that a man should be able to control. Elizabeth Douglas had seen him cry once in his life. That was more than enough.

He had to go. He couldn't stand here another moment, looking at her, wanting her, and knowing he could never have her.

It seemed he'd been looking up since the first day he'd seen her; it was time to look ahead.

Thom turned away, trying to hide the humiliation, hurt, and heartbreak that permeated every corner of his soul.

"Thommy, wait! Oh God, I'm sorry. I didn't mean to hurt you. Please don't leave like this."

He didn't turn around. Grabbing his bag, he slung it over his shoulder and slid over the closest section of the parapet wall. He heard her voice above him as he climbed down, but not once did he look up.

He had his answer, and now he knew what he had to do.

It took a week longer than he intended, but a fortnight after Thom scaled the tower wall of Park Castle, he was putting the final coat of oil on his new sword.

He was about to slip it into the scabbard when Johnny stopped him. "Can I see it one more time?"

Thom's mouth curved up on one side as he handed the gleaming blade to his brother. The lad was unusually strong like Thom and their father, and despite its weight, he lifted it easily with one hand to admire it in the beam of sunlight streaming through the small open shutter.

It was Shrove Sunday, and the brothers had returned to their cottage after mass for Thom to finish packing. Their father said he had to attend to some business at the castle.

"She's a beauty," Johnny said, taking his eyes off the long blade long enough to glance up at him. "It's the finest work I've ever seen you do. Da was right. You could make swords for kings."

Thom laughed for what felt like the first time in weeks before rumpling his brother's shaggy, too-long hair. "I hardly think a king would be content with such a plain hilt of horn without a jewel or bit of gilding to be seen, but 'twill serve for a simple soldier."

"Not for long," Johnny replied with all the fierceness of a boy who had looked up to his older brother for fourteen years. "I know you will work your way up in the ranks quickly. It might have been faster if you'd kept enough of the coin to buy a decent horse."

Thom made a face. Though he'd never trained seriously with a sword, it was riding that might prove the biggest barrier to his goal. He wanted to be a knight, and as had been pointed out to him all those years ago by the Douglases, knights needed to ride. "Aye, well, you know how I feel about horses."

Johnny grinned—his older brother's problems with horses (even when shoeing) was a source of great amusement to him—but then sobered. "Da is grateful, Thommy. Even if he doesn't show it."

Thom nodded. "I know."

But his father was like him: stubborn and proud. He'd thought that Thom realizing he didn't have a future with Lady Elizabeth would keep him here; he didn't realize it would send him away.

Thom was leaving. He'd taken half the money his

mother had left him and used it to purchase a blade blank to make a sword and other armor he would need to join Edward Bruce's army. Under normal circumstances, he would have offered his sword to his lord, but as he would sooner run his new blade through James Douglas's black heart, after what he'd done to Joanna—taking her innocence when he had no intention of marrying her and leaving her alone with an unborn child to mourn—Thom hoped to find a place in the king's brother's army. Not surprisingly, Douglas had granted him leave to go.

The other half of his coin he'd given to his father to expand the forge. It was enough to replace his tools and hire two new apprentices if he wished. At first Big Thom had refused the money, but Thom could be stubborn, too. Besides, he pointed out that half should rightly belong to Johnny. Had she lived, their mother would have wanted him to have something.

"Must you go tomorrow?" Johnny said. "Can't you stay for the Shrove Tuesday feast at the castle?" The day before the start of Lent was one of the biggest feasts of the year.

Thom stiffened. Not just because a mention of the castle inevitably conjured up thoughts of Elizabeth, but because it also reminded him that there was only *one* castle in Douglas now. Shortly after Thom's fateful rooftop meeting with Elizabeth, Jamie had returned to Douglas for the third time to rid Castle Douglas of Englishmen. He'd succeeded, in the process slaying the captain whose sword Thom had just returned and slighting his own castle to the ground. Only embers and piles of rocks remained of the once great fortress.

Thom shook his head grimly. "I've stayed longer than I intended already."

"Jo is better?" Johnny asked.

Thom nodded. It had been Joanna's terrible accident after *Sir* James Douglas's departure that had kept Thom here for the additional week. She'd nearly been killed after colliding with a horse, following an argument with Jamie that she refused to discuss. But it was the loss of the child that he wasn't sure she'd ever recover from.

"She's out of danger," Thom said, though he suspected it would be a long time before Joanna was "better." But he'd done what he could for her, and a glimpse of Elizabeth when he'd gone to visit Joanna at Park Castle had told him he'd delayed long enough.

"I understand," Johnny said, though it was clear that like their father, he did not. Though his brother was excited for him, and wanted to hear all about his adventure, Thom knew Johnny would never follow in his footsteps. His brother had everything he wanted right here.

A knock sounded on the door. Bending over the bed to start putting his extra clothes into his pack, Thom told Johnny to see who it was.

Thom heard the door open and then silence. He glanced over his shoulder and frowned. What in Hades was Johnny doing? He was just standing there with his mouth open. The door blocked Thom from seeing who was on the other side.

Thom stood and was about to ask him who it was, when a familiar voice made his spine stiffen and every nerve ending stand on edge.

"Johnny? Is that you?" She gasped and threw her arms around the stunned lad. "My goodness, you've grown so tall, I would hardly recognize you."

Johnny nodded, seemingly incapable of speech.

Thom's jaw clenched. What the hell was she doing here? He hadn't even been sure she knew where he lived. Not once in all the years he'd known her had Elizabeth ever been to his home. He'd always met her at the forge. He'd never thought about why until now. Seeing her here was . . . *wrong*. She didn't belong in a place like this. She never had. Only now did he realize it.

The simple two-room cottage had never looked as humble as when Lady Elizabeth Douglas in her white—who the hell wore *white* to the home of a smith?—velvet gown stepped across their threshold. The room seemed darker, the walls more black with smoke from the peat, the rushes on the hardened dirt floor seemed more in need of freshening. The simple furniture with the pillows and hangings that hadn't been replaced since his mother died suddenly looked worn and threadbare. No one would ever accuse the MacGowan men of tidiness, and dishes from the previous evening's meal, as well as dirty clothes, were scattered throughout the room.

"What are you doing here, Elizabeth?"

His voice came out harsher and colder than he intended. Her head jerked in the direction of his voice; she hadn't seen him until that moment.

Releasing Johnny, she gave him a fond ruffle of the hair and turned to face Thom. "I need to speak with you."

"Now is not a good time."

Her gaze fell to the open leather bag on the bed, half-filled with his clothing, before lifting those big blue eyes back to his. "Jo said you are leaving."

"Tomorrow morning," Johnny filled in, finally finding his voice.

Elizabeth turned to the awestruck lad. "Would you mind giving your brother and me a few minutes in private? There is something I should like to discuss with him. I think I saw some boys heading down to the river to fish."

Johnny looked to him. Thom was tempted to shake his head but nodded.

A few moments later the door shut behind him, and

they were alone. Someone who didn't know her might think she was as cool and confident as she appeared, but Thom could see from the way her fingers were gripping the edges of the fur-lined cloak draped around her shoulders and the slight quickness of her breath that she was nervous.

He had no intention of easing it. He leaned back against the wall and crossed his arms formidably, waiting.

She looked around. "So this is where you hid yourself all those years. How come you never invited me here?"

As if it weren't obvious. He hadn't missed the tentative way she'd moved into the room, as if making sure she didn't accidentally step in muck or brush her pristine skirts against something dirty. She wasn't comfortable, and it showed.

His gut twisted. "What do you want, Elizabeth? Say what it is you will and go. As you can see, I'm busy."

She frowned. Her nose was not much bigger than it had been all those years ago, and it had only a few more crinkles. He'd never spoken to her so brusquely, and she didn't seem to know how to respond. "We need to talk."

"There is nothing to talk about."

She moved toward him. "Why are you being like this? Why are you so angry with me? I didn't do anything wrong."

"I'm not mad at you."

What right did he have to be mad at her? How could anyone blame her for not considering him as a suitor? No one would. He was so far beneath her as to make a match between them not only laughable but condemned. Aye, he had no right at all.

But he did blame her. He blamed her for being sweet and kind and so generous and funny that he couldn't help falling in love with her. He blamed her for being so damned beautiful it hurt just to look at her. He blamed her for deluding him into believing that he was someone worthy not only of friendship but of love. For making him believe that he was her equal in all the ways that mattered. For all the years he'd wasted waiting for something that was never going to happen.

He wasn't mad at all.

She put her hands on her hips the way she always did when she was angry with him. "I'm more than familiar with your black moods, Thom MacGowan, so don't try to intimidate me with your scowling. I know when you are mad about something."

He stood, letting his arms fall to his sides. "As you pointed out, a lot has changed in five years. Maybe you don't know me as well as you think you do." He took a step toward her, looming over her in the semi-darkness. "Maybe you should be intimidated. I'm not distracted by silly jokes anymore."

The deep suggestiveness of his voice hinted at exactly what might distract him now.

Her chin jutted up, but the flutter of a pulse below her jaw told him that she was not as unaware of his meaning as she wanted to be. He felt a surge of distinctly primal satisfaction. "Don't be ridiculous."

No doubt she didn't mean it the way it came out, but her words only fueled his temper, which like the rest of him was already too hot. The soft, subtle scent of her perfume wrapped around him in a sensual haze, stoking—or maybe he should say stroking—the flames of desire that made his body harden.

He stepped back. "Aye, it's ridiculous, all right. Which is why you should get the hell out of here."

It took her a moment to realize what he meant. "I didn't mean . . ." She scowled. "You know what I meant—that you would never hurt me—but you seem determined to misunderstand me. And don't speak like a churl."

"Don't you mean like the son of a smith? I may not

speak French—or whatever other languages you converse in now—but I understand you perfectly. Which is why we have nothing to say."

She pursed her mouth, clearly trying to exercise patience in the face of his rudeness. "I'm sorry I hurt your feelings, Thommy." Hurt feelings? If a hole could have opened in the middle of the floor to swallow him up, he would have welcomed it. Was two weeks ago not humiliating enough? She'd crushed his dreams, made him feel like a fool for thinking he could matter to her, and she acted like he was an overly sensitive schoolboy. "But you caught me off guard. I had no idea you felt . . . like that."

It embarrassed her even to say it. He suspected his face was as red as hers, and his teeth were gritted so tightly he was surprised he could speak. "That was obvious. But you need not worry that I will trouble you with those feelings again. I was mistaken."

She instantly brightened. "Then we can forget all about this and get back to normal?" She smiled. "I've missed you, Thommy. There is so much I want to tell you about France."

Years ago, he would have listened happily to her stories—actually, he had. Although he had no desire to see France or any of the other places she spoke of when they were younger, he would have traveled there, lived there, whatever she wanted, if that would have made her happy.

Now he stared at her in disbelief. Did she think his feelings were so shallow and malleable that he could turn them on or off like the wick from an oil lamp?

"How do you propose we get back to normal, Elizabeth? I've been waiting for five years for the lass I've loved for as long as I can remember—who I thought loved me—to come home." Her eyes widened at the word "love," but he didn't stop. "And when she does come home, it's to learn that everything I thought was wrong. Not only does she not return those feelings, she considers them 'impossible' and a 'game.' I may be a fool, but even I can see that it can never go back to the way it was."

Her eyes flared. It took a lot to rile her temper, but it appeared his fool comment had succeeded. "Nothing has to change, if you wouldn't be so blastedly stubborn."

Only years of remembering his place, of forcing himself to remember that she was the laird's daughter, prevented him from hauling her up against him. Instead he leaned down to look her in the eye. "Open those pretty blue eyes for once, Elizabeth. Everything *has* changed. Now both of us see that a future is impossible."

She glared at him mutinously. He wasn't the only one who could be stubborn. "That doesn't mean we still can't be friends."

"Yes, it does." They stood glaring at each other angrily for a few moments. His hands flexed at his sides, itching to touch her. To see that anger flare to the passion that he knew was just lurking underneath. But he wasn't good enough to touch her.

Pain stabbed and he turned away. "Now, if you'll excuse me, I need to finish packing."

It was she who touched him. The feel of her hand on his arm set off flares of awareness racing all over his skin. The anger had fled from her face, and she was looking at him with something like panic in her gaze. For once, he didn't feel like comforting her.

"But I don't want you to leave, Thommy. It won't be the same here without you." She'd always been able to tease him out of his bad moods, and she did so again. "Besides, who will be there to catch me when I fall?"

Thommy stared at her. Stared at the achingly beautiful

young woman who'd haunted his dreams for far too long. It had to stop. He wasn't the boy who'd saved her from stumbling more times than he could remember, and he sure as hell wasn't a "knight" who'd saved her from falling out of a tree and was rewarded with the hand of a princess.

But one day he would be. One day Elizabeth Douglas would regret letting him go. One day she would see the man he was and want him with all the longing and desperation that he felt right now, but by then it would be too late.

Their eyes met for the final time, and with all sincerity he said, "You know, Elizabeth, I really don't give a shite."

She gasped, and after a stunned moment, finally did what he asked.

When the door slammed behind her, Thom sat down on the edge of the bed and put his head in his hands.

3

Blackhouse Tower, Scottish Marches,
Ash Wednesday, February 22, 1314

ELIZABETH GAZED OUT the tower window, scanning the surrounding countryside. The bitter cold of winter was evidenced by the unbroken swaths of browns and grays painted across the horizon. It seemed there was not one green leaf or colorful wildflower left in the heavily forested hillsides of Galloway. The only wail was of the wind; the distinctive call of the peewits would not be heard for another few months.

Blackhouse Tower, part of the Douglas patrimony restored to her brother by Robert the Bruce, stood on the edge of a burn in the heart of the Ettrick Forest, the wild, inhospitable land that had served as a favorite base of Scots "rebels" from William Wallace to the Bruce. Beyond lay the rolling hills of Peebles, Selkirk, Jedburgh, Roxburgh, and the other important towns that lined the Scots side of the border.

What she wouldn't do to be in one of them. God, how she couldn't wait to leave this bleak, desolate place. The endless gray days, the monotony of seeing the same handful of faces day in, day out, the droning quiet. In the city there was always something new. There was always noise, entertainment, and something to be excited about. Here, in their remote forest fortress, the most exciting thing to happen lately had been the completion of a new tapestry to adorn the wall behind the dais. And she didn't even like needlework!

But not for much longer. Somewhere out there Jamie and his men were harrying one of the last English garrisons in Scotland at Roxburgh Castle, as part of King Robert's preemptive war against the English. In late October, Bruce had given notice that in a year's time, he would forfeit the lands of any nobles who still had not submitted to his authority as king. The threat to the nobles loyal to the English had finally forced Edward to act. The English king had responded with a call to muster at Berwick Castle in June.

Bruce was using the intervening months to prepare for the upcoming war. In addition to raiding and securing tribute from the English unfortunate enough to live near the border, the king's army was laying siege to the crucial strongholds of Edinburgh and—soon—Stirling, as well as sending out small bands of warriors (such as the one led by her brother) to prevent supplies from getting through to the others still in English possession, such as Roxburgh, Jedburgh, Bothwell, and Dunbar. The Bruce did not have the men or resources to lay siege to them all. When Edward II did march north, Scotland's castles would not be strongholds for the English.

But Jamie was expected to be called to Edinburgh soon to ready for the coming battle, and when he did, he'd promised to take them with him. After the fierce battles that had started the war, it had largely come to a standstill. With thousands of Bruce's men occupying the city, there was no fear of attack by the besieged English garrison of a hundred men. At least two of Bruce's sisters would be there, as would the wives of many of his retinue.

Elizabeth couldn't wait. Edinburgh wasn't Paris, but it was certainly a vast improvement over the Ettrick Forest.

She scanned the countryside, almost as if she might see a colorful banner or the flash of silver mail beneath a surcoat in the distance. But it wasn't the blue and white of Jamie's arms for which she unconsciously looked. Were Edward Bruce and his men nearby as well?

"Watching for someone, Ella?"

Elizabeth startled and turned in the direction of the speaker, her cousin Lady Isabel Stewart, daughter of the hero John Stewart of Bonkyl, who'd died fighting with Wallace at Falkirk, and cousin to the current Steward of Scotland—the 6th—Walter. The 4th Steward had been both girls' grandfather.

Isabel grinned and continued. "Trying to conjure up Sir Thomas out of all that mist? It's a long way to see to Edinburgh."

Elizabeth smiled. "I shall see him soon enough, Izzie."

Although Isabel was easily placated, the other occupant in the room was not. Joanna had known Elizabeth for too long. They weren't just childhood friends anymore. Joanna had become her sister-in-law two and a half years ago when she and Jamie had finally married. They'd gone through a difficult time after Joanna's accident. Elizabeth wasn't privy to all the details, but she knew Jamie had done something horrible, which Joanna had eventually forgiven him for. Fortunately, almost losing one another had seemed to make their love stronger. They'd been lucky.

Her sister by marriage gave her a very knowing look. "I hear from James that with Randolph laying siege to Edinburgh, Edward Bruce will begin the siege of Stirling Castle soon."

Elizabeth held her expression impassive, although she knew it well. "That is very interesting, but is of no import to me."

Joanna quirked her brow. "Isn't it? Hmm."

Elizabeth didn't like that "hmm." Whatever Joanna thought she knew, she was wrong. If Elizabeth spent too much time looking out of windows, it was because she was bored out of her mind and anxious. Not because she was looking—or waiting—for anyone, especially Thommy.

She was curious as to what had happened to him, that was all. Other than hearing that he was fighting with Edward Bruce, Elizabeth had heard nothing from her former friend in three years.

"Is it your argument with Archie that is bothering you?" Isabel asked.

Elizabeth was about to protest that nothing was bothering her, but as they seemed disinclined to believe her, she shrugged. "A little," she admitted. "It's hard with both Lady Eleanor and Jamie away. He doesn't listen to me."

"Nor to me," Joanna said with a wry smile. "But I think it is a function of being sixteen and a Douglas male who thinks he knows everything. I remember that time well."

So did Elizabeth. Her heart squeezed, admitting only to herself how much she missed it. It was before everything had become so *complicated*. Why did Thommy have to go and ruin everything by trying to change things? It had been perfect the way it was.

She'd treasured the bond between them, and the deep, abiding friendship that had weathered war, distance, and time. He'd been her companion, her confidant, her anchor in a maelstrom. He was her one constant, and along with Joanna, the best part of coming home. Thommy *was* home to her. Douglas hadn't been the same after he left.

She'd thought he would always be there. Whether it was rescuing her from a tree when she was six (and saving her from countless bruises, skinned knees, and twisted ankles afterward), providing a shoulder to cry upon after the death of her father at eight, or listening to her teenage tirades against her stepmother after one of their many arguments, he always seemed to know exactly what to say—or not say—to make it better. Even after the worst period of her life, when King Edward had stripped her family of everything after the death of her father, and they'd been forced to beg for a place to stay with relatives—eventually finding it with Isabel's family—Thommy was the only one she'd been able to confide in about the fear and shame that even now she couldn't quite forget.

Which was why Thommy's confession had come as such a shock. If anyone knew how important a good marriage was for her, it was he.

He was her dearest friend. At least she thought he had been. It still infuriated her to think about the way he'd last spoken to her. How dare he be mad at her when he was the one who'd tried to change the rules all on his own! She'd never thought of him like *that* and had no idea his feelings toward her had changed. She'd just turned sixteen when she'd last seen him, for goodness' sake. Hardly a time of great perceptiveness in life.

Admittedly, she hadn't been all that much more perceptive at twenty, and her reaction to his declaration could have been more tactful. Thommy was so infuriatingly *proud*, and she knew how touchy he could be about any reference to his father's position in their household. But she'd been stunned by his admission, and the words had popped out unthinkingly.

But what had he expected her to say? What he'd proposed was impossible on every level. She had a duty to marry to increase the power and prestige of her clan.

She'd never thought of Thommy before in terms of rank, but he'd forced her to acknowledge the vast difference between them. Daughters of important nobles did not marry sons of smiths. Not in Scotland—nor in any part of Christendom, for that matter. Only peasants thought of things like "want" and "love"—although thankfully she'd refrained from blurting *that* out. She could only imagine how he would have reacted to that less-than-sensitive observation. Love was desired in noble marriages, of course, but it was expected to grow, not be the basis of it.

She pursed her mouth. It still grated on her how coldly he'd treated her, and how easily he'd walked away and never looked back. So much for friendship and love.

Still, she hated how it had ended between them. Something about it felt unfinished—incomplete. Maybe that explained the strange restlessness that she just couldn't seem to shake. She wanted to see him—just to make sure he was all right, of course. She couldn't bear the idea of him hating her.

Pushing aside thoughts of her former friend, she returned to the subject at hand. "You mean Douglas pigheadedness changes after sixteen? You might tell my brother. Jamie still seems to think he knows everything." She shook her head. "I admit, I understand Archie's frustration. Were it me, I would be chomping at the bit to get out of here, too."

Archie wanted to join the fight, but Jamie had refused. Not only was he too young, it was too dangerous. The English would love nothing better than to get ahold of the brother—half or not—of the "Black Douglas." But Jamie's promise of "soon" was wearing thin to their sixteen-but-old-enough-to-fight brother, and Joanna and Elizabeth had been left with the difficult task of enforcing Jamie's orders. Last night she and Archie had argued about it.

"You mean you aren't?" Joanna said with a laugh. "I don't think Archie is the only one who wished he could take a horse and ride to Roxburgh—or Edinburgh."

Elizabeth tried to bite back a smile but failed. Joanna was right. "I do wish Jamie would finish up whatever he is doing at Roxburgh," Elizabeth said. "I'm not getting any younger. I'll be four and twenty next month. Now that Jamie has finally found someone who meets his requirements, I want to get on with the wedding."

"Maybe he can just take the castle for you?" Joanna said dryly. "That will get you to Edinburgh quickly."

Both women looked at each other and burst out laughing. Jamie's reputation for taking castles by subterfuge was becoming legend, but Roxburgh was one of the most heavily defended castles in the Borders.

"Well, it might have taken cousin James awhile to find

you a husband, but he did find one of the most important men in the kingdom," Isabel pointed out. "Not to mention a newly created earl. I should hope cousin Walter does half as well for me."

As Jamie held Elizabeth's wardship and marriage rights, the young Steward of Scotland held Isabel's.

Elizabeth flushed with pleasure, not bothering to hide her excitement among her friends. Jamie *had* done well for her—extremely well. "I can't believe I will be the Countess of Moray," she said in a low voice, as if saying it too loud might jeopardize it.

Jamie had proposed a betrothal with Robert the Bruce's nephew, and Jamie's close friend and rival, Sir Thomas Randolph. The Douglases were also related to Bruce—through their great-grandfather the 3rd Steward of Scotland—but Randolph was the son of Bruce's mother's half sister.

"There is so much to do, I cannot wait to get started," Elizabeth continued. "It's been too long since we've had the excitement of a celebration to plan for, and since Jamie thinks the king will insist on holding the wedding feast at one of his castles, it will likely be the biggest since he became king. Music, dancing, the best wine and food . . . It will be like being in Paris again. I'll have a beautiful new dress made—I know just what I want—and matching slippers, and—"

"A husband," Joanna interjected. "Don't forget that after this fantastic wedding and beautiful dress you'll have a husband."

Elizabeth shot her a chastising frown, refusing to let her sister-in-law dampen her excitement about the prospect of a wedding.

Although nothing had been settled yet, the trip to

Edinburgh was a mere formality. She had met Sir Thomas a few times, and there was no reason to think they would not suit. He was handsome and charming enough to make any young woman's heart race. She scrunched her nose. Hers hadn't as yet, but she was sure it would once they got to know one another better. More important, as the favored nephew of the king and an earl, he had enough lands to ensure her security for the rest of her life. Neither she nor her future children would ever have to rely on the charity of relatives again.

Aside from the Bruces, there might not be a more important man in the country than Thomas Randolph. Although Jamie might disagree about that. "I would be hard-pressed to find anything to object to in Sir Thomas," Elizabeth pointed out.

"Aye, he's a handsome rogue," Joanna agreed. "As well he knows. Women certainly seem to love him, but do you?"

Elizabeth gave her an odd look, taken aback. "What does that matter?"

It was Jamie's decision whom she married. Though he would never force her, Elizabeth knew her duty.

"It matters a great deal," Joanna said quietly. "I know James is excited about the prospect of this alliance, but don't let him push you into anything. He will want you to be happy—even if you need to remind him of it."

Elizabeth smiled with understanding. Jamie and Jo were so happy now, sometimes she forgot that it hadn't always been so easy for them. Jamie had married "beneath" him "for love," but it hadn't been without some struggle on her ambitious brother's part.

For a man in James's position, marriage was a duty, and marrying for love opened him to public censure. It offended not just the social order but was viewed as giving in to lust rather than honor. Elizabeth blushed. Who would have thought her fierce, strong brother would neglect his duty for base desires?

Although Jamie had weathered the scandal well, he could afford to do so with the king's rewards, and Elizabeth knew her duty. Unlike her brother, she did not have the ability to fight her way to greatness with a sword. Her only path to a secure future was through marriage.

Of course she didn't begrudge her brother his happiness—and she loved Jo like a sister—but that path was not for her. "What you and Jamie have is rare, Jo. It's not like that for most women in our position. Nor is it something that has ever been important to me. I'm not romantic like you are. But don't worry, I'm sure I will come to love the earl well enough. What's not to love?"

Joanna looked at her as if she wanted to argue, but decided not to press. Instead one corner of her mouth lifted. "Plenty, if you listen to James. Although until you are safely wed, I expect he'll be singing his praises."

Elizabeth laughed, having heard more than one of her fearsome brother's tirades against the "pompous" knight, when Randolph had bested him at something. The men were fierce rivals, always trying to one better each other in feats of battle, but surprisingly also were good friends.

"I can't wait to meet this paragon," Isabel said. "If half the things I've heard about him are true, he must be an impressive man."

Izzie would get her wish sooner than they anticipated. As if on cue, the sound of hoofbeats below signaled the arrival of a rider.

A few minutes later, Joanna was holding a message from Jamie in her hands. Her eyes bulged as she started to read it, and she muttered something like "God in heaven!"

Elizabeth was concerned until her sister-in-law started to laugh.

"What is it?" she asked.

There were tears of joy and pride in Joanna's eyes as she handed the parchment to her. "Read for yourself, but your future husband isn't going to be very happy when he hears about this."

Elizabeth read it in stunned disbelief. Near the end she let out a cry that mirrored Joanna's and threw her arms around her in celebration. Jo was right. Randolph wasn't going to be happy. He was almost two months into his siege on Edinburgh Castle, and James had just taken Roxburgh Castle in one night.

They laughed until tears ran down their cheeks. The miraculous feat that they'd jested about moments before had come true. Jamie had done the impossible once again. In a move that no one—including the Bruce—was expecting, he'd seen an opportunity and had taken the castle by subterfuge the night before during the Shrove Tuesday celebrations.

And almost as wonderful to Elizabeth's mind, after seeing to the destruction of the castle, her brother would arrive at Blackhouse within a fortnight to escort them to Edinburgh.

Overjoyed, Elizabeth went to share the news with Archie and her youngest brother, Hugh.

She only found one of them.

The bastard was toying with him. Thom attacked from the left and then from the right, but each time the captain deflected Thom's sword with a deft twist of his hands, first slapping—hard—the flat of his blade to Thom's shoulder and then his thigh. Letting him know that were they not sparring, his blade would have cut.

Thom didn't need to look at his opponent's face to know that he was gloating. The captain had been his enemy since Thom had stopped him from accosting Eoin MacLean's wife last year. The bastard should be thanking him. The captain—Sir John Kerr—had suffered a beating at MacLean's hands, instead of the slow death he would have had had Thom not intervened before he did more than grope.

But the captain didn't see it that way, and he looked for any opportunity he could to make Thom look bad— especially, like now, when their lord was watching.

Over the past three years Thom had quietly been making a name for himself, and Edward Bruce, Earl of Carrick, had taken notice. The king's only remaining brother had taken a personal interest in Thom's training, and let him know that despite his late start and humble beginnings, Thom could rise high in his army. This offended the captain's sense of order, and the earl's favoritism only increased his resentment.

Thom had suffered for it. And not just from the captain. For the past three years he'd been subject to every kind of humiliation, heard countless crude comments about his birth, and endured every kind of drudgery and physical demand that were calculated to wear him down—to prove that a "peasant" couldn't compete with men who'd been born to the battlefield. He'd wanted to quit more times than he could remember—usually when his bruised and battered muscles were burning, sweat was pouring from every orifice of his body, and he had taken another mouthful of dirt—but the thought of returning home in defeat had always stopped him. So he'd suffered and endured and eventually he'd earned their grudging respect. Most of them, at least.

"Perhaps you should stick to the hammer," the captain taunted. "The sword is the *noble* weapon of a knight. Brute strength won't get you very far if you don't learn how to use your edge." Thom was used to the snide remarks about his birth and didn't rise to the bait, which only served to annoy the captain. "Again," Kerr (or as the men aptly called him, "Cur") demanded, holding his sword out in front of him in a defensive position. Thom clenched his jaw and raised his hands to the right of his temple, preparing to attack.

"Don't think so much," one of the men gathered around watching suggested.

It was exactly Thom's problem. He was not without strength or skill, but even after three years of constant training, he had not found the instinctive movements that seemed burned into the muscle of men who'd held a sword since youth.

As much as Thom hated to say it, the captain was right: brute strength would only take him so far. Which was why he was subjecting himself to Kerr's humiliation at every opportunity. The captain might be a bastard, but he knew how to wield a sword.

Thom didn't want to just be good, he wanted to be among the best. If that meant cramming fifteen years of training into a handful of years and listening to the captain's slurs and taunts, he would suffer it gladly. He would do whatever it took.

With grim determination, Thom heeded the advice of the man who'd spoken and tried not to think too much as he stepped forward. He turned his hands, as if he meant to swing underhanded across, but then at the last minute, he rolled his wrist and used a downward motion. The captain was too good to be fooled. He blocked the blow, but when he did, Thom reacted, using the edge of the blade to roll over the captain's sword and tap his ribs, signifying a cut.

Thom betrayed none of his satisfaction, but it was there in Kerr's furious expression.

A few of the men clapped and cheered. Despite his rank, the captain was a crude braggart and not popular around camp.

The most important spectator clapped among them. When he finished, Carrick called Thom over. "Not bad, MacGowan. I see you are improving in your sword skills."

Thom accepted the compliment with a nod. "The captain has taught me much."

Carrick lifted a dark brow. "I see you've learned some diplomacy as well. You may become a knight yet." His mouth twisted with amusement. "Assuming your horsemanship skills have progressed, that is?"

Thom didn't bother hiding his grimace. His lack of fondness for horses (and theirs for him) wasn't exactly a secret. He rode, but through sheer grit and determination. "I'm afraid not, my lord."

Carrick laughed uproariously and clapped him on the back. "We'll find you a sweet filly to tame yet. Which reminds me . . ." He gave Thom a knowing look. "You made quite the impression on our hostess with your heroics a few days ago."

Thom winced a little at Edward Bruce's attempt at humor. Like most men in camp, Carrick could be crude when it came to talking about women. Big Thom would have skinned him alive, if he'd heard Thom say half—a quarter—of the things that were said about women at camp. Thom might be of low birth, but he'd been raised to treat lasses—all lasses—with respect. Despite their supposed code of chivalry, from what Thom had seen, not all knights took it to heart.

But Carrick wasn't all bad. Thom knew that many men didn't like the king's second-in-command, but he wasn't one of them. Edward Bruce could be hotheaded and impulsive, but he was also bold, fierce, and aggressive on the battlefield. If he was in the shadow of his older brother and at times jealous, perhaps Thom understood. He knew what it was like to always be looking up.

"It was nothing, my lord," Thom said.

"Well, Lady Marjorie doesn't think so. I wish I'd seen it. Did you really climb all the way up there?" The earl pointed to the spine of the pitched roof of the tower house.

Rutherford Castle was of the simple stone peel tower construction that was common in the area. It had served as a base for the earl and his men as they raided England and harried the garrison at Jedburgh to prevent any provisions from getting through.

"It's easier than it looks, my lord."

Edward Bruce glanced at him as if he were crazed. "How the hell did the cat get up there anyway?"

Thom shrugged. "Lady Marjorie said one of the children was chasing him around the ramparts and the cat was trying to escape. He was probably too scared to try to come down."

"I wonder why," Carrick said dryly. "I sure as hell wouldn't risk my neck for a cat, but Lady Marjorie is grateful. *Very* grateful. The lovely widow has requested that you be among the men to provide her escort to her lands in Yorkshire." When Thom didn't immediately respond, he added, "She specifically asked me what your position was in the army, and whether you were wed. I told her you were one of my most promising soldiers, and that you were as yet unmarried. The lady is definitely interested. Move your pieces right, and you'll capture your 'queen,' and be lord of this castle in a few months."

With the amount of attention Lady Marjorie had been showing him the past few days—and the suggestive touches and brushes—Thom wasn't completely surprised by the earl's news. "Thank you, my lord. I will do my best. When do I leave?"

"The day after tomorrow."

"You do not need me here for the raids?"

Carrick shook his head. "We'll be leaving for Stirling by the end of the week. You can meet us there." The earl paused, eyeing him thoughtfully. "You surprise me, MacGowan. I thought you would be more excited by the prospect of a rich wife. You've made no secret of your ambition. The alliance will elevate your standing among the men and make your path to knighthood much easier. 'Tis a good match. Better than most in your position could hope for—although I suspect your countenance helps. I've noticed how popular you are with the lasses." Thom withheld comment, as there wasn't much to say about that. Carrick frowned. "Is there another match you hoped to make?"

Thom shook his head. "Nay, my lord. I am pleased—*very* pleased," he added, furious at himself for his reaction. Carrick was right: he should be cheering from the rooftops at his good fortune. Lady Marjorie Rutherford was the widow of a respected knight with significant dower lands on both sides of the border, including this castle near Peebles. For a man in his position, it was a good match—a *spectacular* match—indeed.

If the lady herself was a little bold in her advances and reminded him of the feline to which she was so attached (more than her children, he couldn't help noticing), she was reasonably young, attractive, and, from what he could tell, an excellent chatelaine. Lady Marjorie was more than he could have hoped for.

He wasn't a lovesick fool anymore. A broken heart had proved to be a powerful eye-opener, curing him of all his illusions. He knew exactly where he stood, and what he needed to do to move up the ranks. A good marriage—a good *alliance*—was part of that.

Elizabeth had taught him well. Thom didn't think much about the past. He'd moved on. But when he did think of her, it was no longer with anger and hurt. It was no longer a raw, festering wound upon which the slightest touch would make his insides scream in agony. Nay, now it was more of a dull sense of loss and disappointment. A hole in his heart that would never be filled.

Not that he blamed her. He must have been half-crazed to ever think she would look at him as a potential suitor— even if she had returned his feelings. Elizabeth wasn't the widow of a minor baron. She was a *Douglas*. With everything that meant.

His mouth fell in a tight line. Unfortunately, he hadn't been able to put all of his past or all Douglases behind him. It seemed like every time he turned around, he was running into his former friend-now-nemesis or being forced to listen to some tale of whatever amazing feat the Black Douglas had managed on the battlefield. He was damned tired of it.

Joanna might have forgiven "Sir" James, but Thom wasn't as forgiving.

Perhaps the journey to Yorkshire would prove a boon in more ways than one. In England the Black Douglas was feared, not revered, playing more the role of bogeyman than great hero.

"I will be ready, my lord, and I look forward to escorting Lady Marjorie," Thom said with much more enthusiasm this time. "You can be assured, I won't waste this opportunity."

Carrick nodded. "Good. Resume your training."

A squire ran up and handed a missive to Carrick as Thom started to walk away. He took only a few steps before Carrick called him back. "MacGowan, wait." He finished reading the piece of parchment and lowered it. "I'm afraid your pretty widow is going to have to wait."

"My lord?"

"It seems Douglas has performed another miracle." If there was anyone who enjoyed hearing about Douglas's feats less than Thom, it was Edward Bruce—and perhaps Thomas Randolph. "He's taken Roxburgh Castle, and we've been ordered to help him destroy it."

4

ARCHIE CERTAINLY WAS going to have some ex-plaining to do. Elizabeth was exhausted by the time she and Joanna's brother, Richard, rode through the gate of Roxburgh Castle late the following morning. She dropped off the horse before someone could help her down and winced, putting her hand on the small of her back. The sixteen-year-old scamp had much to atone for, indeed. Not just for her exhaustion, but also for the crick in her back after one of the most horrid nights of sleep in recent memory. The ground had been about as warm and comfortable as a block of ice. Had she known what she was in for, she might not have been as eager to follow her runaway brother to Roxburgh.

Her mouth twisted. Who was she trying to fool? The long ride, ache in her back, and lack of sleep were well worth the prospect of a little excitement. She wanted to retrieve her miscreant of a brother, of course, but if there *happened* to be a feast or two to celebrate Jamie's taking of the important castle while she was here, she wouldn't be *too* disappointed.

Upon learning that Archie had ridden out shortly before the messenger had arrived, Elizabeth had called immediately for her horse and gone after him. It wasn't the first time she'd had to hunt down one of her half brothers and drag them back by the ear (fifteen-year-old Hugh was proving just as stubborn and muleheaded as other Douglas males). The difference this time was that she knew where Archie was going.

She did not consider it dangerous. What was left of English authority in Scotland had been whittled down to a few castles: Bothwell, Berwick, Jedburgh, Dunbar, Stirling, and Edinburgh. Bruce's and Randolph's siege blockades around the latter two castles, preventing the garrisons from leaving, made it the safest time around them in years. At least until June, when Edward II had threatened to march on Scotland again.

Nonetheless, she'd taken an escort, which was a good thing, as they'd seen a party of English knights on patrol east of Selkirk. Joanna's eldest brother (another Thomas) was fighting with Jamie, but twenty-year-old Richard was one of the handful of warriors Jamie had left behind to defend the castle.

The men were a mostly unnecessary precaution. The English knew better than to venture into the "haunted" Ettrick Forest. It was said to be the lair of Bruce's infamous Phantom warriors. The men were not phantoms, of course, but were extraordinary warriors. Their identities were cloaked in mystery, but as the sister of James Douglas, she had unique access to information. Listening at doors was definitely beneath her, but it did prove enlightening.

A second man at arms had been with her and Richard as well, but when they hadn't caught up with Archie by the time they reached St. Boswell's and the Newtun road, Elizabeth had sent him back to Blackhouse to inform Joanna of their plans to ride on to Roxburgh.

She frowned, thinking it odd that Archie had been able to evade them. At sixteen, her brother was more passion and impulse than skill and subterfuge. Richard had picked up his trail easily enough, but lost it at Selkirk. Assuming Archie would stop when it grew dark, they'd journeyed on until a few hours past nightfall. By that time they were more than halfway to Roxburgh, and she decided to bed down for the night and ride the rest of the way in the morning.

After handing off the reins to a stable lad, Elizabeth turned to Richard, who looked just as exhausted as she. "Find some food and get some rest. I'm sure Jamie will allow us a few days' respite before we must return."

She spoke with more confidence than she felt. She'd be lucky if her brother didn't send her right back. Jamie would undoubtedly be furious with her for riding—anticipating his words—"halfway across Scotland" (which was an exaggeration as it was a quarter across at most) with one man for protection. But, as she intended to remind him, it was his own fault. She'd warned Jamie about Archie doing something foolish, and he was the one who'd left her in charge of their brothers while Lady Eleanor was visiting relatives in England. Besides, Jamie was the one who'd taught her how to ride, and he wasn't the only Douglas who knew how to take advantage of the countryside.

She and Richard had stayed off the main roads, and except for the party of English they'd seen from a distance, they'd encountered nothing more dangerous than peddlers and pilgrims. The latter were all over these roads with the important abbeys of Melrose and Dryburgh so close.

Richard didn't put up much of an argument. "If you are certain you don't need anything else? I'd like to find my brother and hear all the details of the capture." He shook his head. "I can't believe I missed it."

Elizabeth grinned. "You sound like Archie, but aye, go find your brother while I go find mine—both of them."

He gave her a rueful grin. Like Joanna, Richard was blond and took after the Vikings who were undoubtedly in his ancestry. "I must admit the laddie impressed me. He's more skilled at riding and evasion than I thought."

Her as well. She frowned again, as Richard hurried off in the direction of what she assumed were the barracks. The celebrating must not have gone on too long last night—it *had* been a holy day, she supposed—because the yard was already bustling with activity.

The porter who had admitted them was finally coming out of his shock at her announcement of her identity. He offered to escort her to her brother, who was in the North Tower, but she'd declined. The fewer people who saw her brother lose his temper the better.

Elizabeth had seen many fine castles in her three and twenty years, but even including the magnificent palaces in France, Roxburgh was among the finest.

Situated on a hill between the Tweed and Teviot rivers, surrounded on three sides by a moat, it possessed a large dungeon and eight—she'd counted—towers. The curtain wall around the castle must be thirty feet high and eight feet thick. The castle was a walled city unto itself. The sheer magnitude of what her brother had accomplished became clear as she walked across the yard toward the impressive North Tower.

Dear Lord, how had he done it? She couldn't believe her brother had taken this massive fortress with sixty men. Richard wasn't the only one eager to hear the details.

A sound of banging grew louder as she approached the large circular tower. From the clouds of dust that greeted her as she entered, she realized Jamie wasn't wasting any time. His men were already beginning the slighting of the castle.

Though she understood why it must be done, it was sad to think that an architectural masterpiece like this must be destroyed. It was one more sin to lay upon the feet of the English. It still hurt to think about her own home, Douglas Castle, which had been destroyed for the same reason—by its owner.

Three years earlier, Jamie had taken the castle back from the English and destroyed it to prevent it from being garrisoned by the enemy again. Losing her home in such a way had been horrible. She'd been hurt and furious with Jamie for weeks, but eventually she'd come to understand the reasoning behind it—even if she didn't like it.

Standing in what must be a guardroom, Elizabeth looked around and saw nothing but men with shovels, hammers, and picks digging and tearing apart walls. Jamie certainly wasn't meeting here with his men. She must have gone to the wrong tower.

She started to back away when something caught her eye. Or rather *someone* caught her eye.

Good Lord! The blood seemed to drain from her body and then rushed back in a strange, fuzzy heat that made her skin prickle. One of the workers had taken his shirt off while he labored. He was a big man, and very—*very*—powerfully muscled. He had his back to her, and every time he swung the tool in his hand—a hammer, she realized, when she could tear her gaze away long enough to look—his heavy, thick muscles rippled all across his torso. All across his broad shoulders, his narrow waist, and his bulging arms. Her breath caught as her eyes remained fixated on his arms. They looked as strong as battering rams; she wondered that he needed the hammer at all.

A rush of warmth spread to her cheeks at the primal display of brute strength and raw physicality. Her reaction didn't make sense. She had no cause for embarrassment. She'd seen other muscular men without their shirts. Albeit none so . . . *so*.

But it wasn't embarrassment, she realized, it was something else. Embarrassment didn't heat other parts of her and make her body feel too heavy for her legs. Embarrassment didn't hold her breath and catch her pulse. Embarrassment didn't make her shiver.

Suddenly, realizing that she was gaping, she looked away. But something on his arm caught her attention and made her glance back. It was a red scar about three inches in length and half an inch in width on his left forearm. It was a scar you might get from being burned by a hot piece of iron.

She frowned, taking in details she hadn't noticed before. He was tall. About as tall as her brother at four or five inches over six feet, which was rare enough to be remarkable. His dark hair was cut too short to reveal any wave, but it was the right shade of almost black. The fluttery feeling in her stomach buzzed up her spine. It couldn't be . . .

But indeed it could. He turned and an achingly familiar pair of piercing blue eyes pinned her to the ground.

Thommy! My God, it *was* him! Except that he looked so . . . *different*. Rocked, she felt her legs buckling and put her hand out to catch herself on a nearby post.

That was a mistake.

Thom didn't know what was worse. That James Douglas had added one more incredible story to his ever-increasing arsenal of incredible stories and having to watch him bask in the glory, or being forced to do all the backbreaking work to clean up after it.

It turned out that brute strength was worth something after all, particularly when it came to slighting castles. Over the past two years, as castle after castle had fallen to the man they all called "the Bruce," Thom had been prized indeed.

If he thought to escape the hammer by being a soldier, he'd failed. Doubly. Not only was he swinging one to take down walls, he was taking odd jobs repairing weapons when he could to make enough coin to purchase one of the four-hoofed fiends. *A warhorse.*

In between swings, he shuddered.

As if riding one of the Devil's spawns wasn't enough, he'd be expected to learn to fight on one of them. Christ, he had a hard enough time keeping his seat with *two* white-knuckled hands gripping the reins. It seemed even the most docile of beasts turned into a wild, bucking stallion when Thom was around. Even the small hobby-horse he'd ridden here had tried to nip him.

By the time he'd arrived late last night, he'd been in a foul mood. A mood that hadn't improved any on coming face-to-face with the hero of the hour. Hell, after what Douglas had done, probably of the year.

Decade.

Age, blast it.

There had already been some dramatic tales of trickery and subterfuge in the retaking of castles by Bruce and his men the past few years—including three by Jamie at Douglas Castle, Randolph (with James's help) at Linlithgow, and Bruce himself at Perth Castle—but this one was the biggest, most important yet. Maybe more so because it had surprised everyone.

Even the Bruce.

The assault on the castle had been a rogue mission. Douglas had watched the garrison, seen an opportunity, and seized upon it.

With Edinburgh Castle under siege, the garrison at Roxburgh had assumed Bruce's attention was focused in that direction. It was, but Douglas's wasn't. Taking advantage of the Shrove Tuesday "carnival"—the farewell to meat—Douglas and about threescore of his men disguised themselves in black cloaks, crawled on their hands and knees across a field to mix in among the grazing oxen, and scaled the walls with their newly invented rope ladders. Taken by surprise, most of the garrison had surrendered. A handful of men, including the Gascon keeper of the castle, Guillemin Fiennes, had attempted to take refuge in one of the towers, but a one-in-a-million arrow shot by the Highlander Gregor MacGregor had struck the commander below the eye as he attempted to peek out an arrow slit.

He'd surrendered, and the garrison had been permitted to slink back to England in defeat.

Thom had lifted a brow at that. A brow Douglas had seen and asked if he had a problem with it. To which Thom had been unable to stop himself from sarcastically questioning whether all the larders had been full. A reference to Jamie's most famous "black" deed, where he'd tossed the bodies of the English garrison into the larder of Douglas Castle and set it on fire.

Douglas had been livid, and for one moment, Thom thought they would come to blows again. Hell, after a lifetime of having to keep his thoughts to himself and deferring to the "lord," he would have welcomed it. He wouldn't last two minutes against Douglas with a sword, but when it came to brawling, he could hold his own with anyone.

Brute strength.

Aye, he had that, which is why it had grated when Douglas had ignored him and turned to Carrick to tell him where his men could find the *hammers* and other tools to get to work, while they went to the Hall to accept homage from the nobles and other landowners in the area.

Thom took another powerful swing with the blasted hammer against the section of wall and heard a crack. Good, it was finally loosening.

They'd been working on this section of the wall all morning, digging a deep trench underneath, and then loosening the stone with the hammer and picks. They were almost ready to set fire to the wooden supports. With a little luck, the whole thing would buckle and collapse into itself. But it was by no means exact. He just hoped he was far enough away when it all came down.

"Careful," he said to one of the men. "You don't want to hit that section too hard. It's already weakened."

The man had stopped to look at him, and his eyes widened at something over Thom's shoulder. "If that lass is real, I'd give my left bollock to have her looking at me the way she's looking at you. Is she yours?"

Thom looked over his shoulder and froze. The sight that met his eyes was so unexpected he didn't have time to prepare himself. For one moment, he was that lad again who looked up at the tower and thought he saw a princess. And all the longing, all the admiration, all the feelings came rushing back to him in a torrential wave.

Ella.

He stiffened, remembering. Nay, not Ella, Elizabeth. *Lady* Elizabeth to him. That part of his life was over. "She is not mine."

She never had been.

But what the hell was she doing here? In the middle of his work site, damn it! There were unstable walls everywhere; didn't she realize how dangerous it was?

And why the hell was she looking at him as if he were a beast in a menagerie?

She started to sway as if she was woozy. Instinctively—as he'd done it so many times before—he lurched forward, thinking to catch her. But she was too far away.

He must have realized what she was going to do, because he was already running toward her as she reached out to brace herself on a post. A post that had been set up to support an unstable wall.

He shouted for her to get out of the way, but it was too late. In slow-moving horror he watched as a section of the wall gave way.

She stood there, frozen in horror as dust, rock, and debris came flying down upon her.

Oh God, the stone was going to hit her head. Heart in

his throat, Thom leapt forward, shoving her harshly out of the way and taking her to the ground.

They landed hard, his body on top of hers, braced protectively to take the brunt of the falling stone. He grunted in pain as a sizable rock hit the edge of his shoulder. A few smaller rocks peppered his back, legs, and the arm that was protecting his head. Next time, he would remember not to remove his helm. But it was hot work, and he'd been getting sweaty . . .

Sweaty.

Ah, hell. All of a sudden he realized two things at once. The dust was settling, she was safe, and he was living out one of his fantasies.

He had a lot of them.

But one of his favorites, especially in those first few months after leaving Douglas, had been seeing her in that white gown again and running his dirty hands all over her. What was it about all that pristine perfection that made him want to mess her up a little? That made him want to take his big, callused smith's hands and slide them all over that flawless, milky-white skin?

He imagined her soft, naked body under his, their skin hot and slick as he drove into her again and again. He imagined that icy cool facade hot and flushed with pleasure—maybe a little sweaty—begging him to take her harder, rougher. He imagined her fingers digging into his shoulders, as urgent moans came apart in a violent scream. And after, he imagined her strewn over him, naked limbs twisted in the sheets with a messy, well-tumbled look on her face.

She wasn't wearing white, but he was half-naked, sweaty, and her fingers were digging into his shoulders. With her under him, it was pretty damned easy to imagine everything else. He was thick and hard, and for one agonizingly perfect moment, he notched himself between her legs. Blood rushed and pounded. The urge to push—to thrust—was nearly overwhelming.

He raised his chest enough to look into her eyes. It was a mistake. Hers were filled with shock . . . and something else. Something that made him think—just for a moment—that he hadn't been wrong. That what she felt for him was more than friendship. That she was just as aroused as he.

And that she was finally seeing him.

She cupped his jaw with one of her tiny hands, and it felt like a brand upon his skin. "You are always riding into my rescue, aren't you, Thommy? How shall I reward you this time?"

It was a game they'd played as children.

A *game*, damn it. Nothing had changed. Except that he'd outgrown games years ago.

He was about to tell her exactly how she could reward him—explicitly—when he heard a familiar voice say, "Get the hell off my sister, you filthy bastard!"

Saying she was stunned was putting it mildly. For a moment, Elizabeth forgot how to breathe. The air was trapped in her lungs somewhere near her heart, which also seemed to have come to a screeching halt. Apparently her head wasn't working very well either, as the first thought that popped into it wasn't relief at not lying crushed under a pile of rocks, but the inane realization that he was handsome.

She'd blinked a few times, trying to clear the confusion. But it wasn't a mirage. The piercing blue eyes, strong jaw, hard cheekbones, broken-more-than-once nose, heavy brow, and not-quite-black hair were all Thommy, and he was undeniably *handsome*.

Breathtakingly so. And heart-stoppingly and head-confusingly so, as well. Good Lord, how had that happened? *When* had that happened?

"Grateful to be alive" wasn't her second thought either. Or her third, for that matter. The thoughts that followed were rather occupied by the awareness of the big, slightly sweaty, half-naked body on top of hers, which looked and felt about as hard and solid as all those rocks that had been about to tumble down on her, and that by all rights due to his size *should* be crushing her but wasn't. He actually felt good. *Really* good. Even though he was heavy and hot. As in standing-too-close-to-the-forge hot. Her fingers were practically burning as they dug in—or tried to dig in—to the steel ball of muscle on his upper arms.

God almighty, he was strong! She'd known that, of course. How could she not with as many times as she'd watched him work or do his chores? But it was quite a different thing to see it and another to experience it viscerally over every inch of her body.

Indeed, everything about what she was feeling right now was visceral. Her senses were heightened, her nerve endings prickling, her skin tight and sensitive, and hot. Did she mention hot? All over hot. Drenching hot. Rushing to strange parts of her body hot.

Good gracious, what was wrong with her?

It was only when she looked into his eyes that she felt her sense of equilibrium return. The familiar gaze gave her an anchor in a storm of confusion.

Thommy.

She sighed with relief and made a jest. A jest that from his expression hadn't been received very well.

She was still trying to figure out what she'd said wrong this time, when her brother intruded.

Thommy was pulled off her, and she was left . . . bereft. Not to mention cold and strangely let down.

"What the hell do you think you are doing?" Jamie shouted at Thommy.

There were very few men who could appear completely nonplussed to have the Black Douglas shouting at them, but Thommy was one of them. Even as a youth, he would stand up to Jamie in a way that none of the other village boys dared. He would face him just the way he was right now, with a calm, expressionless look on his face that drove Jamie crazy. Though there was nothing outwardly challenging or defiant, simply by the level of control it was exactly that.

He was a rock. Solid, steady, and unflappable. No matter how much Jamie egged him on to fight back—no matter how angry Elizabeth could sense Thommy was—he never would. At least that's the way it had been in Douglas and before the argument that had ended their friendship. But now, she wondered if something had changed.

This time, Thommy broke his stoic facade with a cocked brow. "What did it look like I was doing?"

There was a subtle taunt in his voice that Elizabeth didn't understand. But Jamie did. He made a sound low in his throat like a growl and moved toward Thommy. "I'm going to kill you, I don't care what Carrick says."

After getting herself to her feet—the two men were too busy breathing fire to remember her—Elizabeth stopped him. "Wait, Jamie!" She stepped in front of Thommy, who was still standing there lazily with his arms crossed in front of him, as if he didn't have a care in the world (especially that he was a moment away from having Jamie's fist in his jaw). "He was saving my life, that's what he was doing," she said. She moved her hand, gesturing to the rocks all strewn around their feet. "Did you happen to miss the wall that just came down? Well, it would have been on my head had Thommy not pushed me out of the way." She bit her lip, turning around to face Thommy. She had to dip her head back to look up. "Are you hurt?"

He held her gaze for a long heartbeat. There was an intensity there that she couldn't decipher. She would have given almost anything at that moment to know his thoughts.

"No."

She wasn't sure whether to believe him, but he was making her feel kind of funny with the way he was looking at her—her heart was fluttering oddly—so she turned back to Jamie and glared. "You should be thanking him."

Unable to deny the evidence around him, Jamie stepped back.

She waited. Unlike Thommy's, her brother's expression hid few of his thoughts, and right now "stubborn" was besting what was "right."

She put her hands on her hips. "Well?"

For the first time, Elizabeth was aware that there were other men with Jamie, and that with the men working on the wall, they now had quite an audience. Thus at least a dozen men witnessed the rare sight of James Douglas apologizing. He might be drawn up as tight as a bow, his hands might be curled into fists at his sides, and his mouth might look like he'd just drunk curdled milk, but he said, "It seems I owe you an apology. I didn't realize—"

All of a sudden he did realize.

He spun on her with all the anger that had been directed at Thommy. "You could have been killed! God damn it, Elizabeth, don't you know how dangerous this is? What the hell are you doing in here?"

Apology apparently forgotten, he eyed Thommy suspiciously, and she felt him stiffen behind her.

Elizabeth frowned at her formidable brother. She knew his anger was out of concern, but he was wrong with what he was insinuating. "I was looking for *you*. I was told you were in the North Tower."

"I was. This is the Guard Tower."

"Aye, well, I realized that too late. I was leaving when I accidentally knocked down the wall."

She decided it was more prudent not to explain she'd grabbed the wall to brace herself from the shock of seeing a half-naked man.

Not just any half-naked man.

Her brother's eyes darted to Thommy, and then back to hers again. "Why are you at Roxburgh at all? As I recall, I told you to stay put, and I would be at Blackhouse to fetch you when I'd finished here. This is no place for a lady."

Was it her imagination, or had he emphasized that last word for Thommy's benefit? The tension between the two men was palpable.

Jamie was acting like she'd come to Roxburgh to find Thommy. But that didn't make sense. He should have guessed why she was here. She frowned. "I came after Archie, of course. To bring him back."

Jamie wasn't looking back and forth to Thommy anymore; his gaze was firmly fixed on hers. "What are you talking about?"

Her heart sank, as the first hint of panic spiked her

pulse. "Archie took a horse and rode out yesterday to join you. I followed him to bring him back, but didn't catch up with him in time. I thought to find him here with you."

Jamie shook his head, and she knew from his grim expression what he was going to say. "Archie isn't here."

5

AFTER JAMIE'S OMINOUS pronouncement, Elizabeth and her brother retired to the king's solar in the North Tower—the actual North Tower, this time, which was connected to the Guard Tower by the aptly named North Range.

Jamie had led her away so quickly she hadn't had a chance to speak with Thommy—not that the blank stare he gave her invited conversation—but she would seek him out later.

First, she had Archie to worry about. She was trying not to overreact, but she could sense Jamie was anxious as well. He'd called for Richard, and along with Joanna's other brother, Thomas, they were gathered around the table on benches with a few of Jamie's other household guardsmen.

Her brother's eyes seemed to have turned black as they felt like pinpoints on her. "You rode halfway across Scotland with *one* guardsman for protection?"

Truly, he was so predictable. "I'm not the one who matters right now. We need to find Archie. Where else could he have gone?"

She didn't doubt there would be hell to pay later, but Jamie's worry for the sibling who was currently in danger won out. "Are you certain he was making his way here?"

Elizabeth bit her lip, her hands twisting anxiously. "Nay, but I assumed after our argument"—she'd filled him in on the disagreement she'd had with Archie the night before—"he would come here. It's what he'd threatened to do." She looked to Richard for help. "He was headed in this direction—at least until Selkirk."

"Aye, my lord," Richard put in. "I tracked him easily enough but lost him in the city."

Jamie swore, dragging his fingers through his hair. His eyes fell on her accusingly. "You were supposed to be watching him."

Elizabeth gave him a harrowing look. She knew he was upset, but she wasn't going to let him turn this on her. "Other than lock him up, I don't know what you expected me to do. He's a stubborn, pigheaded, sixteen-year-old lad who wants to prove himself and thinks he is indestructible. You wouldn't know anything about that, would you?" Jamie's mouth twisted, trying not to smile. "I gave orders that he wasn't to leave the castle, but he stole a horse while most of the men were hunting, and no one noticed that he was gone until I went to look for him. He had no more than a few hours' lead time on us."

Jamie stood and came over to pull her up into his arms. He squeezed her tight. "Hell, I'm sorry. I know this isn't your fault. Don't worry, I'm sure we'll find him easily enough."

Elizabeth felt the tears gathering behind her eyes as she

stared up into her big brother's handsome face. "Do you think so?"

He pressed a kiss to her brow. "I know so. I will lead the search party myself."

Relieved, Elizabeth stood to the side and listened as he gave orders to his men. If Jamie said he would find him, he would. When it came to warfare, there was no one she trusted more.

Although under the circumstances, maybe it wouldn't hurt to make doubly sure. She waited for him to finish and drew him aside for a private word. "Are any of the Phantoms here?"

His expression went tellingly blank. "What are you talking about?"

She rolled her eyes. "Really, Jamie, it's not that hard to figure out. Although I don't know why you didn't join, since you are always fighting with them anyway." She rattled off the names of the men most often in his company: Gregor MacGregor, Kenneth Sutherland, Magnus MacKay, Ewen Lamont, Eoin MacLean, and Robbie Boyd. She knew Alex Seton had been a member as well, but he'd recently switched allegiance to fight with the English.

"How the hell . . . ?" His eyes narrowed. "God damn it, Ella, you are too old to be listening at doors." He gave her a hard look, meant to intimidate. Although impressive, it was thoroughly wasted on her.

He stormed off without confirming or denying anything, but she was relieved to see that when he rode out of the castle less than an hour later, four of the men she'd mentioned rode with him.

It would be all right. Her brother and Bruce's Phantoms—or as they called themselves, the Highland Guard—would find Archie. She retreated to the room provided for her to bathe, eat something, and rest, confident that when she woke, she would be giving her young brother a scolding like he would not soon forget for scaring her so horribly.

Elizabeth tried not to be alarmed when her brother and the other men still had not returned by the evening meal. She'd hoped to have a chance to talk to Thommy, but he hadn't been among the two hundred or so warriors who'd gathered in the Great Hall for the light repast.

She'd missed him the past few years, but hadn't realized how terribly until she'd seen him. There had been a void in her life since Thom left, and now that she'd been given the chance, she was determined to put it right between them. They couldn't go on like this. They'd been friends for too long.

When she'd inquired of Edward Bruce where she might find him, he told her he hadn't seen MacGowan since the men had finished the work on the tower for the day a few hours earlier. He'd shrugged indifferently and suggested he might have gone into town with some of the others. He was a popular man in town. From how Carrick said it, she took it to mean with the women.

At that point, a man seated nearby interrupted. "He's not in town, my lord." He turned to her. "If you are looking for MacGowan, my lady, he was waiting to see the healer."

"The *what*?" She didn't realize she'd jumped to her feet until everyone turned to stare at her.

The man—who was really more of a lad at seven or eight and ten—blushed. She suspected he was one of the earl's squires. "I didn't mean to alarm you, my lady. It is nothing serious." He frowned. "MacGowan wouldn't have been able to swing a hammer all day if his shoulder were broken."

Elizabeth didn't need to hear anything more. "Where?" she demanded.

The lad—Henry—pointed her in the direction of the apothecary, which he said was located near the kitchens on the other side of the castle garden.

It was dark and cold out as she fled the warmth of the Hall, but she didn't take time to fetch her cloak. The directions weren't as easy to follow as she thought, so she was forced to stop and ask a few times, but eventually she found the right door and burst into the small building windblown, breathless, and half-frozen.

But none of that mattered when she caught sight of the man seated on the stool with his back to her. He had his shirt off again, but this time she didn't notice the broad shoulders, narrow waist, and wide expanse of muscle. This time all she could see was the patch of horribly bruised and swollen skin that covered a large portion of his right shoulder.

A sharp cry strangled in her throat.

He turned at the sound, and their eyes met.

"You're hurt!" she exclaimed accusingly.

"It's nothing," he replied, a hint of annoyance marring the overly polite tone. "I thank you for your concern, my lady, but you should return to the Hall."

He didn't wait for her response, turning his head and giving her his back. Apparently, she was supposed to leave. Well, she was about to disappoint him. Undaunted by the cold clip of his voice and undeniable air of unwelcomeness, she closed the door behind her and crossed the room.

Although Thommy was ignoring her, the healer was not.

The young, very pretty healer, she suddenly realized. The red-haired, green-eyed, pixie-faced woman was looking at her with unabashed curiosity.

"Elizabeth Douglas," she said by way of introduction. "The injury is my fault. Is it broken?"

"Ah," the healer said with a smile. "You are James's sister. I thought you looked familiar. We met a long time ago when the Highland Games were held at your uncle the Steward's castle on the Isle of Bute. My father was the Earl of Sutherland. I'm Helen MacKay."

MacKay. It took Elizabeth a moment to make the connection. "Ang—" She started to say Angel, but stopped, realizing she wasn't supposed to know that Lady Helen was the unofficial physician of the Phantoms. The woman's eyes widened; she'd caught the slip. "You are Magnus MacKay's wife," Elizabeth said instead. "I've heard James speak of you."

Thommy was in good hands indeed.

Helen's mouth twisted. "It seems you have. But to answer your question, it is not broken. Although, as I was explaining to Thom here, he made it much worse by working all day after he was injured. I'm sure it must have hurt like the devil to swing a hammer or pick with this. If something hurts," she explained, as if talking to a bairn, "that means you shouldn't keep doing it."

"It was fine," Thommy said stubbornly.

Both women acted as if he hadn't spoken. Men were so ridiculous when it came to admitting pain. Elizabeth didn't need a physician to know that. She had three brothers.

"Now, he will need to keep it bound for at least a few days until the swelling goes down," Lady Helen continued. "I've applied a soothing salve, which should be reapplied in the morning and evening before he goes to sleep. He'll need someone to help him wrap it."

"I can—"

"I will have one of the men in the barracks see to it," Thommy said, cutting her off with a sharp glance. "You should go back to the Hall, Lady Elizabeth, you don't belong here."

If Helen was surprised by his rudeness, she did not show it.

"As it was my fault you were injured, I certainly do," Elizabeth replied.

"I doubt your brother would agree. Should we go ask him?"

Elizabeth smiled sweetly at the threat. "You are welcome to when he returns."

Helen's head was going back and forth following the exchange, and she seemed to be fighting hard not to smile when Elizabeth finished.

"Would you show me how?" she asked the healer. "That way I can make sure it is done properly."

"Damn it, I don't want—"

"I'm sure Lady Helen has other patients who need help," Elizabeth said, cutting off his protest. "Do you want to waste time arguing or will you let me do this? Good gracious, Thommy, it's not as if I haven't touched you before."

Helen's eyes shot up at that, and when she realized how it sounded, Elizabeth's cheeks heated. But at least Thommy seemed to understand she would not be shooed away. He snapped his mouth closed, gave her a hard glare, and turned away from her to face the wall. From the way his jaw was clenched, she was surprised his teeth weren't cracking.

If she didn't know him better, she might think that he

wasn't just being stubborn but that he *really* didn't want her here. But she did know him . . . didn't she?

She had to admit this indifferent stranger attitude was slightly disconcerting. He wasn't just acting like he didn't know her, he was acting as if he didn't *want* to know her.

Lady Helen handed her the strip of cloth and showed her how to wrap it around his shoulder and then around his ribs to secure it. Despite what she'd said about touching him before, Thommy wasn't the only one who jumped when she pressed the strip of linen to his skin. She felt like she'd been buzzed with lightning.

"I'm sorry," she said, recovering from the shock. "Did I hurt you?"

He mumbled nay, something that sounded like a curse, and gruffly told her to hurry up and finish.

Now, *that* sounded like Thommy. She muttered something back about rude, grumpy, overgrown little boys who were too proud and muleheaded to admit they were hurt.

With Helen's help, it didn't take long to wrap the linen around the injured shoulder. Satisfied, Helen told Thommy he could put on his shirt, which due to the loose cut, he was able to do on his own—despite not being able to lift his right arm more than a few inches. Elizabeth suspected that keeping him from lifting was the reason for the binding. Donning his leather surcoat was a bit more difficult, but he managed with Helen's help.

Without looking at Elizabeth, he thanked Helen, grabbed his plaid and weapons, and started for the door.

Elizabeth exchanged a surprised glance with Helen and went after him. "Thommy, wait! I wanted to—"

Talk to you. But her words were cut off by the sound of a door closing.

Elizabeth blinked, almost as if she couldn't believe he'd just slammed the door on her.

After a hastily muttered apology to Helen (although why she was apologizing for his rudeness, she didn't know), she went after him. Actually, as he was walking so fast, she had to run after him.

"Thommy!" Her voice grew louder. "Thommy, wait!"

There were a number of people milling about the yard who turned to look at her. Unfortunately, Thommy wasn't one of them. He didn't stop walking until she came up next to him, grabbed his arm, and forced him to acknowledge her. They were a few feet away from what she suspected was the barracks, and the torches near the door provided enough light to see his face. "Good gracious, Thommy, I asked you to wait. Did you not hear me?"

"I heard you fine—the English on the other side of the border probably heard you fine—but I did not hear a question."

She frowned. "You did not give me a chance. I was going to ask to speak with you."

"No, thank you," he said in the same overly polite tone he'd used earlier. He started to move away. *Would* have moved away if she hadn't stepped around to block him. Or tried to block him, but as soon as their bodies came into contact, she realized the futility of that. It was like running into a stone wall. Actually, it was like having a stone wall run into her. He was forced to catch her to prevent her from falling on her backside.

He set her on her feet and let her go about as quickly as a burning pot. "Bloody hell, Elizabeth, do you ever look before you step? I've never known someone to have such a difficult time staying upright."

It sounded so much like something he would have said

years ago that she grinned back at him. "I tie my boots together, remember?"

It was what he'd always teasingly accused her of doing to explain her frequent stumbles as a girl. She didn't stumble so often anymore, although the last time she had, it was the first time he hadn't been there to catch her. She'd ended up with a twisted ankle.

She'd always been able to lighten his moods with a silly jest or gentle tease, but it was clear that wasn't the case anymore. His expression was not one of amusement. Ambivalent, mildly annoyed, and impatient was probably a more accurate description.

Darkly shadowed and strikingly handsome was another. She couldn't seem to stop staring at the familiar features and wondering how it could be that he looked so *different*.

But it wasn't just his appearance that had undergone changes in the past three years, she realized. The changes were deeper—far deeper. The grim, taciturn warrior with the merciless mouth and eyes as cold and sharp as steel was nothing like the reserved, if sometimes stoic, childhood companion she remembered. If she didn't know him so well, she might think he looked intimidating. Maybe even *fierce*.

But it was clear that the past few years had been hard on him, and suddenly she wanted to hear everything about it. Everything about *him*. Just like it had been when they were young.

"What is it that you wanted, Elizabeth? Say what it is you have to say. I'm tired and want to get back to the barracks."

She looked up at him, scanning his face for any vestiges of the man she remembered and wondering how she was going to break through this impenetrable shell he'd put up around him. She couldn't let it go on like this. He was too important to her. He'd always been the one person she could count on, the one person who was always there for her—even when he wasn't. The thought that she might never see him again—never talk to him again—was inconceivable. She needed him in her life. She just hadn't realized how much until now.

She tried not to sound hurt. "I just wanted to speak to you."

"And what I want is immaterial?"

She stepped back, unsure of what he was accusing her. "Of course not. But it's been three years, Thommy. I thought you might wish to speak with me, too? I had hoped you would still not be angry with me after what happened last time. You never gave me a chance to apologize."

"I am not angry with you at all. Why should I be? The fault was mine." He spoke so calmly—so indifferently—it was hard to believe this was the same man who'd burned with such *passion*. She almost wished he was still angry with her. At least then she would know he cared a little. "You have nothing to apologize for. I'm sorry if I offended you. You need not fear it will be repeated. I see things very clearly now."

She didn't know what he was trying to say. Did that mean he no longer had feelings for her? She was relieved. Of course, she was. That meant they could go back to being friends. "I never meant to hurt you, Thommy. Surely you know that?"

He stared at her intently, as if wanting to deny it, but ultimately, he seemed to concede her sincerity. "Aye."

It was the first crack in the steely facade, and rather than step back and be patient as she should have, she pressed forward. "Does that mean we can still be friends?" She reached up and put her palm on his cheek, the stubble underneath thicker and rougher than it had been before. Something about that sent a shiver over her skin as she said, "I've missed you."

He flinched away from her touch. She could feel the hard calluses on his palm as it wrapped around her wrist to drag her hand to her side. "You can't touch me like that anymore, Elizabeth. We aren't children. Someone might see and get the wrong idea. Your brother, for one."

She frowned. "Jamie can go to the Devil. I don't care what he thinks."

"I wish I could say the same, but in this case he's right. You and I . . . There is no you and I. We cannot go back to the way it was. I haven't been Thommy for a long time—and you aren't Ella. We have different lives. I'm a soldier, and you are the sister of the Black Douglas. We live in two different worlds. You need to go back to yours and leave me to mine. I've moved on, it's time for you to do the same."

Her lips parted with a gasp that never came; it stayed lodged in her chest, where it started to burn.

He turned on his heel and walked away. This time she let him go.

Elizabeth told herself that Thommy—*Thom* (how was she supposed to think of him that way?)—didn't mean it. He couldn't want to cut her out of his life completely. Forever. They would get past this. They *had* to get past this.

Time . . . that's what he needed. She vowed to give him that before seeking him out again.

But it didn't take her long to regret that vow.

Only one hour later, she stood gazing up at her brother. "What do you mean, there is no sign of him? There *has* to be a sign of him. He couldn't have just disappeared." Jamie's expression was too still. Too expressionless. "What is it? What are you not telling me?"

"Nothing," he said.

Tears sprang to her eyes. "Tell me, Jamie, I know when you are hiding something."

He shook his head and sighed, dragging his fingers through his hair. "I'm not. But you were right, we were unable to find any sign of him after Selkirk. Archie isn't usually so careful, and it bothers me."

She'd thought the same thing. "Perhaps you could use a different tracker?"

Jamie quirked his mouth in a half smile. "I used the best. Trust me, if Lamont can't pick up his trail no one can."

"Then what do we do?" She started to pace in front of him. "We can't just stay here and do nothing."

"We aren't. I've sent a few men back to Blackhouse to see if he's returned there, Lamont and MacLean are still out searching for signs, and a couple of friends have ridden to Edinburgh to fetch someone who might be able to help find out more information."

"Lachlan MacRuairi?"

"Bloody hell, Ella, just how often were you listening in on my conversations?"

She decided it prudent not to answer that question. "It's not exactly a secret. MacRuairi was named as one of Bruce's Phantoms years ago."

Jamie wasn't fooled. "Aye, well, that may be true, but not everyone knows why I might have sent for him."

"So you did send for him?"

He shook his head. "You are incorrigible. I almost pity Randolph." His wicked smile, however, suggested otherwise.

"When will you know more?"

"I hope by tomorrow." Sensing her distress, he pulled her into his arms and gave her a comforting squeeze. "I know it's hard, but try not to worry too much, little one. For all we know, Archie decided to return home, or he took a wrong path and is turned around."

Neither of them believed that. Something was wrong, and they both knew it. But Jamie was right. It wouldn't help to imagine all the horrible things that could have happened. They would have to wait for his "friends" to return with information.

Until then . . . she had to resist the impulse to run straight to Thommy. *Thom*.

It wasn't easy. The next twenty-four hours were some of the longest of her life—especially after MacKay and Sutherland returned from Blackhouse Tower the following morning to report that Archie hadn't returned there. It was Lachlan MacRuairi they were waiting for now, and it wasn't until after the bells for vespers had rung that he finally rode through the gate with a handful of the other Phantoms.

They looked like they'd been in the saddle for hours, and if the grim expressions on their faces were any indication, the news was not good.

The men immediately retired to the king's solar with Jamie—the same room where she'd met with him yesterday. Jamie posted a man outside the door, but she'd noticed the day before that the room also had a fireplace with a chimney, which was shared with the room above. Before the castle had been taken, the third-floor chamber would have been occupied by one of the English nobles—or perhaps noblewomen—in the castle, but fortunately for her, it was empty. She had no intention of waiting for Jamie's edited and condensed version of what the men had to tell him. It was a little smoky with her head almost in the chimney, but due to the late hour and lack of noise in the yard she was able to hear most of the conversation.

She almost wished she hadn't.

"An English patrol of men wearing De Beaumont's arms was seen rounding up men suspected of being rebels near Selkirk and Jedburgh on Wednesday morning after news reached them of the attack on Roxburgh."

Her heart sank hearing the words from the man she assumed was MacRuairi.

She heard her brother use a vile curse she'd never heard him use before. "Was Archie among them?"

Another man spoke. "We can't be sure, but it seems likely. The timing fits and the lad's tracks disappeared not far from where the patrol was seen."

"They will have taken him to Jedburgh," Jamie said. "It's one of the only castles in the area we've been unable to take."

"Aye," the man she'd identified as MacRuairi said. "That is what we assumed as well. But there's more."

Elizabeth braced herself, gripping the edge of the bench she was seated on until her fingers turned white, sensing that what he was about to say wasn't going to be good.

It wasn't.

MacRuairi explained how he was able to get inside the castle with a group of villagers and merchants that morning, but there was no sign of the prisoners. Unable to find out any information, he'd had to ride to their contact at Carlisle Castle to learn the rest.

Elizabeth wasn't surprised they had an English spy, but she was surprised when MacRuairi referred to a *her*.

"She was able to find out that the men were taken to Bamburgh Castle in Northumberland for imprisonment."

"Northumberland?" Jamie repeated. "Bloody hell, why take them that far? Do they know who he is? Do they know they have a Douglas?"

"She doesn't think so. She thought it was a precaution. With your men in Roxburgh, the English patrol didn't want to take a chance with Jedburgh being so close."

Elizabeth felt the blood drain from her face. She'd been to Bamburgh Castle once as a child when her father had been keeper of Berwick Castle, and the knowledge of where they'd taken her brother filled her with despair and horror. She didn't need to hear the men below discuss the difficulty of a rescue; she understood it. Bamburgh's location perched on a steep, rocky cliff made it virtually inaccessible and the perfect place for a prison.

But these were the Phantoms; surely if anyone could free Archie from an impossible place they could?

"We can attempt a rescue," MacRuairi said. "But we've never done anything like this before. Without a long siege, our only way in is up that cliff. It's not like climbing a thirty-foot wall with grappling hooks and a ladder. It's over a hundred and fifty feet of sheer basalt rock without a tether. Success is far from guaranteed, and we could make the situation worse."

Jamie echoed the question in her head. "How could it be worse? He might as well be in the Tower of London, damn it."

"A rescue attempt could alert the English to the importance of one of the prisoners. If they start questioning your brother, how long will it take for them to discover his identity? And if they do . . ."

He didn't need to finish. They all knew what that would mean. If the English learned they had the brother of one of the most hated men in England in their possession, the man blamed for countless "black" deeds and reviled as the Devil, they would hang Archie from the nearest gallows—or worse.

But what if they already knew? What if the prisoners were already being questioned? Tortured? How long did Archie have then? He was only sixteen!

The men went back and forth, but Elizabeth knew they couldn't take a chance and wait. They had to try. Especially when there was someone who could help them. As soon as MacRuairi had mentioned the sheer rock, she'd known. Jamie would know, too.

She kept waiting for her brother to say something, but when it was clear he wasn't going to, she knew she had to act.

She didn't give the man at the door a chance to stop her. She brushed by him, ignoring his protests, and burst into the meeting.

Ignoring the men looking at her with surprise, she stared right at her brother. "You know someone who can help. You have to ask him."

The guard spoke at the same time. "I'm sorry, my lord. I tried to stop her."

"Not very well, it seems," James said, addressing the man first. He sniffed in the air, his eyes narrowing on the fireplace. The smoke had given her away. "I will speak with you later, Elizabeth. Now is *not* the time."

The calm, low voice didn't fool her. She knew he was furious at her for eavesdropping—she didn't blame him—but this was too important. "But Thom can help."

"No, he can't. This has nothing to do with him."

"But—"

"Damn it, there are no buts! We don't need his help. Climbing trees and hills around Douglas is a far cry from trying to sneak into one of the most formidable castles in England. MacGowan has been a warrior for three years. He isn't cut out for something like this. These are not normal missions. His inexperience will only make the rest of our jobs more difficult and could put the rest of us in danger."

Jamie was blind when it came to Thom. She knew her brother was too proud to ask Thom for anything, after the falling-out between them. She started to argue but he stopped her.

"This is supposed to be *secret*, and it's important that it's kept that way. There are many lives at stake, including Archie's. Do you understand?"

Wide-eyed, she nodded. Suddenly conscious of all the eyes upon them, she turned around to leave. She wasn't about to give up, but she knew her brother well enough to know that she would not convince him like this.

But he knew her well, too. He followed her to the door and said in a low voice so that no one else would hear, "Stay away from him, Ella, I mean it—I don't want you anywhere near MacGowan. You will be on the first horse back to Blackhouse in the morning, and he will be on the other end of my sword."

Her brother's warning echoing in her ears, Elizabeth hesitated for about thirty seconds. She did not doubt that Jamie meant what he said, but she would gladly return to Blackhouse if it meant Archie was safe. And although Jamie was irrational when it came to Thommy, he would not kill him just for talking to her. Besides, she was confident she could prevent a battle between the two men if need be. She'd done so many times before.

No matter what Jamie said about Thommy's lack of experience, there was no question in her mind that he could help. He could climb anything. How many times had she watched him scale cliff sides when they were younger? Not to mention the tower houses. He could help the Phantoms, she was certain of it. Just as she was certain he would help.

6

BLOODY HELL, IT was cold. The padded wool arming coif that covered Thom's head and neck beneath the steel bascinet was scant protection against a wintry Scottish wind. Hell, it wasn't much protection against a *summery* Scottish wind, which could be almost as frigid. His ears were frozen.

Why the hell hadn't he brought an extra plaid? He paced the ramparts as much to keep warm as to keep watch on the darkened countryside.

Guard duty at night was a special kind of hell. Long, lonely hours trying to stay alert and not freeze to death. Who would have thought he'd be longing to swing a hammer? But this was his "reward" for saving the princess. Unable to help with the taking down of walls for the next day or two while he rested his blasted shoulder, he'd temporarily been re-assigned to the night's watch. But in a day or two, as soon as additional men arrived from Edinburgh,

Carrick had given him leave to return to Rutherford Castle and Lady Marjorie.

Focused on movement beyond the castle walls, he didn't pay much attention to the footsteps coming up the guardhouse stairs, assuming it must be the officer in charge. It was, but Carrick's lieutenant wasn't alone.

"MacGowan. You are needed below. Peter will take your place until you return."

Thom didn't argue. He was so glad to be relieved he didn't question the cause. It wasn't until he was led into a small guardroom built into the stone wall—probably a place where the English had temporarily kept prisoners—and saw who was waiting for him that he wished he could return to his frigid post.

Elizabeth.

She didn't greet him right away, but turned to the lieutenant with a grateful smile. It was a smile to make men silly, even humorless old warriors like Sir Reginald Cunningham. "Thank you for finding him. I promise this will only take a moment." When it looked like the man intended to stay, she added, "What I have to say to Thom is of the utmost secrecy. If you could see that we are not disturbed, I would greatly appreciate it."

The old warrior looked uncertain. "Does your brother know you are here, my lady?"

She gave him a dazzling smile. Having been on the other side of that smile more than once, Thom knew a falsehood—or at least a misleading statement—was on its way.

"He knew exactly where I was going."

Which answered precisely nothing.

Thom's mouth fell into a hard line as Sir Reginald, still

in a bit of a blinded stupor, grinned back at her and left them alone.

She immediately spun around to look at him and raced into his arms.

He was so startled that they instinctively closed around her. She melted against his chest, her soft feminine curves pressed against him in all the right places. He inhaled the delicate scent of her perfume and felt the memories crash over him. She'd always smelled so sweet and fresh.

For one treacherous heartbeat, he forgot everything. Where he was. That three years had passed. How hard it had been to get over her. That he didn't still love her.

For that one treacherous heartbeat, he thought she'd reconsidered. He was so overcome by the rush of emotion that when she looked up at him and said, "I need you," he heard, "I want you."

Lost in the entrancing sea of her eyes, he'd felt himself falling. His mouth lowered, and it was only when her eyes widened in shock at what he was going to do that he snapped back to reality.

"I need *your help*," is what she'd said.

She hadn't reconsidered. She didn't want him, she wanted something *from* him.

With a sharp curse, he let her go. But the emotion—the lust—pounded through him like a bitter drum.

They stared at one another for a long moment. Elizabeth in surprise, and he in anger—at himself. He'd moved on. He didn't love her with every fiber of his being anymore. Elizabeth Douglas was his past.

Seeing his expression, she took an instinctive step back.

He forced his anger to cool. She'd lost the power to hurt him three years ago. "What do you want, Elizabeth? I'd wager a week's wages that Jamie not only doesn't know you are here, but explicitly told you not to come here."

She bit her lip guiltily, and he had to force his eyes away from the sight of those tiny white teeth with that plump lower lip in their tight grasp. It made him think of taking the velvety red softness between his own teeth. It made him think of sliding his tongue over the marks and then into her mouth, finally tasting her.

Past, he reminded himself.

Instead, he focused on trying to control the temper that was threatening again. "Did you listen to nothing I said before? I asked you to let me be, and now you are dragging me away from my duty. You can no longer come running to me whenever you want. This is my job, Elizabeth. I have responsibilities and people who are counting on me. I am no longer yours to command."

She blinked at him, wide-eyed, obviously taken aback. "I never thought you were. And I wouldn't have come to you if it weren't an emergency. I need—*we* need—your help. It's Archie."

Thom didn't know her younger half brothers very well, but he knew how much she cared about them. "Has he been found?"

"No . . . Yes . . . I don't know." With tears glistening in her eyes and emotion thick in her throat, she blurted out a garbled explanation. From what he could tell, Archie had been taken by Henry de Beaumont's men to Bamburgh Castle, and Jamie and a small group of warriors were planning an attempt to rescue him.

"But the only way into the castle is up a steep cliff, and I thought . . ." She looked up at him expectantly.

He knew exactly what she thought. "You thought I would drop everything, ride not just halfway across

Scotland but also across the enemy lines, climb not just a dangerous cliff but also the wall of one of the most fortified castles in England, and then somehow find your brother—in *prison*, no less—release him, and get him to safety without being discovered by an entire garrison of English soldiers. Does that about sum it up?"

Big blue doe eyes lifted to his in a face that had lost some color. She stared up at him wordlessly, making him feel like he was kicking a blasted puppy.

But this wasn't his problem—*she* wasn't his problem—and he wasn't going to let himself get sucked back in. It had been hard enough to get over her the first time.

But it wasn't just that. He'd worked hard to be where he was, and he wasn't about to let her interfere. She'd pulled him from his duty, damn it, without a thought. What would she do next time she "needed" him?

She finally found her voice. "I know it's a lot to ask, but Jamie will be with you along with . . ." She chewed on her bottom lip as if contemplating how much to say. "Some *very* good warriors. The best." Suddenly, she gasped and covered her mouth with her hand as if something had just occurred to her. "Of course, your shoulder! It must be causing you pain."

"My shoulder has nothing to do with this." It was still sore, but he could climb if he wanted to. "*I* have nothing to do with this. So why come to me, Elizabeth?"

"I thought you would want to help."

He lifted one brow in challenge. "I very much doubt you thought about me, or what I wanted, at all. You just assumed that all you would have to do was ask, and I'd come running like I always have. Well, I'm sorry, but I can't. Not this time. You'll have to find someone else who *wants* to help."

She gazed up at him, stunned. "You are saying no?"

She looked so incredulous that if it wasn't at the expense of his pride he might have laughed. "It probably never occurred to you to think I would refuse, did it?"

The guilty flush that pinkened her cheeks put the first crack in his composure. He took her by the shoulders, forcing her to look at him and hear what he said. "I don't have to play the doting servant to your princess anymore. Nor do I have to hold my tongue around my 'betters' and jump to you or your brother's bidding. Let James work another one of his miracles, or better yet, have him ask me himself." He laughed as if he knew it would snow in hell before her brother ever came to him for help. "I have other things to do."

He tried to turn away, but she reached out to catch his arm. The injured one, but that isn't what made every muscle in his body seize. "That is not why I am here. You are being unfair, I've never thought of you like that."

"Haven't you? Am I not someone to rely upon? Someone who has always been there for you?"

"Yes, that is why I came to you. That is what friends do."

"Don't you mean that's what *I* do? Your idea of friendship sounds rather one-sided."

She blinked up at him. "I . . ." Tears welled in her eyes. "I didn't realize . . ." She drew in a ragged breath that made his heart skip. "I'm sorry, Thom, I didn't mean to be such a burden to you."

She'd let his arm go, and he raked his hand back through his hair. Bloody hell. He hated this; hated refusing her anything. It made him feel as if spiders were crawling all over his skin. "You weren't a burden. But you just have to understand that I just can't be there like that for you anymore."

He didn't want to hurt her, but he couldn't let himself get distracted or be diverted from his goal. Lady Marjorie was waiting for him, and he wasn't going to let this opportunity pass him by.

He knew Elizabeth. If he let her in even an inch, she'd do something sweet to burrow her way into his heart again. He wasn't going to let that happen.

"I understand."

But she didn't. She turned to leave, but this time it was he who stopped her. He took hold of her arm and turned her back around to face him. He had to make her see, or she'd be right back the next time the impulse struck. "I have something else to do. Someone is waiting for me."

"Who?"

"The woman I hope to marry."

Marry? The word echoed in her head, and Elizabeth felt suddenly dizzy.

She caught herself from swaying and looked up at him. Something in her chest squeezed. Her lungs felt as if she'd just inhaled a cloud of acrid, gritty smoke.

"You are getting married?"

He arched a brow. "You sound so surprised. Did you think that because you did not want me no one else would?"

The subtle chastisement in his voice was like a slap. "I never thought that at all. Why are you putting words in my mouth to think the worst of me? I'm *shocked,* not surprised, although you are right—I shouldn't be. Any woman would be lucky to have you."

Actually, it was more surprising that he wasn't married already. Just look at him. He was gorgeous. One of the best-looking men she'd ever seen. He must have dozens of women clamoring for his attentions. Something she ate must not have agreed with her, because she suddenly felt ill.

"Not any woman," he said flatly. Then, as if angered by his own words, he made a movement with his shoulders that wasn't quite a shrug. "Nothing has been formalized."

"But?"

"But I have reason to believe a betrothal is imminent. I hope to leave in the next day or two to escort her to her estates in Yorkshire."

Why was she finding it so hard to breathe? The air seemed to have grown cold and icy in her lungs. *Estates*? "I see. C-congratulations. I am happy for you. She is a v-very lucky woman."

She meant it, even if the words seemed to stick in her throat.

"It's a good match," he said matter-of-factly. "She is the widow of a minor baron who holds a castle near Peebles."

A castle? The widow of a baron? It *was* a good match—a very good match. She should be proud of him for making such a beneficial alliance. Which didn't explain why a strange sinking feeling had settled low in her stomach.

She forced a smile to her face and hoped it didn't look as tremulous as it felt. "I'm happy for you. You deserve the best, Thommy—*Thom*," she quickly corrected.

Their eyes held for one long heartbeat before he looked away. "Aye, well, it will make knighthood an easier reach."

She smiled. He was the most noble, honorable man she knew. He'd always had a keen sense of right and wrong. He'd been a knight to her for a long time, but she didn't think he'd appreciate hearing any more childhood memories from her. He was getting on with his life just as he'd said.

She just hadn't realized . . .

Married.

Wasn't she hoping to do the same? Had she forgotten about Randolph?

She was ashamed to say she had.

She took a deep breath, forcing air through her dry lungs. Maybe they both had moved on. "You were right, I shouldn't have come."

Thom wasn't the boy from the village anymore. He wasn't her childhood companion and confidant. He hadn't been for a long time. He was a soldier. A man she didn't even know anymore.

His face was taut, his expression grim. He seemed pained when he spoke, as if he were waging some kind of fierce internal battle. "Jamie will bring your brother home safely, Elizabeth. He's a good climber."

It was true. After the near disaster in the tree all those years ago, Jamie had been determined to become just as good a climber as Thom. He'd pushed past the fear that she wasn't supposed to know about—she'd figured out what had stopped him that day a few years later—and become very good. But no one was as good as Thom. She'd seen him scale sheer rock faces that would make a spider hesitate.

Nonetheless, she forced a wide smile on her face. He was right, this wasn't his battle. "I'm sure you are right."

They stared at one another in the semi-darkness, neither knowing what to say, but both understanding that it was goodbye.

She wished, she wanted . . .

She took a deep breath and broke the silence. "Goodbye, Thom."

"Goodbye, Elizabeth."

With one last look to hold on to, she opened the door and left.

Elizabeth scanned the horizon, willing a group of riders to appear. The vantage from the East Tower chamber of the castle afforded a broad view of Roxburgh and the stark, gently undulating countryside beyond. There were hundreds of people bustling along the narrow wynds and roads of the important burgh, but none were the men she sought.

God in heaven, how much more of this must she endure? It seemed all she did of late was stare anxiously out of tower windows, waiting.

She sighed with frustration. Two days! James and Bruce's famed Guard been gone two long days, and not one word. Had it taken them longer to reach the castle than they expected? Or had something gone wrong?

Not knowing was agony. With nothing to do but wait, she felt like a lion in a cage.

Or a *princess* in a tower.

Her heart squeezed as it had every time she thought of Thom since their parting two nights ago—which was often. His accusations had stung. She'd never realized what it had been like for him. Never glimpsed the resentment and bitterness that must have been lurking underneath the stoic facade, and she'd been digging through her memories to see whether there was something she could point to—something she might have done to cause it.

But she'd come to realize that maybe it wasn't any specific occurrence that had fueled his resentment; it was simply a natural function of the separation between them in rank. It was something that had never mattered to her because she didn't *have* to think about it. Thom, on the other hand, didn't have that luxury. He would have always been aware of the differences in rank between them, and precisely what that meant. The laird's daughter and the smith's son; the laird's heir and the smith's son—there was no question of who took precedence and who had authority.

They weren't equals. Even if she had never thought of it that way, she'd always implicitly understood it, and perhaps their relationship had been forged on that uneven foundation—just as Thom's had with Jamie. Her brother didn't have to toss his authority around or force Thom to take a knee before him; the fact that he *could* do so would be difficult enough to swallow for a man like Thom. A strong, proud man whose natural authority made him a leader in his own right. The village boys had always looked up to him as their leader unless Jamie was around. Then it was her brother to whom they deferred.

For the first time she wondered what their relationships would have been like had they been born of similar rank. Her perception shifted. It was no longer clear that Jamie would have been in charge, just as it was no longer clear that she would have never thought of Thom as a potential suitor. She suspected she would have thought of things quite differently. It was a disconcerting realization.

That there was undoubtedly some truth to Thom's accusations made her feel horrible. She *had* taken him for granted and assumed he would always be there for her. She could acknowledge that.

But he was wrong about the rest. She'd never thought of him as a servant who must jump to do her bidding, and she hated that he could think that of her. But as important as it was to her for him to know that, she also knew that the only way to prove it to him was to heed his request and leave him be.

She had her own plans for the future to think about, didn't she?

She had to let him go.

But her chest squeezed as she glanced out the window. This time her eyes scanned the yard below. Had he gone to his widow yet?

She hadn't seen him since the midday meal yesterday, but she hadn't been able to find the courage to ask Edward Bruce about him at today's. She feared the answer.

A soft rap on the door drew her gaze from the window. Expecting her maidservant, she was surprised by the woman who entered.

Immediately, her heart jumped. "Have you heard something?"

Lady Helen gave her a wry smile and shook her head. "Not yet." Shifting the wiggly bundle in her arms, she added, "Willie and I thought you might be in need of some company." Her gaze shifted meaningfully to the window Elizabeth stood before. "I've spent many hours staring out of windows."

Elizabeth could only imagine. What must it be like to be married to one of Bruce's Phantoms? To the men who were called upon for the most difficult, dangerous missions? She shuddered. "How do you manage?"

The pretty healer smiled while struggling to keep hold of the wee laddie who, in addition to wiggling, had started verbalizing his displeasure at being held. "This stubborn little ox for one. I also have my work, which keeps me busier than I'd like."

Elizabeth understood. Helen tended to the men who were injured on the battlefield. Crossing the chamber, she held her arms out and smiled. "He's adorable. May I?"

Helen looked relieved. "Do you mind? My arms feel

like they are about to fall off. He's already so heavy, and he doesn't like much being held right now."

"He wants to crawl?"

Lady Helen nodded. "Aye, and he doesn't like being told no. I'm afraid he's as muleheaded as his father." She grinned, noticing how Elizabeth's arms sagged with the weight. "And built as solid as his father as well. I must admit I'm looking forward to him walking."

"But be careful what you wish for," Elizabeth said with a laugh, bounding the adorable fair-haired child in her arms. "I remember how it was when Hugh started to walk. It seemed we were forever chasing him to prevent some sort of disaster."

The little boy seemed to like her bouncing and gurgled with laughter, revealing a handful of pearly white teeth. He was a cute little devil with a cherubic round face, big green eyes, long lashes, feathery soft blond hair, and sturdy little limbs.

"He likes you," Lady Helen said with a smile. "He seems to have a fondness for pretty lasses already."

Elizabeth grinned and laughed as he started to play with one of her plaits. "How old is he? Ten months?"

Lady Helen's brows lifted. "Yes, next week. I'm impressed. You'd think with all I know about healing I'd be better at this. But Willie has a knack for revealing just how ignorant I am. I never seem to know what to do with him. I can't believe I actually thought this would be easy."

Hearing the very motherly frustration in her voice, Elizabeth had to smile. She remembered Joanna's similar travails during Uilleam's first year. Her nephew would be two in June. "He is your first?"

Helen nodded. "I've heard from some of the other wives

that it gets easier. Since a few of them have more than one child, I guess I'll have to believe them."

It must have for Jo, Elizabeth thought with a smile, if the recent greenish hue to her skin in the morning meant anything.

Elizabeth suspected she was referring to the other wives of Bruce's secret Guard. "Your husband doesn't mind you and the baby being here?"

Lady Helen's mouth twisted. "I wouldn't say that. I think he'd rather Willie and I were at Varrich Castle in the far north of his lands in Sutherland, but he knows I may be needed, so we try to find a balance. Willie and I stay far away from danger, but as soon as Magnus deems it safe we are with him. With the victories the king has been having of late, I hope it won't be long until most of Scotland is safe." She glanced down in horror at Elizabeth's wrist. "Willie, no!"

The little boy had moved on from trying to poke his chubby fingers through Elizabeth's plait to gnawing on her bracelet.

"It's all right," she said with a laugh. "He isn't doing any harm."

"Are you sure?" Lady Helen said, watching uncertainly. "It's very beautiful." She peered closer at the thin, etched piece of metal. "And unusual. I noticed you holding it when I walked into the room. It must be special to you."

Elizabeth must have been twisting it again. Joanna had pointed out more than once—as if she should signify something by it—that she did so often when she was anxious or nervous about something.

"It is," Elizabeth answered. Thommy had given it to her for her saint's day right before she'd been forced to leave for France at the start of Bruce's war. She rarely removed it.

The small cuff was simply designed, consisting of two half-circles of brass (likely remnants from making the quillons from a sword) hinged on one side and secured by two clasps on the other. The workmanship was exquisite. It was etched with ancient symbols, such as those that were on the old cross at St. Mary's in Douglas said to have been from the time Christianity was first introduced by the Irish missionaries St. Finian and St. Columba. Thommy was so talented, which is why she'd never understood why he wanted to be a knight. Although perhaps she had a better idea now.

"May I see it?" Helen asked.

"Of course," she replied, trying to wrestle it from the baby's gummy grasp. When he started to argue the way that babies do, she distracted him from whining by putting him down on the ground. He took off exploring right away. The room was sparsely furnished—so not much for him to get into—but she kept a close eye on the fireplace.

With one eye on her son, Helen marveled at the design.

"I read once about the Romans giving armbands to their soldiers for military distinctions," Elizabeth said. "It has always reminded me of that."

Something in Helen's gaze sparked. "It does! I've heard of those as well. Armilla, I believe they were called. Hmm . . ."

Elizabeth would have followed up on that hmm, but Helen handed the bracelet back to her at the same time as she darted forward to cut off Willie's path to—of course—the fireplace.

"What is it about babies that makes them see danger and head right for it?" Elizabeth said with a shake of the head while Lady Helen gently admonished her son.

"I don't know," Lady Helen answered. "But not all of them outgrow it. My husband, for one."

Lady Elizabeth laughed, but she sobered when Helen turned from the window where she'd moved over to point out things to distract Willie.

"What is it?" she asked.

The healer's relief was visible. Until that moment, Elizabeth hadn't realized how anxious she was. "They're back."

7

THOM HANDED SIR David Lindsay the sword. The important knight, and one of Bruce's closest companions, held it out in front of him to examine. He turned it over in his hand, sliced through the air a few times, and looked at every angle of the handle as if he were searching for something, while making short exclamations along the way.

"Bloody hell, MacGowan, how did you do this so quickly? It feels like an entirely new sword. The balance is incredible, and the handle feels as if it was made for my hand."

Thom shrugged. "If I'd had a pair of fullers I could have fixed the blood groove. It could use a little more taken out near the tip to lighten it. But the English armorer wasn't thoughtful enough to leave all his tools behind."

The castle forge appeared to have been hastily abandoned after Douglas had taken Roxburgh. Thom had decided to make use of it when he wasn't attending to his duties for Carrick. God knew, he wasn't sleeping; he might as well make some extra coin in those wakeful hours.

He had nothing to feel guilty about. But damn it, seeing Elizabeth's pale, anxious face from across the Hall or courtyard the past couple of days had eaten away at his resolve. Indeed, he'd skipped the midday meal today as much to finish the sword as to avoid seeing her.

Not that it helped. He could still see those big doe eyes right in front of him as she'd looked up at him and pleaded with him to help her.

The pull to go to her aid was so strong it physically hurt not to do so. His chest had been aching for two days.

He cursed inwardly and turned his attention back to Lindsay, who paid him the coin they'd agreed upon and thanked him. "I could send a few more men your way, if you think you'll have time. I know many of us have had a difficult time finding a good smith with as much time as we spend sleeping on heather." Thom stiffened. Not noticing, Lindsay laughed. "It seems of late that the only time we are in a castle, it is to destroy it."

Us, the men who fight, and *you*, the men who serve. Thom knew the knight didn't mean anything by it, but it still reverberated. He wasn't one of them, and maybe he was a fool to try to change that. Damn it, what did he have to do? For three years he'd been killing himself to become one of "us," and all he had to do was pick up a hammer and once again he was "you."

But he had to admit there was something about being back in a forge that was oddly comforting. He felt more at home in this unfamiliar building than he had in any of the places he'd stayed in the past three years.

He'd been back to Douglas only once since he left, and

it had been horrible. Although it had been good to see Johnny, the short time he'd spent with his father had been awkward, uncomfortable, and filled with pain on both sides. It was as if neither of them knew what to say to one another anymore. His father thought Thom was ashamed of his background, and Thom didn't know how to explain what drove him to try to do more. Hell, he wasn't even sure he could explain it to himself. But it was the same thing that drove him when climbing. He liked the element of danger and pushing himself to the extreme. He wanted to see how far he could go.

"I wish I could," he said truthfully. He needed the money. "But I'm leaving in the morning."

The additional men had arrived earlier this afternoon and Edward Bruce had given him leave to return to Rutherford to escort Lady Marjorie to Yorkshire. Unfortunately, the escort would be small, as Carrick could only afford to spare a few men. The earl and the rest of his army would be leaving at the end of the week to begin the siege at Stirling Castle.

Out of habit rather than necessity, as the forge would undoubtedly be destroyed by the end of the week, Thom cleaned out the ash and replaced the tools after Lindsay had departed. It was dusk by the time he closed the door of the forge behind him and crossed the yard to the barracks. He was filthy, and despite the chill in the air, he was going to head down to the river to bathe before finding something to eat and trying to get some sleep. He had a long day ahead of him in the saddle tomorrow.

With a grimace, he was about to open the door to the barracks when the sound of a party of horsemen riding through the gate drew his attention.

He recognized Douglas in the lead, as well as a handful

of the men who accompanied him. Thom had crossed paths
with Boyd, MacKay, Sutherland, MacRuairi, and MacLeod
a few times in the past three years; Elizabeth hadn't exag-
gerated: the warriors who'd accompanied Douglas were
among the best of Bruce's army. He frowned as something
struck him. Both Boyd and MacRuairi were reputed to be
members of the king's secret "Phantoms." If there was any
truth to it, he wouldn't be surprised that these other men
were as well.

Was Douglas?

The very idea of his former friend being a part of something so illustrious grated. But it made sense. Too much
damned sense. Whatever Thom's personal feelings, he could
not fault Douglas's skills as a warrior.

He was about to turn away when he looked closer at the
riders. He swore aloud, realizing who was missing: Archie.

One look at her brother's face, and Elizabeth knew—even
before she scanned the men who were walking into the
Hall behind him for the gangly auburn-headed youth.

"Archie?"

Jamie shook his head grimly.

Out of the corner of her eye, she noticed Lady Helen's
reunion with her husband. The big Highlander took his son
from his wife's arms as if he weighed nothing and enfolded
Lady Helen against his leather-clad chest. The deep affec-
tion between them reminded Elizabeth of her brother and
Jo. She'd thought their love unusual, but maybe it wasn't as
uncommon as she thought.

"What happened?" she asked her brother.

He shook his head, indicating not here. Jamie con-
ferred for a few minutes with one of the most fearsome,

imposing-looking warriors of the Phantoms—which was saying something. Though she'd never met him, Elizabeth knew he was the leader of the impressive band of warriors: Tor MacLeod. All ten members of the Guard had answered Jamie's call to rescue his young brother; it was out of their respect for Jaime that they'd put aside their other duties. It also said much about the king's regard for Jamie that he'd let them go with the greatest test of his kingship coming in a few months' time. The coming of the English host in summer was a specter haunting them all.

"I will send word to the king about our delay and speak with Carrick," MacLeod said in the native tongue of the *Gall-Gaedhil* Islanders.

Jamie nodded. "We will reconvene in the morning. Get something to eat, and my steward will direct you to your chambers. We can all use some rest."

After seeing to the food, Jamie led her into the king's solar. Seeing his exhaustion, she forced him to sit and fetched him a goblet of wine before taking a seat on the bench next to him to hear what had happened.

He explained how they'd arrived and spent the first day surveying the castle and trying to gather information about the prisoners. They'd learned the Scots were being held in the guardhouse in the tower near the edge of the bluff. MacRuairi had tried to enter the castle with some villagers, but the porter was checking everyone, and he'd had to turn around rather than take a chance at being recognized. Apparently, MacRuairi had a lot of enemies in the Borders. From what she'd heard, the infamous West Island chieftain turned pirate mercenary had a lot of enemies all over.

Jamie had waited until the wee hours of the night to attempt to scale the cliff.

"It should have been easy," Jamie said, clearly frustrated. "That side of the castle is woefully undefended—I didn't see one guard in the area the entire night. All we had to do was climb that cliff, toss the scaling ladder over the wall, and we would have been in and out with no one the wiser." He shook his head. "Even the cliff didn't look as bad as we thought. It was steep, but there were plenty of foot- and handholds. For the first hundred and twenty feet or so, I thought we would make it."

"And then?" she asked.

Jamie's mouth fell in a hard line. "Then we hit thirty feet of sheer rock. I tried, but I could not get more than a few feet up. MacRuairi managed to climb to within a dozen feet, but then slipped and came within a handhold of falling the rest of the way off the cliff."

Elizabeth's eyes widened in horror.

"You are to keep that information to yourself, by the way. I doubt his wife would appreciate how close she came to becoming a widow."

She nodded. MacRuairi was married to Bella MacDuff. The former Countess of Buchan was regarded as a great Scottish patriot and hero.

"We don't think anyone in the castle heard, but we can't be sure. A handful of our men stayed at Bamburgh to keep watch, while the rest of us returned to Roxburgh to regroup for another attempt."

Thank God. Elizabeth couldn't hide her relief. "You are going back?"

"Aye, and this time we will be successful. I probably should have listened to you in the first place."

Elizabeth was so shocked at first she didn't understand. "You should have listened to *me*?"

"You were right." Her brother grinned at her expression

and tweaked her nose the way he'd done when she was a girl. "Aye, I *do* know how to say those words. It would have saved me a long journey back and forth, if I'd taken him in the first place."

All of a sudden, she realized what he meant. "Thom?"

Jamie nodded. "Aye. Those rocks would have been nothing for him. I've seen him climb far more difficult cliffs with ease."

Elizabeth shook her head dumbly. "It's too late. You'll have to think of another way."

"There is no other way." He frowned, studying her. "What do you mean it's too late?"

Elizabeth bit her lip and made a sheepish face. "I already asked him."

He exploded off the bench. "You did what?" Well over six feet of angry warrior loomed over her intimidatingly. She combated it by sitting there serenely with her hands folded in her lap. Thom had taught her that. "Damn it, Ella, I told you to stay away from him."

Her eyes narrowed right back at him. "You are my brother, not my father. Thom is my *friend*, and I will see him if I want."

"Until you are married, I might as well be your father. It is your duty to obey me, and you will do as I say." They stared at one another for a few minutes, angry gazes crossing like swords, waging a silent war of wills. Jamie was right, but he also must have realized that if he forced the issue, it would change the relationship between them forever. He was the first to stand down. "I should send you back to Blackhouse right now, as I promised."

Her heart clenched. He couldn't send her away—not until Archie was safe. "But you won't," she said with more certainty than she felt.

He held her gaze for a long pause before relenting. "Damn it, Ella. You don't understand."

"Then why don't you explain it to me?" she said quietly.

"MacGowan doesn't want to be your friend. He hasn't for a long time. He wants *you*."

She shook her head. "He might have at one time, but not anymore."

Jamie's expression hardened. "Do not argue with me about this, Elizabeth. No matter what he's told you, he wants you, and he'd do anything to have you. Hell, why do you think he's here?"

"He wants to be a knight. He's wanted to be a knight for as long as I can remember."

"Because of *you*, damn it. He's under some misguided belief that if he raises himself high enough he'll be worthy of you. But he'll never be worthy of you. I didn't realize his feelings at first, but it became clear that night I found you on the tower. God knows what would have happened had I not put a stop to it. He took advantage of both of us, Ella. Me for our friendship, and you for your innocence. He thought that because we were friends I wouldn't object to the son of the smith courting my sister." His eyes blazed with anger. "Can you imagine? Christ, he would have made a laughingstock of us both—and ruined you in the process."

Elizabeth winced at the harshness of it, though she knew it was the reality. "He wasn't taking advantage of me, Jamie. Thom is one of the most noble men I've ever known. You know him. He would have never done anything to dishonor me."

"I know from experience what passion can do to an honorable man." Elizabeth realized he was referring to himself and that the memory pained him. "Aye, I know the kind of man Thom was," he admitted grudgingly. "And I would have trusted him with my life. But trusting him to be able to control himself with my sixteen-year-old sister when I saw the way he looked at you?" He shook his head. "No way in hell. I wasn't going to take any chances. I'm still not, which is why I want you to stay away from him. I will see to the situation with Archie."

She shook her head. "You don't understand. I already asked him to help, and he refused."

She'd managed to surprise him. "He refused *you*?"

She nodded.

He frowned. "Was it his arm? I didn't think he was seriously injured."

She shook her head. "He wasn't. He just didn't want to do it. He said he was leaving in a day or two—I'm not even sure he's still here." She paused, taking a deep breath through tight lungs. "He said there is a woman waiting for him. A woman he hopes to marry."

If she'd surprised him before, she'd managed to shock her brother dumbstruck now. "Married? You are serious?"

She nodded.

"To whom?"

She shrugged, looking down at her hands. She was gripping her bracelet so tightly, she realized, the imprint would probably be dug into her skin. "He didn't say. Only that she's a widow of a baron."

Jamie quirked a brow, obviously impressed. "It's a good match for him."

Why did hearing her brother say it only make her feel worse? Marriage had always been about making the best alliance to her—why wasn't it in this case? "Aye," she agreed.

Jamie didn't say anything, but she could feel his eyes on

her. After a moment he said, "The widow will have to wait, and if he's gone already, he can be brought back."

"Nay, you don't understand. The widow was only an excuse. He doesn't *want* to help, Jamie."

"What he wants is immaterial. I'm not giving him a choice. MacGowan is a soldier, he will do what he is told."

Elizabeth's eyes widened in horror, thinking about what Thom had said. Jamie forcing him would only reinforce every horrible thought he had about being their "servant."

"No! You can't order him, Jamie." She thought back to her conversation with Thom. "Maybe if you ask him personally, and explain the situation . . ."

"So he can have the satisfaction of refusing me?" He made a sharp scoffing sound, and said, "I don't think so. If he refused you, he sure as hell isn't going to do it for me."

"But—"

He put up his hand, stopping her. "This is our best way—maybe the only way—of getting Archie back. What's more important, your brother or MacGowan's tweaked pride?"

Both. Nothing Jamie had said was wrong, but Elizabeth knew Thom wouldn't see it that way. He would be furious.

She couldn't let him think the worst of them. What he wanted *did* matter to her.

She stilled. Maybe there was a way. Maybe if she asked him again and could convince him to help, Jamie wouldn't need to order him to do it. She just prayed that he was still here.

"Report to Douglas at first light. You will be under his command for the entirety of the mission."

It took everything Thom had to keep his expression

neutral while listening to Carrick, when rage boiled inside him like a pot with a too-tight lid.

He couldn't believe it. He was being forced on the very mission for which Elizabeth had come to him the night before last. His answer, and what he'd wanted, hadn't mattered. Either she or Jamie—or maybe both—had gone directly to Carrick.

Though this smacked of Jamie's methods, he knew how desperate Elizabeth must be feeling. Was she not giving him the opportunity to refuse again?

It didn't matter who it was. He had anger enough for both of them. Thom was a damned pawn, to be moved about at Douglas's will. He was the village boy again who had to bite his tongue and not defy his "lord."

That he'd been about to volunteer for the mission to which he'd just been assigned only proved what a bloody fool he was. He couldn't believe he'd actually been feeling *guilty* for refusing to help.

He fought to keep his emotions in check as he responded to Carrick. "I should not like to keep Lady Marjorie waiting, my lord. I understood I would be permitted to leave in the morning."

The earl frowned. "This mission takes precedence. The lady will have to wait a bit longer." He smiled wolfishly. "I'm sure you will think of a way to make it up to her."

Thom's jaw clamped. "And if I were to refuse?"

Carrick's eyes narrowed. "This is not a request. The king has ordered that Douglas be given whatever he needs to free his brother. Douglas seems to think that you may be of use to him—and I tend to agree based on the rooftop service you performed for Lady Marjorie." Carrick studied him a little longer, perhaps suspecting the rage that Thom was fighting hard to contain. "I know there is bad blood between you and Douglas, and he would have seen you gone from this army well before now. I haven't let him interfere because I see a lot of promise in you. Succeed on this mission, and you can prove to both of us that that belief is warranted."

Thom didn't need to prove anything to the "Lord" of Douglas, but he nodded, only too aware that he didn't have a choice. Douglas had seen to that.

"Good," Carrick said. "I will look forward to hearing of your exploits when you get back. You can return to the barracks or wherever it was that you were heading when Henry found you."

"The river, my lord." He was still covered in soot from his work in the forge earlier.

"To wash?"

Thom nodded.

"It's as cold as a witch's teat out there," Carrick said with a shiver.

Thom would take his word for it.

Carrick waved his hand, signaling for Henry to come forward. "Have a bath prepared for MacGowan in the kitchens. If one cannot be found, have them use mine."

The squire's eyes rounded, but he nodded.

Carrick's generosity surprised Thom as well. He supposed it was meant to ease the sting of being forced not just on the mission but also under Douglas's command.

It didn't, but he wasn't fool enough to refuse the rarity of heated water. "Thank you, my lord," Thom said, taking his leave.

He retrieved the drying cloth, soap, and fresh clothes that he'd left outside Carrick's chamber in the dungeon after Henry had chased him down, and followed the squire to the kitchens.

While the water heated in big iron pots over the fire, he tried to ease the tempest swirling inside him with drink. Lots of it. He downed cup after cup from the jug one of the serving maids had brought him. It was *uisge beatha*, and from the raw, throat-searing taste of it, he better not put his cup too close to the fire or it would combust.

The liquor did its job, however, taking the violent edge off his anger so that when the same serving maid offered to help him remove his clothes—with a look that promised more—he agreed. A lass was exactly what he needed to take the rest of the edge off.

Carrick's squire returned to his duties and left them alone in the corner alcove of the kitchens where the bath had been set up.

The lass was probably a few years older than him, buxom, dark haired, and pretty enough with a wide mouth that spoke of experience and pleasure. He'd wager this wasn't the first time she'd made a similar offer to a man in this castle.

Thom let her undress him. Let himself slink into the warm water. Let her hands roam all over his body with the soap, scrubbing the dirt and grime from his skin as she made little sounds of pleasure and anticipation at all she found.

He wanted to like it. He wanted to harden in her hand. He wanted to lie back, close his eyes, and let her stroke some of the lust and anger from his body.

He sure as hell wasn't the untried lad he'd been three years ago. He'd stopped waiting for Elizabeth the moment he'd left Douglas. None of which explained why he gently unfurled the serving girl's hand from around him and shook his head. "Just the bath, lass. I think I've had too much of the cook's spirits."

The lass didn't concede defeat easily, but when it became clear she wasn't going to change his mind, she helped him wash his hair, and then fetched the linen drying cloth to wrap around his waist as he stepped out of the tub.

The drink had been helped along by the warm water, and she had to steady him when he nearly slipped by putting her hands around him.

At first he thought she was the one who'd gasped. It wasn't until he'd peeled her now damp chest (and impressively hard nipples) from his that he looked over and saw they were no longer alone.

Elizabeth stood in the entryway, blocking the view of the rest of the kitchens, staring at him.

Stricken was the best description of her expression. From her quickness of breath, the hooded cloak, and rosy cheeks, he guessed she'd just run in from outside, but her eyes were wide and glassy, and her skin underneath the chill was pale.

He wasn't doing anything wrong, damn it—though in that one look she managed to make him feel as if he were.

How long had she been standing there? Had she seen him emerge from the tub? And why did the idea of her eyes on his body suddenly make the part of him that had been indifferent to the serving maid's attention suddenly feel very heavy and very thick?

The dangerous tempest of emotions simmering inside him came roaring back. Rage, resentment, and something else. Something far more dangerous right now. Lust.

"What do you want?" he said sharply. "As you can see, I'm busy."

He kept his arm around the serving woman. She was blocking his mostly naked body from Elizabeth's view. The now damp drying cloth didn't hide much. One glance of those big blue eyes on his cock, and he'd be hard as a rock.

But he was just angry enough—egged on by the drink— to actually think about setting the woman aside. He wanted to shock her. Wanted her unbalanced. Wanted her to see a man's lust—a man's desire. *His* lust, damn it. *His* desire.

"I-I," she stuttered. "I need to speak with you. It's important and cannot wait. Please . . ."

He should have sent her away right then. He should have realized that he was playing with fire.

But he didn't.

8

ELIZABETH WAS REELING. The relief she'd felt on learning from Carrick's squire where Thom was fled the moment she entered the kitchens and saw . . .

Everything. Her mouth went dry. Heat flooded her cheeks and spread over her skin in a prickly swath. He'd been naked. For one mind-numbing, breath-stealing, blood-heating moment she'd seen every inch of his body, and it had been incredible. The rock-hard muscles of his arms and chest had continued down past his narrow waist to his flanks and legs. There didn't seem to be a spare ounce of flesh on him; he was lean, chiseled, and honed to a razor-sharp blade of masculine power and strength.

Good gracious, how could he have been hiding all *this* from her? For a moment she felt a spark of anger, feeling as if she'd been duped.

And then there had been that other part of masculine strength and power. The long, thick proof of his manhood that she'd glimpsed for only an instant before the drying cloth had been wrapped around his waist.

She'd felt something strange low in her belly. A flutter of awareness. A tiny contraction that made her body quiver.

With little privacy in a castle, she'd seen a number of backsides and male parts and never given it much thought. But she was thinking now, and she didn't think she'd ever forget the sight of him. Just as she would never forget the lash of pain that had splayed through her chest when she saw the woman plastered to his chest and realized what she'd interrupted.

Were they . . . ?

Panic rose in her chest. Panic that put to shame the fear she'd felt on thinking that she wouldn't be able to find him before Jamie did.

But her brother was still in the Hall eating; she still had time to convince Thom to help before he was ordered to do so. Trying to ignore the arm he had looped around the woman's waist, she repeated, "Please, Thom."

She stared into his eyes and felt a strange shiver run through her. There was something different about him. Something dangerous. Something hot and edgy that she didn't understand. He wasn't calm and indifferent anymore.

Their eyes held, and she almost backed away. Something wasn't right. There was a strange energy crackling between them that instinctively she knew she could not handle. It was like trying to harness a maelstrom, trying to capture lightning, or trying to silence thunder.

"Very well," he said.

She detected a slight slur in his voice and frowned. Was he drunk? Thom didn't drink to excess. At least the Thom she'd known didn't, but how much did she know about the man before her?

If she thought too much about that question, she might be more nervous than she already was. She *was* nervous, she realized. Which was ridiculous. This was *Thom*, she reminded herself. She'd known him for most of her life. He was like a brother to her.

The rejection of that thought was instant and visceral. He wasn't like a brother to her at all. Not anymore, at least—if he ever had been.

He removed his arm from the woman's waist. "Thank you, lass. But I think I can manage from here."

The serving maid looked like she wanted to argue, but glanced in Elizabeth's direction and seemed to think better of it.

Elizabeth stepped to the side to let the woman pass. A moment later, she and Thom were alone. Or virtually alone, as there were still a few people in the kitchens. But this corner was fairly secluded. No one would bother them. Why did that knowledge suddenly make the air between them fire even hotter?

She turned away to give him some privacy while he dressed, although she knew it was as much to stop herself from looking at him again.

When he'd donned a linen shirt and breeches, she crossed the room to stand before him. The heat and smell of soap from the tub infused her senses. At least that's what she told herself. But she knew it probably had more to do with his heat and the fresh scent of soap that emanated from his skin. He smelled good. *Really* good.

She still couldn't get used to how big he was. Standing this close to him, his chest a broad steely shield before her, it made her want to reach out and . . .

She cleared her throat, trying to shake off her errant thoughts. She had to focus on why she was here. "Jamie is back."

She could almost feel him stiffen as every muscle in his body seemed to flex. Good gracious, why did she suddenly feel the urge to trace the chiseled contours with her fingertips and see if they were as steely as they looked?

"I know; I saw him ride in."

"Then you must have seen that Archie wasn't with him? It didn't work, Thom. Jamie couldn't climb the cliff. There was a sheer section near the top and he couldn't do it. But you could. He said it would be easy for you. That you've climbed far more difficult before. I know it's asking a lot, I know it could be dangerous, but he said there weren't any soldiers guarding that section, and the other warriors will follow . . ." He wasn't saying anything. Indeed, she couldn't help noticing how eerily quiet he was while she rambled on. *Something is wrong.* But she didn't listen to that little voice and pressed on. "I know you refused. I know you have no reason to help, but please, I'm begging you to reconsider."

She had to convince him. After what he'd told her about feeling like a servant and being at their "command," she couldn't let him think he didn't have a choice. He'd worked so hard to make a new life, and if Jamie forced him to do this, it would be a blow to his pride that he might never forgive.

She hadn't realized her hand had fallen on his arm as she'd spoken until she noticed him staring at it. She tried to pull it back self-consciously, but he wouldn't let her. He circled her wrist and drew her closer.

Their bodies were almost touching. Good Lord, it felt like she'd walked into the forge. Heat bellowed over her, weakening her knees. She felt strange. Light-headed—as if she might faint.

What was happening to her? This was *Thommy*.

"How badly do you want it, Elizabeth?" His voice was low and husky, and so ripe with meaning, she wondered if they were still talking about Archie. "What are you willing to bargain?"

Bargain? Suddenly, she understood. Money! Why hadn't she thought of that before? If it seemed unusually mercenary for Thom, she reminded herself that things were different now. For a man to be a knight, it took coin. "Name your price, and you shall have it. I do not have much silver of my own, but I'm sure Jamie will pay you whatever—"

"I don't want your brother's blasted money!"

"But I told you, I have little of my own that is not in my tocher—" She stopped, looking at him in shock.

Was that what he was proposing? *Marriage?*

He laughed harshly. "Don't look so horrified, *that* will not be required of you. As I said, I have other plans."

She frowned, not just at the reminder of his betrothal, but at how quick he was to assume he knew what she was thinking. She'd been surprised—not horrified. "Then I don't understand."

"Don't you?" His voice was husky again as his gaze slid down her body. Slowly. Intently. Leaving an imprint in its wake. "Can you think of nothing else with which to bargain?"

She gasped. The heat in his gaze left no doubt as to his meaning.

Jamie was right. Thom was not the noble boy with the

fierce sense of right and wrong whom she remembered. He'd been prone to brooding moods at times, but this was a dark, angry side that she'd never seen before. "You would force me to give you my virtue?"

His eyes found hers. The hot flash of blue sent a blast of heat all the way to her toes. But it was the sultry smile that made her limbs start to melt. "Force?" He pulled her body snugly against his. "I won't need to force anything."

The fierce sensations that shuddered through her made her wonder if he might be right.

As a man who'd been around fire his whole life, Thom knew better than to play with it. But he wasn't just playing with it, he was fueling it, stoking it, daring it to burn him. But he couldn't stop. He finally had Lady Elizabeth Douglas where he wanted her. Seeing him—*really* seeing him—and the burgeoning awareness shuddering through her was irresistible.

He'd only sought to bargain with a kiss, but when she'd assumed more . . . well, he was not exactly in the right state of mind to set her right.

But why her assuming he wanted money angered him more than her thinking he was bargaining with her virtue he didn't know.

He never should have touched her, and he especially never should have brought her body against his. The feel of her breasts crushed against his chest, the dart of her nipples, the flush of desire on her cheeks, and the sweet gasp and parting of her lips drove him out of his mind with lust. It took him to a place that was dark and deep and impossible to find his way out of. It was the place of erotic dreams and fantasies. The place where he finally tasted her.

Finally touched her. Finally had her flush with desire and weak with surrender.

"You aren't serious," she managed nervously. "I know you, Thom. You don't mean it."

Her certainty only fueled the flames hotter. She didn't know him at all. "You knew a boy who knew his place. A boy who only let you see what he wanted you to see. A village lad who wouldn't dare to touch the perfect little princess for fear that he might sully her."

Her eyes widened and flickered with what looked like fear. He didn't know whom he hated more at that moment. He let her go and set her away from him, needing to put distance between her and his surging body. His fists clenched and re-clenched at his sides as he fought for control. "Is the thought of having my hands on you so offensive?"

She blinked. "No! I mean yes . . . I mean no, of course not! Why are you trying to confuse me?"

His mouth set in a hard, unforgiving line. "Is that what I'm doing? I thought we were bargaining. But since my terms didn't appeal to you—"

"A kiss," she said, cutting him off.

His heart might have stopped beating. His breath, however, had definitely stopped. All he could do was stare at her and wait for her to explain.

"I will let you kiss me, and then you will agree to help rescue Archie."

Let you. His jaw clenched. "How gracious of you, but I'm afraid that isn't good enough."

She flushed, obviously surprised by his rejection of her terms. Did she think him that desperate for a taste of her?

So what if he was, damn it!

"What *do* you want, then?" she demanded, her own temper flaring.

"I will let you kiss me," he said.

Her brows drew together. "That's what I said."

He didn't correct her. "*And* we will see if you can persuade me that it is worth the risk."

The furrow between her brows deepened. "How am I to do that?"

"Make it good." His voice gave no hint of the rapid heating of his blood. "I'm sure you've been kissed before?"

Her eyes narrowed, as if she suspected there was more behind the question than there first appeared. She was right.

"Once or twice."

The rage that rose inside him was so fast and furious it could only be bloodlust. His muscles flared. The thought of someone else touching her drove him to the very edge of his restraint. Who? When? *Kill.*

Somehow he managed to respond without growling. "Good. Then you will know what to do."

Elizabeth had no idea what to do. Thom—the person she thought she knew most in the world who it turned out she didn't know at all—was standing there obviously waiting for her to begin.

She eyed him warily, sensing that there was far more to this conversation than she was hearing.

It had seemed like a good idea, but now that she was actually looking at him, knowing what she had to do, it felt . . . bigger. *Much* bigger. And daunting. And somehow important—as if she were about to do something that she knew could never be undone.

She licked her suddenly dry lips and took a small step forward. But her entire body seemed to shake. Her knees were wobbling, her legs had turned to jelly, and her stomach seemed to be flipping around inside like a fish out of water.

That's what she was. She had no idea what she was doing. She had been kissed before—twice, actually—but somehow she sensed a kiss like the quick pecks stolen by a particularly bold French suitor was not going to suffice.

Make it good.

She looked up at him, feeling her heart rise to her throat.

If only he weren't so imposing.

If only he weren't so tall, and so outrageously handsome.

And if only she hadn't just seen him naked. Dear God, it was no time to think about that! Her heart was hammering so loudly she wondered if he could hear it.

His arms were crossed as he watched her move infinitesimally closer. "I don't have all night."

She scowled at him. This wasn't easy for her, blast him. Straightening her shoulders, she wiped her hands on her skirts and closed the distance between them.

She stopped about a foot away.

His mouth curled with a smile that made her feel like a plump, juicy lamb. "I won't bite," he said, and then so softly that she wondered if she heard him right added, "Unless you want me to."

Her eyes flew to his. But although he was still smiling that wicked "come closer if you dare" smile, his meaning and thoughts were indecipherable.

Good Lord, it was hot in here! There was a sheen of perspiration on her brow, and her skin felt as if it were fevered.

The tension between them was so thick she couldn't

breathe. Although there might be another explanation. Maybe she was scared to inhale because she feared his scent would wash over her and penetrate her senses again, confusing her.

He had to realize how nervous she was, yet he just stood there watching her with that inscrutable, impervious, annoyingly calm expression on his face. She felt a strange twinge of sympathy for her brother, recalling how many times Thom had used the same expression on him. It was how he'd fought back. How he'd defied his lord without doing so outright.

Was that what he was doing? Fighting back with indifference? The flare of anger gave her just the burst of courage she needed.

She was making more out of this than there was, she told herself. It was only a kiss. She could do this.

Putting both of her hands on his chest to brace herself, she lifted onto her toes.

But she still wasn't tall enough. His mouth was still a few inches away, and clearly, he wasn't going to make it easier on her by lowering it.

Blackguard!

Pursing her mouth, and bolder now with anger, she slid her hands around his neck, stretched against him, and dragged his head down to hers.

Their lips met in the softest, most delicate brush. The shock that ran through her, however, was not. It was jolting. Nerve flaring. Heart-stopping.

She almost drew back. But his body was warm, and despite being so hard, it was remarkably cozy, and the spicy scent of whisky on his breath was strangely intoxicating, drawing her in for more.

He *had* told her to make it good.

9

EIGHTEEN YEARS. THOM had had to wait almost eighteen fucking years for her to kiss him again, and damned if it wasn't worth it.

The sweet press of her lips to his cheek that she'd given him as a child in gratitude for rescuing her from that tree, however, was nothing compared with the sensation of her very grown-up, very sensual mouth brushing against his. The kiss was still sweet, but his response—and the yearning that surged through him—was not. It was about as far from sweet as it could get. It was raw and primitive and intense, blinding him with a white-hot bolt of lust that reverberated through his body like a thunderstorm.

A thunderstorm he had to fight to contain. His hands were planted firmly at his sides, every muscle in his body flexed and rigid with restraint. Restraint that had been burned in over years of wanting what he could not have.

You can't touch her. She's not for you.

Words that were so ingrained in him that even now, even now when her mouth pressed against his more firmly, when her body rubbed against him innocently and invitingly, when she made a soft sound in her throat that practically begged him to respond, he didn't.

Bloody hell, it was almost as if he was scared to touch her. Scared that maybe the rest of the world was right—maybe he wasn't good enough. Scared that putting his rough, callused hands on her would somehow mar all that creamy perfection. And most of all, scared that after so many years of holding back, his passion, once released, would be impossible to contain.

His restraint infuriated him. He didn't need to stop himself anymore. Why shouldn't he kiss her, damn it? There was no one to stop him. No one to tell him he couldn't have her.

He'd been waiting for this for too damned long. Waiting for her to come to him, to recognize what had always been between them, and to show her exactly what she'd forsaken.

No more holding back, damn it. He started out slow, as if testing whether his body would follow his mind's command. *Put your hand on her waist. Gentle, damn it. Don't bring her in too tight. Move your other hand up easy. Cradle her head.*

Ah, Christ. He bit back a groan as the smooth silk of her hair slid over his knuckles and sent a fresh wave of sensation racing over his skin. It taunted him. Tempted him. He wanted to lace his fingers through it, twist it around his hand, and bring her mouth in hard against his.

He wanted to slide his tongue into her mouth and kiss her hard and deep. He wanted to kiss her until her taste melded with his, until her tongue circled and thrust wildly—passionately—against his, until she felt the same insatiable hunger that was burning inside him.

Blood rushed like molten ore through his veins, urging him to devour, urging him to open those achingly sweet lips under his and taste her fully. But he forced his pulse to slow, forced his hands not to grip but to caress, and forced his mouth to sweep and entreat, not ravish and plunder like an uncouth villein.

As if she were the most fragile piece of porcelain, he

drew her infinitesimally closer. The hand on her hip slid around her waist and the hand cupping her head brought her mouth more firmly against his.

He didn't move. Didn't trust himself to do anything other than let the sensations roll over him in a hot, heavy wave. But the honey sweetness of her breath, the velvety softness of her lips, the feminine lushness of the curves sinking into him dragged him under.

It was too much. It felt too good. The instincts firing through him were too powerful, the urges too primal. He was too damned hot. He couldn't do this. He had to pull back.

But whatever rationality he might have possessed fled when she made a moan low in her throat. A moan that moved from her mouth into his. A moan that shattered every bone of restraint he had in his body and opened the damned floodgates.

He pressed her into the curve of his body, gripped the back of her head, and brought her mouth decisively to his. There were no more gentle brushes and sweeping entreaties; he opened her lips with his and sank into her deep and hard. Kissing the innocence from her mouth with bold, authoritative strokes of his tongue that demanded a response.

And she gave him one. Christ, how she gave him one. Her response undid him. Tentative and innocent at first—proving that she'd never been kissed like this before—and bolder and more passionate as desire took over.

Desire for *him*.

Aye, she wanted him, and the satisfaction of being right, of knowing that the connection between them was far more than friendship, was nothing to feeling it shudder through her, hearing it in her soft moans, and tasting it in the frenzy of her mouth and tongue sliding against his.

It was even better than he'd imagined—and what he'd imagined had been damned spectacular. But he hadn't been able to dream up the incredible feel of all those womanly curves fitted against him, the delicate sweetness of her mouth, the silkiness of her hair, the fresh scent of soap that clung to her baby-soft skin. He sure as hell couldn't have known how it would feel to have her hands digging into his back and shoulders as the kiss intensified, as if she were struggling to hold on. And he hadn't had a damned clue what it would be like when her body rubbed against his trying to get closer. When his hand slid around the firm swell of her bottom to lift her against him. To feel his cock hard and snug in that one place he wanted it, and then feel her rock innocently but instinctively against him.

He damned near lost himself. The pleasure was so acute, the pressure so intense, he could have come right there.

He didn't know how much longer he could hold on. His hands were no longer capable of caressing; they were too busy covering every inch of her. The soft swell of her hips, the lush curve of her bottom, the heavy swell of her breasts.

He couldn't hold back the groan when he finally took those perfect mounds of flesh in his hands. Christ, they were spectacular. Lush and round and generous. Too much to hold in one hand generous. Bury your face generous. Wreak havoc with his nights generous. How many times had he dreamed of this? Dreamed of cupping her. Squeezing her. Circling his thumb over the turgid peak until she arched in his hand. Dreamed of making her gasp and moan.

If he'd ever had a doubt about the nature of the connection between them, it was gone. Passion like this couldn't be denied.

Nor could it be controlled.

Elizabeth didn't understand what was happening to her. Well, in theory she understood that Thom was kissing her—and she was kissing him back—but the sensations assailing her body, the sensations turning her brain to porridge, and her legs to jelly, *those* she didn't understand at all.

She'd never imagined a kiss could be so . . . overwhelming—so utterly and thoroughly consuming. That it could make her feel as if she never wanted to do anything else. As if her body had suddenly come alive, and yet at the same time make her feel as if she would die if his hands didn't keep touching her and his tongue didn't keep stroking her.

His kiss was incredible. He seemed to know exactly what he was doing, and he was doing it perfectly—expertly. She'd never imagined he could be so assertive. Bold. Dominating. Where had he learned . . . ?

She didn't want to know.

He tasted so good—dark and spicy laced with whisky. The intoxicating combination poured through her senses in a hot, melty rush that made her drunk with pleasure and so weak she would have slid to the floor (despite her grip on his rock-hard shoulders) had she not felt the sturdy edge of a small table behind her.

The added support was even more welcome when he took her breasts in his hands and her entire body went liquid. The hot rush of pleasure that coursed through her forestalled any pretense of shock or maidenly modesty. The warmth of his touch branded her with sensation. Her breasts had taken on a purpose: to be in his hands, to be squeezed and caressed, to have her nipples plied between his fingertips. To have his mouth . . .

Oh God. She made a sound of pure molten pleasure as he broke the kiss to cover her breast with his mouth.

Somehow, while she was lost in the delirium of their kiss, he'd managed to loosen her gown and move the bodice to the side enough to reveal the pink tips of her breasts to his gaze . . . and to his mouth. His hot, wet mouth that was now sucking her hard and deep while his tongue circled the turgid, throbbing tip.

Any resistance she might have felt, any glimmer of sanity that might have broken through the drunk-with-pleasure haze, was lost the moment his mouth covered her.

A bolt of pleasure shot all the way down to her toes, but it gathered between her legs turning hotter, wetter, and more insistent.

Her body knew what she wanted, and even as her back arched deeper into his mouth, her hips began to press against his manhood. The thick column of flesh was so big and hard, and the pressure so exquisite, she would have given him anything—or everything—to keep it going.

Which is exactly what she did, when he slid his hand under her skirts and touched her in that warm, wet place that quivered so anxiously.

Thom was caught in a dark whirlpool of lust and desire that sent him deeper and deeper to the point of no return. He didn't know if he could pull himself out—even if he wanted to.

He sensed the exact moment she surrendered to him, the exact moment she was his. He could hear it in her gasp and feel it in her limbs as his finger slid over that warm, sensitive place between her legs. Any resistance simply melted away and her body succumbed to the force of desire surging between them.

The heat . . . the dampness . . . She was so wet for him he couldn't stand it. He lifted his head from her breast to stare into her half-lidded eyes.

She wanted him, and the warm, honey-sweet proof was slick around his fingers. He plunged into her, holding her gaze to his, watching as the pleasure and surprise transformed her features.

He was going to make her come. She was achingly close already. Her breath started to quicken with sharp little gasps, her eyes grew hazy, and the soft pink flush on her cheeks darkened as he stroked her.

His already throbbing cock throbbed harder as his finger slipped in and out of that tight, warm glove. God, she was so sweet. So beautiful. Her response so innocent and free as she gave herself over to the pleasure he was bringing her.

She was almost there, her body squirming, her gasps muffled with frustration, her eyes closed, as she tried to find what she was looking for. He took pity on her innocence and left her without a choice, pressing his palm against her as he found the sensitive spot that could not resist. She started to shudder and cry out.

It was the most beautiful thing he'd ever seen.

And also the most painful. The urge to take his own release gathered at the base of his spine and pounded. He wanted to be inside her so badly, wanted to feel those spasms tightening around his aching cock instead of his finger, wanted to feel all that warm dampness flooding him. He had to bite back the pulse that brought a milky drop to his tip, and the roar of blood surging through his veins and blasting in his ears: *take her . . . finish it . . . she can be yours.*

She is *yours.*

He might have done just that had she not lifted her eyes to his. Eyes that were filled with wonder, tenderness . . . and trust.

It took Elizabeth a moment to realize something was wrong. She felt as if she'd just catapulted to the stars. As if she'd just ridden across the sky in Apollo's blazing chariot. As if she'd died for a moment and glimpsed heaven.

The pleasure of Thom's touch had consumed her, and then it had wound tighter and tighter until it snapped and broke apart into a shattering array of light. It was pleasure and sensation unlike anything she'd ever imagined. And she rode out wave after glorious wave until the last tingling pulse had ebbed from her body.

She opened her eyes and looked into the familiar face of the man who'd brought her to such heights and felt something strange swell in her chest. A warmth of emotion that she'd never felt before. The intimacy—the closeness—of the moment seemed to wrap around her and squeeze.

She would have smiled had the veil of euphoria not lifted enough for her to realize that the sweet tenderness of emotion, the warmth in her chest, and euphoria were not shared by the man leaning over her. Rather he seemed pulled as tight as a bowstring, teetering on the edge of some dark, violent precipice he was fighting not to fall off of.

"Thommy?" she asked uncertainly, forgetting he'd asked her not to call him that. Her hand went to his face, cupping the hard lines of his jaw. The stubble grated against her palm and she could feel the heavy pulse just below his cheek. "What's wrong?"

His gaze hardened to blue chips of ice, but she yanked

her hand back as if scalded. A breath of cool air spread over her skin, and all at once she became aware of her wanton state. She was collapsed on a table, her breasts were half-spilling out of her gown, her skirts were bunched around her waist, and he had his hand between her spread legs with his manhood positioned only a few inches away. Her gaze slid to the thick column of his erection, and she knew that all he had to do was loosen the ties of his breeches and he could be inside her.

She wouldn't resist. She was pretty sure she would welcome him.

He seemed to know that, too, and for one pulse-stopping moment she thought he was going to do exactly that. Her heart even slammed against her rib cage in anticipation.

But then he pulled back harshly, removing his body and his hand from her in what felt like a cold slap.

A cold slap that was matched by the sting of his words. "Keep your virtue, my lady. It was not part of the bargain." His eyes skimmed over her. "Although you present a tempting invitation, a kiss was all that was required."

Elizabeth gasped as a sharp knife of pain slid between her ribs. She sat up and quickly pulled down her gown to hide her nakedness. "I wasn't . . ."

But they both knew she was. She'd offered him her virtue and he'd refused it.

His gaze held hers unyieldingly, his mouth pulling into a tight smile. "You needn't worry. The kiss was good enough. I'll honor your ardent *request* to help free your brother." She didn't understand the snide turn he put on the word. "But in return you will honor mine."

"What?"

"To leave me the hell alone."

The harshly uttered words spoken with such vehemence cut off her breath. Her chest squeezed with a pain sharper and deeper than she'd felt before. How could he touch her like that one moment, and then the next act as if he wanted nothing to do with her? She'd just experienced something extraordinary, yet it seemed to be nothing to him at all. And that made her feel oddly vulnerable, confused, and precariously close to tears.

Her eyes scanned his face, looking for any sign of weakness, any crack in the formidable, handsome facade. Finding none, they came to rest on his. "If you are certain that is what you want?"

With her gaze, she argued, pleaded, and begged for him to disagree. But her silent words had no effect.

With one last long look, he gave her a sharp nod and said, "Aye, that's exactly what I want."

The words had barely left his mouth before he was gone.

10

THEY'D RIDDEN THROUGH the day—and most of the night—but not thirty-six hours after that disastrous kiss, Thom stood in the shadow of the formidable Bamburgh Castle, listening to Douglas go over the plan that would send Thom 150 feet up a cliff and into one of the most formidable castles in England.

Though his former friend had avoided him over the long, harrowing ride across the dangerous Marches, Thom had felt Douglas's scrutiny more than once.

Douglas was a suspicious bastard. Thom's silent acceptance of the order to accompany him—rather than the anger Douglas had undoubtedly been expecting—hadn't sat well with him. Douglas was probably wondering whether his sister had anything to do with it.

If he only knew.

Douglas would kill him. And it would probably be deserved. Thom had been one thrust away from taking her innocence and destroying them both.

He'd acted dishonorably, and he knew it. For his entire life, Thom had prided himself on always doing the right thing. In a world that only cared about *who* you were, not *what* you were, he'd always told himself that it was actions that made a man noble—not blood. But he'd acted as base as the world wanted to make him.

And all for what? To prove a point? To make her see what was between them? To make her realize what she'd forsaken?

Well, he'd succeeded. He'd proved that there was a hell of a lot more than friendship between them. He'd proved just how incredible it would be between them. He'd proved that she wanted him just as badly as he wanted her.

But at what cost? The hard-wrought peace he'd found, and the new life he'd built for himself, had been shattered. He would hear the cries of her release in his dreams for the rest of his life. He would hold the memory of her kiss, the sweetness of her mouth, the softness of her skin, and the perfection of her breasts forever. Any woman he took to his bed in the future would suffer by comparison.

For a few precious minutes he'd had everything he'd ever wanted, and it had been better than he'd ever imagined.

He never should have touched her. He still couldn't believe he'd lost himself like that. But he'd had plenty of hours over the long journey to recall in vivid detail exactly how close he'd come to giving Douglas a reason to stick that blade in his gut.

But Thom didn't give a shite about what Douglas thought or suspected. He was here to do a job. The sooner the better, which was one of the reasons why Douglas's decision to wait until the following night to make their ascent didn't sit well.

"There is no reason to wait. I'm ready now," Thom insisted. "There are still three or four hours before dawn." He had already inspected the cliff below the castle. "It won't take me longer than three-quarters of an hour to climb. Even with the additional time to secure the rope, have you and the rest of the men climb that last section, and hoist the rope ladder to climb the wall, we will have Archie out of there well before the sky begins to lighten. Besides, the mist is thick tonight and will shield us from any soldiers who happen to pass."

Douglas's eyes narrowed. He wasn't used to being contradicted—especially by someone in Thom's position. But it was bad enough that he'd been forced under his former friend's authority again, he would be damned if he'd keep his mouth shut when he didn't agree with something—especially when that something involved his life and area of expertise. He and Douglas would never be equals, but they were both warriors, and the field of battle had a way of leveling.

"The rocks are damp from the rain earlier," Douglas pointed out.

"As it rains almost every night this time of year, they'll likely be wet tomorrow as well. At least today it is relatively warm. Tomorrow it could be colder and the wet could turn to ice."

Ice would make that last section of the cliff impassable—too dangerous for even him to attempt.

"I thought you would need time to recover after the ride."

Thom's jaw tightened. "I'm fine."

He'd had to work hard to keep up with the rest of the men, but his struggle with riding—usually a source of amusement—wasn't when it came from Douglas.

"MacGowan's right," MacLeod said. Thom was more pleased by the support than he wanted to let on. Over the past day and a half he'd been impressed—maybe even awed—by the warriors who rode beside him, and none more so than by the man who appeared to be their leader. "If MacGowan says he can do it, we should let him try. The lad has already been in there for six days."

Jamie's expression darkened, and despite the bad blood between them, Thom felt a twinge of compassion for his former friend. He could well imagine the dark thoughts that must be racing through his head. Christ, if Johnny were in Archie's place Thom would be going half-crazed wondering what kind of tortures and hardships he was suffering. Actually, he had to admire Douglas's clearheadedness and ability to prevent his personal demons from interfering with his decisions.

Thom's tone lost some of its combativeness. "Let me try, Jamie. If it looks like it will take longer or the conditions worsen, I'll turn around. You know I can do this."

Jamie held his gaze and eventually gave a terse nod. "Don't take any unnecessary chances. We can't afford anything to go wrong. If we lose the element of surprise . . ."

He didn't need to finish. They all knew that without surprise they had virtually no chance of rescue. The only way to get Archie out of there would be a direct attack on the castle or a siege—neither of which was going to happen. Bruce was focused on taking Scotland's castles, not England's.

"We won't," Thom replied, the decisiveness of his voice adding assurance. "We'll be long gone before the English realize we were there."

Douglas's mouth quirked. It was probably the first time he'd smiled at Thom in eight years. "Aye, well, I wish I shared your confidence. But I've been doing this too long and have learned that if something can go wrong, it will. Just ask MacGregor about the dog at Berwick," he added dryly.

The famed archer overheard him and told Douglas to do something to himself that was physically impossible.

The rest of the men laughed, and Thom was already looking forward to hearing the story on the return journey to Roxburgh.

He took Douglas's words of caution to heart. His former friend might be an arse, but he was an experienced, battle-hardened one who'd been on God knew how many dangerous missions. This was Thom's first, and no matter how it had come about, he was determined to prove himself among his companions. If that meant casting himself in the role of pupil to Douglas's teacher, he would do so gladly. Whatever his personal feelings, Douglas was one of the greatest knights in Scotland; Thom would be a fool not to heed his advice.

Fortunately, Douglas's trepidation proved unwarranted. The plan proceeded without a hitch—or a barking dog, as Thom was to hear about over the campfire the next evening.

Thom climbed the cliff and scaled the last thirty feet of sheer rock without any trouble. Jamie and Elizabeth had been correct in their estimation of his skills. He wouldn't characterize it as easy, but neither had it been difficult. Had he not ridden almost nonstop for the last twenty hours or so, and had a sore shoulder, he would have climbed it in even less time than the forty minutes it took him.

The most difficult part of the mission turned out to be finding somewhere to tie the rope that he dropped to Douglas and the six others who'd accompanied them into the castle—MacRuairi (who supposedly would be able to open the gate), Sutherland (who apparently had some knowledge of black powder that might give them extra time if they needed it), MacKay (who like Thom didn't have any fondness for riding and also like Thom apparently possessed some skill with working iron), Boyd (who didn't need to tell him what he was there for—his physical strength was obvious), MacSorley (whose easygoing presence and seafaring skill were put to use throwing the grappling hooks of the specially made wooden ladder they used to scale the wall), and MacLeod (whose unrivaled skill with the sword would be needed if they stumbled on any trouble). Campbell, MacGregor, Lamont, and MacLean had remained outside the gate to keep watch and alert them from below if anything appeared amiss.

Eventually Thom decided to secure the rope by winding it around a large rock and using his own body to provide extra leverage as the men climbed the last sheer section of the cliff.

MacSorley threw the grappling hooks over the wall with barely a sound, and to Thom's surprise, after Douglas, he was the next man sent up the ladder. It was an unexpected honor, and Thom knew it was MacLeod's way of letting him know it was a job well done.

Once in the castle, they encountered no resistance in their search for Archie. He was exactly where he was supposed to be: in the prison tower at the edge of the cliff. The two soldiers in the adjoining guardroom had been dispensed with quickly, and within a matter of seconds MacRuairi had the iron bar of the door unlocked.

It was pitch-black in the small chamber, and MacSorley had fetched a torch from the guardroom. Three filthy, bloodied faces stared back at them from a corner of the room; one of them was Archie's. Thom's stomach rolled, and bile rose up the back of his throat.

Douglas didn't say anything, but Thom knew what he was feeling because he felt it, too: rage. Archie was only sixteen, damn it, but the lad had obviously suffered a vicious beating. He was covered in bruises and cuts, and the eyes that looked back at them were white with terror.

But with no time to take inventory of the wrongs committed against his brother—wrongs that Thom had no doubt would be accounted for in the not-so-distant future—Douglas simply gave the lad a quick embrace and helped him out of the hellhole in which he'd been trapped. They'd taken the other two men (who weren't much older than Archie) with them as well.

Though in bad shape—weak from hunger and the beatings they'd suffered—the former prisoners nonetheless found a boon of strength to aid in their escape. They managed to climb the ladder and descend on their own, albeit with some help and the support of the ropes.

By the time the group was riding away from the castle, there was still nearly an hour of darkness remaining.

Lamont and MacLean had found additional horses, but Archie and the two others were too weak to manage them on their own. Douglas took his brother, and Campbell and MacGregor took the other two behind them for the first few hours of hard riding.

Once they'd crossed the border near the English-occupied Berwick Castle, Douglas slowed the pace. After the first break, where the prisoners had washed, had their wounds tended by MacKay, eaten, and drank a good draught of *uisge-beatha*, they were able to ride on their own.

But rest is what they most needed, and by early afternoon, Douglas halted for the night. Unlike the ride the day before, they had no cause to press. With the rain, sodden ground, and taking to the hills whenever possible to avoid the main roads and running into any English patrols, the ride was slow-going and treacherous to say the least.

They'd stopped somewhere in the Cheviot Hills, near what appeared to be an old hill fort. Archie and the other two lads were asleep on bedrolls in the canopy of the forest, while Thom relaxed with a skin of ale and some of the other warriors around the fire. MacLean and Lamont were on guard duty, and MacLeod and Douglas had gone somewhere—probably to hunt for food—but the other men were enjoying their well-earned rest. Thom was content just to listen to the conversation (most of which consisted of pointed barbs and needling), but he found himself drawn in more than once.

He'd already heard the story of how a dog had foiled the taking of Berwick Castle (when MacGregor hesitated to shoot it), and how they'd narrowly escaped capture afterward due to a resourceful young girl from the family who was hiding them deciding to sell tickets to see "the most handsome man in Scotland," when the conversation turned to the most recent—and more successful—mission.

MacSorley, whose wicked smile was matched by his sense of humor, clearly liked to needle the others. His current target, however, was surprising. From everything Thom had heard of Lachlan MacRuairi, he was not a man to prod. His reputation as a black-hearted scourge and the most feared pirate in a Western Isles kingdom of pirates was well known. Thom had been shocked when MacRuairi had been unmasked as one of Bruce's Phantoms and assumed he had been paid a fortune for his sword. But after watching him for the past couple of days, Thom was no longer certain his loyalty had been bought. Still, MacRuairi wasn't a man Thom would want to cross swords with in a dark wynd or close.

MacSorley, however, seemed undaunted by the infamous mercenary's reputation. "I think that pretty wife of yours and all those bairns you were never going to have made you soft, cousin." They were kinsmen? Thom couldn't hide his shock. The two couldn't have been more different in appearance and temperament. "I thought you said climbing that cliff was 'impossible.'" The big, fair-haired seafarer who would have made his Viking ancestors proud grinned. "MacGowan here didn't seem to have any problems."

"Sod off, Hawk. I think you are confused. I'm built like a rock, but that doesn't mean I am one."

MacSorley—Thom wondered where the name Hawk came from—chuckled and turned his gaze to Thom assessingly. "Interesting theory. Rock. I like it. It fits."

Thom had no idea what he was talking about, but the others seemed to, as he saw more than one man smile.

MacRuairi wasn't finished. "Anytime you want to show

me how it's done, cousin, be my guest. But I didn't hear you volunteering to lead the way."

MacSorley gave a dramatic shudder. "Nor will you. Christ, I didn't even like being up that high with a rope. Be it good old terra firma or the wooden planks of a ship, I need something under my feet."

MacRuairi leaned back, kicked his legs out, and crossed his arms, eyeing his cousin slyly. "I didn't think you were scared of anything, cousin—other than your wife."

A few of the men laughed, and MacSorley grinned. "And people say you have no sense of humor." He shook his head. "Let's just say I have a healthy respect for both." He turned to Thom. "So, *Rock*, how the hell did you learn to climb like that? I've never seen anyone scale a cliff so high or sheer."

Thom smiled at the name—understanding the others' amusement earlier—and shrugged. "I don't know. It was just something I enjoyed, so I kept doing it. I like the challenge, I suppose, and the satisfaction of doing something no one else has before."

A few of the men exchanged glances, and Thom wondered what he'd said.

"Well, that's an understatement. I'd wager the English are still scratching their tails, wondering how we got in there."

Tail was a slur for coward, and Thom chuckled along with the others.

The Highlander Magnus MacKay, who was leaning against a tree next to Thom, gave him a long look. "I have to admit I share Hawk's healthy respect for heights."

"And for your wife?" Sutherland quipped.

MacKay grinned; his wife, Helen, was Sutherland's

sister. "Aye, with her knowledge of plants, I'd better." He turned back to Thom. "How do you get past it?"

"The height?" Thom asked.

MacKay nodded.

He wasn't aware Jamie had come up behind them until he heard him answer. "He doesn't look down."

Surprised—actually, shocked as hell—at the easy reference to the day of their first meeting and what had solidified their friendship, Thom snapped his head around to look at him.

There was something odd about Douglas's expression. It took Thom a moment to pinpoint why: he wasn't looking at him as if he was contemplating ways of sliding a blade between his ribs.

"Can I speak with you for a moment?" Douglas asked.

Thom nodded and stood from the rock he'd been sitting on. It wasn't without some effort. His limbs ached from the long hours on horseback.

He was sure Douglas noticed, but he refrained from making a remark. They moved a short distance away toward the small stream where they'd watered the horses. It wasn't exactly a comfortable silence, but he waited for Douglas to break it. When he did, he said the last thing Thom expected.

"Thank you," Douglas said, stopping at the edge of the water and turning to face him. "I owe you . . ." His voice fell off, and when he spoke again, Thom could hear the emotion. "You saved my brother's life."

Maybe he should have just accepted his thanks and left it at that. But too much had passed between them, and the past burned with too much resentment. "I wasn't left with much of a choice, was I?"

There was still enough light left to see the pulse below

Douglas's jaw tic, but it was clear he was making an effort not to lose his temper. "I couldn't take any chances."

"You could have tried asking."

"You refused my sister, I didn't think you would do it for me."

"That's a pile of shite," Thom said angrily. "You didn't ask because you couldn't stand the thought of lowering yourself to ask me for anything."

The anger and animosity were back, filling the air between them as they faced off in the semi-darkness.

"Maybe because I knew how much pleasure you would take in refusing me," Jamie snapped back.

They knew each other too well—knew their weaknesses and the pride that was the source of the tension between them even when they were the closest of friends. Douglas was right. Thom would have refused, and after how they'd found Archie, the realization shamed him.

The anger seeped out of him. He drew back and raked his fingers through his hair in frustration. "No matter how it came about, I'm glad that I could help, but I wasn't alone."

Douglas gave him a wry look, apparently amused that Thom was seeking to share the credit. "Nay, but we wouldn't have been able to do it without you." His expression cracked, revealing the torment underneath. "Christ, if I hadn't been so stubborn—if I'd listened to Ella and brought you in the first place we could have saved him two or three days of suffering. What he went through . . ."

Archie had told them that they hadn't had food in days, and the only water they had was from the rain that backed up from a drain in the floor. They'd been left to freeze every night, and the only time they'd seen light was when they were taken out to be beaten by the bored soldiers. Three of the men they'd arrived with they suspected had been killed.

"MacKay said he will have no lasting injuries. He is fortunate nothing was broken."

Why the hell was he trying to give him comfort?

"Maybe not his bones, but the spirit does not recover so easily. Christ, Archie told me they were planning to torture them. If we'd waited until tomorrow, God only knows in what state we might have found him."

Both men were silent for a while, staring at the slow-moving water before them. There wasn't much that could be said. Finally, Douglas straightened and turned back to him. "Anyway, I meant what I said. You acquitted yourself well today, and we wouldn't have been able to do it without you. For what it's worth, you have my thanks."

Surprisingly, it was worth a lot. Thom nodded in acknowledgment, feeling as if an uneasy truce formed between them.

"I probably should be thanking you," he said after a minute.

Jamie didn't hide his shock. "For what?"

"Giving me a chance to fight alongside the best warriors in Scotland—hell, probably in Christendom."

Only someone who knew him as well as Thom did would see the hint of wariness that returned to Jamie's expression. But he needn't worry; Thom wasn't looking for confirmation. He didn't need it. If these men weren't Bruce's illustrious Phantoms (and at least two were), then they might as well be.

Perhaps recognizing that, Douglas relaxed. "Aye, they are that."

"They?" Not Douglas, too?

Jamie lifted a brow. "If I didn't know you better, I would think that was a compliment."

"And if I didn't know you better, I'd think that was you being modest."

Jamie laughed, and Thom found himself smiling as well. For a moment, it almost felt like old times. The easy exchange, the jests, the prodding—he'd forgotten how it had been. It was probably why despite the danger he'd been enjoying himself so much the past couple of days. These men had a bond not unlike the one he'd had with Jamie all those years ago.

He'd never let himself acknowledge how much he'd missed it.

"What will you do now?" Jamie asked as they started to walk back.

"Nothing as exciting as this. But thankfully not taking down any more castle walls—at least for a while. Although with the weeks of boredom ahead at Stirling during the siege, I might be wishing for an excuse to swing a hammer."

Jamie frowned. "I thought Ella said that you had something else to do first? Something about an engagement to the widow?"

The reason for the frown became apparent. Undoubtedly, the knowledge of his betrothal had been met with considerable relief by Jamie—which might explain some of the easing of tensions between them—and he wanted to make sure what Elizabeth had told him was the truth.

Thom nodded, allaying his fears. "Lady Marjorie Ruth-erford."

Douglas lifted both brows, clearly impressed. "I've met her before—you have done well for yourself."

Thom shrugged. "Nothing has been formalized."

"But it will be?"

If the question was more intense than the situation warranted, Thom pretended not to notice. "Aye."

A broad smile spread across Jamie's face, and once again, he was relaxed. "Well, then you have my congratulations. Jo will be beside herself with two betrothals to celebrate."

"Two?"

Jamie stopped to stare at him, his expression recovering some of its wariness. "Ella didn't tell you?"

Thom heard the irritation in his voice. "Tell me what?"

Sensing he wasn't going to like what Douglas had to say, Thom braced himself.

"My sister is to be betrothed to Randolph."

No amount of bracing could have prepared him for the blow. For the white-hot ball of pain that had shot into his chest and exploded.

He flinched—maybe even staggered.

Elizabeth was getting married.

Why hadn't she told him?

Because he had nothing to do with it. She'd never looked at him as a potential suitor. Christ, why should she? She was about to marry one of the most important men in the realm. And he was just a lad from the village.

Damn it, he'd thought he was immune. He thought she'd lost the power to hurt him.

Anger at his own weakness made him stiffen. Pride schooled his features into a hard mask, but he knew Douglas had seen the toll his words had taken.

Forcing the bitterness from his voice, Thom said, "She did not mention it. But when you see her, please give her my congratulations. To you both," he amended. "An alliance with the new Earl of Moray . . ." He let his voice fall off. Not even Douglas with his well-known ambition could have reached much higher. "You must be thrilled."

Douglas swore. "Fuck, Thom, I'm—"

But his apology—if that's what he intended—was lost when Thom walked away.

For good.

11

"YOU'LL MAKE YOURSELF sick if you don't eat," Joanna said. A small smiled turned her lips, and she placed her hand on her stomach. "And take it from someone who has had her head in a basin for the past couple of weeks—there are far more pleasant ways to spend your day."

Elizabeth's eyes widened. "Oh, Jo, a new babe? I'm so happy for you!"

She was thrilled to hear her suspicion confirmed, although beneath her smile of joy was a fresh wave of stomach-churning, chest-twisting horror.

Pregnant. Dear God. In the long list of horrible consequences that had paraded up and down her mind (relentlessly) over the past two and a half days, she hadn't considered a child. In addition to ruin, disgrace, and the loss of her virtue—which she'd so narrowly avoided—she might have been left with a far more lasting reminder of her temporary loss of sanity. For that was the only thing that could explain her utterly irrational, illogical, foolish behavior.

Still, she felt a sharp stab in her chest as the image of a tiny, pink-cheeked cherub with piercing blue eyes and almost-black hair flashed before her.

If she didn't know better, she would say it was longing. Which was silly. She wanted children, of course. They were her duty. But unlike Joanna, she hadn't been counting down the days from the time she turned sixteen until she could be a mother.

Joanna had always been the type of girl who had to hold every baby in the room. She loved nothing more than being at home surrounded by her family.

Elizabeth had never been like that. She liked children (some better than others), but she didn't need to hold every one. She'd never seen herself in a big Hall surrounded by nothing but her children. She saw herself at court surrounded by excitement, entertainment, and lively conversation.

But . . .

But *nothing*, she told herself firmly. Nothing had changed because of that ill-advised kiss. Except that she'd learned a powerful lesson in tempting sin.

She should have listened to Father Francis! From the time she was a little girl, it had been drummed into her head to hold fast to her virtue. To be chaste until her marriage. To not let the Devil tempt her into immorality and wantonness.

She'd thought a kiss was nothing. Because the two kisses she'd experienced before *had* been nothing. She hadn't anticipated how persuasive the Devil could be—or rather, how skilled he could be with his tongue!

Good Lord, when she thought about it, her knees still felt weak.

Thom's kiss was nothing like the two that had come before. It hadn't been simple and chaste, it had been carnal, and sensual, and overwhelming. It was a side of him that she'd never seen before. A bold, authoritative, and aggressively masculine side of him. A dominating side of him.

It had aroused feelings—sensations—in her that she'd never imagined let alone experienced before. Most of all it had made her feel good. *Too* good. As in "I've lost my mind good." As in "here is my innocence for your taking" good.

She still couldn't believe how quickly a kiss had spun out of control. How one minute she'd been thinking how warm and soft his mouth was, and how good he tasted, and the next she'd been sprawled on a table, half-naked, with his mouth on her breast, his hand between her legs, and practically begging for him to take her virtue.

She was glad he refused—of course she was. She just wished he hadn't done it so harshly, when she'd been feeling so dazed and happy. If he'd thought her an untouchable "princess" before (where he got that ridiculous notion, she didn't know), it was clear he no longer thought of her that way. She'd never realized how much he'd been keeping from her, and how much he'd been holding back. All that passion . . .

Sensing her sister-in-law's eyes on her, Elizabeth forced herself to take a big spoonful of the beef pottage they were enjoying for the midday meal. She chewed slowly, making sure Joanna saw, and then asked, "Does Jamie know about the baby?"

Joanna shook her head. "I wasn't sure when he left, and I didn't want him distracted by anything."

Elizabeth understood. Jamie had been unbearable with worry when Joanna was pregnant with Uilleam, as Joanna had suffered a previous miscarriage. Not that it had made her brother's over-protectiveness any easier to bear.

Her cousin, who was seated on Joanna's other side, interjected. "Perhaps your happy news will soften the blow of our 'surprise'?"

The three women looked at each other and broke out into laughter. They all knew that Jamie was going to roar like an angry lion when he heard that his wife—his *pregnant* wife, no less—and "dear" cousin had ridden "halfway across Scotland" without an army for protection.

Jo and Izzie had arrived yesterday, much to Elizabeth's relief. She'd been climbing the walls (what was left of them), waiting for Jamie and Thom to return with Archie. Her fear for her brother mingled with fear for Thom. It was only after Thom left that she fully considered the danger he would be facing. He wasn't Jamie. He wasn't used to fighting scores of Englishmen or performing death-defying feats of bravery at every turn. He'd only handled a sword to forge one until a few years ago.

What if she'd sent him to his death with that kiss?

If anything happened to him . . .

Her heart twisted, and the smile fell from her face. She would never forgive herself.

"James will recover," Joanna said matter-of-factly. "I had to come. As soon as I received his missive that Archie was missing, I began to make preparations. When I learned that Archie had been imprisoned . . ."

Her voice fell off, and Elizabeth reached over to put her hand over hers to give it a comforting squeeze. "He will be all right," she said firmly. They *both* would be all right.

"Of course he will," Izzie said from her other side. "The smithy's son will help."

"Thom," Joanna filled in, with a sidelong glance at Elizabeth.

Elizabeth made a great show of dunking a chunk of bread in the broth and pretended not to notice. Joanna had been very interested to hear that Thom had not only been here, but had been conscripted into helping with the rescue. Elizabeth had provided an edited explanation, but she knew that Joanna sensed there was more to the story.

Izzie wrinkled her nose. "How did a smith's son from Douglas end up fighting with Edward Bruce?"

"It's a long story," Joanna said.

There were a lot of turnips and onions in the soup, Elizabeth noticed from the intense study she was doing of it.

"You were all friends growing up?" Izzie asked.

Joanna didn't answer, so Elizabeth was forced to look up from her bowl. "We were."

Were, but not any longer. Thom had made that perfectly clear. And after what had nearly happened, Elizabeth wasn't inclined to challenge him.

Not that she was worried about *that* happening again. She was sure it had been a one-time loss of sanity. Now that she was experienced and knew what to expect, she would not succumb so easily. It was her innocence that had been to blame, she told herself. It could have happened with anyone.

Of course, it would have been much more appropriate if it had happened with Randolph.

She bit her lip. But now that she had tasted passion, she was sure it would. Of course it would.

Still, prudence dictated a certain amount of caution around Thom. She would not tempt sin unnecessarily. He was so blastedly handsome, and all those muscles had felt surprisingly good—wonderful—against her.

Something in her voice had caused Izzie to frown. "Did something bad happen with the smith's son? You tense up every time he is mentioned, and cousin Jamie turns outright *black* with temper."

"Nothing happened," Elizabeth responded quickly. Perhaps too quickly. And with far too much insistence. Her cheeks flushed. "Nothing specific. He and Jamie . . . they grew apart. We all did."

Jo looked like she wanted to argue, but pursed her lips and studied *her* barely touched pottage instead.

Izzie seemed to understand. "I suppose it's only natural. The friends we have when we are children aren't always suitable when we get older."

Elizabeth bristled. "Thom is perfectly suitable. He's a wonderful man. He was always the best among us. I wasn't the one who ended our friendship."

Izzie held her gaze for a moment. "I see."

But she didn't; she only thought she did.

Elizabeth would have corrected her, but at that moment there was a commotion at the door to the Hall as one of the guardsmen rushed in. Barely had he announced that the men were back when Jamie came striding into the room.

The three women seated at the dais rose in unison. Elizabeth clutched a hand around her throat as if it might help her to breathe, but her chest was frozen as her eyes scanned the men behind him.

Her knees buckled, and she was forced to grab the edge of the table to keep from falling. Right behind her brother, initially hidden from her view by the sizable warrior who walked beside him, was Archie.

It had worked! Her brother was safe, and . . .

The cry that bubbled from between her lips was more of a sob. Even among the group of exceedingly tall, broad-shouldered, and muscular warriors, she picked him out easily.

Thom was as well.

Despite her hold on the table, her legs gave out. She collapsed back on the bench. The relief was too much, and the emotion of the past few days caught up with her all at once as she burst into tears.

Realizing her tears were only causing Archie more guilt and distress, Elizabeth quickly got her emotions under control. But after days of fearing she might never see her young brother again, she was reluctant to take her eyes off him or let him be pried from her side.

But the lad was exhausted, and once she'd assured herself that he had eaten as much as he could—his beaten, starved appearance had shocked her—she resisted the urge to follow him to the barracks and watched him walk out of the Hall with Joanna's brothers.

Tears swelled in her eyes and throat, the tumult of emotion ranging from relief to heartbreak.

Jamie, who had been fixed to Archie's other side throughout the meal (also, it seems, reluctant to let him out of his sight), put his hand over hers. "He'll be fine, El."

She turned to meet her brother's gaze. "Will he?" she challenged, anger flaring inside her. "I'm not so sure. He is not the same mischievous, overly confident young brother who snuck away from Blackhouse a week ago. He has aged ten years since I saw him last."

She knew it was unfair to take her anger out on Jamie,

but he seemed to understand. "No, he is not," he admitted. "But he is alive and safe, and we can be grateful for that. The rest will work itself out in time."

The tears finally slid down her cheeks. "It's not fair. Whatever he's gone through . . ." She had figured out the basics and wasn't sure she wanted to know the details. "He's only a boy, Jamie."

"Aye, and he's not the only young person who has suffered in this war. But he's more fortunate than most, so remember that."

"I'll try."

Jamie nodded. "I'm sending him back to Blackhouse with Richard and Thomas tomorrow."

Elizabeth's heart jumped. "But I thought he would come to Edinburgh with us."

With the castle mostly dismantled, James was anxious to return to the king, who was currently at Holyrood with his nephew—her soon-to-be fiancé, Thomas Randolph, the new Earl of Moray.

"He can join us when he has recovered, but Lady Eleanor will be returning from England at the end of the week. She will know what he needs."

Elizabeth wanted to argue, but she knew Jamie was right. Their formidable stepmother had been through many difficult times in this war with many husbands, including her father when he'd been returned from prison. She would know how to help her son.

Elizabeth nodded and turned her head back to her plate, pushing the small pieces of bread and cheese she'd broken off but hadn't eaten around the trencher with her finger. She cast a quick glance in Joanna's direction a few tables away but drew her eyes back sharply. She wasn't sure what the tight, prickly feeling was in her chest, but she didn't like it. If she didn't know better, she would think it was jealousy. Which was ridiculous. Joanna and Thom had been friends since before Elizabeth had met them. They were like siblings. Why should she care that they were talking, laughing, and so clearly happy to see one another?

So what if when Joanna had cried on seeing him and thrown herself into his arms he'd laughed, spun her around, and hugged her tight. So what if every time Elizabeth heard him laugh, she remembered how it used to be, and it felt as if a knife was sinking deeper and deeper into her heart. So what if he hadn't looked at her—not once—and acted as if she weren't even there. As if he hadn't held her in his arms three nights ago, kissed her, and made her feel something she'd never felt before.

Who was she trying to fool? His indifference, especially compared to how he was with Joanna, hurt. It hurt a lot.

She wasn't the only one casting glances to the other table. Jamie, too, could barely hide his annoyance. But he was too smart to try to do something about it. Those who didn't know Joanna well only saw the gentle and sweet outside, but her sister-in-law had steel in her spine that was every bit as rigid and unbending as Jamie's. When it came to Thom, she would defend him as fiercely as she would Uilleam. Jamie knew better than to try to interfere.

"You were right," Jamie said, catching her last glance. "We wouldn't have been able to free Archie without him. No one else could have climbed that cliff. I'd forgotten how good he was."

She suspected Jamie had forgotten quite a bit when it came to his old friend. "We are fortunate he agreed to help. I should thank him."

Although she was fairly sure the last thing Thom wanted from her was her thanks. *"Leave me the hell alone."*

He'd made his wishes quite clear.

"I already thanked him," Jamie said.

She couldn't hide her surprise. "You did?"

Jamie shrugged. "It was the least I could do after not giving him any choice in the matter. I already told you that he was ordered to go, and from what Carrick said, he was furious."

"But I thought—" Her mouth slammed shut, all of a sudden realizing what had happened.

Thom had lied to her. He'd let her think he still had a choice. He'd let her try to convince him, let her bargain her virtue, and let her kiss him, while already knowing that he had been ordered to go.

He'd tricked her. Used her desperation for her brother in some kind of misguided form of vengeance for perceived wrongs at Douglas hands. The irony of course was that she'd done it for him, trying to salvage his pride.

And how easily she'd succumbed. How satisfying it must have been for him.

Her eagle-eyed brother hadn't missed any of her reaction. "You thought what?"

She didn't say anything, pressing her lips together tightly.

"You spoke to him, didn't you?" He swore. "I knew there was something odd going on. Damn it, Ella, I told you to stay away from him."

Elizabeth glared back at him. "I thought a request from me would be easier to swallow than an order from you."

"And he agreed this time?" His eyes narrowed suspiciously. "Why?"

Elizabeth didn't flinch. She wasn't going to give her dogged brother any bone to sniff. "I don't know why. Maybe he liked hearing me beg. Does it really matter?"

Jamie watched her a little longer and then shrugged, apparently satisfied. "Nay, I suppose not. But as grateful as I am for what he did to help with Archie, I can't say I'll be sad to wave him off tomorrow when he leaves to fetch his widow."

Tomorrow? She glanced over one more time and willed Thom to look in her direction. When he didn't, she turned away.

It's for the best, she told herself.

Then why did it hurt so terribly?

"I've missed you, Thommy. We've all missed you."

Thom gave Jo a small smile that was surprisingly wistful. "I've missed you, too," he said. It was good to see her— really good. He paused, his eyes meeting hers intently. "You are happy? He treats you well?"

Joanna's mouth split into a wide grin. "I am obnoxiously happy, and James treats me like a queen."

Thom studied her a few moments more, and seeing nothing to dispel the truth of her words grumbled, "He'd better. 'Tis how you deserve to be treated. After what he did—"

She put her hand on his arm to stop him. "That was a long time ago, Thommy. James has changed."

Thom held her gaze a little longer before nodding. If Joanna's state of bliss was any indication, Thom was willing to concede that Douglas had changed—at least in some ways. In others, he was exactly the same. His ambition where his sister was concerned, for example. *Randolph*. Thom gritted his teeth and tried—unsuccessfully—to prevent the muscles in his neck from bunching.

Mistaking the cause of his reaction, Joanna squeezed his

arm and forced his gaze back to hers. "Truly, Thom." She smiled. "And I don't need a 'big brother' to watch out for me anymore, I know how to fight my own battles."

He suspected she did. But it would never stop him from watching out for her. "Aye, well, that's the thing about siblings. You have them whether you like it or not."

She laughed, but then after a moment sobered. "I wish you would come home more often. Johnny misses you—and so does your father."

Thom didn't say anything. What could he?

Sensing Elizabeth's gaze on him again, it took everything he had not to look in her direction. He didn't trust himself. When she'd seen him walk into the Hall a short while ago and burst into tears, he'd nearly forgotten everything and gone to her.

He was a bloody fool. For three years he'd had to work to put the past behind him, and just when he'd finally succeeded, he lost his damned mind and kissed her.

You did a lot more than kiss her. He fought a pained groan as the memories assailed him again.

He might have resisted the temptation to look at her, but Joanna hadn't missed Elizabeth's one-sided exchange. "She misses you, too. More than she wants to admit." Thom's mouth fell in a hard line; he didn't say anything. "Has it helped?" she asked. "Has staying away made it any easier?"

He was tempted to pretend he didn't know what she meant. If it had been anyone other than Jo, he would have. But she knew him too well. She'd been there. She'd seen his broken heart and understood because she'd had one, too. And for the same reason: Douglas pride and ambition. Hers might have turned out differently—and Thom didn't begrudge Jo her happy ending—but she had to realize that not all bards' tales came true. And unlike Jamie, who had loved Jo since almost the first day they'd met, Elizabeth had never loved him. She'd never even been aware of him like that.

But she was aware of him now, he thought with not a small surge of satisfaction. *Very* aware.

There be dragons . . . He pushed the dangerous thoughts away.

"Aye," he said. "It has made it easier." At least until recently.

"And you are happy?"

A wry smile turned his mouth. "I'm a soldier fighting in a war; there is not much cause for happiness. But I like what I'm doing, and I am satisfied with how things have progressed so far."

"You have done well for yourself," Joanna said. "The earl speaks highly of you." She paused and glanced over at her husband, who sat with Elizabeth and some of the other men, including MacLeod and Boyd, at the high table with Carrick. "James said you acquitted yourself well on the mission, and *that* lot," she said with a nod in the direction of the Phantoms, "are hard to impress." She smiled. "I'm proud of you. It couldn't have been an easy adjustment when you first arrived."

It hadn't been. The other men-at-arms had made it about as difficult on him as they could. But the blacksmith's son had withstood everything they'd thrown at him and proved that he had a place among them. He'd earned his right to be there, even if some thought his blood should have barred him from any consideration of knighthood.

Perhaps sensing that he would rather not talk about it,

Jo added, "What will you do now? Will you journey with the earl to begin the siege at Stirling, or will you go with us to Edinburgh? I hate to say goodbye when we've only just said hello. I'm sure James could be persuaded—"

"Neither," he said, cutting her off before she could say it. He'd rather die of boredom laying siege to a thousand castles than put himself under Douglas's authority—one successful mission or not. "I have an errand that has already been delayed too long."

"Ah, yes, your widow. Ella mentioned that you were considering marriage."

His mouth fell in a hard line. Would that *Ella* had been as forthcoming about her own nuptial plans. He gritted his teeth. *Randolph* . . .

Bloody hell.

"Do you care for her?" Joanna asked.

He looked at her sharply, but then realized she meant the widow. "I barely know her, but she is pleasant, attractive, and wealthy. I'm sure we will get along well enough. It is a good match."

"I'm sure it is on parchment," Joanna said. "But there is more to marriage than tochers, alliances, and advancement. Or there can be if you find love." He stiffened instinctively, a steel wall dropping down before him. But Jo paid it no heed and punched right through it. "Are you certain you and Ella . . . ?"

"Absolutely certain," he said in a voice that brokered no argument. "There is no me and Ella and there never has been."

He made the mistake of looking over at her, and for one perilous heartbeat, their eyes met. The bellow of heat that blasted his chest burned a hole right through him. Feelings he didn't want, feelings that had taken years to be rid of, poured over him in a hot, penetrating wave and threatened to take hold.

He looked away sharply, breaking the connection. Breaking *any* connection. No way in hell was he going to let it start all over again. He'd had enough of his insides ripped out getting over her the first time.

Suddenly, he couldn't wait to get out of there. Rutherford Castle and Lady Marjorie were waiting for him. He pushed back from the table and stood before Jo could respond. "Carrick is calling for me."

The earl wasn't even looking in his direction.

Joanna knew he was lying, but nodded and stood to return to her husband. "You won't leave without saying goodbye?"

He shook his head and leaned over to press a kiss to her cheek. "I won't."

"Promise?"

He quirked a smile. "Aye, I promise. Although I hope you like being woken at dawn."

She smiled back at him. "I don't mind, although James isn't overly fond of early risings."

Like his sister, Thom couldn't help remembering. Ella had always bemoaned his having to get up so early to start the fires and carry the coal when he was a lad. He hadn't minded, but she'd thought it must be torture.

Memories, blast it. This had to stop.

He left Jo laughing with a promise to make it nice and early and approached the dais where Carrick was seated. He caught his eye and was pleased when the earl immediately called him forward.

"Ah, MacGowan, I was just going to send for you."

He arched a brow in surprise. "You were?"

"Aye, you are a popular man."

Thom frowned, having no idea what he was talking about. But from the glance Carrick sent to MacLeod, who was seated a few feet away from him, Thom suspected he'd been hearing about the mission.

"My lord?" he asked, seeking clarification.

The earl held up a folded piece of parchment. "Not an hour after I receive a message from my brother requesting your presence in Edinburgh, MacLeod comes to me with a similar request." One side of his mouth lifted. "I also received a rather annoyed missive from Lady Marjorie this morning. Apparently the lady's patience is wearing thin. She is growing tired of waiting for an escort and wonders if she should find other arrangements."

Thom swore under his breath.

Carrick heard it and laughed. "Aye, the lady is far from subtle, isn't she? I'm afraid you are going to have some explaining to do to her when you can convince my brother to give you leave."

Thom pushed aside his worry about Lady Marjorie, still reeling from the news that the king wanted to see him. "Do you know what this is about, my lord?"

"I suspect it is about the same thing that caught MacLeod's attention, but you'll have to ask him."

Thom nodded, not knowing what to say. He was honored and, if he could admit the truth to himself, not a little nervous. *The* Bruce wanted to see *him*? The smith's son had indeed climbed high.

It was just when his chest had started to swell like a pig's bladder filled with air that Carrick took out a pin. "I understand you are close with Douglas's wife and sister? You'll be pleased to hear that you will be riding with them to Edinburgh."

Pop.

12

IF ELIZABETH WAS secretly pleased that Thom was journeying with them to Edinburgh (and *not* riding to his widow), she refused to admit it—even to herself. She knew her brother was less than thrilled—to put it mildly—but there was nothing for him to worry about. There was nothing between her and Thom. Not even friendship.

All right, maybe that wasn't quite true. There was *something* between them. Something that fired her blood and made her skin hot whenever she saw him. Identifying it as awkwardness and embarrassment, she was sure it would fade when she became accustomed to seeing him again.

Although how she was supposed to be accustomed to seeing him when all she seemed to be able to notice was how ridiculously *attractive* he was, she didn't know.

And she wasn't the only one. She didn't understand. It had never bothered her before when the village girls used to flirt with him; why did it bother her now to see practically every unmarried female in the vicinity batting an eye—or two!—in his direction?

Perhaps because he couldn't trouble himself to lift one or two in *her* direction. Not once since the night he'd returned with James two days ago had he spoken to her or even glanced her way. But with them leaving for Edinburgh in the morning, she knew that she had to do something to ease the awkwardness between them. She couldn't see him for hours on end—it would take at least two days, maybe three if the weather was bad, to reach Edinburgh with their large train of carts—and let this continue. People would notice. Like Jo and Izzie, who were already watching her with far too many raised brows and knowing looks.

His words came back to her as she walked across the cold, torchlit yard. *"Leave me the hell alone."* She would. Just as soon as they reached Edinburgh, and once she'd had a chance to say her piece.

She found him in the stables. He seemed to be talking to someone—and not in a very nice tone. "So listen up. This is how it's going to be."

She stopped and stood on her tiptoes to try to peek around him, but his shoulders blocked her view. Not that she was suffering from the scenery. They were quite impressive shoulders: square, broad, and stacked with thick slabs of round, hard muscle. Or maybe that was considered the tops of his arms? Those were rather impressive as well. She could remember how hard they'd felt when her fingers had tried to dig . . .

"You try to throw me off or bite me tomorrow, and the next time I need you, it will be for the fellmonger. Do we understand each other?"

The horse—to which she now realized he was speaking—made a loud snorting sound, apparently not too worried about its hide.

Elizabeth couldn't hold back her laughter. "I see you haven't lost your charm around horses. I don't think he believes you. Rather than issuing threats, you might try a lump of sugar."

Thom scowled at her, whether for the interruption or for simply being there, she didn't know. Probably both. "I tried that. The demonic beast nearly took off my hand."

Elizabeth stepped forward, moving around him, having care not to let their bodies brush. The warm, sultry air of the stables was not conducive to forgetting what had happened in the kitchens. *Concentrate on the smell*, she told herself. But the pungent earthy aroma of animals wasn't distracting her flaring nerve endings.

"He probably senses that you don't like him," she said. "I've told you a hundred times horses are sensitive creatures."

Thom made a sharp sound. "Sensitive my ars—" He stopped, remembering his company. "Not this one. He's stubborn, pigheaded, ornery, and foul tempered."

Elizabeth shot him a look that said the horse might have something in common with someone else she knew.

Making a cooing sound as if she was gentling her nephew, she reached out her hand—palm turned up—and let the horse sniff her for a moment. Telling him that he was a good boy, she stroked his neck and muzzle. The horse showed his pleasure in the stroking by lowering his ears and giving a soft nicker.

"Aye, I can see what you mean," she said, her mouth twitching. "He's a real black-hearted devil, isn't he?"

Thom stood back, watching her with glaring eyes and crossed arms. "Do you charm snakes as well?"

She grinned. "I'll let you know."

His eyes narrowed, and she laughed again. God, she'd missed this. She'd missed *him*.

Elizabeth held the horse's mouth down with the lead rope and continued petting him, while Thom grumbled (something about the horse being a traitor), finished putting out some fresh hay (peppered with a few carrots and apples, she noticed), and checked the saddle and reins for the following day. He obviously took his riding seriously.

When he was done, he finally turned to her. "Did you want something, Elizabeth?"

The note of impatience in his voice made her bristle; it also reminded her of her purpose. "I wished to thank you for what you did for Archie."

"You're welcome. Now if that is all . . ."

He tried to walk past her but she stepped in front of him, putting her hand on his chest. It was a mistake. She could feel the beat of his heart under the solid shield of steel. That heady, warm feeling came over her again.

She jerked her hand back and shook off the haze. "No it is *not* all. Why did you lie to me? Why did you let me think I could persuade you, when you'd already been ordered to go?"

He didn't have the decency to look ashamed by her discovery. In fact, he looked amused. "As I recall, I wasn't the one who was bargaining. You were. If you didn't like the terms you shouldn't have *offered* them."

Elizabeth's cheeks fired. "But you said . . ."

She gazed up at him stricken, realizing the truth. He hadn't said anything.

"Did I?" he asked idly. "Or did you just make a lot of assumptions?"

The latter. She was the one to put her body and then a kiss into the negotiations. But he'd still tricked her. "You could have told me it wasn't necessary. Instead you let me . . ." She was too embarrassed to get the words out and looked away.

"Lower yourself?" he filled in, although that wasn't what she'd been about to say. *Act like a wanton.* "Aye, well, I wasn't in the best state of mind. I was furious. You found me at an inopportune time."

She remembered exactly how she'd found him, and the

woman who'd been touching him. "You mean I interrupted your plans so you just decided to take advantage of another opportunity?"

He looked confused for a moment, but then one corner of his mouth lifted. "Aye, something like that."

She stared at him, feeling as if a big, heavy lump of ore was burning in her chest. "You've changed, Thom."

The disappointment in her voice seemed to spark his temper. "Why? Because I didn't keep my hands to myself like a good lad? Because I took you up on your offer? Or because I made the perfect little princess feel something as base as lust?" She gasped, outraged, but he continued. "What you are seeing now has always been there; you just haven't wanted to see it."

"You're wrong. The boy I knew would never try to purposefully hurt me. I know you are angry, but this is not who you are—you are better than this."

The locking of his jaw was the only indication he'd heard her. "Maybe you didn't know me as well as you thought you did."

"Maybe you are right," she threw back angrily. "I knew a young lad who mourned the loss of his mother but who was too proud even at 'almost nine' to let anyone know that he cried for her. I knew a lad who would laugh for hours at horrible jokes to make a little girl happy. I knew a lad who comforted an eight-year-old child who had lost her father and been left penniless in a cruel world. I knew a lad who never once asked what happened in those difficult years, but seemed to understand anyway. I knew a lad who would clear a place for me by the forge and let me watch him work, who climbed towers to spend hours telling me stories under the stars, who was a good son, a good brother, and a good friend—the best. Who was honorable and kind, and always did what was right. That was what I saw in you, Thommy. God, I never even noticed how ridiculously handsome you are! I was so dazzled by the person on the inside—the person who I thought was my friend—that was all I could see."

Thom was thunderstruck. He didn't know what to say. He'd wronged her, he realized, blaming her for not loving him, when in fact she had. Not the way he wanted her to perhaps, but she'd loved him all the same.

He swore and raked his fingers through his hair, feeling like an arse. A ridiculously handsome one—which shouldn't please him as much as it did.

She was right. This wasn't who he was. He'd cut off her attempts to re-establish the friendship between them to protect himself. But there was a difference between self-protection and how he'd lashed out at her in the kitchens. He'd had a right to be angry—but not at her.

But Elizabeth was caught up in her own anger and didn't give him a chance to apologize. "Maybe it is *you* who doesn't know *me* as well as you thought you did. You claimed to love me, but what you loved doesn't exist—it never has. You saw a little girl in a castle and held her up as some kind of unattainable object. Something out of reach and untouchable, like a pretty statue of painted marble. But I've never asked to be on a pedestal, you just put me there. I don't sit on thrones wearing gold robes or float around in a faerie garden with butterflies flittering around my head always smiling and happy. And I'm sure as Hades not perfect." She shuddered with disgust. "Sometimes I'm stubborn, sometimes I'm too proud, sometimes I get angry and say things that are insensitive, and sometimes I make unwise decisions—which you should be well aware of after what happened the other night." She paused to take a deep breath. "I think that also proved that I'm far from untouchable—actually, quite the opposite; I rather like being touched." He barely heard the next words, as his head had just exploded. "So who knows who best, *Thom*?"

He ignored the subtle taunt of his name, grabbed her by the elbow, and hauled her up against him. "What do you mean you rather like being touched?"

She sputtered, clearly exasperated. "After everything I just said, *that* is what you focus on?"

Damned right it was. He might have growled and drew her a little closer with a shake. "Like being touched by whom?"

She blinked up at him.

"Randolph?" Thom demanded furiously. "Or do I call him Moray now? Do you 'like' when your betrothed touches you?"

Elizabeth jerked out of his hold. "Randolph? He hasn't . . ." She pursed her mouth angrily. "I meant you." Thom relaxed—marginally. "And he's not my betrothed," she pointed out.

"Yet."

"Yet," she agreed.

"You did not think to mention that little detail to me?"

"I wasn't hiding anything," she said, clearly trying not to sound defensive—and failing.

"Weren't you?"

Her mouth flattened in a stubborn line he recognized only too well, as he'd been seeing it since she was six. "My betrothal has nothing to do with you and me."

The muscles in his neck were drawn so tight he could

feel them twitching. "I think your soon-to-be betrothed might disagree. I suspect he'd be very interested in what happened between 'you and me' in the kitchens."

She flushed guiltily, but then straightened her spine. "That was a mistake. It won't happen again."

The fact that he agreed didn't make it any easier to hear. He clenched his fists at his sides so he wouldn't be tempted to draw her back into his arms and wipe that haughty purse off her mouth.

"And the fact that you like when I touch you? Does that have nothing to do with him either?"

His voice was huskier than he intended. The damned warm air in the stable was getting to him—as was the soft scent rising up from her hair. She always smelled so good.

But the warm sensations fired by her closeness were quickly banished by her next words. "Why should it? I'm certain I shall like it when he touches me as well."

Thom didn't think he'd ever moved that fast. He spun her around and had her backed up against the wall in seconds flat. With his hands planted on either side of her head, he leaned in threateningly. "What the hell do you mean by that?"

She glared at him, her eyes spitting blue sparks. If he'd been trying to intimidate her, it clearly hadn't worked. He was one of the biggest, strongest men in camp, and she pushed him back with one dainty finger on his chest. Christ.

"Why shouldn't I? Now that I know what to expect, I imagine it will be even more pleasant. From what I've heard, he's had enough practice."

Could a head explode twice? His was certainly in danger of doing so. He could feel the hot pressure pounding in his skull. "It's that simple, is it? Now that you've experienced passion, it's all the same, is that it? It doesn't matter who is touching you?"

"No, of course not!" She frowned. "Why are you always trying to confuse me and put words in my mouth? I just meant there was no reason to think I won't enjoy—"

"Don't say it," he warned darkly, his mouth only inches from hers. If he heard one more word about her and Randolph, he was going to forget every vow, every promise he'd made to himself not to touch her again.

He knew it was her innocence speaking—that she'd convinced herself that what had happened between them wasn't anything special. Just as he knew that what had exploded between them, what had made a kiss descend into nearly mindless passion in a matter of minutes, was a rare gift. But *knowing* didn't make it any easier to hear.

Wisely, she closed her mouth. She must have realized how close he'd been to kissing her, because this time when she edged away, she eyed him cagily.

Slowly the rush of blood surging through his veins stopped pounding and his pulse returned to normal. Air— as opposed to fire—was once more blowing in and out of his lungs.

"I don't want you to hate me, Thom," she said in a small voice. "I never meant to hurt you."

"I know—and I don't." It would be infinitely easier if he did.

She brightened, and the pure radiance of her smile was like a beam of sunlight streaming through his chest.

The ice that had been encased around his heart for three years began to melt, and God help him, he didn't know how to make it stop.

13

IT DIDN'T TAKE ELIZABETH long to realize what Joanna was up to—her sister-in-law would never be characterized as subtle.

The slighted walls of the once great Roxburgh Castle were still visible on the horizon behind them when Joanna caught sight of Thom riding by with a few of Bruce's secret warriors and called him over under the pretext of introducing him to Izzie. The exchange would have been brief had Joanna not proceeded to regale her cousin with a seemingly endless stream of tales from their youth. "Oh, Thom, you must tell her about . . ." and "Elizabeth, don't you remember when . . . ?" were uttered so many times she lost count.

She might have been grateful—the time forced riding together eased a great deal of the lingering awkwardness between her and Thom—were it not for her kinswoman's reaction. Her pretty cousin, who was as clear-eyed, hard to impress, and seemingly impervious to charm as any young woman of her acquaintance, was utterly and completely dazzled.

Thom was barely out of earshot (after he was called away by Tor MacLeod and Joanna finally had to let him go—apparently even Joanna hesitated to defy the intimidating Island chief), when Izzie turned to her accusingly. "Good, gracious! *That* is your smithy's son?"

Elizabeth glared at her. "He is not my—"

"You neglected to mention that he is jaw-droppingly gorgeous."

Elizabeth pressed her lips together, not quite sure why she was so annoyed by the observation. Was it because it had taken her so long to realize the same thing? "I hadn't noticed," she grumbled.

Izzie looked at her as if she must be blind—something that Elizabeth was beginning to wonder herself. But her eyes had been opened. They were *wide* open, blast it.

Fortunately, her cousin shifted her attention to Joanna. "My God, those eyes—those unbelievably *blue* eyes—contrasted against that black, wavy hair." She sighed dreamily.

"It isn't black," Elizabeth said unthinkingly. Both sets of eyes turned to her, and she could feel the heat staining her cheeks. "It's almost black, but when the sun is shining on it, you can see that it's more a dark sable brown . . ."

Izzie's brows shot up in perfect tandem; Joanna's smile was so wide she'd best have care not to swallow a bug.

Feeling their scrutiny, she blurted, "Randolph is dark haired as well. *And* exceedingly handsome."

"Is that so?" Izzie said thoughtfully.

Elizabeth nodded. It was definitely dark—although she'd be hard-pressed to say the shade.

"And his eyes?" Izzie asked curiously. "Are they dark or light?"

Elizabeth tried to picture him, but the image wasn't very sharp. Realizing Izzie was trying to make some kind of point, she scowled at her. "Light."

"Blue like your smithy's son's?"

Elizabeth gritted her teeth, refusing to be baited. He wasn't hers, blast it. And what did it matter what color eyes Randolph had? Or that she'd never noticed. "Yes," she said, hoping she was right.

"Hmm."

Apparently her cousin was taking "hmm" lessons from her sister-in-law.

Ignoring them both, Elizabeth rode in miffed silence for the remainder of the morning, mostly talking to Helen MacKay, who was having difficulty with her fidgety young son and fortunately hadn't heard the earlier conversation. Elizabeth didn't know why she was so annoyed, only that she was. By the time they stopped to water the horses, however, her good humor had returned. She was laughing with Izzie about Uilleam's latest antics—apparently, he'd decided that food tasted better *after* it was dropped on the floor—when she heard Joanna exclaim, "Oh no. I thought something was wrong. Look at that"—she pointed to his left rear hoof—"my horse is losing a shoe."

Joanna could see the faintest edge of metal sliding out from under the horse's hoof.

She turned to Elizabeth. "Be a darling and see if you can find Thommy. He may have a hammer."

"Have you ever seen Thommy shoe a horse?" It wasn't a pretty sight. "I'm sure one of Jamie's men—"

Joanna waved her off—*seemingly* uncaringly. "Izzie can go if you are too tired."

"I'd be happy to . . ." Izzie started.

"I'll do it," Elizabeth said over her. The sly fox.

So she went to ask Thom if he could help. Knowing how much he despised shoeing, he agreed with a surprising lack of hesitation. Of course, it *was* for Jo.

After he'd fixed the shoe—with Elizabeth unconsciously taking her position as horse distracter as she'd done when they were young so he wouldn't get kicked—Joanna insisted he share some of the sugared biscuits the cook had given her, which were accompanied by more reminiscing, until Jamie came upon the cheerful scene and promptly sent Thom away to scout ahead of them.

The first time might have been by chance, the second by coincidence, but when they finally made camp for the night, and Joanna insisted over Jamie's objection that Thom dine with them "after all his help," her brother wasn't the only one who realized what was going on. But Joanna was impervious to his dark glares and Elizabeth's chastising frowns.

As she'd noted, subtlety wasn't one of her sister-in-law's strengths.

But Elizabeth couldn't pretend that she minded Jo-anna's efforts to throw them together. It was nice to be around Thom again—even if it wasn't quite as easy and uncomplicated as it used to be. At least for her. She was far too aware of what had happened between them. Every time she looked at him, she remembered how his mouth had felt on hers, how he'd tasted, the heat of his tongue sliding in her mouth, the feel of his hands on her body— and then the more wicked memories hit her. The feel of his hardness between her legs, the weight of his body pressed against hers, the intimate stroking, the burgeoning plea-sure, and the shattering euphoria that had followed. How did one act normally with a man when they had shared something like that?

She didn't know.

But when the time to fetch him came, Joanna didn't need to ask her, Elizabeth volunteered.

She found him down by the riverbank fishing and took a seat on a rock beside him as if it were yesterday rather than eight years ago that she'd done the same. "Catch any-thing?"

He shot her a sidelong look. Of course he'd caught

something. He was one of the best fishermen in the village. Goodness, how it used to drive Jamie crazy.

"How many?"

He shrugged and nodded to the bucket a few feet away that she hadn't seen before. "A half-dozen or so." He paused. "Is it time?"

"Soon. We'll just have time to drop those fish off with the cook before Jamie sees them."

His mouth quirked, which she supposed was a promising start.

He pulled the line in, stood, and held his hand down to her. As if it was the most natural thing in the world—and in so many ways it was—she slipped fingers into his. She'd forgotten the strength of his grip, the hardness of the calluses on his palms . . . and the warmth. It flooded her senses as she came to her feet before him.

They stared at one another for a long heartbeat, the intensity of his gaze making her wobble.

He had to grab her arms to catch her when her unsteady legs nearly made her slip. "Bloody hell, Elizabeth, be careful. I assure you, that river is every bit as cold as it looks."

She didn't tell him that it wasn't clumsiness, it was *him*. "Th-thank you," she stammered. Good gracious, what was wrong with her? Why was she so nervous? Why was she so . . . *fluttery*? Why was she so aware of the closeness of his body, the hard lines of his face, the brilliance of his eyes, the softness of the lips that were a short tiptoe-rising distance away from her? Why did she feel so warm—like she was standing too close to the forge and might get burned?

Apparently she wasn't the only one affected. He stared down at her. Her eyes. Her mouth. "Elizabeth . . ." he started, half in warning and half in anger.

He was going to kiss her. She felt the muscles in his arms tighten as he drew her incrementally closer. Felt the heat of his breath as his mouth lowered. Felt the slam of her heart against her ribs in anticipation. And then she felt . . .

Nothing.

He drew back, set her carefully away from the slippery edge of the muddy bank, and let her go.

"We should go," he said calmly, as if he hadn't been moments away from putting his mouth on hers.

As if she hadn't been moments away from letting him.

A flush heated her cheeks, but she, too, acted as if nothing had happened—or nearly happened. It was much harder pretending that she wasn't disappointed it hadn't. "Yes, Joanna will wonder where we are."

He gave her a dry look that was so wonderfully *Thommy* her chest swelled with happiness. "I doubt she'll wonder anything, as I suspect that was rather the point."

Apparently he'd caught on to Joanna's little game as well. She gave him a small smile of shared understanding, and they walked back together through camp. They didn't talk, but their pace was slower than it might have been.

Thom glanced up as the shadow fell over him. But he'd been aware of her the moment she came into view on the bridge. She was like a damned beacon for his senses. Or maybe it was the other way around—his senses lit up like a damned beacon whenever she was near.

The men had made camp across the bridge from Newbattle Abbey in a small clearing along the banks of the River Esk. But Douglas had arranged for his handful of women traveling with them to stay in the abbey. Although the traveling party had thus far managed to avoid rain—and therefore the soggy, muddy roads that could have severely delayed their journey—the temperature had dropped to near freezing over the last few hours, and the women would be much more comfortable with the Cistercian monks.

In other words, Douglas wasn't taking any chances.

Joanna's efforts the past two days to bring Thom and Elizabeth together had not gone unnoticed by her husband—or anyone else for that matter. But Douglas didn't have anything to worry about. As much as Thom had enjoyed spending time with his old friends—and he had enjoyed himself, perhaps more than he wanted to—no matter how many errands, dinners, and loose horseshoes Joanna arranged, it wouldn't make a difference. It was too late for him and Elizabeth. They'd both moved on.

Elizabeth might want him physically, but Thom did not delude himself that she wanted more from him than pleasure. Not when she could marry one of the most important men in the realm. A man like Randolph could give her something Thom never could: position, wealth, and security. And he maybe better than anyone knew how much those things meant to her.

Although it would have saved him a whole hell of a lot of heartbreak had he recognized it earlier.

Elizabeth was too practical, with too much of her brother's ambition in her to risk a marriage to someone in Thom's position. She and Jamie had both been scarred by their father's death. Maybe if those difficult years had never happened, it would be different. But when her father had died in prison after being declared a traitor, his lands and wealth stripped by King Edward, his widow and children had been left with nothing. They'd been "little better than beggars," Elizabeth had once said.

Edward's hatred of Sir William "the Hardy" Douglas had been extreme—even by the king's notorious Angevin standards. With Edward's mercurial temper, no one had wanted to chance taking in the "traitor's" widow and children and risk having his vitriol turned toward them. Finally, half-starved, with little more than the "rags on their shoulders" and "one step away from an almshouse," Isabel's family had taken them in. The situation had been both "humbling and humiliating."

Elizabeth had laughed when she'd told him that, but now he realized how telling that had been.

Eventually Edward's temper had cooled toward the widow (if not the "traitor's spawn") and some of Lady Eleanor's dower lands had been restored. By the time the family had returned to Douglas a couple of years later, the situation wasn't nearly so dire. But the experience had left a lasting imprint on Elizabeth. From that point on, it seemed she was always looking beyond the little village of Douglas to something bigger.

Randolph was one of the biggest. She wouldn't let him go. No matter how much she lusted for Thom.

All Jo's machinations had succeeded in doing was make the inevitable parting when they arrived in Edinburgh tomorrow more difficult.

Fortunately, he'd had a bit of a respite today. He had no doubt Joanna would have found countless pretenses to seek him out, but the Phantoms hadn't given her a chance. MacLeod had asked him to ride out with Sutherland and MacKay to check on a bridge ahead of them that might need repairing from a storm a few weeks ago (it had), and then he'd ridden ahead to scout with Lamont and MacLean. Finally, on hearing that he was skilled with the making of swords, MacRuairi had asked him to take a look at one of his arming swords—he fought with two that he wore crossed at his back. All of which had taken him well away from the ladies for most of the day.

But it appeared his respite was over.

Elizabeth was smiling down at him, so beautiful it almost hurt to look at her. Actually, it did hurt, damn it. The heavy blue wool cloak she wore was trimmed with fur around the hood, framing her fair face like a snow queen—

He stopped, her earlier accusations coming back to him. Had he made her into something she wasn't? Holding her up as something "perfect" and unattainable? A pretty porcelain poppet in a shopwindow?

He had to concede that there might be more truth to her accusation than he wanted to admit. He had always seen her through the window of that little girl he'd first mistaken for a princess. The embodiment of everything he wanted but thought he couldn't have.

She wasn't perfect—he knew that. She could be stubborn, opinionated, and defensive—especially when it came to her family. She sometimes spoke without thinking and could be blind to what was right in front of her—he better than anyone knew that. She sometimes focused so much on the goal that she lost sight of everything else. And God knew she could watch where she stepped more often.

But she was also sweet and kind, generous (visiting not just almshouses but also lazar houses), always saw the good in those around her (sometimes naively), strong willed, confident, and despite what she said about sometimes being in a bad mood, almost always happy and cheerful. She had always been able to make him smile—even when he'd slipped into one of his "dark moods," as she called them. She truly cared about the people around her, including him. Especially him.

So she might be right, but she was also wrong. He *had* truly loved her.

"I thought now that you wielded a sword you didn't make them anymore," she teased.

He paused, putting down the file he'd been using to answer her. "Aye, well, it seems I've somehow managed to find myself doing both."

"I'm not surprised."

He frowned, not knowing what to make of her comment. "You're not?"

She shook her head. "You are too talented. Someone was bound to notice at some point." The matter-of-factness of her tone was oddly flattering. "Johnny said you only got better after I left and had developed a following not just in Douglas but in the rest of South Lanarkshire as well."

He quirked a brow. "Asking after me, El?"

A pretty dusting of pink appeared on her snowy cheeks, and she quickly changed topics. "Is something wrong with the handle?"

He wasn't surprised that she'd guessed. God knew she'd watched him do something similar dozens of times. "It shifts a little with a hard blow."

She looked down at what he was doing. "Are the guards too flat or are they uneven?"

He smiled and shook his head. He wondered how many highborn ladies knew so much about swords. He'd venture a very few. "A little of both. I don't like the shape of the tang either."

"But you can't fix that without a forge."

"Exactly."

"Whose sword is it?"

"MacRuairi's."

She lifted a brow. "I'm impressed. He keeps limited

company—to say the least. I knew him for two years before I swallowed my fear enough to talk to him. Meeting his wife helped." She shook her head. "Who would have ever thought Scotland's most famous heroine would wed one of Scotland's most infamous pirates?"

He, too, had been surprised to learn that Bella MacDuff had married Lachlan MacRuairi, the notorious bastard-born West Highland chieftain. Thom shrugged. "He heard I might be able to fix it, and asked me to look at it. We aren't exactly blood brothers."

She gave him an odd look, as if something was just occurring to her. "You spent a lot of time with them today."

"Who?"

"MacLeod and the others. I wonder . . ."

She shook off whatever it was she'd been about to say, but he could guess. He'd been wondering the same thing. Were the Phantoms singling him out for a reason? MacLeod had asked him a few questions about his training and battle experience, but had not been forthcoming about why he'd asked Carrick to send Thom to Edinburgh. He'd been watching him though—closely.

"No matter," she said. "I'm afraid I have an errand I must attend to for Joanna." Seeing his expression, she laughed. "Don't worry, it's nothing to do with you. Have you seen Jamie?"

"Awhile ago. I think he went hunting with some of his men."

"Ah, well, then Joanna's favorite blue gown will have to wait." At his look of incomprehension, she explained. "She needs one of her trunks."

"So that she can impress the monks?"

She giggled. "Hardly. I think it rather has to do with the other travelers who arrived. Lady Mary of Strathearn—the earl's daughter. Joanna never liked her. She thought she had designs on James before she married Sir John Moray of Drumsagard."

Thom shook his head. Women. "If I see him, I'll let him know."

"Thanks." She stood there staring at him as if she wanted to say more, but after a moment she left, and he resumed his filing.

But he was distracted, and the work wasn't as satisfying as it had been.

There had been nothing particularly remarkable about the conversation with Elizabeth, but each time he was with her, it was becoming more and more difficult to keep his heart hardened against her.

Christ, he'd nearly kissed her the other day by the river, and God only knew how that could have ended. If it was anything like last time, there was a good chance it would have been with her pushed up against a tree and him deep inside her.

Honor and nobility had once meant something to him. They were qualities he'd always prided himself on because of his actions, not because of some "sir" or "lord" in front of his name. Elizabeth had made him forget once, but he would not do so again.

"What is between you and Douglas's sister?"

Thom turned, not realizing MacLeod had come up behind him. Christ, no wonder they were known as Phantoms; the man moved like a ghost. With his strength and build it was especially impressive. "Nothing," he said automatically.

The fierce Island chief studied him intently. Thom wasn't easily intimidated, but he had to admit it was damned unsettling.

"It didn't look that way to me," MacLeod said.

He had obviously been watching him again. Thom's gaze hardened. "However it looked, I'm not sure why it is any business of yours."

MacLeod arched a brow as if Thom's bold reply had surprised him. Perhaps it should have. Given MacLeod's reputation, Thom probably should have responded with quite a bit less hostility in his tone. Rather than MacLeod being offended, however, Thom sensed he'd impressed him again.

"Depending on what happens in Edinburgh, it might be very much my business. Douglas is an important man in the Bruce's army—and someone I respect. We often work together. I lost a man last year to discord; I won't lose another. And that lass, I suspect, would cause quite a lot of discord."

To put it mildly. Thom and Douglas had reached a tentative truce, but Thom did not delude himself that that truce wouldn't turn back into full-fledged war again if Douglas suspected anything between Thom and his sister.

"We?"

MacLeod gave him a look that made him feel stupid for asking.

"Elizabeth and I are old friends," Thom said, answering MacLeod's original question. "We've known each other since we were children."

"Douglas said she is to marry Randolph."

"Aye."

"Good," MacLeod said. "Keep it that way, and there won't be a problem."

The man who Thom suspected was the leader of the band of Phantom warriors—who'd struck fear in the heart of their enemies and become the fodder of legend—walked away, leaving Thom certain of two things. One, he was possibly being recruited by the most elite guard in the army, and two, whatever chance he had to be part of the Phantoms was contingent on him not angering Douglas.

In other words, if Thom wanted a chance to fight among the best warriors in the kingdom, Elizabeth Douglas was off-limits.

The Phantoms? Thom still couldn't believe it. Even after a long night of thinking about little else—while trying to repress the building excitement—he wondered if he'd misunderstood.

But he hadn't. MacLeod was considering him for the Phantoms.

Christ, if Thom needed any more incentive to stay away from Elizabeth—which he didn't—he had it. That wasn't to say that he wasn't damned glad their journey and forced togetherness was almost over. Powerful incentive or not, he wasn't exactly rational when it came to her.

Unfortunately, their early morning departure had been delayed by a heavy downpour of rain that had started at dawn and now, two hours later, was still going strong. When it was discovered that one of the travelers taking respite at the abbey was also traveling to Edinburgh in a carriage—which was rare due to their impracticality on Scottish roads—Douglas decided, over his wife's objections to the proposed company, to wait so that the ladies might join her and avoid a very cold and uncomfortable ride.

After another hour of waiting for Lady Mary and her carriage, they traveled barely a mile before the "road" narrowed, one of the wheels slid on the uneven ground, and the blasted thing became stuck in the mud—thus proving the impractical nature of carriages in Scotland. Fortunately, the rain had waned a bit by then, so the women were not soaked while the men labored to fix it. When they had, it was time for the midday meal, and the group spread out to eat. Thom lost sight of the ladies, until Joanna came rushing up to him as he was packing his saddlebag.

"Have you seen Ella?"

She looked mildly worried, but suspecting another of her ploys, he didn't pay too much attention. "Not for a while."

Joanna frowned. "Neither have I. She wandered off after the meal and hasn't returned."

"How long ago?"

"Fifteen, maybe twenty minutes."

Realizing this wasn't a game, Thom frowned. "She went by herself?"

"Aye, I thought . . ." Joanna blushed. "She might need privacy."

"She isn't likely to get lost around here. Which way did she go?"

She pointed in the direction of the river. "Downstream a little."

"I'll fetch her," Thom said.

When Joanna smiled, he wondered if he'd been tricked again.

It didn't take him long to realize that he hadn't. He called her name a few times as he picked his way through the dense trees and brush. But he'd only gone about fifty yards when he noticed that the bank of trees along this side of the river hid the edge of a ravine. The kind of ravine that it would be easy for someone to slip down.

Ah, hell. His stomach dropped, but his pulse took off

in the opposite direction. Dread twisted in his gut as he retraced his steps and walked back and forth along the edge shouting her name, looking down into the abyss of foliage with his heart in his throat and fearing what other tangled limbs he might see among the branches and vines.

Finally, he heard a soft cry. "Here. I'm here."

He looked down, and when he saw the two big blue eyes staring up at him, the heart that had been in his throat jammed. She was about twenty feet below him, clinging to a small tree that wasn't much more than a sapling about halfway down the steep embankment. The steep, *unstable* embankment.

Damn. From the visible roots and large chunks of missing dirt, he could see that part of the hillside had already come away.

He followed what must have been the path she'd taken down the hill with his gaze. With the wet rock, mud, and dried leaves, she would have been sliding fast. That thin twig of a tree was likely the only thing that had stopped her from sliding all the way down to the rocky bottom. And it was the only thing preventing her from continuing.

She could be lying in a twisted, bloody pool . . . God, he thought he might be sick.

He did a quick scan of her person, and aside from a few scratches, dirt, a missing veil that he could see about ten feet down the slope, and a mussed plait, she didn't appear to be seriously injured.

But he didn't like the look of that tree. Not wanting to alarm her, he forced a lightness to his voice that he did not feel. "Are you all right?"

She nodded, her eyes getting a little wider. "I slipped."

He couldn't help smiling. "I can see that."

"I tried to pull myself up, but I didn't want to let go."

"Don't!" he said, unable to completely mask his alarm. Then more calmly, he added, "I'm going to come down to get you."

"But shouldn't you get a rope first?"

Aye, but he didn't think he had time. The roots of that tree were not very deep and the rain coupled with her weight had loosened the grip it had on the hillside. He could already see the dirt lifting around the base.

"I'll be careful," he assured her, starting down.

With very little to grab on to that was sturdy enough to support his weight, he half-scrambled, half-slid down the embankment, keeping his body as parallel to the ground as he could, using his right hand for leverage and left for support. With one eye on her and the other on the base of that damned tree, he made his way toward her with precision and speed born not so much of skill but of determination. There was no way in hell he was going to fall—not when she needed him.

By the time he reached her, he knew they would never be able to climb back up. They would have to go down. It had only been a handful of minutes since he started looking for her, and he knew it would be awhile before Joanna sent someone after them.

He'd devised a plan, but it was going to take a leap of faith on her part.

He could see the pale terror mixed with panic on her face as he approached, and it tore at him. The urge to comfort—to protect—her overwhelmed him.

He stopped a few feet away, not wanting to get too close lest she reach for him or he put strain on that tree. The whole patch of ground looked in peril of breaking away.

"Hi," he said, smiling as if they were meeting on a stroll through the forest.

"Hi," she replied softly. Her eyes sparkled with the edge of tears. "You found me. I didn't think anyone would come in time."

"Joanna sent me. She was worried when you didn't return."

"I was on my way back but then I saw a baby hare. I thought it had been injured in a trap and tried to follow it. But I guess it didn't want to be followed, as it led me over this embankment."

"I guess not," he agreed. He paused and thought for a moment. "How do you know which rabbit is the oldest?"

It only took her a moment to catch on before she smiled. "I don't know."

He grinned. "Look for the gray hare."

She giggled, and then scrunched her nose. God, he loved it when she did that. He always had.

"That isn't a very good one."

"And yet you laughed," he pointed out. "But if you think you can do better, be my guest."

"You're trying to distract me."

"Is it working?"

One side of her mouth curved up. "A little."

"I need you to try to concentrate now—and I need you to trust me."

"All right." She agreed without hesitation, and it made his already compressed chest squeeze a little tighter.

There was a tree at the bottom of the ravine with sturdy branches that overhung just a few feet from where they were on the hill. He told her what he wanted her to do, and her eyes went perfectly round.

"I can't jump!"

"Yes, you can. It's only a few feet, and I'll help you. We'll do it together. I'm going to come toward you, you let go of the tree, grab on to me, and I'll do the rest."

"What happens if it breaks?"

"It's too thick to snap, but if it bends we'll ride it all the way down to the bottom. All right?"

She didn't say anything, just stared at him mutely as if he'd lost his mind.

"El? I need you to do this. The ground is too slick with too many rocks. It's too risky to try to slide down."

She gave him an incredulous look. "And jumping on a tree limb isn't risky?"

His mouth twisted. "*Less* risky."

He'd kept an eye on the tree she was holding and saw it move another inch. She must have felt it, too, because her face suddenly drained again, and she nodded. "We better do it quickly."

He looked into her eyes. "Don't think, just look at me." He held her gaze. "We go on three. Ready? One . . . two . . . three."

He moved, she let go, latched on, and together they leapt. He needed both hands to grab the upper branch, but as soon as he felt the lower under his feet, he let go one hand and drew her in tight against him, until both the branch they were standing on and the one he was holding on to for support steadied. But the wild fluttering of her heart beating against his took a little longer.

Her eyes held his the whole time, and the knot in his chest grew and grew.

He knew she was still scared, but a small smile had started to work its way up the corners of her mouth. "I seem to recall being in a similar position once before, except at the time you weren't quite so tall."

He feigned a struggle to hold her. "And you weren't quite so heavy."

Her brows shot up in outrage. "Heavy! I may have put on a few extra pounds the past couple of years"—she sent him a glare—"but you would, too, if you lived with Joanna and all her sweets. I swear, every time I turn around there's a new cake that I 'must try.'"

He was trying not to laugh, which only served to further infuriate her. The lass was ridiculous. The only "heavy" places on her body were in exactly the right places. Two in particular were temptingly crushed to his chest. If he looked down . . .

He didn't look down.

She gave him a little huff, and probably would have peered down her nose if she hadn't been plastered to his side. "Obviously you aren't as strong as all those muscles make you look."

There was something admiring in her voice that heated his blood and sent all jests to the wayside. She liked his body.

She must have felt the change in him, because the gaze that was turned to his grew suddenly soft. Aroused. *Hot*.

Had he not been perched in a tree, with her wrapped around him, he might have kissed her. He *would* have kissed her. Nothing could have stopped him.

Instead he shuffled her around so that she was on the inside closest to the trunk. From there he loosened his hold around her so that she could grab the branch.

"Do you think you can get down the rest of the way from here?" he asked.

She peered at the grid of limbs below here feet. She only needed to climb down a handful, and she would be close enough to the ground to drop.

"I think so."

"I'll go first and guide you down."

She nodded. They were on familiar ground, and it didn't take long before they were on solid ground as well.

He caught her to him and let her go. Or rather, he intended to let her go, but she kept holding him.

He didn't know who moved first, but one minute he was staring into her eyes, and the next his mouth was on hers. All the heat, all the passion, all the desire that had been simmering in the air between them since that night in the kitchens boiled over.

He pushed her back against the tree they'd just climbed down, cupping her head with one hand to protect it from the bark, and lacing his other under her leg to wrap around his hip.

It was as close to heaven as he could imagine. Their tongues sparred, circled, and stroked, harder and faster. Deeper. It was as if they were starved for one another and were now feasting, devouring, consuming.

He couldn't breathe, but he didn't care. She tasted so warm and sweet, all he wanted was her.

And she wanted him.

He could feel it in the fervor of her response, in the stroke of her tongue, in the way her hands gripped the muscles of his arms and back, her leg tightened around his hip, bringing his cock into that sweet little juncture, and her hips moved against him.

Aye, he could definitely feel that. It made him groan and throb, and pulse in anticipation. For an innocent, she sure as hell knew how to drive him wild. Instinct was a powerful weapon, and she wielded it with the skilled precision to bring him to his knees.

He was out of control. His mouth was on her neck, his

hand was cupping her breast, squeezing, rubbing his thumb over the taut peak. The erotic sounds of her gasps and breathy moans egged him on.

Too fast . . . not fast enough.

He had to touch her, had to feel all that heat and dampness on his fingertips. He slid his hand under her skirts and groaned with pure molten pleasure. She was so warm and silky, and ready for him. He wanted to make her come. He wanted to be inside her.

Honor? Nobility? He didn't care about either right now. All that he cared about was making the girl he'd wanted his forever.

A cry stopped him. Not her cry, but her brother's. "Elizabeth!"

He heard his own name, too. He thought it was Mac-Leod's voice.

He swore and pulled away. He wished he could say the shock was like a bucket of ice water poured over his senses, but his body was still on fire, desire still fisted like a ball at the base of his spine, and his head still roared with the primitive call to mate.

"Down here," he managed to respond tightly, moving out from the canopy of tree branches that he hoped had been enough to shield them from view.

From Jamie's expression, it appeared they had been. He looked more concerned and suspicious than ready to kill. "Where's Ella? Is she all right?"

Elizabeth stepped out beside him. "Right here, and I'm fine."

One glance at her ravaged appearance and *now* Jamie's expression was ready to kill. "What the hell are you doing down there?"

"I *fell*, Jamie," she said angrily, guessing what he'd been thinking. "Thommy *saved* me from cracking my head open on these rocks." He didn't miss the "For goodness' sake!" added under her breath.

"Get a rope," Thom said, conscious of MacLeod's presence. He didn't want him to think he hadn't heeded his warning—which he hadn't, damn it. "I will fill you in on all the details once Elizabeth has been seen to."

14

I'M FINE," ELIZABETH SAID, brushing off her brother's concern. After being pulled up the hill with the help of the rope, Jamie had ordered a tent to be quickly set up for her to be checked over. "'Tis my pride that is bruised more than anything else. I can't believe I was so careless."

"You could have been killed," Jamie said. As it was wont to happen once the threat of danger was over, some of his concern gave way to anger. "Damn it, Ella, you know better than to wander off on your own like that."

Joanna hurried to her defense as she usually did when Jamie lost his temper with her. Putting herself between the stubborn siblings who often butted heads was something she'd been doing since they'd first met. "It was an accident, James. Elizabeth didn't mean to slip. And she didn't wander off, she was looking for privacy, which everyone needs a few times a day."

If Joanna had always been the loyal defender, then Izzie had always been the clever diplomat. She turned the conversation away from Elizabeth's part in the day's events. "You are so fortunate Thom found you when he did," Izzie said. "I can't imagine having to jump like that. You must have been terrified."

She had been—at first. But the moment Thom had his arm around her, she'd felt secure. A calmness had descended over her, which given the situation was preposterous. "I was," she said. "But I knew Thom wouldn't let me fall."

There was a moment of silence as her brother, sister-in-law, and cousin stared at her with varying degrees of interest, from Izzie's curiosity, to Joanna's "I knew it!" to Jamie's eagle-eyed suspicion.

Self-conscious under their scrutiny, Elizabeth added, "I just meant that he is so good at climbing there is no one I would rather have with me in that situation."

"He *has* done it before," Joanna pointed out with a smile.

"He has?" Izzie said. "You never told me," she said to Elizabeth accusingly.

Joanna proceeded to rectify the matter, recounting the tale of their refusal to be left out of the boys' game and the dangerous aftermath.

Unfortunately, the story had not distracted her brother. "Did anything else happen, Ella?"

The image of her plastered against Thom's big, hard body, her leg wrapped tightly around his waist as he pressed his manhood against her shuddering body, his hand touching her as their mouths devoured and tongues lashed . . .

"Elizabeth?"

She startled at her brother's voice and blinked incredulously. Good God, she couldn't think about that! She should *never* think about that. What could she have been thinking to kiss him again?

No matter how incredible it felt.

She forced a calmness she did not feel to her expression and hoped the guilt was not plain on her face. "What are you implying, Jamie?"

He gave her a hard look. "You know exactly what I'm implying."

Joanna intervened again. "It is really none of your business, James."

"Damn right, it's my business! She's my sister and my responsibility. And she's marrying Randolph."

"Nothing has been decided," Joanna said.

"Yes, it has," Elizabeth insisted. "We're going to Edinburgh to meet my betrothed, and my sliding down a hill has not changed that. But Thom is my friend, Jamie, and nothing will change that either."

Except it had changed. Elizabeth was beginning to realize that first kiss—and the one that had followed—had changed everything. What she didn't know was how to change it back.

Despite the late start, once he was assured Elizabeth was uninjured, rather than spend another night on the road, Jamie decided to press on to Edinburgh. It was only a handful of miles, and with a break in the rain, he hoped they would reach Holyrood Abbey—where the king had set up his temporary court—by vespers. Elizabeth suspected a big part of his decision was to prevent her and

Thom from any more "chance" encounters on the road—with or without Joanna's intervention.

Elizabeth couldn't fault his reasoning—or the need. As much as she'd loved spending time with Thom, and a return to some vestige of their former friendship, she knew it was probably best to put temptation out of temptation's reach.

And he was temptation personified.

Why had he kissed her, blast it? Why had he made her feel . . . she didn't know what she felt, but whatever it was she didn't like it. It made her anxious. Unsettled. Confused. It made her heart jump whenever she caught sight of him. It made her ache to finish what they'd started.

What was wrong with her? She'd narrowly avoided disaster twice, and she was looking for another opportunity? She must be out of her mind.

From her bench in the carriage, Elizabeth stared out one of the small openings. The rain had stopped, and despite the cold, she'd pulled back the leather flap to feel the air on her face. The bumping and tossing of the carriage over the rough terrain were making her slightly nauseous.

Fortunately, Joanna, whose stomach didn't need any additional cause for nausea, had fallen asleep—as had the others—on some of the pillows and cushions that had been piled on the benches and floor of the carriage to make it more comfortable, which given the constant jerking and jostling was definitely relative.

Elizabeth sighed, watching the darkening countryside roll by in a bumpy panoply. Every now and then she could make out snippets of conversation coming from the men who rode ahead and behind, but the clatter of the carriage prevented her eavesdropping and relieving some of the boredom.

She would rather be riding, but having accepted an offer to ride in the carriage, they felt obliged to keep Lady Mary company for the duration of the journey.

Thank goodness they would be arriving in Edinburgh soon. It was what she wanted, wasn't it? She'd been counting the days to be back in a big city, far from the monotony of the countryside. She'd been eager to begin preparations for the wedding that she'd been so excited about.

A wedding she had barely thought about since she'd left Blackhouse Tower.

There had been so many other things to think about, she told herself. Archie, for one. She was sure all the excitement would come back to her once they arrived, and she and Randolph came to their understanding.

Her stomach lurched, which she attributed to the jostle of the carriage. The lurching of her heart, however, could only be explained by the man who'd just ridden past. Her chest squeezed at the sight of the familiar frame, the broad shoulders ensconced in dark leather and strapped down with a multitude of weaponry, the inch of wavy dark hair visible beneath the steel edge of the helm, the powerful legs gripping the horse tightly—perhaps too tightly, she thought with a smile. Would he ever be comfortable on a horse?

He was so achingly familiar and yet so different. The village boy who'd been her closest companion was a powerful warrior now, and he looked it. The change was difficult to grow accustomed to.

"I remember you, you know."

Elizabeth startled at the sound of their hostess's voice. Lady Mary had woken, and if her thoughtful expression was any indication, she'd been watching her.

"I'm sorry?" Elizabeth said, perplexed. "Have we met before?"

Lady Mary smiled. She was very pretty, which perhaps explained some of Joanna's irrational jealousy, and had been nothing but kind and gracious to them. Although perhaps to Joanna it was more politeness than graciousness. The subtle difference in how Lady Mary addressed Joanna would not have been noticeable had Elizabeth not been looking for it. But it was there. As it was with most ladies of noble birth. It was a level of reserve. An invisible raising of the hand to keep a distance between them. Joanna wasn't one of them, and she never would be—no matter whom she married.

"We have, though I'm not surprised you don't remember. We were both children. I was visiting my aunt and uncle, the Earl of Angus, when your stepmother sought refuge with him after your father's death."

Elizabeth paled, but Lady Mary appeared not to notice.

"I was only a couple of years older than you at the time, but you made a big impression on me. You were such a beautiful child, and I remember thinking that if someone who looked like you could find yourself in such dire circumstances, I could as well." She laughed. "Isn't that silly? Children are so superficial and inclined to see the world only as it relates to them, aren't they? But I remember feeling so sorry for you. It was such a scary time, and everyone feared doing anything to offend King Edward. I overheard my uncle and aunt arguing about it. My aunt wanted to help your stepmother, but my uncle was terrified Edward would come after him. Did she want to be in the same position? he asked her." Lady Mary shook her head. "I know they both deeply regretted turning you and your brothers away—James was being fostered, wasn't he?"

Elizabeth nodded. With William Lamberton, but she

was afraid to speak, lest the mortification she was feeling
be made obvious.

Lady Mary smiled. "I thought so. A blessing, I suppose,
for him. At ten or eleven he wouldn't have been much help.
Anyway, I'm sure they would apologize if they could. I
hope you do not blame them."

"Of course not," Elizabeth said honestly. They had not
been alone, and their reaction had been understandable.
King Edward might well have sought retribution against
anyone who helped them.

*"I'm sorry." Elizabeth could hear the Earl of Angus's voice
as he spoke to her stepmother in the laird's solar while she and
her baby brothers waited on a bench before the fire in the Great
Hall. "But you have to understand . . . we can't risk it."*

*Why would no one help them? Tears filled her eyes, though
she'd heard the words before. It was the same thing the others
had said. This was their third castle. Their third friend "who
couldn't refuse them." But they had. She was only eight but she
knew they were running out of places to go—and money to get
there. She was tired and hungry, and didn't want to sleep in
another church.*

The memories came back. The fear. The helplessness.
The darkness and hunger. Feeling like they were lepers.
God, she hated thinking about it. Hated talking about it
even more. She wasn't an eight-year-old little girl anymore
who'd been one bag of coins away from an almshouse.
Were it not for the generous abbess who'd taken pity on
them and given them a bag of silver that was meant for
the convent, that's where they would have ended up. The
thought of being in a position like that again . . .

She repressed a shiver.

Unconsciously, her hand went to the purse of coins at
her waist. It was almost full, and when it was, she would

start again. "It was a long time ago," she said to Lady Mary. "I barely remember it."

"And you've come a long way from that time, haven't you? I hear a rumor that you are to marry the new Earl of Moray? I'd venture to say there isn't a more highly prized unmarried man in all of Scotland."

Elizabeth smiled tightly. Good gracious, she made it sound like Elizabeth had won a contest, landed the biggest fish, or brought down the most pheasants. It wasn't a game!

Or was it? Wasn't the game of marriage all about "winning" the best alliance?

Lady Mary didn't seem to mind Elizabeth's lack of response. She continued on, adding in a low voice, "At least one Douglas will make a good match."

Elizabeth stiffened; her spine felt as if a steel rod had been stuck down it. "I'm afraid I don't know what you mean."

Lady Mary gave her a chastising frown. "Come now, Lady Elizabeth, your loyalty to your sister-in-law is admirable, but surely you realize that a daughter of an obscure local knight is not a fitting wife for one of the most powerful lords in Scotland?"

Of course she did in *theory*, but it sounded so horrible when put like that. Though Lady Mary wasn't saying anything that wasn't accepted belief and something that nearly every person of their acquaintance had probably thought, it made Elizabeth want to cringe and rage at the unfairness. Joanna was perfect for James, why couldn't everyone else see it? Why did society have to put barriers of rank between them? It was so silly. But it was the way it was. It was the way people thought. And nothing could change it.

Jamie had known what would be said of his marriage, and he'd gone through with it anyway. Because he loved

Joanna. But the world had not changed with him. Nor would it during their lifetime.

"The Dicsons have been very important retainers for the Douglases for years. Joanna's grandfather gave his life for my brother's cause. My sister-in-law is eminently suitable. Indeed, I can't think of anyone more suitable for my brother."

Lady Mary put up her hand. With a wry smile, she said, "I see I have offended you. It was not my intent. It is obvious you are very loyal to your sister-in-law. She is fortunate to have you."

Elizabeth shook her head. That was where she was very wrong. "We are fortunate to have her."

After the awkward conversation with Lady Mary, Elizabeth was relieved a short while later to be freed from the confining walls of the carriage—although she did wish her freedom hadn't come at the expense of Joanna's stomach.

"Are you sure you are all right?" she asked her sister-in-law, who was riding beside her looking considerably less pale than she had when she'd rushed from the carriage looking as if she might lose the contents of her midday meal.

"I'm fine," Joanna assured her. "The fresh air is doing wonders." She looked over her shoulder to make sure Jamie wasn't listening—he wasn't—and lowered her voice. "Truth be told, it wasn't my stomach. But I needed to think of something that James wouldn't object to so that I might get out of the carriage."

Elizabeth's mouth twisted. "I wish I'd thought of it earlier." Then more earnestly, she added, "But you have nothing to worry about, Jo. I don't think my brother has even looked at another woman since he was nine."

Joanna chuckled softly, but then shook her head. "There's just something about that woman that gets under my skin. Maybe it's that I know James might have married her, and she would have been the perfect wife for him."

"You are the only perfect wife for him. Anyone who sees you together knows that."

He would have been miserable with a woman like Lady Mary.

Joanna smiled. "Thank you for saying that. No matter how many unpleasant carriage rides I must endure, there has never been a day—an hour of a day—that I've regretted marrying your brother. Never," she repeated adamantly as if for Elizabeth's benefit.

The reason why became immediately apparent. Joanna paused, her gaze flitting momentarily to Thom, who was riding near the front of the group with a few of the Phantoms. Elizabeth had to force herself not to follow her sister-in-law's gaze. Hers had strayed to the front too many times already. She was doing her best to avoid looking at him, since it caused so many *problems*. But she was discovering that she didn't need to look at him. Just knowing he was there made her feel funny.

Joanna looked back at her. "I just want the same happiness for you."

"I shall have it," Elizabeth said determinedly. "Sir Thomas will make me very happy. Just because we did not start out desperately in love as you and James does not mean it won't grow that way."

Joanna held her gaze, clearly wanting to believe her. "I hope so. I just don't want you to regret—"

"I won't."

It wasn't the same. Elizabeth didn't love Thom. Well, maybe she loved him, but not in the way Jo loved Jamie. It was the other part that troubled her. The lusting part.

Clearly realizing that she'd said enough on the matter, Joanna let the matter rest.

Elizabeth was more relieved than she wanted to admit. She didn't want to talk about Thommy with Joanna. She didn't want to talk about Thommy with anyone. All she wanted to do was reach Edinburgh, where she was sure everything would fall back into place.

She would be back in a city again, with all the entertainment and excitement that had to offer. Even in the midst of a siege, the city would be a buzzing beehive of activity. There would be markets, shops, music, noise, and so much to keep her busy with planning for the wedding she wouldn't have time to think of anything or any*one* else.

The incessant awareness—lust, whatever it was—that she felt every time she thought of Thom would disappear.

It would be perfect.

And as the lights of the city came into view on the horizon ahead of them, it seemed to be true. Her heartbeat quickened with excitement. It was so beautiful. The imposing castle perched high on the rock above the twinkling lights of Scotland's biggest and most important city (at least since the English had taken Berwick-upon-Tweed). It looked magical—like some enchanted kingdom from a child's faerie tale.

By the time they reached the famous abbey built by King David I after a cross miraculously appeared from the sky and saved him from being gored to death by a hart, Elizabeth could barely sit straight in her saddle she was so excited. Or at least mostly excited. A small twinge of trepidation was to be expected, wasn't it?

If the stench of the city had perhaps taken some of the enchantment out of the moment, it was soon replaced when not a minute after the king came out of the abbey to greet them, a man came galloping through the gate as if riding straight out of that same faerie tale. He shimmered from head to toe in a magnificent suit of mail that must have cost a king's ransom. The rich velvet surcoat of gold and yellow bearing the arms of Moray also adorned the most impressive-looking warhorse Elizabeth had ever seen. It was a big, ferocious beast that looked as if it should be pulling Satan's chariot rather than Apollo's. But somehow the juxtaposition of dark against all that blazing light worked.

When the man dismounted and tore off his helm, revealing tousled dark waves of thick hair and a face so finely featured and classically handsome, by all rights Elizabeth should have gasped.

Her cousin did. "Good gracious," Izzie whispered. "Is he for real?"

There was a slight edge of wry amusement to her cousin's voice that made Elizabeth smile. He was almost too faerie-tale perfect to believe. Lancelot to Bruce's Arthur without the complication of Guinevere.

The king must have been standing closer than they realized. "My nephew certainly does know how to make an entrance," he added dryly. "He will never be accused of modesty or meekness."

Elizabeth smiled at the man who'd defied the odds and wrested the throne of Scotland from the iron grip of the most powerful king in Christendom, Edward of England. "Perhaps not, sire, although perhaps he has no cause for either."

The king laughed. "I suspect you are right." James had

gone forward to greet him. They'd exchanged a cross grip of the forearm, and Randolph said something that sounded like "Where is she?"

James pointed in her direction, and through the crowd Randolph's gaze found hers. Their eyes met and held. It was a significant moment—and undeniably a romantic one—and she forced herself to feel something. But her heart didn't stop, her breath didn't catch, and her chest didn't squeeze. The most she could manage was a tentative smile.

He broke out into a broad grin in return and crossed the distance between them, the men falling back out of his way to create a path like the sea parting before Moses.

All except one. He had his back to her, but she didn't need to see his face. It was etched on every inch of her memory.

Now all those things happened: her heart stopped, her breath caught, and her chest squeezed; she feared that he would not move at all. That he would stand there like a dark sentinel and block Randolph's path to her. That he would confront or challenge the man she meant to marry. One of the most powerful men in the country.

Oh God, Thom, don't . . .

At the last minute, he moved out of the way, taking a deliberate step back.

Elizabeth exhaled, finally releasing the breath she'd been unconsciously holding. She hoped no one else had noticed, but from the look of worry on Joanna's face, she knew she'd seen it as well.

The smile fell from Randolph's face long enough to frown in Thom's direction, but it quickly returned to hers with a smile.

What he did next was the kind of thing that wee lasses

dreamed of—the kind of thing that when she had been married for years she would tell her grandchildren. Instead of taking her hand or bowing, he stopped before her and dropped to his knee.

Izzie muttered something that sounded distinctly like "Good grief."

Elizabeth could almost hear her eye roll. She would have shot her a glance, but Randolph did it for her. Her cousin simply met his frown with an innocent smile. Frowning harder, he turned back to Elizabeth and held out his hand.

Realizing she'd forgotten her part, Elizabeth placed her hand in his. He bowed over it and said, "My lady. I'd hoped to be here when you arrived." Standing, he did not release her hand right away as he looked into her eyes. "I hope your journey was uneventful?"

Elizabeth thought of the ravine and her eyes unconsciously sought Thom's. Their gazes held for only a fraction of an instant; she felt seared by the contact, the flash of heat was so intense.

All of a sudden, he turned and left without saying a word. He didn't need to. The look of pain on his face said everything. He'd lied. Thom did still care about her, and unintentionally she'd hurt him again.

"My lady?" Randolph inquired.

Elizabeth jolted, brought sharply back to reality. *Uneventful.* "Aye, my lord, perfectly uneventful. Although we did get stuck in the carriage, and I managed to fall down a ravine."

His brows lifted for a moment in surprise before he laughed and shook his head. "I'd hate to think about what warrants eventful. But come, we shall hear all about it."

With that the king led them all into the Hall. But

Elizabeth was painfully aware of the man who was absent. The man whose tortured expression would haunt her sleep for too many nights to come.

15

"WHAT DO YOU THINK?"

It took Thom a moment to respond. It wasn't only the "did I just fall down a faerie hole?" daze brought on by the identity of the man posing the question (the king of Scotland was asking *his* opinion?), or that he was surrounded by five of the most powerful men in the country (the king's oldest and most trusted advisor, Neil Campbell, Randolph, Douglas, MacLeod, and MacRuairi), it was also that he was trying to figure out whether the king was jesting. But from the serious expressions of the men watching him, he realized the king was very serious.

Jesus.

"Can it be done?" the king added, obviously impatient for his response.

Thom was glad he hadn't laughed or blurted out "by a dead man" as had been his initial reaction. Instead, he gave the question the respect due the questioner.

Bloody hell.

Nudging his mount forward, and then back and forth to the left and right, he looked over the infamous "Castle Rock" of Edinburgh Castle from every possible angle from where they were positioned at the base of the steep rock face. He pushed aside the knowledge that climbing the Rock had never been done, pushed aside the words "impossible" and "suicide," and tried to look at it objectively. But almost three hundred feet of nearly-sheer basalt cliffs didn't give quarter.

Thom had never contemplated climbing anything of the like. It made the cliffs at Bamburgh look like child's play. He followed cracks and crevices in the rock up the face, but they all disappeared into dead ends of solid, unyielding, impenetrable rock. There were handholds and footholds, but they were few and far between. Short distances could be managed, perhaps, but almost three hundred feet?

He shook his head. It would likely be suicide. But *could* it be done?

He turned back to the king. "I don't know."

The Bruce's dark eyes gleamed. "Does that mean it's possible someone could climb it?"

"No one ever has before, but at this point, I'm not saying it's *im*possible. I'd need a closer look to scout it from different vantages to see whether there is a way up."

Something that he wasn't seeing right now.

"You shall have whatever you need," the king said quickly. "My nephew will see to it."

Thom stiffened reflexively. Maybe the only thing worse than being under Douglas's command would be being under Randolph's. The sting of last night's arrival at Holyrood was still too fresh. He'd felt like he was watching some kind of damned farce. A play torn from the pages of Arthur and his knights, featuring the perfect shining knight and the beautiful princess for all to admire.

Except that it hadn't been a play; it had been too damned real. And the beautiful princess was his, damn it.

For Thom, standing aside in silence as Elizabeth greeted the man she planned to marry was like a slap in the face and all too reminiscent of his youth. *Remember your place. Don't reach too high. Keep your mouth shut.*

Stepping back had been the only prudent thing to do. But why did he feel that in doing so he'd conceded something he didn't want to concede?

Perhaps sensing the direction of Thom's thoughts, MacLeod said, "It would have to be done at night. We will see to it that no one from the castle is alerted."

The king lifted a brow. "You want MacGowan with you?"

The Highland Chief nodded. "Aye."

Thom almost heaved a sigh of relief.

Randolph shot Douglas a surprised look, at which his old friend just shrugged. They all knew what MacLeod's command meant: Thom was being recruited by the Phantoms.

"Very well," the king agreed. He turned to Thom. "You may be able to help with a few other missions I have in mind."

Thom nodded. "I'll do whatever I can, sire."

"My brother says you wish to become a knight?"

"Aye, sire."

"Do well, and I will personally see to it," he said. Thom was still reeling from the king's words when Bruce added with an enigmatic laugh in MacLeod's direction, "Although not everyone sees the value, knighthood still has much to recommend it." He glanced down at Thom's horse—a pathetic beast compared to the fine horseflesh ridden by the other men. "You will need to find a better horse."

Thom repressed a groan. "I'm working on it."

More than one man laughed as they turned their mounts and headed back through the forest to return to the abbey.

Fortunately, it would be a short stay. With his release from Douglas's temporary command, Thom would leave the abbey for the siege encampment at the base of Castle Hill—the elevated rise from the west that provided the only accessible entrance to the castle—about a mile away. Staying at Holyrood, being forced to watch Randolph woo his bride, would have been unbearable.

Thom needed to put his head down and concentrate on the opportunity being given him with the Phantoms. Christ, the king had offered to knight him if he proved himself.

He was riding at the back of the group with MacRuairi and MacLeod going over a plan to try to get a closer look at the cliff that very night, when he took the opportunity to ask about the king's earlier remark. "What did the king mean when he said you did not see the value in knighthood?"

The two West Highland chieftains exchanged a look.

"We're Highlanders," MacLeod said as if that were explanation enough.

"We have our own code," MacRuairi added. "The chivalry of knights may make for romantic tales," he said with an eye to Randolph. Apparently Thom wasn't the only one not impressed by Randolph's performance. "But it is not reality, nor does it win wars." He gave him a slightly evil smile. "You'll see."

Thom frowned. "There are no knights among you?"

"A few," MacLeod answered. "But it is secondary to their place in the Guard."

The Guard. Thom stored the information away for later.

"There was another among us for whom it was not secondary," MacRuairi said with a deadly look on his face. "He lost sight of his place and betrayed us. He fights for the English now." He practically spat the last.

Whoever the man was, Thom wouldn't want to be in his boots if he ever came face-to-face with Lachlan MacRuairi again.

Thom realized that Sir Neil Campbell, who in addition to being one of Bruce's oldest friends was also brother to one of the Phantoms, must have overheard some of their conversation when he started prodding Randolph. "I hear you made quite an impression last night, Randolph. I'm surprised you did not call out the trumpeters."

Randolph said something Thom didn't hear, but he suspected it was a suggestion for Campbell to do something that was physically impossible.

The older battle-hard warrior just laughed. "Douglas's sister seems too levelheaded to be charmed by such theatrics. That shining knight on a white charger routine isn't likely to get you very far. I hope you have another plan in the works."

Randolph might be arrogant and a bit pompous—if not priggish—but he could give as good as he got. "If it doesn't, I suppose I can always try your method of wooing."

"The hell you will," Douglas said, obviously not appreciating the jest—Sir Neil had abducted his young bride a few years back.

Randolph smiled. Thom could see he enjoyed getting a rise out of his friend and rival. "I won't need to. I think your sister and I see eye to eye on everything."

There was something about Randolph's arrogance—his cocksure confidence—that made Thom want to put a fist through his gleaming white grin.

But it was the fierce surge of possessiveness that gripped him, which told him he wasn't quite as over Elizabeth Douglas as he wanted to be.

The question was, what was he going to do about it?

Would he take another step back? Concede? Stand aside and do what he was supposed to do? What he'd been doing his entire life?

Or would he fight for what he wanted?

Fight for what now seemed possible. As a knight and a member of Bruce's secret army, he would have something to offer her. And maybe, just maybe, a life together wasn't a complete fantasy.

"Are you looking for someone?"

Startled, Elizabeth turned to the man seated next to her at the high table. She plastered what she hoped was a relaxed smile on her face, although she was anything but. "Who would I be looking for when all of Edinburgh is gathered in this very room?"

Sir Thomas chuckled. "Aye, you are right about that. My uncle has invited most of the city—well, anyone of import, that is, for today's meal." He lowered his voice, a mischievous smile turning his mouth. "I might even call it a feast if this wasn't the middle of Lent."

Elizabeth laughed. It was hard not to be charmed by the vaunted knight. Sir Thomas Randolph, Earl of Moray, was witty, sophisticated, enjoyed the same things she did, knew the same people, and was just wicked enough to make things interesting. She was fortunate indeed. So why was she staring at doorways?

"Anyone of import."

Not quite everyone—at least not to her. She hadn't seen

Thom since the night they'd arrived two days ago. She learned from Jo that he'd left the abbey to join the men in camp laying siege to the castle.

It was for the best, she knew. But why didn't it feel that way? Why did her chest squeeze every time she thought of his face that night?

Was it guilt?

Whatever it was, it was affecting her interactions with Sir Thomas, and she knew it had to stop. He might begin to think she wasn't interested, and she couldn't have that.

He'd probably talked to her cousin Isabel more than he had her—which was her fault, as she'd made it a point to keep Izzie close to her side whenever he was around. Her cousin, however, didn't seem very impressed with her soon-to-be-betrothed, and unfortunately Randolph sensed it. He went out of his way to charm her, but it had rather the opposite effect. Izzie watched him with an amused detachment that was halfway between rolled eyes and polite tolerance. Needless to say, Randolph didn't like it, and Elizabeth sensed his growing frustration with her cousin. She certainly didn't want that frustration extended to her.

Turning her full concentration to the man at her side, Elizabeth responded to his irreverence with mock shock. "A feast on a Wednesday during Lent? The abbot would never condone such a thing."

Sundays were the only break from fasting during Lent.

They both glanced down the table to where the abbot sat beside the king with a huge trencher of food before him, and at least one very large goblet of wine. There was no meat, but with all the lampreys, oysters, and fish it was hardly missed.

Meeting each other's gazes, they burst into laughter. When more than one person stared at them—including her cousin, who frowned disapprovingly at their loss of decorum—they managed to get themselves under control.

Randolph took a long swig of wine from his own goblet. "Lent or not, I'm grateful for the distraction. I'm going out of my mind with boredom. How much longer can the blasted garrison hold out? It's been over two months."

Elizabeth couldn't resist teasing him. "Is that what I am, my lord, a pleasant distraction from the tedium of the siege?"

If he was surprised that she was flirting with him—the first time she'd done so—he hid it quickly. "The siege is undeniably tedious"—it was well known that the Bruce had no love of laying siege to castles, which inevitably involved long periods of waiting and inactivity, and clearly his nephew shared his view—"but you are *far* more than a pleasant distraction."

The huskiness of his voice and the knowing look in his eyes—his dark *brownish-green* eyes, blast it (as her cousin had pointed out more than once)—should have made her pulse quicken and her skin prickle. Instead it made her regret changing the mood between them. She was comfortable with Randolph as long as they kept it light and friendly. But the first hint of amorousness was making her distinctly *un*comfortable.

Fortunately, she did not sense any real feeling behind his suggestive tone. Actually, it felt a little bit practiced and rote—like this was something he'd done hundreds of times before. With his roguish reputation, she didn't doubt it.

"There has been no movement, then?" she asked matter-of-factly, clearly departing from any hint of flirtatiousness. "No indication that the English might be getting ready to surrender?"

If he'd noticed her shift in tone, he did not show it and shook his head. "Since Lubaud's imprisonment there have been no talks at all." Elizabeth knew that the former Gascon commander of the castle's earlier negotiations with King Robert had sparked a riot among the garrison inside the castle, leading to his imprisonment by his own men. He'd been replaced by an Englishman. "But they must be getting dangerously low on provisions," he continued. "We've intercepted every shipment and attempt by King Edward to resupply them."

"And there is no other way to take the castle?"

She thought she saw something flicker in his gaze, but then realized it must have been the candlelight. Even in the middle of the day the abbey's refectory was dark, and the king had ordered oil lamps and candelabra to illuminate every corner of the otherwise plain and sparsely decorated room.

He shook his head and said dryly, "Not unless your brother can conjure another miracle." Randolph apparently had taken the news of his rival's latest feat with remarkable good grace—not that she didn't think he would give his eyeteeth to better James by taking Edinburgh Castle in some equally dramatic fashion. "The garrison at Roxburgh were caught unaware; unfortunately the same cannot be said about the garrison here. We will not surprise or trick them into opening the gates."

He sounded so frustrated Elizabeth reached out and put her hand on his arm. "I'm sure you will think of something, my lord."

He covered her hand with his and smiled at her warmly. "And until then, I shall have you to distract me."

He really was incredibly handsome, she thought. It was easy to see why the women at court were so besotted with him. Wealth, power, connections, charm, and extraordinary good looks. . . . it was a rare combination.

Although not as physically overpowering as Thom, the earl was still quite tall—at least a couple of inches over six feet—and well muscled. His build was leaner—more tightly honed from years of wielding a sword than the thick, heavy slabs of hard muscle forged from physical labor and swinging a hammer that made Thom so physically overpowering.

She'd never noticed it before, but the two men actually looked quite a bit alike. Both had dark hair, piercing eyes, and classically handsome features. Randolph's were slightly more refined and arrogant perhaps, but there was something about Thom's thick, long lashes, the dark shadow that appeared on his jaw within hours of shaving, the hint of a dimple in his left cheek, and the slight bump on the bridge of his nose from a boyhood fight with Jamie that gave him a not-quite-so-polished look that appealed to her.

When Thom turned those smoky blue eyes on her . . . the shiver of awareness that ran through her awoke other feelings—other sensations that she'd never experienced before. Her nipples hardened, her breasts grew heavy, and warmth tingled between her legs.

His mouth, too, was so perfectly wide and sensual. She couldn't help but remember how soft and warm it had felt on hers. Randolph's mouth was nice, but it was hard and perhaps a little cold. It didn't make her think of hot, passionate kisses . . .

Dear Lord. She stopped, realizing what she was doing. She'd been staring at Randolph comparing him to Thom, and Randolph had mistaken her interest—particularly when her eyes had dropped to his mouth.

His gaze didn't actually heat, but she detected a flicker, and perhaps the first real indication that he might be contemplating kissing her.

Cheeks ablaze with mortification, she shifted her gaze decidedly *away* from his mouth.

But the heat in her face didn't last for long. No sooner did she look away from Randolph than her gaze met another. This one was definitely blue.

She drew in her breath in a sharp gasp, and all the heat slid from her face in horror and what felt like guilt, although she'd done nothing wrong.

Thom stood in the doorway with some of the other Phantoms. He'd just arrived, but he'd obviously been there long enough to witness at least some of what had transpired on the dais between her and Randolph.

Good God, he thought . . .

She wanted to push back from the bench, race across the room, and tell him he was wrong.

She might have. But he didn't give her a chance. He turned, said something to one of the Guardsmen who stood next to him—it appeared to be Magnus MacKay—spun around on his heel, and left.

Only Randolph's voice stopped her from going after him. "Do you know MacGowan well, my lady?"

She dropped back down the inch she'd risen off her seat.

He'd obviously caught the direction of her gaze. But there didn't seem to be any suspicion in his tone, merely interest.

She schooled her features in what she hoped was nonchalance. "Very well. We've been friends since childhood."

It was the truth, but such a small part of what was between them it felt like a lie. "He's impressed my uncle with what he did to help free your brother. He thinks he might be useful."

Elizabeth frowned. "For what?"

"A few missions here and there," Randolph said vaguely

with a dismissive wave of his hand. "What is your impression of the man? Can he be counted on? He is of low birth, is he not?"

"His father is the village smithy, but his mother was the daughter of a knight. Thom is one of the most noble men I know, and there is no one I would count on more. The king is fortunate to have him in his army."

She didn't realize how she'd bristled or how forcefully she'd spoken until Randolph apologized. "I'm sorry, I meant no offense. I was merely curious, that is all." He smiled. "MacGowan is fortunate to have such a valiant defender on his side. I know your brother didn't like him, so I just wondered."

"He and Jamie used to be as close as brothers."

Clearly, she'd surprised him. "They were?"

She nodded. "They had a falling-out years ago."

"Over what?"

Me. "I don't know," she lied, hoping he didn't pursue the matter.

Fortunately, her cousin interceded. "I wonder if the king will chance some music tonight, my lord?"

Randolph's gaze sharpened as it fell on Izzie. "I doubt my uncle will press his luck with the abbot tonight."

Izzie's eyes twinkled with mischief. "How disappointing. I was hoping you'd sing for us. Lady Mary said you have the voice of a troubadour. Truly, my lord, is there no end to your accomplishments?"

There wasn't even a hint of sarcasm in her voice, but Randolph knew she was laughing at him—and didn't like it. He drew as tight as a bow, his mouth pressing in a flat white line.

Aye, he definitely didn't like it—and her cousin, she suspected, even less.

Elizabeth shot Izzie a chastising glare for prodding him, but she just smiled with pretty, wide-eyed innocence.

Randolph's gaze narrowed even more on that smile, and for once Elizabeth thought he might lose his composure, but he stared at Izzie for a long pause before turning back to her. "Do you sing, my lady?"

"Horribly. I play the lute a bit, but it's Izzie who is the gifted musician in the family. She sings like an angel."

He didn't hide his skepticism, turning back to Izzie with a brow so sharply arched it almost came to a point. "Is that so?" he drawled. "Lady Isabel hides her accomplishments well."

The statement could be taken two ways, but they all knew exactly how it was intended. Isabel stiffened at the slight, which Elizabeth hastily tried to smooth over. "While we were in Paris, she sang for King Phillip himself, and Monsieur de Vitry permitted her to sing one of his chansons."

"Really?" If he was impressed that the man considered the greatest musician of his time had considered a woman worthy of one of his songs, he did not show it.

Elizabeth nodded, while Izzie's cheeks burned. "She made the nuns weep when we took alms to St. Mary's Wynd Hospital yesterday and she joined them in a hymn. They asked her to come again tomorrow." Suddenly she had an idea. "Perhaps you would care to join us after morning prayers to hear for yourself?"

Women were forbidden from singing in church, as they were thought to be unclean and inherently wicked, although nuns were permitted to sing as part of their duties in a convent.

"I will look forward to it," he said, with only polite enthusiasm.

As soon as she could, Elizabeth excused herself, pleading a headache. When it looked like her cousin would attempt to go with her, Elizabeth stopped her. "Nay, they will be bringing out the confections soon, and you must stay and hear the rest of the earl's story. He was telling me all about the taking of Perth Castle, and you must tell me every detail when you get back to the chamber."

Izzie gave her a look that promised retribution, and Randolph looked as if his wine had just turned to vinegar.

Elizabeth smiled back sweetly at them both and tried not to laugh. Clearly they'd gotten off on the wrong foot, but she was going to make them like each other whether they wanted it or not.

At last, Elizabeth was able to make her escape. She just hoped she wasn't too late.

16

"HAVE CARE," MACKAY had warned him as they stood in the entry of the refectory. "Your thoughts are not difficult to read, and I don't think Bruce would be too pleased if you put a dirk in his nephew's gut."

Thom looked away from the dais and schooled the anger from his features, furious that his thoughts had been so transparent. He sure as hell wasn't going to impress the Guard if he didn't learn to control himself. Hiding his reaction wasn't usually a problem. At least it hadn't been until he'd run into Elizabeth Douglas again. Fortunately, MacKay was the only one who had noticed.

But by the king's invitation or not, Thom's joining the others for the midday meal at Holyrood had been a mistake. He'd known that the moment he'd stepped through the door and saw the couple on the dais. For the first time, that is what they'd looked like: a couple. Bloody hell, Randolph seemed to be thinking about kissing her right there in the middle of the damned meal.

Thom had to get away. MacKay had offered to come with him, but he'd declined—wanting to be alone. He'd thought about returning to camp, but the moment he stepped outside on the cool but sunny day and glanced up, he'd changed his mind.

A few hundred yards beyond the gate of the abbey stood the massive formation that dominated the landscape and seemed to watch over the burgh like a stony sentinel. Actually, the shape was more reminiscent of the drawings of the massive Egyptian sphinx carvings that had been brought back from the Holy lands after the Crusades. The locals called the hill Arthur's Seat; it was purportedly once a place that King Arthur went to watch over the city. From the top there were supposed to be panoramic views for miles.

Thom had been anxious to climb it since they'd arrived, but with the nightly scouting climbs of Castle Rock (so far yielding no feasible path up) and his daily duties with the Phantoms (which mostly consisted of him being tossed around and having the shite beaten out of him while "training"), he hadn't had time.

It wasn't a difficult hill to climb. It could be walked fairly easily from the east up a grassy slope. But Thom needed the release of pent-up energy, so he took the more difficult route up the rocky crags from the south.

He'd left most of his armor and weapons with the stable lad, but the climb was more strenuous than he'd expected, and despite the coolness of the day, his leather *cotun* was tied around his waist as he pulled himself up the last stretch of rock.

He stood atop the hill ready to enjoy the fruits of his labor by taking in the magnificent views all around him. Instead, he got one of the biggest shocks of his life.

Sitting about twenty feet away on a small rise was a mirage. A mirage that looked a hell of a lot like Elizabeth— or at least a flushed-cheeked, glowing with perspiration, wrinkled and dirty-hem gown wearing, shimmering blond hair loosed from its plaits and tearing across her face with the wind version of Elizabeth.

She was beautiful. More beautiful than he'd ever seen her before. She didn't look like a princess at all. Mussed and warm from the walk up the hill, she brimmed with energy and life.

God, how he wanted her.

Why was she torturing him? His already strained and well-worked muscles tensed with a flood of anger. "What are you doing here?" he demanded.

"I . . ." The question seemed to trouble her—as if she didn't know the answer. "You didn't say goodbye." She sounded pleased to have come up with something.

"When?"

"The night we arrived."

"You were busy."

She bit her lip. "Thom, I . . . I had to see you."

"Why?"

She looked down, embarrassed. "You looked upset."

Elizabeth had always been able to read him better than anyone, but in this case he hadn't exactly been hiding his feelings. He'd looked like he wanted to kill someone; like a man who was being dragged through the four corners of hell. His fists clenched at his sides. "So you followed me?"

"Not exactly. You'd already left the abbey by the time I was able to get away." His mouth hardened, recalling what—or who—she'd been getting away from. "When I stepped into the courtyard and saw the hill"—she shrugged—"it wasn't hard to figure out where you might go. I took a chance. But it took me longer to walk up here than I anticipated, and I feared I'd missed you."

He looked around, already knowing what he'd see: nothing. "So you walked all the way up here alone? Christ, El, what in Hades were you thinking? You could have tripped or fallen."

She stood, shook out her dusty skirts, and walked toward him. "You sound like Jamie. It's not as if I haven't climbed a hill before—you know that as well as anyone— and I was careful."

He made a sharp sound of disbelief, and she glared at him.

"You forget," he said. "I've seen what happens when you are 'careful.'"

She sniffed haughtily and looked past him down the cliff. "Was it a difficult climb?"

Taking her by the shoulders, he forcibly moved her back a few feet from the edge. Christ, was she trying to kill him? "No."

Shaking off his hold, she put her hands on her waist. "I wasn't going to fall."

He crossed his arms before him. "Let's just say I was making sure of it." Elizabeth and edges of cliffs didn't mix.

She rolled her eyes, and he put a hand on one of her bent elbows. "Come, I'll walk you back down."

She spun on him. "I'm not ready to go back."

His grip tightened along with his mouth. "Yes, you are. You shouldn't even be here. If anyone learns you followed me . . ." He swore, realizing what would happen if MacLeod found out. "What would your betrothed think?"

"He's not my betrothed, and I doubt he'd care overmuch. Sir Thomas doesn't strike me as the jealous sort."

Then he was a fool. Because if he had any inkling what Thom was thinking about right now, he'd have cause to be very jealous indeed.

"Maybe not," Thom agreed. "But Randolph doesn't strike me as a man who would like the rumors and innuendo that would follow from the woman he's chosen for his bride being discovered alone with another man."

Her chin took that stubborn tilt that he knew so well. "We aren't doing anything wrong. We're friends."

That was all it took. He snapped, hauling her up against him. "That is shite, and you know it. There is a hell of a lot more between us than friendship. Do you need me to remind you of exactly how much more?"

Her eyes widened. "No."

"Say it," he practically growled. "I want to hear you say it."

She stared up at him wide-eyed. "There is more between us than friendship."

He let her go, realizing how close he was to losing control. How close he was to crushing her in his embrace and making her his the easy way. It took a moment for the fierce beating of his heart to slow and the lust that had curled its way through his limbs start to ebb.

She'd said it. He had his admission. Now what?

He dragged his fingers back through his hair. "Why are you really here, Elizabeth?"

She studied his face, her gaze deep and probing as it met his. "You still care for me."

Thom felt like he was being raked over the coals all over again. Like he'd been flogged until the skin had been stripped away from his bones. Months—years—of suffering and he was right back where he started.

"I *love* you. I've probably never stopped loving you. I will probably always love you. Is that what you need to hear? Does that make it better? Do you have the answers you need now?"

She looked stricken. "No . . . I . . . I don't know." Tears glistened in the corners of her eyes. "Why are you trying to confuse me and make this so difficult?"

Seeing the torment and struggle taking place inside her, Thom felt some of his anger and frustration dissipate. This wasn't easy on her either. Admitting she had feelings for him would force her to contemplate things that would be scary for her. But marrying a man she didn't love only to realize she loved another would be far worse.

In his heart he knew she loved him. He just had to make her see it. He had to make her realize that whatever difficulties they faced, whatever scorn, censure, and condemnation, wouldn't matter if they loved each other.

Is that what he thought? He realized he did. Seeing her with Randolph had made him realize that he couldn't stand down. He was going to fight for her—for them. No matter what the risks.

Thom wasn't Randolph, but if all went well with the Phantoms and Bruce made him a knight she would be able to hold her head up high. He might never be "worthy" of her in society's eyes, but he would be able to provide for her and give her the security she craved. She just needed to give him a chance.

A wave of tenderness rose inside him. He took her chin between his fingers and gently tilted her face to his. "If you are confused, it is only because you are not listening."

"To what?"

Thom had made his decision. He wasn't going to step back again. He was going to fight and reach for the damned stars. He was going to show her that he was the right—the *only*—man for her.

"To this." He lowered his mouth and kissed her.

Elizabeth didn't want to hear what he was trying to tell her, but the moment his lips touched hers she felt it. The aching tenderness. The heartfelt emotion. The sweet, invisible pull that reached inside, grabbed hold, and wouldn't let go.

This wasn't a kiss of possession, a kiss of unfettered passion, or a kiss of mindless abandon. It was not about anger, or loss of control, or lust. It was controlled, gentle, and intended to show her exactly how he felt about her.

With each soft caress of his lips, with each slow stroke of his tongue, she felt the wave of emotion growing inside her surge higher and higher. It wrapped around her chest, coiling tighter and tighter until it almost hurt.

It did hurt. It was sharp, poignant, and so beautiful and sweet she couldn't bear it. It made her feel things she didn't want to feel—face feelings she wanted to escape. Feelings that overwhelmed her.

He overwhelmed her. The softness of his lips, the faint taste of clove on his breath, the warmth of his body radiating through the linen of his tunic. He smelled of sun and heat, which, mixed with the heather of his soap, was an intoxicating combination to her senses, lulling her deeper and deeper into his tender embrace. He cradled her against him as if she was the most precious thing in the world to him. As if this were meant to be.

You are not listening . . .

She didn't want to listen. She didn't want to feel. She didn't want tenderness and emotion. She wanted him to do what he'd done before. To bring her more pleasure, not more confusion.

She gripped his shoulders, her fingers digging into the thick bulge of muscle to bring him closer.

She fought tenderness with passion, parrying the slow stroke of his tongue with deep thrusts and carnal twists. She heard him groan and felt his arms tighten around her in response to her sensual entreaty.

She thought she'd won.

She moaned at the increased contact, feeling the tips of her breasts harden as they were crushed against the steely warmth of his chest. She loved the way he felt against her. Loved the feeling of all that strength wrapped around her.

This was exactly what she wanted.

She pressed even tighter, letting her hips rock against his. The feel of his manhood riding high against her stomach, so hard and thick . . .

She wanted him to move against her. Wanted the pressure—the friction—the frantic energy pulsing through her. She didn't want time to think.

But he wouldn't give it to her. He seemed impervious to her attempts to spark the lust that simmered between them ready to burst into flames at the first flare. He blocked the carnal thrusts and twists of her tongue with long, loving strokes.

He took control and didn't give it back.

She almost cried out in frustration as he met her wicked onslaught not with the speed and frenzy she craved but with deft control and gentle caresses. His hands did not cup her bottom to lift her against him, they smoothed over her hips and waist as if he were sculpting a fine piece of porcelain.

The ache in her chest returned. The tenderness mixed with passion combined to make an even more powerful drug. One that beckoned and tempted. But she fought against it, using the only weapon at her disposal.

Slowly, she started to slide her hand down his stomach.

Thom knew what she was trying to do. She was scared and determined to deny the tender feelings he roused in her with passion.

But he was equally determined to win this sensual battle that had sprung up between them; to prove that it wasn't just lust but something far deeper that bound them. He wouldn't let her win. *Couldn't* let her win.

But when her hand began to inch down his stomach he started to sweat. He had to grit his teeth against the pleasure that he knew was a few sweet strokes of her hand away. Just the thought of her touching him, of having those dainty, white fingers wrapped around his thick, throbbing cock . . .

Oh God. The pounding at the base of his spine, and the tight throbbing of an already too-hard erection, intensified.

He concentrated on kissing her. Concentrated on the gentle strokes of his tongue delving lovingly into her mouth. Concentrated on the soft brushes of his lips against hers, on the velvety softness of the delicate cheek under his hand.

He tried not to think about the hard tips of the generous breasts digging into his chest or the hips innocently pressing against him, or the hand . . .

The hand that was now at his waist, damn it.

He stopped breathing, sensing her hesitation. She was innocent. A maid. Not a wanton. She wouldn't be bold enough to touch him. Christ, at least he hoped she wouldn't. But knowing Elizabeth . . .

He muffled a curse even as temptation beckoned. It would be so easy to put his hand over hers, slide it over him, and show her what to do. Show her how to wrap her fingers around him, grip him tight, and milk him until the pleasure exploded. Release—relief—was only a few pumps away.

But he couldn't, damn it. The feel of her hand on him . . . he didn't know if he would be able to stay in control.

He was about to find out. She was bold enough all right—God, help him. He couldn't stifle the groan that tore from deep inside his lungs when her hand tentatively skimmed over the swollen head. Instinctively—because what else could he do?—he thrust into her hand, and she molded her fingers and palm around him.

He stilled. He might have stopped breathing for a moment while he thanked every god he'd ever heard of and tried to find the strength to stop the powerful urges surging through his body. It felt so damned good, so damned right, a few thrusts of his hips, and the pleasure would be pulsing through him.

But the relief—no matter how great—would only be temporary. And it wouldn't bring her any closer to recognizing and accepting her feelings for him—with everything that might mean.

A moment now or a lifetime? It wasn't hard to decide.

So he let her hand stay there. Ignored it (as if that were

possible) while he concentrated on kissing her, showing her with his mouth and tongue how much he loved her. Even when she mewled in frustration, when her hand accidentally tugged him in a motion that if it wasn't a stroke was a damned fine imitation of one, he didn't give in.

But the instant he was certain he'd made his point, he pulled back. He knew it was only a matter of time—probably not much—before the fact that she was warm and willing against him would wreak havoc with even the most steely of control.

He didn't say anything, but just stared into her eyes, holding her close and watching the frustration and turmoil play across her faerie princess features. The big blue eyes framed by curly, long lashes, the tiny, slightly upturned nose, the high pink cheeks, and soft red mouth.

"Why are you doing this?" she begged in a half-plea, half-cry of desperation.

He knew why she was fighting him so hard. She was scared. Scared of what admitting her love for him might mean. Scared of what she would have to give up. And she was resisting her feelings for him with everything she had. "You don't need to be scared, El."

She pulled back as if he'd uttered a horrible slur. "I'm not!"

"Then why are you trying to deny what is between us?"

"Are you sure it isn't you who are doing that?"

Realizing what she meant, he released her and stepped back. "There is more to what is between us than lust, Elizabeth. Lie to me if you want, but don't lie to yourself."

One kiss might not have proved it to her, but he wasn't going to give up. He would make her see it whether she wanted to or not. Elizabeth Douglas loved him. She had for a long time, and soon they would both know it.

17

"I'D WAGER IT has been some time since the nuns and the residents of St. Mary's have been treated to such a beautiful recital," Elizabeth said as she left the almshouse with her cousin and Randolph. "I can't say I've ever enjoyed the Lenten hymns as much. But I didn't know who to listen to; it seemed that as soon as Izzie took a breath, you filled it right in, my lord." She tried not to smile, pretending that she didn't know what they'd been doing. But after Izzie forced him to sing upon mentioning how good he was to their audience, it had been obvious that they were waging some sort of battle. "Perhaps you might consider singing a chanson together sometime for a feast?"

Izzie's eyes narrowed, aware that her cousin was needling her. "What an extraordinary idea, Elizabeth." She smiled sweetly at Randolph. "But I would never think to compete with such prodigious talent as the earl's."

The ever-chivalrous knight gave a short bow of his head. "It is I who would be honored, Lady Isabel. Your cousin did not exaggerate your talent, you have a beautiful voice."

It was simply stated without his usual grandiosity.

Izzie seemed taken aback, whether from the compliment or from the sincerity with which it was given, Elizabeth couldn't tell.

Truth be told, Elizabeth had been grateful for the distraction they provided. Though her visits to almshouses and lazar houses were important to her, they could sometimes be difficult, evoking memories that she would rather forget of how close she came to one herself. She'd felt the cold shadow of memory before Randolph and Izzie's war of song had reminded her of where she was.

They continued down the wynd, proceeding down the high street to the abbey located at the bottom end. The morning mist had yet to lift off the hills to the east, and although the day was off to a cool start (she and Isabel had both worn their warmest fur-lined cloaks), she sensed it was going to be another beautiful day. At this time of year, anything that didn't involve ice, snow, or rain was reason for celebration.

Once through the gate, they paused opposite the massive facade of the abbey entrance. She turned to Randolph. "Will you be able to join us in the refectory to break your fast, my lord?"

The first meal of the day was eliminated during Lent except for on Sundays.

He shook his head. "I wish I could, but I must return to the castle to see whether any progress has been made."

"Progress?" Izzie repeated with a frown. "At night? Do the English like to parley in the dark, my lord?"

Randolph's smile turned brittle. The détente between them was apparently already at an end. "I meant in general," he said dismissively. But Elizabeth sensed rather the opposite. Did they have something planned at night? An attack on the castle perhaps? But given what he'd said before, it didn't seem likely. "My uncle will be waiting—" He stopped suddenly, frowning. "That's strange."

"What's strange?" Elizabeth asked.

"He should be at camp. Excuse me for a moment."

Both women turned as Randolph started off in the

direction of the gate. It was then that Elizabeth saw the man who'd caught his attention: Thom.

Her heart jumped, obviously having not quite recovered from yesterday's overworking.

She hadn't thought to see him so soon. He'd seemed eager to be rid of her, marching her down the hill and watching stoically from the trees as she made her way safely through the gate. He hadn't even waved; she'd looked.

They'd said little on the way back down the hill. Thom once again wore that blank look he'd perfected in his youth when facing an angry Jamie, and Elizabeth had been, well, angry. At herself, at him, maybe it didn't matter.

When she thought about how she'd touched him . . .

She didn't think about that—*couldn't* think about that—especially standing outside an abbey with her soon-to-be betrothed only a few feet away.

Don't lie to yourself . . .

Her mouth pursed at the memory of the challenge he'd tossed down at her feet like a gauntlet. He had a lot of nerve, thinking he knew her better than she knew herself. Elizabeth knew exactly how she felt. She cared for him—deeply—and wanted him—irrationally—but she did not love him. At least not in the way he meant.

She wasn't Joanna. She didn't think with her heart. She was far too practical to fall in love with someone she could never marry. She'd been exiled from society and treated like a leper once before; she would not go through that again—at least not willingly. She had a secure future in her grasp, she wasn't about to let it go.

So what if she dreamed about the way he kissed her and touched her, and wanted him to do it again? It didn't change anything. And there was nothing to say she wouldn't feel the same way about Randolph . . . in time.

But how long will it take? Shouldn't there be at least a tiny spark by now?

"I wonder what they are talking about?" Izzie said thoughtfully. "What exactly is it that MacGowan does in Bruce's army?"

Elizabeth was wondering the same thing herself as she watched the two men converse intently. "Jamie said the king had some special missions for him in mind."

"And those missions involve Randolph?" Izzie made a face. "Makes things rather awkward, doesn't it?"

Elizabeth stared blankly at her cousin. "Why would it be awkward?"

The implicit warning didn't deter her cousin one bit. Izzie laughed and rolled her eyes. "Oh, I don't know, like maybe having the man you claim you don't want show up to see you right under the nose of the man you say you do?"

"I'm sure Thom isn't here to see me," she said primly, but her cheeks were blazing.

What if he was? Would he be so bold (and foolish!) as to pursue her right—as her cousin had said—under Randolph's nose? Not to mention her brother's. Surely he would be more circumspect?

"Don't look now," Izzie whispered out of the side of her mouth. "Your Thom and Sir-Too-Good-to-Be-True are headed this way. But don't worry, I'm sure this won't be awkward at all."

Right now, Elizabeth was finding it difficult to remember why she usually found her cousin's dry sense of humor so amusing.

Seeing the men walking toward them made her heart

start to race. Despite the cool air, she could feel a distinct sheen of perspiration on her brow. She had nothing to feel guilty about—which didn't explain the frantic drumming of her pulse.

If only Thom wasn't so handsome. She couldn't seem to look away.

He met her gaze and nodded. "Lady Elizabeth, Lady Isabel."

Before she could catch her breath to respond he moved off. Apparently he *wasn't* here to see her. She was relieved. Of course she was. It only felt like disappointment.

"Is everything all right, my lord?" Izzie asked Randolph, covering the admittedly *awkward* moment, as Elizabeth stood there with her mouth agape.

"Fine. I thought MacGowan might have been here for me, but it seems he is on a personal mission."

"He is?" Elizabeth asked in what was intended to sound disinterested but came out as something of a squeak.

Personal as in a woman? There were many staying at the guesthouse—most of them were the wives of the men in Bruce's retinue, but there were a handful of unmarried ones—like Lady Mary—as well.

"Aye," Randolph said. "To see Douglas's wife." *Joanna?* "But I have some good news. It seems there is no reason for me to rush back, so I will be happy to join you for the meal after all. Assuming the invitation is still open?"

The roguish smile and charming twinkle in his eye were undeniably calculated to make her knees weak. But hers didn't shake—not even a little.

Joanna?

"My lady?" he asked.

Elizabeth snapped back to attention. "Of course the invitation is open, my lord. We are delighted. Aren't we, Izzie?"

"Thrilled," her cousin said, her tone making Randolph's mouth tighten.

He ignored Isabel for most of the meal, which was rather inconvenient, as it forced Elizabeth to do more of the talking than she would have liked.

It was strange. She could talk for hours about Paris with Thom, who'd never been there, but with Randolph, who'd spent time there over the years, she struggled to keep the conversation going. Only when they returned to the subject of music did she finally have a reprieve. Izzie couldn't resist interjecting her opinion, and an enthusiastic discourse— which sounded better than argument—between her and Randolph followed, for which Elizabeth was blissfully excluded.

Her gaze, however, kept sliding to the door.

When the short meal finally ended and Joanna still had not appeared, Elizabeth gave up any pretense of not wondering why and went to find her sister-in-law.

Thom's plan worked better than anticipated. He knew Elizabeth wouldn't be able to resist seeking him out, but he underestimated her irritation.

Thus, when she materialized in camp less than two hours after he'd left Joanna at Holyrood, he was caught by surprise and suffered an unpleasant blow to the ribs from Sutherland's hammer as a result.

He swore and grimaced with pain but didn't let it stop him. Ignoring Elizabeth, who stood near the edge of the practice yard with Helen MacKay doing a horrible job of pretending not to watch him, Thom gave his full attention to the contest with Sutherland and returned the blow with one of his own.

Sutherland grunted from the strike and the battle intensified. Blow after blow was exchanged and blocked, the exertion and effort it took wearing the combatants down to the point of exhaustion. But both men were too stubborn to yield.

The hammer was by far Thom's best weapon, and his most comfortable with on the practice yard. He could hold his own against the elite warriors—even Sutherland and MacKay, who vied for title as the best.

Thom couldn't say he was disappointed that she'd caught him with the hammer in his hand rather than the sword. Compared to most men-at-arms, he was good with a blade—maybe even really good—but compared to MacLeod and the elite warriors of the Highland Guard he had a long way to go.

But training with the Guard had given him a new perspective. The Guardsmen were strong with most weapons, but unlike the training he'd undertaken with Edward Bruce to become a knight, where the focus was on his skill with the sword, these men focused on their individual skill and were valued for it. Each warrior had been picked for what they excelled at, whether it was seafaring for MacSorley, archery for MacGregor, or scouting for Campbell. Thom was being recruited not for his skill with a sword (or a horse, thank God), but for his ability to climb. If he won a place among the vaunted warriors, it would be because he was the best.

Who would have thought that when he was climbing rocks as a lad and his mother was yelling at him to get down, it would someday be his path to greatness?

He had no doubt he qualified, but unfortunately he hadn't yet been able to prove it. The nighttime forays at Castle Rock had failed to identify a possible route up the cliffs. He thought he might have found a way last night, but after spending hours trying to figure out a way to span a twenty-foot section that didn't have useable foot- or handholds, he'd been forced to admit defeat.

It wasn't something he did easily, as the current battle with Sutherland demonstrated. Sweat was dripping from every inch of Thom's body, his muscles felt like jelly, and the hammer seemed to weigh three hundred pounds, but knowing Elizabeth was watching him gave him the added strength to keep fighting, and the edge he needed to win.

In the end it was Sutherland who raised a hand to yield after Thom took him off his feet with a well-timed blow and twist of his foot.

Thom nearly collapsed beside him, but managed to reach down and help the other man to his feet.

"Nice move, Rock," Sutherland said with a wince as he rubbed his neck. "I see you've been paying attention to Raider's lessons."

Thom's mouth twisted. "Maybe a few."

The man with the war name of Ice laughed. "I'd say more than a few, but well done." He clapped him on the back. "Of course, you'll have to best MacKay tomorrow or I'll never hear the end of it."

Thom grinned; the fierce contests between the two brothers by marriage had become legend in the Guard. "I'll do my best."

"Aye, well, just to be sure, I think I'll speak to Lady Elizabeth and make sure she plans to be in camp tomorrow as well."

Thom's smile fell. He was glad none of the other men were close enough to overhear.

"Don't worry," Sutherland said. "I know all about the added incentive of an appreciative audience. If my wife had been watching, I would be the one helping you to your feet." Suddenly he frowned. "Damn."

"What is it?"

"Saint knows as well," he said, referring to MacKay by his war name. "I'll have to make sure Helen is away from camp when you fight him."

The two men looked at each other and laughed.

Thom would have given three months' wages for a warm bath before a fire, but instead he went to the stream to wash before seeking out Elizabeth, who had headed into the infirmary tent with Helen.

Although Thom was glad Elizabeth had sought him out so quickly, he wished she'd done so in a more circumspect fashion. Having her come to him in the middle of camp, surrounded by men who would be very interested to know why she wanted to see him—MacLeod, Douglas, and Randolph, to be specific—wasn't exactly what he had in mind when he'd sought out Joanna.

Knowing he wouldn't be able to keep his wooing of Elizabeth secret without help, he'd gone to Joanna, who'd been only too eager to agree to his plan, despite the fact that she'd be going against her husband's wishes. She seemed to think that Jamie—like his sister—was being willfully stubborn about the matter and would "come around."

Thom wasn't so sure.

But he did have reason to hope that MacLeod might eventually understand and perhaps soften his stance. Although it was hard to believe by looking at the fierce, seemingly emotionless warrior, MacLeod had married for love. From Hawk—MacSorley—Thom had heard the story of the rogue mission MacLeod had led to rescue his wife from English hands—an act that launched the first strike in Bruce's war eight years ago.

Still, Thom didn't underestimate the risk in what he was doing. MacLeod had been damned clear about what was at stake. He didn't want another Alex Seton. Thom had learned of the warrior whose discord with the others (Boyd, in particular) had caused him to leave the Guard. In deciding to pursue Elizabeth, Thom knew he was jeopardizing his future as a knight and his place in the Guard. He was also jeopardizing whatever chance he might have with the widow Rutherford—if she hadn't gone tired of waiting for him.

But he couldn't let Elizabeth go again. What they had together was worth fighting for. He realized what he was asking her to give up to marry him. Nor did he underestimate the difficulties they would face. But he had to make her see that he was worth it—*they* were worth it.

But he also knew he was waging a losing battle against time. The betrothal could be announced any day.

The very thought sent rage surging through his blood. He almost regretted not giving in to their passion on the hill yesterday. It sure as hell would have sped things up. But he wouldn't give her the excuse he knew she was looking for. He didn't want her to marry him because he'd taken her virginity, he wanted her to marry him because she realized she loved him.

Moving quickly, he removed his clothes and walked into the small, knee-deep stream that the men were using to wash. Unable to fully dunk himself, he used his hands to splash the icy water over him and rinse away as much of the grime and stench of practice as he could. It was cold as hell, and he made short work of it, getting in and out in a couple of minutes. Which was fortunate, as he'd barely finished tying his braies when Elizabeth came bursting through the trees that provided privacy from the camp.

"You can't—" She stopped, seemingly unable to find her

tongue. She gaped at him, eyes widening to take in more of the chest she was so blatantly admiring.

He'd been about to pull on his shirt but instead he picked up the black leather chausses he'd been wearing earlier.

"I can't what?" he asked calmly.

She blinked a few times, tearing her gaze from his chest long enough to meet his eyes, only to slide it back to his chest again.

He fought a smile. The lass was clearly flustered.

Good. He liked her flustered.

Finally she shook her head and returned her gaze to his. Remembering what she'd been so eager to tell him, she held up the scrap of parchment he'd left with Joanna. "You can't make this."

He lifted a brow, pretending not to understand. "Jamie won't know it's from me."

"That isn't why."

"Jo said there is a forge near the abbey that I can use—there will be no chance of Jamie discovering what I am doing that way. The sword she wants me to make for him will be a surprise. It's all arranged. I spoke to the smithy earlier, and he's agreed for a small fee to let me use his tools after he is done for the day. I should be able to work for a few hours after my duties are done before retiring for the evening. I will have to clean the forge, but it isn't anything I haven't done before."

She narrowed her gaze, as if she suspected he was purposefully reminding her of all those late afternoons she'd sat and watched him do the same.

Guilty.

"It's not the forge." Her eyes fell to his chest again,

but this time her mouth tightened. "Will you put on your shirt?" ,

Amused, he crossed his arms and gave her a lopsided smile. "Why? It's not like you haven't seen me before. More of me, in fact."

Her cheeks heated at the memory and her eyes seemed to dip against her will.

Hell. Despite the cold, he started to swell and almost regretted teasing her—almost.

More determined this time, she clenched her fists and forced her blazing blue eyes back to his. "The design for the sword is all wrong. It's far too simple. Don't you remember all those discussions we had about design and embellishment?"

"I like simple. What does it matter what it looks like as long as the sword does its job?"

She groaned with the weary frustration of generations of women who'd tried to make a man see something that was obvious to them. "We've talked about this before. You can charge more, for one, and by making something special—something unique—you will create an object of desire and increase your reputation. You need to make a sword worthy of your skill and of Jamie's position. A sword that people will envy."

She'd been preaching the same message to him for years—which is exactly why he'd left the crude drawing for Joanna to show her. Just as he'd known she wouldn't be able to resist finding out why he'd come to see Joanna, he'd also known she wouldn't be able to resist finding him to complain about the design he'd come up with.

She came around to stand beside him, holding the drawing out for them both to see. "There needs to be scrollwork on the crossguard and hilt, which should be covered in silver gilt, with maybe a large ruby here"—she pointed to the tip of the pommel—"there should be a design etched on the blade, and the scabbard should be inlaid with gold and more precious stones."

She looked so outraged he had to fight not to laugh. Instead he acted as though he'd barely heard her and continued putting on his clothes—finally donning his shirt.

"Draw something up if you like," he said, as if it didn't matter to him one way or the other.

She glared at him angrily, clearly annoyed by his indifference. "I will!"

She started to stomp back off toward camp but he stopped her. "Wait. I'll take you back. You shouldn't be walking around camp by yourself."

She shook her head. "Someone might see us. I'm just supposed to be fetching . . ." Her voice dropped off, and she looked around. "There it is! I must have dropped it when—"

She stopped, her cheeks heating again. She quickly ran back to the edge of the trees where she'd first seen him and apparently had dropped the excuse she'd given for heading down to the stream. "I'm fetching a fresh bucket of water for Helen. I volunteered to help her look after the wounded men today."

He lifted a brow, impressed by her resourcefulness. Although he probably shouldn't have been given how often they'd devised ways of being alone when they were young. She also seemed to understand the risk.

"I'll watch you from the trees all the same."

She nodded and hurried back to the infirmary tent, the bucket of water jostling back and forth at her side.

He smiled, wondering how long it would take her to show up at the forge with the drawing.

18

*T*HERE! ELIZABETH THOUGHT with satisfaction as she drew the final scroll on the drawing. *Now* that *is a sword!*

Not for the first time this afternoon, she felt a presence over her shoulder. "Are you done yet?"

She glanced up at a hovering Joanna. "Yes. What do you think?" she asked, handing it to her.

Joanna studied it for a moment before looking back at her in amazement. "It's spectacular. You think Thom can do this?"

"If he can get the materials."

Joanna waved off her concern. "I'll procure whatever he needs."

"It will be expensive," Elizabeth warned.

Joanna just gave her a look. Jamie had become a very wealthy man in the past few years. The cost would not be a hardship, although it might be difficult for Jo to explain to her husband why she needed all that coin.

Elizabeth's mouth twisted. Or maybe it wouldn't be. Her sweet, uncomplicated, probably never told a lie in her life sister-in-law was proving a rather devious fellow conspirator.

She'd already agreed to cover for Elizabeth later when she went to find Thom at the forge and had even arranged a guard for her from among Jamie's men—someone who she thought wouldn't be prone to ask too many questions. The forge was just up the high street from the abbey, but she was taking no chances.

"Thank you again for helping with this, Elizabeth. James will be so surprised."

Elizabeth couldn't resist a wry smile. "He will indeed, especially if he learns who made it. I must admit, I'm rather surprised you were able to get Thom to agree to do it."

"It wasn't so hard," Joanna said with a knowing smile. "I think he has cause to want to improve his relationship with James."

Elizabeth pretended like she didn't know what Joanna meant and folded the drawing into quarters before tucking it in the purse she wore attached to her girdle.

"Are you ready?" she asked, standing. "I want to return these to Brother Richard before I go." She held up the quill, ink, and small knife that she used to cut the tip of the quill and make small corrections to the drawing.

They found the young monk in the scriptorium, and after thanking him, they were heading to the stables to meet the guardsman who would accompany Elizabeth to the forge when they saw Izzie and Randolph hurrying toward them.

"There you are!" Izzie said, her relief obvious. "The earl was waiting in the refectory for you when I came in from my walk around the gardens. I've been doing my best to keep him entertained, but we decided we better come look for you."

In other words, her cousin had exhausted pleasantries and had run out of nonirritating things to say to Randolph. Although if Randolph's expression was any indication, it might be too late.

"You didn't forget, did you?" Randolph asked her.

Elizabeth looked at him blankly. "Forget?"

"We were supposed to go riding this afternoon. I was going to show you Samson's Ribs in the park."

Elizabeth cursed inwardly while pasting a smile on her face. He'd spoken to her about the strange rock formations yesterday. "Of course, I didn't forget, it's just that . . ."

As "I'm sneaking off to see another man" didn't sound like a great excuse, she tried to think of an alternative explanation.

Joanna came to her rescue. "I'm afraid it's my fault, my lord. I didn't realize Elizabeth had other plans when I begged her to help me with an errand. I'm not feeling very well, and you see . . . well, it's a private matter, I hope you understand."

Randolph looked properly discomfited and vaguely panicked that she might try to explain. "Of course. We will do it another day."

"But you've come all this way," Elizabeth said, suddenly—belatedly—struck with a few pangs of guilt. Pangs that grew in number when she noticed the leather bag he carried, which, from the smell of fresh-baked bread, she suspected was stuffed with food. "Why don't you take Izzie?"

It was hard to say who looked more horrified.

"But I should come with you," Izzie protested.

"I should return to camp," Randolph said at the same time.

"It's best if I do this alone," Elizabeth said meaningfully. She gave her cousin a look that pleaded for agreement. *Please*.

Izzie returned the look with one that said she was going to owe her—a lot—but she'd no doubt suspected the source of Elizabeth's dilemma. "I would love to see this rock formation, if you would show it to me, my lord."

Randolph could do nothing but agree. He looked at her cousin for a long moment and then gave her a short nod. "We should not delay; it will be dark soon."

Elizabeth exhaled slowly as the two walked off. It was hard to say between both of them who appeared less eager.

"Thank you for doing this for me, Ella. I didn't mean to cause you any trouble with Randolph."

There was something about the way Joanna said it, however, that made Elizabeth think her sister-in-law wasn't bothered by the idea at all, and indeed might even be happy if this project for Jamie caused plenty of trouble with Randolph and pushed her toward Thommy.

Her eyes narrowed. Was that what this was about? Was this sword just another of Joanna's attempts to push them together?

If so, she had to admit, it had worked. Elizabeth was fully involved; she couldn't wait to see how the sword turned out.

"It was my fault, I forgot about our ride today," she said.

Fortunately, Joanna chose not to comment about that—although much could be said. Instead, she frowned pensively, watching a stiff-backed, tensed-shoulders Randolph lead away an unusually morose Izzie. "Do you think . . ." Her voice dropped off, and she shook her head. "Never mind."

Elizabeth was too distracted to follow up on it. "I hope Randolph doesn't question your man waiting in the stables."

Joanna shrugged. "Even if he does, it won't matter. You are running an errand for me. I did not speak an untruth."

No, but she certainly had left out a few salient details.

Fortunately, there was nothing to worry about. Elizabeth's "escape" from the abbey went smoothly, and a short while later she was pushing open the door of the forge.

She'd forgotten the blast of heat, the smoke, and the smell of burning metal, but the memories hit her the moment she entered.

Thommy was already hard at work and didn't immediately hear her come in, giving her time to observe him as he pulled the red-hot blade blank from the forge and set it upon the anvil to hammer.

She felt a wave of powerful emotions pulling her down a path of bittersweet longing for a time when life was far less complicated. When a friendship between the lord's daughter and the smithy's son didn't matter.

Her heart squeezed. How many times had she come on something like this before? How many times had she come bursting into the forge excited to tell him something? Excited to see him?

So many things had changed, but in that one fundamental respect she was forced to admit they hadn't. She was still excited to talk to him and still excited to see him. Far more so than she'd ever been with anyone else, and far more so than she should be.

If anything, the childhood memories paled in comparison to what she felt now. For now her feelings were complicated by other reasons for excitement. Like noticing the way the linen of his shirt stretched over broad shoulders and powerfully muscled arms as he hammered the hot metal, or noticing the damp tendrils of dark hair at his temple or the bead of sweat running down the hard lines of his cheek and jaw. Or noticing how the wide mouth that had kissed her so tenderly was pressed in a taut line of concentration as he worked.

As a girl, she'd been unaware of the primitive appeal of a tall, handsome, powerfully muscled man who was hot with sweat swinging a hammer before a fire. But she was aware of it now—achingly, painstakingly, *rousingly* aware of it.

Why was she here? Why was she putting herself in temptation's grasp?

She might have turned around had he not looked up and noticed her. The boyishly happy smile that curved his mouth prevented her from doing anything other than just stand there and stare at him with her breath firmly locked in her chest.

He put down the hammer, removed one of the leather gauntlets he wore to protect his hands from the fire, and wiped the back of his hand over his forehead. "That was fast. Finished with the drawing already?"

Elizabeth's mouth quirked. "Aye, well, I wanted to get it to you before you messed anything up."

He laughed and crossed the room to stand beside her. The forge wasn't a large building, and with him standing next to her, it suddenly felt even smaller. He was so blastedly big! The fire that powered the furnace seemed to grow even hotter. She could smell the heat of his body, but it was not an unpleasant scent. Rather the opposite. The faint hint of muskiness brought a sensual edge to the heather from his soap.

"Let's see what you've come up with," he said easily, having no idea of the havoc he was wreaking on her senses—or her pulse for that matter. It seemed to have shot up through her throat.

She pulled out the drawing and handed it to him, feeling unaccountably anxious all of a sudden. She wanted him to like it, she realized.

She need not have worried. His expression shifted from one of study to one of incredulity. "You drew this?"

She nodded.

"Why have you never told me you knew how to draw?" He was frowning at her as if she'd kept something important from him.

She shrugged, inordinately pleased by the implicit compliment. "I didn't know myself. But I was inspired."

He'd turned unusually serious. "This is very good, Elizabeth. Very good."

Her cheeks heated with pleasure, but she couldn't resist teasing him. "You sound so surprised I don't know whether to be flattered or offended."

He grinned lopsidedly. "Flattered. Definitely flattered." He pointed to the etching on the blade. "What is this?"

She turned over the parchment. "I drew a more detailed part of that section here. It's oxen and a castle."

It didn't take him long. "Roxburgh."

She grinned. "Aye, I thought Jamie would like immortalizing one of his greatest achievements on his blade."

"He will indeed," Thom said wryly.

They both knew that James liked nothing more than to have the name of Douglas remembered for generations.

They spent the next half hour going over the details of the design. Thom asking questions and then them discussing alternatives if he thought one of her design elements might interfere with the function.

When they were both satisfied, Thom stepped back. "I should get back to work. This sword of yours is going to take quite a bit of time, and Joanna wants it next week."

Elizabeth nodded, strangely reluctant to go. It had been so nice being with him again like this. She wasn't ready for the moment to end. "Do you mind if I stay awhile?"

∞

Thom stared down at that beautiful upturned face and wanted to tell her she could stay forever.

No longer wrapped up in the discussion about the drawing—she'd surprised the hell out of him with that—Thom was thinking about being wrapped up in other things. Like her legs around his hips as he drove . . .

Hell.

"I'm not sure that is a good idea."

She looked so crestfallen he had to force his arms to his sides so as to not pull her into them. "Why? I just want to watch a little while, I promise I won't get in the way."

"Because if you stay, I'll want to touch you."

She didn't appear taken aback by his bluntness. "Would that be so horrible?"

Her soft voice was like a siren's song, drawing him in. He wanted to answer it. Actually, he wanted to sweep her into his arms, push her back on the table, and ravish her senseless—but he forced himself back from the edge of the precipice.

"Aye, it would. I'm not going to do that while you are letting another man court you—even if he is doing a piss-poor job of it."

She looked mildly offended. "What do you mean?"

He gave her a long, penetrating look. "If you were mine, you can be bloody well sure you wouldn't have time to sneak away to meet another man."

She lifted her chin. "I'll have you know Randolph and I were supposed to go riding today."

Thom tried to dim the hope that swelled in his chest at what she'd unintentionally revealed. "So you could have been with Randolph, but you are here with me instead." He stepped closer, not caring that he might get soot over her fine cloak, took her arm, and pulled her to his leather-apron-covered chest. "Does that not tell you something?"

She looked startled, and then maybe a little cornered. She tried to pull away. "I wanted to get you the design." He gave her a look that told her he knew that wasn't everything. "You are right. I shouldn't be here."

She broke away and headed for the door. But Thom wasn't going to let her go so easily. "You can't marry him, Ella. You don't love him."

She paused for a moment. "Nay, but I *like* him. And there are other reasons to marry—far more important ones."

"Such as fear? That isn't a reason. Don't tie yourself forever to a man you don't love because of things that happened in the past."

She bristled as he knew she would. "You don't know what you are talking about."

"I know you think Randolph's lands and money will protect you from ever having to be poor again. That his position as the king's nephew and one of his chief lieutenants means that no one will ever close a door to you. But there are no guarantees in life, El."

Alarm took away some of her anger. "Are you saying you think Bruce is going to lose the war?"

"No one knows the future. I think he's got a fighting chance, which is a hell of a lot more than anyone else has had, but England is the most powerful nation in Christendom. What I'm saying is that whether Bruce wins or loses the war won't change what you went through as a child or erase those memories."

She tried to brush away his concerns. "That was a long time ago. Yes, it was horrible. But I was a child. I hardly even think about that time anymore. And if you haven't noticed, with his lands restored and the additional rewards from the king, Jamie has become very wealthy in the past few years. I've hardly been suffering."

Thom eased back one edge of her fur-trimmed plaid cloak to reveal the embroidered purse she had tied to her waist. Reaching between them to lift it, he weighed it in his hand. "That feels like a lot of coins to be carrying around town."

"I thought I might go to the market later."

He held her gaze. "So you aren't still saving coins to bury under bushes and rocks?"

Her face went stark white. "What are you talking about?"

"Do you think I didn't know? Christ, you were only a wee lassie when I realized what you were doing. I wasn't going to let you go wandering off unprotected—especially carrying that kind of silver." For a moment he saw a flash of panic in her eyes and understood. "It's all there. I never touched any of it."

She looked away, ashamed. "I never thought you would." Her eyes glistened. "You must think I'm a fool . . ."

He took her chin, forcing her gaze back to his. "I think you were a scared little girl who did what she could to make herself feel secure in a world torn apart by war. And I still think you are scared and trying to protect yourself. But marrying Randolph isn't the answer."

"And you are?"

He stiffened at her tone. It wasn't a scoff, but it had enough attitude to be damned close.

He gritted his teeth but kept a rein on his temper, dropping his hand. "I can't promise you the lands and wealth that would come from marrying Randolph, but I am not without means or prospects. I will be able to provide for you. Perhaps not in the manner you are used to, but we won't be living in a hovel either. And I can promise you one thing—one thing that Randolph will never be able to give you. I can make you happy."

"How can you be sure he won't when there is every reason to believe we will suit fabulously?"

"Why, because he's rich, handsome, and charming? Because he has a handful of castles, speaks French, and knows the same people as you? None of that means shite if you don't want to bed him at night, Ella."

He'd angered her. Her face flushed red and her eyes shot off little sparks of fire. "And you're so sure I don't?"

He knew she was trying to prod him into reacting, but he wasn't going to do it. He wasn't going to push her back against the door and prove it to her. Not that it wasn't *damned* tempting.

But he did back her up a little, closing the distance between them to a hairbreadth. He could practically feel the furious beat of her heart against his chest. "I think the only bed you want to climb into is mine."

She tried to push him back. "You arrogant—"

"Why else are you here alone with me when you know well what happens whenever we are together?" He caught her wrist and wrapped it around his waist so their bodies were just touching. "Why else did you follow me up the hill? You want me, El, just as badly as I want you."

As if to prove the truth of his words, her body shuddered against his. It reverberated through him like a lightning bolt, setting off every primal instinct in his body. *Take her. Make her yours.*

But he couldn't give in. She had to come to him on her own—not blindly with eyes clouded by lust. Not that he didn't intend to use the passion between them to his advantage.

"Does he do this to you, El?" His voice was low and husky. "Does he make your body tremble for his touch? Does he make your breath quicken and your lips part for his kiss?" He moved the pad of his thumb over the velvety pillow of her lower lip, wishing it were his mouth. He wanted to drink her in. He wanted to slide his tongue in deep and taste every inch of her.

He leaned closer, brought his face to the side of her neck, inhaling the soft floral fragrance of the soap she used to wash her hair and blowing softly into her ear. She groaned, melted, and he almost forgot himself—almost.

He slipped one hand under the edge of her cloak, cupping her breast gently in his hand as his thumb rolled over the taut peak. After holding back for so long, he still couldn't get used to being able to touch her exactly as he wanted. "Does he make these sweet little nipples hard? Do you want his mouth on you, sucking you?" She gasped at his wicked words, and he skimmed his hand to her waist to slide between her legs. "Does he make you hot and wet? Do you want him to put his hand right there"—he pressed—"and slide his finger into all that creamy softness?"

The gasp turned to a whimper, a deep whimper that egged him on. He was so damned hot; his body was on fire.

His tongue flicked in her ear. "Does he want to lick you up? Does he want to taste you until you shatter against his mouth?" She froze, and he chuckled. "Does that shock you? That is only one of the things I want to do to you. There are so many things I could show you about pleasure. I want you standing naked before me so I can see every inch of that beautiful body, I want you to ride me, I want to feel your mouth on me."

Her whimpers were coming harder now, and he was not unaffected. The sultry haze he'd spun had wrapped around them both. He'd never talked like this to anyone in his life. But he wanted her to know everything he could bring her—everything she'd be giving up. But he was hard as a hammer, his blood pounding, close to the edge of his restraint.

He molded his hands on her breasts before turning her around and nestling her in the curve of his body. "Or maybe you'd like it from behind." She arched into his hands, her bottom instinctively pressing against his hardness. "Aye, do you like that, sweetheart?" He kept one hand on her breast while the other dipped down in front between her legs, showing her how it would be. How he could pleasure her.

Unfortunately, she was also showing him, and it took everything he had not to move his hips against her and let the friction of that sweet bottom pressing against his aching cock release the pressure threatening to explode from the base of his spine.

He should never have started a game that he knew he could not finish. But, Christ, it felt good. And the knowledge that she liked what he was saying to her . . .

He swore and pulled back.

She stared at him mutely, cheeks flushed, lips parted, and eyes heavy with arousal.

"Marry me and you will have all that and more. I will spend every day for the rest of my life making sure that you never regret it." He took her hand and put it on his chest over his heart. "My heart beats for you, Elizabeth. It has always beat for you. And I think yours beats for me. That's why you'll never be happy with Randolph."

"You're wrong!" She yanked her hand back as if scalded, looking as if she was close to tears.

But in doing so, she gave him his last argument. "Am

I?" He looked down at her wrist, where beneath the edge of the sleeve of her cloak and velvet surcoat he could see the thin layer of brass resting against her wrist. "Then why do you still wear a cheap piece of metal when your wrists could be covered in gold and rubies?"

She didn't say anything for a moment but just stared down at the bracelet as if she'd never seen it before. A lifetime of emotions crossed her lovely features before her eyes lifted to his again. "What you want is impossible, Thommy."

"I know. There is every reason for you to refuse me and only one to say yes."

"What is that?"

"When you know, you will have your answer." He stood back. "You should go."

This time she didn't argue. She put her hand on the door before turning to look over her shoulder at him. "I will be back tomorrow or the next day with everything you need." Seeing his expression, she added, "Don't worry, I won't stay."

"It's not that. I won't be here."

Her eyes rounded in panic that was fantastically revealing. "You're leaving?"

"Only for a day or two. Bruce has a mission for me."

The king had been disappointed but not surprised when Thom told him that even if he attempted to climb Edinburgh—with the result being almost certain death—there would be no way to safely get others up after him. With a surprise attack on the garrison at Edinburgh unlikely—at least from the cliffs—Bruce decided to focus on other missions. The first was an attempt to free a handful of men being held prisoner at Dunbar, another allegedly invulnerable castle located on an "inaccessible" rock. Thom had no intention of disappointing the king again. If it was physically possible, he was going to do it.

Elizabeth's relief that he wasn't leaving was so palpable he told himself it was only a matter of time before she realized the truth of her feelings. "It isn't dangerous?"

"Nay," he lied. "You don't need to worry, I will return hearty and hale before you even have time to miss me."

She looked at him as if she didn't believe him. "You will be careful."

"Always."

Their eyes held and something deep and powerful passed between them. "Then Godspeed, and I will see you when you return."

She could damned well count on it.

19

ELIZABETH HAD PLENTY OF time to think over the next two days. But really there was not much to think about. The answer—the only possible answer—was clear.

Thom was wrong. She wasn't going to marry Randolph because she was scared, she was going to marry him because it was her duty and the smart—indeed the *only* rational—thing to do. Any woman in her position would do the same. He was refined, handsome, charming, and would soon be one of the most wealthy and powerful men in the kingdom. He would bring prominence, added wealth, and prestige to the Douglases. He was the king's nephew, for goodness' sake! She would be a fool not to accept his proposal when it came.

Marry me . . .

The sharp tug in her chest did not lessen no matter how many times the words echoed through her head. Why was Thom doing this to her? He had to know what he asked was impossible. She couldn't marry him. Even if there was no Randolph the gap between them was too wide. Why was he forcing her to hurt him again?

But those were not the only words echoing in her head. Her cheeks heated every time she thought of the way he'd spoken to her. The things he'd said. The things he'd done.

She could still feel the warm pressure of his hand between her legs as her bottom pressed against the steely column of his manhood. Could he really . . . ?

Aye, she knew he could. Just as she also knew he was right: she would like it. She suspected she would like anything and everything he did to her.

Blast him for confusing her! For distracting her. For trying to turn her from her course. How was she supposed to think of anything else when all she could think about was his naughty words and wicked promises?

She wanted him—there was no denying that. But he was wrong if he thought it was enough to make her happy. She would never be happy with the life he proposed—one where she would be ostracized from many of the other nobles. Where the money she'd hidden wouldn't be enough to keep them from the threat of poverty. Where she would be tucked away in some small cottage in a small village with nothing to do. She would go mad.

Randolph and she were perfectly suited. They would get

along well enough. And Elizabeth was determined to prove it. For the first time since arriving in Edinburgh she threw herself wholeheartedly into getting to know him better and enjoying the city, which included Sunday's outing to the market after mass.

Elizabeth was aware of the number of eyes that followed her and Izzie as they made their way through the crowded stalls. It wasn't surprising, given their escort. She imagined it wasn't often that a knight in full mail and arms with entourage strode through mercat cross in Edinburgh. That it was the king's nephew made it all the more unusual, and the excited whispers buzzed through the crowd like a hive of bees. But Elizabeth paid them no mind; she was having too much fun.

It had been a glorious morning, in large part due to Randolph. So far he'd stuffed them full of pies and tarts, bought them more ribbons than they could wear in a lifetime, and made them laugh as he jested more than bargained with the merchants.

Surprisingly, even Izzie seemed to be having a good time. She'd barely spoken two words to Elizabeth when she'd returned from her ride to the park. Deciding that she would rather not be questioned about her own activities that day, Elizabeth hadn't asked what went wrong. Suffice it to say, Izzie and Randolph weren't going to be friends. Elizabeth had been surprised when Izzie had agreed to come along with her today—as had Randolph upon seeing her. But as the day went on, the sunshine and festive atmosphere worked its magic, and whatever tension she'd sensed between them had faded away.

The group stopped to watch a merchant selling apples juggle the fruit high up in the air, the women clapping each time he added an additional piece. When he finally missed at eight, Randolph insisted on buying the whole basket and had one of his men take it back to camp.

"I think I smell plum tarts up ahead," he said as they ambled away from the applemonger.

Both women groaned. "I couldn't eat another bite," Elizabeth said.

"Nor could I," Izzie added, putting a hand over her stomach. "I will not eat another sweet for a week."

Randolph and Elizabeth exchanged a glance and smiled. They both knew what a sweet tooth Izzie had. She would probably be raiding the monks' kitchens in a few hours.

"Well, if not more tarts, perhaps we can find something else you might like?"

He had a knowing smile on his face as he stopped before a jewelry merchant. As Sir Thomas had come straight from the siege camp, he had been carrying his helm under his arm, but he put it down on one of the tables to pick up a cameo brooch. He said something to the merchant she could not hear, and the man appeared very excited when he nodded and pulled something out of the purse he wore at his waist.

It was a bracelet. A very beautiful one. The thick rope of gold was designed in an intricate woven pattern. Every half inch or so was a large stone—alternating rubies and garnets.

Randolph held it out for her approval. "How about this?"

Elizabeth's stomach dropped with something suspiciously like dread. Her heart started to pound. "I couldn't," she said. "It's much too fine."

"Nonsense. It is nothing."

Nothing to him could feed a family for a year or two— maybe longer. But it wasn't just the cost, it was what it signified. A bracelet of gold and precious stones was not a ribbon or a tart. There was only one occasion on which it was acceptable to give an unmarried woman this kind of jewelry, and that was on a betrothal or wedding. Indeed, the giving of jewelry was expected to befit the new bride-to-be's standing.

Sir Thomas was essentially making a public declaration of his intentions.

The irony of him choosing a bracelet did not escape her.

Elizabeth wanted to refuse, but she knew what that would signify. And she did want to marry him. Of course she did. Today had proved they would suit quite well. *Even if I don't want to bed him at night . . .*

Her mouth pursed. The bed part would come later.

So after another polite but halfhearted protest, she allowed him to put the bracelet on her wrist. It was heavy and foreign feeling. And for one ridiculous moment she heard what sounded like the clap of irons ring in her ears.

"Thank you," she managed. "I don't know what to say."

"It is a mere trifle. There will be more—much more— I hope soon," he said with a gallant bow over her hand.

It was just as before on the first night they arrived. It was a perfect moment—or what should have been a perfect moment—but it was almost as if it was for the appreciation of those around them more than for each other. Sir Thomas knew what was expected of him as one of the most renowned chivalrous knights in the kingdom and acted accordingly.

That wasn't to suggest that it was in any way disingenuous or fake; rather that there was no real sentiment behind his actions.

Is sentiment what she wanted? Was it fair to expect from him what she was not demanding from herself?

They visited a few more booths, laughed, and continued to enjoy the bustle of activity around them, but a strange pall had been cast over the day. Indeed, Izzie had grown noticeably quiet.

Elizabeth couldn't claim to be disappointed when one of Randolph's men found him to say he was needed back at camp.

It seemed Edward Bruce, the Earl of Carrick, had arrived from Roxburgh to meet with his brother the king on the way to begin the siege at Stirling.

Making his apologies, Randolph left without delay, promising to see them at the abbey later. "If I know my uncle Edward, he'll expect a feast."

"Good thing it's a Sunday," she replied with a teasing smile.

A smile he returned, recalling their earlier conversation. "I hope we shall have more to celebrate in the next few days?"

She did not miss his meaning. He was going to formally propose the betrothal. Oh God. "Perhaps," she managed in what she hoped he mistook for shy rather than uncomfortable.

The two women visited a few more booths—with Elizabeth purchasing some fabric for a new veil—before deciding to return to the abbey. It would be time to get ready for the midday meal soon.

"Is something wrong?" she asked Izzie as they walked down the hill, two of Jamie's men following discreetly behind them.

"Of course not."

"You seem upset."

Her cousin shook her head. "Surprised perhaps. I thought you might be reconsidering."

"I know you do not like him."

"I like Sir Perfect well enough. What's not to like?" she teased, repeating Elizabeth's words from Blackhouse with an added note of dry amusement. Elizabeth tried not to laugh at Sir Perfect, not wanting to encourage her sobriquets—no matter how funny they were. "I merely thought you might be interested in someone else."

Elizabeth sighed deeply in almost a groan. "Is it that obvious?"

Izzie's mouth turned wryly. "To me and Joanna, perhaps."

"Please do not tell me I will be hearing it from you as well."

Izzie laughed and shook her head. "No." But then she sobered. "Do you love him?"

That was a question she wouldn't ask herself. She *couldn't* love him; it was as simple as that.

Izzie would understand. She wasn't like Joanna—she was practical like Elizabeth. "That's an unusually sentimental question from you, cousin."

"Maybe I'm feeling unusually sentimental."

Elizabeth gave her a challenging look. "Does it matter?"

"I suppose not," Izzie admitted. "The match with Randolph is a good one—an excellent one. The one with your smithy's son is not just a bad match, it's a horrible one. There would be consequences." She gave a sharp laugh as if something had just occurred to her. "To refuse Randolph for a smithy's son? Lud, I almost wish you could do it just to see Sir No-One-Has-Ever-Refused-Me's face. I can't say that I wouldn't enjoy seeing him knocked down a peg or two."

They stopped talking as they walked through the gate, noticing a commotion in the yard. A group of riders had just ridden in.

Elizabeth's heart jumped, realizing who they were. She'd

suspected Thommy's mission was with the Guard, but it wasn't until she saw him standing to the side with a couple of the men laughing that her suspicions were confirmed. But a quick glance at the group and a longer study of Thom told her much more. It was just the members of the Guard—no other men had gone with them. And the close camaraderie among the group that had always struck her . . . it extended to Thom.

They *are* recruiting him, she realized. And she had to admit the realization awed her a little. Was Thom really good enough to fight beside some of the best warriors in Christendom?

It seemed so.

She was proud of him. Immensely proud of him. But she frowned, suddenly realizing something else. He'd lied to her! If he was on a mission with the Guard, she could be sure it was dangerous.

She was tempted to stomp over there and berate him for the untruth—and indeed might have done exactly that—if someone else hadn't beaten her to him.

She stopped in her tracks as a woman, a very beautiful dark-haired woman, rushed forward to greet him. She must have come out of the refectory.

Thom had his back to her, so Elizabeth couldn't see his expression, but the one on the woman's face was enough to make her heart seize in an icy hold.

It was the coy, flirtatious look of a lover—or a woman determined to make him so. She looked at Thom as if he belonged to her and she couldn't wait to get her hands all over him.

"Who is that?" Izzie asked at her side.

Elizabeth shook her head. "I don't know." But her heart squeezed; she suspected it was his widow.

❦

"Lady Marjorie Rutherford," Edward Bruce confirmed later at the midday meal. Elizabeth was pretending not to listen to his conversation with Jamie. "She grew tired of waiting for MacGowan so she decided to take matters into her own hands, so to speak. I do admire a woman with determined hands." He laughed at the ribald jest, ignoring the censorious look from the abbot a few seats away, and took another long drink from his goblet, which from the loudness of his voice—and his jests—Elizabeth suspected contained something stronger than wine.

The jest might be inappropriate, but it was painfully accurate. The beautiful widow did indeed have determined hands. Every time Elizabeth glanced at the table across the aisle, the "lady" had her hands on him. Nothing too overt: a brush of the arm, a graze of his fingers, a "thoughtless" touch of his shoulder when he said something that amused her, which seemed to be often, and one time when her hand had slipped beneath the table to—Elizabeth would swear—rest on his leg.

Something akin to panic had taken hold. A cold sweat broke out on her brow, her pulse spiked, and nausea swam in her stomach.

She didn't know whether she wanted to throw up or march over there and toss the woman off the bench— probably a little of both. It was the anger—which was both unjust and irrational—that made Elizabeth realize the emotion was jealousy.

If only the woman wasn't so pretty. But with her dark hair, tilted eyes, and striking red lips, she had a sensuality and exotic appeal with which Elizabeth couldn't compete.

Her reaction—her distraction—hadn't gone unnoticed.

"Lady Elizabeth?" Randolph said. "Are you unwell?"

She shook her head. "Perhaps a bit tired." She smiled. "And maybe all those tarts are catching up to me." He looked so concerned she regretted the jest. "I was only teasing. Now, you were mentioning something about your new lands in Badenoch?"

In addition to the earldom of Moray, Randolph had been given the old Bruce lordship of Annandale, the Comyn lordship of Badenoch, the lordship of Man, and the lordship of Lochaber. Only the king's brother had been granted more. The knowledge should please her—thrill her. She couldn't have hoped for a better marriage.

I can make you happy . . .

"Aye, Lochindorb Castle is quite an impressive structure—Comyn might have chosen the wrong bed to lie in, but he did know how to build a place to put it—but the interiors will need some modernizing. A woman's touch, if you will. I hoped that you might be willing to help?"

The panicked feeling came over her again and this time it had nothing to do with Lady Marjorie and her wandering hands. She knew what he was asking and knew what she should say. But the response was harder to form than it should be.

Unable to meet his gaze, she looked down. "I would be honored, my lord." Her voice came out far softer than she intended.

If he noticed her tentativeness, he did not let on. He had the answer he wanted. She had as good as agreed to marry him. She half-feared he might get down on his knee and make some spectacular proposal right in the middle of the meal. Horror washed over her. Good gracious, would he do that?

She was saved from finding out when Joanna asked him

a question. "Did I hear some prisoners were freed from Dunbar, my lord?"

"Aye," Randolph said. "Although I'm not sure you are supposed to know about that. But it seems your friend MacGowan is a highly skilled climber. I'd wager the English think those men flew out of the prison tower." He explained that the prisoners at Dunbar were kept in the base of a tower on a separate rock from the rest of the castle, accessible only on one side. Unless—that is—you approached from the sea and climbed the rock.

Elizabeth wasn't sure she wanted to hear anything else. God in heaven, he could have been killed! Just what Thom considered dangerous she didn't want to contemplate.

"Too bad he can't climb Castle Rock," Randolph added with a wry smile. "Maybe we could finally put an end to this accursed siege."

Elizabeth had felt the blood leech out of her face at his words, which she prayed were in jest. "But an attempt to climb Castle Rock . . . that would be akin to suicide, my lord. It is unassailable."

Thom wouldn't be so foolish, would he? Please tell me that is not why the Guard is recruiting him?

She chanced a glance in his direction, feeling a stab in her chest when she saw the two dark heads bent together, obviously deep in conversation.

Randolph grew at once contrite, offering her a comforting smile. "I didn't mean to cause you concern. I'm not that eager to best your brother's recent escapades at Roxburgh. Climbing that rock isn't an option. We'll have to take the castle the old-fashioned way—with patience. Though I wish I had more of it."

He'd obviously mistaken the source of her concern, but he'd eased it all the same.

She smiled back at him. "I'm relieved to hear it, my lord." She could say something about finding ways to distract him from his boredom, but flirting with him felt . . . wrong. Instead, she said, "I'm sure they will surrender soon enough. From what you've said they cannot hold out much longer without being re-provisioned. And I think you have men in place who will see that doesn't happen?"

Randolph met her gaze, knowing to which men she referred. Men whom no one was supposed to know about. "Aye, I do indeed."

"After the past few years, I think you deserve a bit of a reprieve from battle. Perhaps you might look at the siege as a rest for what is to come?"

He gave her a long, appreciative look. "That is indeed a good way of looking at it. I shall try to remember that when I'm cursing the mud, endless trenches, and staring at closed gates willing them to open." He looked down the table. "Where is your cousin today? I hope she is not feeling the ill effects of our morning indulgences?"

Elizabeth shook her head. "She said she had some letters to write and would join us later." She frowned, realizing the meal was almost over. "I guess she had more to do than she realized."

"Your cousin writes?"

"Aye, as well as a scribe. My aunt insisted. I was fortunate to share her and her brothers' tutor for a while, although I'm afraid I never took to learning as well as Izzie. If she had been a lad, my uncle said she could have gone to Oxford."

He laughed at the very idea. A woman scholar? "Strangely, I can almost see it. She is unusual, your cousin."

It almost sounded like a compliment.

She would have said as much if she hadn't caught

movement out of the corner of her eye. A corner of her eye that had unconsciously been fixed on the other table.

She sucked in her breath. Thom and his widow were leaving. Together. Alone.

Her lungs felt like they'd been filled with molten lead. She felt the crazy impulse to go after them, and knew her thoughts must have been plain for all to see when Joanna asked her a silly question with a worried look on her face and a quick shake of the head. *Don't.* "Do you have any plans for the afternoon, Elizabeth?" her sister-in-law asked.

"Nay."

"Good, I was hoping you might help me with something."

Elizabeth took her meaning. She could find Thom later—at the forge.

But it was small consolation for wondering what he was doing right now.

This was harder than he'd anticipated. Thom had asked to speak to Lady Marjorie privately, but now that they were outside the abbey guesthouse—where the king and others were staying—he didn't know how to start.

To say that he'd been shocked to see her was an understatement. No doubt Edward Bruce thought he was doing Thom a favor in escorting her here, but it had only made the situation more awkward.

He knew he wasn't going to be able to marry Lady Marjorie—marrying her for the wrong reasons would be just as bad as Elizabeth marrying Randolph—but he would rather not have had to tell her that after she'd journeyed all this way to see him expecting a proposal.

Bloody hell.

"Perhaps we should sit?" he suggested.

There was a bench looking over the side garden where he led her, and they both took a seat. He'd put some space between them, but she eased up next to him and put her hand on his arm—the lass seemed to have a dozen of them. He had to force himself not to shift out of her hold.

"There is no reason to be nervous," she said coyly. "I think we both know why we are here."

He smothered another curse, his mouth falling in a grim line. This was only getting worse. He had to put a stop to it before she said something that would cause her embarrassment.

Perhaps something in his expression alerted her. A hard glint appeared in her eye. "If I didn't know better, I might think that you aren't happy to see me."

"I was surprised," he hedged. "But I'm always pleased to see a friend."

She leaned closer to him, putting her hand on his thigh. *High* on his thigh. "I would have thought we were rather more than friends."

The invitation was clear. But he wasn't going to take it. Instead, he removed her hand. "I'm afraid all we can be is friends."

She drew back, her eyes narrowing. She was a beautiful woman, but again the feline resemblance struck him. If she'd hissed and arched her back, he wouldn't have been surprised.

"I don't understand. I thought we had an understanding."

"I'd hoped that something more might be possible, but I'm afraid that is no longer the case. I apologize if I led you to believe otherwise."

"You apologize?" she practically spat, her face tight with outrage as she sprang up from the bench and turned on him. "I cannot believe I'm hearing this. *You* no longer think anything more with *me* is possible? Do you have any idea the honor I was doing you to even consider such a match? If anyone should be doing the refusing it is me. You should be on your knees thanking God for your good fortune."

Thom felt his face flush and jaw clench, but he took her verbal lashing and didn't try to defend himself. She had a right to her anger, and by most standards she was probably correct.

A cold, calculated gleam appeared in her slitted eyes. "Am I to be told the reason for this sudden change of heart?"

"It would not be fair to you. I do not care for you in the way that you deserve."

She looked at him as if waiting for him to finish a joke. After a long pause, she laughed. "By God, you are serious? Love isn't what I wanted from you." Her eyes slid over his body in a way that could not be misunderstood. She wanted him in her bed. He flushed again in anger, feeling not unlike a stallion at market. "You really are a peasant, aren't you? Only peasants think of love as a reason for marriage."

The disparagement struck surprisingly hard. Thom stood, his jaw as hard as a block of ice. "Again, I apologize for any trouble I might have caused you. But I think it better if I take my leave now."

Before he said something they both regretted.

She stepped to the side to block him. "You are a fool. She'll never marry you." His gaze shot to hers. "Aye, you didn't think I noticed the way you stared at James Douglas's precious little sister every time she turned away? I noticed, but I didn't give it a second thought. Do you know why? Because there was no reason. There is no way in Hades the illustrious Lady Elizabeth Douglas would consider marrying someone so beneath her—and even if she was inclined to lower herself, her ambitious brother would never allow it. By God, she's rumored to be almost betrothed to the Earl of Moray!"

He felt the muscle below his jaw start to tic. "You are wrong."

He didn't specify about what, hoping she would take his answer and let it go.

Instead it only seemed to increase her amusement. "I almost feel sorry for you. When you realize what you gave up . . . all for *nothing*." She shook her head, her smile telling him she was relishing the thought. "You could have been a knight, living in a castle, ruling over substantial lands, and instead you will be lucky to still be carrying that sword if Sir James gets wind of your intentions. He'll probably see that Bruce kicks you out of his army and sends you right back where you came from."

Thom wished he could say she was wrong about that, too. But she wasn't. Douglas's reaction wasn't something he hadn't considered—he just hoped to be in a better position with the Guard and have help from Jo and Elizabeth when the time came.

Finally, she stood back to let him pass. "Go. We are done here. And do not bother coming to find me when you realize she will not have you. I wouldn't take you if you came crawling on your knees naked and begging—not that I wouldn't appreciate the view." Her eyes scanned him again. "What a waste."

What a narrow escape.

Wanting to put the unpleasant exchange behind him, Thom was only too eager to do as she bade. But her words stayed with him longer than he wanted them to.

20

IT WAS LATE afternoon before the opportunity arose for Elizabeth to sneak away. Jamie had been uncharacteristically slow in leaving them to return to his duties after the midday meal. He was supposed to accompany the king on a hunt, and for a while, she feared he might beg off to stay at the abbey with them.

"Go," Joanna said a few minutes after he finally left. "Take this." She handed her a small but heavy bag containing the stones and gold that could be melted down to use on the sword. "I will cover for you if James returns while you are gone."

Elizabeth looked at her uneasily. "Are you sure? I don't want to cause any trouble between you."

Jamie had been asking a lot of questions about their plans for later today. It could be nothing, or it could be he suspected something. Elizabeth didn't want to put Joanna in an awkward position or force her to lie to her husband.

"Let me worry about James. I know you are anxious to see that Thom has everything he needs."

They both knew that wasn't the reason for her anxiousness, but Elizabeth appreciated the pretense.

After leaving the guesthouse, she met Simon, the same young warrior who'd taken her last time, in the stables and made the short walk to the forge.

This time Thom heard her when she entered. He looked

up but didn't stop what he was doing right away, finishing hammering out the metal while it was hot before sticking it in a barrel of sand to cool. He was already working on the tang.

He stared at her, obviously waiting. Remembering the reason for her visit, she pulled the bag with the gold and jewels and handed it to him. "Here. Jo was able to purchase everything that you requested."

He didn't bother looking inside, but nodded and put the bag on the workbench. "Thanks." They stared at each other in silence for a few moments. "If there is nothing else, I should get back to work."

That was all he had to say? He wasn't going to explain . . . *anything*? Her hands fisted in the wool fold of her cloak. In her flustered state, she blurted, "I saw you with Lady Marjorie."

One brow arched in mild surprise. "Aye."

Elizabeth gaped at him. "Aye? That is all you have to say?"

"What else am I supposed to say?"

She marched across the room toward him, stopping a few feet away with her hands on her hips. "She's the widow you were planning to marry."

"Is that a question?"

She gritted her teeth, feeling the distinct urge to stomp her foot. How could he be so nonchalant? Was he being purposefully obtuse? He was acting as if nothing had happened. As if he hadn't spent a couple of hours with another woman practically on his lap—as if he hadn't left with her . . . *alone*.

"No, it is not a question." Her foot might have indeed moved up and down. "Yes, it's a question. Are you marrying her?"

He wasn't kind enough to betray any of his thoughts

with his expression. God knew, he probably thought she was a crazy woman—she was certainly acting like it.

"Is there any reason I shouldn't?"

"I thought . . ." *Marry me.* She flushed. "You don't love her."

There was more of a question in her voice than she intended. This time both brows shot up in surprise. "I wasn't aware that was a prerequisite for marriage. Indeed, I seem to recall you telling me differently."

The challenge in his eyes never let up. Only when she shifted her gaze to the floor did it release her. She stood there miserable, wanting to cry, but unable to deny his words.

He was right, and she had no right to interfere. Lady Marjorie would make him a good wife. She didn't want him to change his plans for her, did she? What about Randolph?

His accusations at Roxburgh came back to her. Was she still thinking of him as hers? Still assuming he would always be there for her?

He wasn't hers, and she shouldn't be here.

He crossed the distance between them, lifting her face to his with the back of his finger under her chin. His voice was husky and tender. "I'm not marrying her, Elizabeth."

She scanned his face, blinking back tears. "You're not?"

He shook his head. "I told her circumstances had changed, and it was no longer possible."

"Oh."

"Aye, oh."

The sense of relief that she had no right to feel was overwhelming. She stared into his eyes, not knowing what to say.

His hand was still holding her chin, but one thumb had moved over to caress her lower lip. "I want you, sweetheart.

Only you. And my marrying Lady Marjorie for the wrong reasons when I love someone else would be just as wrong as you marrying Randolph. Besides, in case I wasn't clear the other night, I've already asked you to marry me."

"Thom, I . . ." *Can't.* But before she could get the word out to refuse, his mouth was on hers, and all she could think was that nothing had ever felt more right.

Their first two kisses had been an explosion of passion, their third a tender expression of love, and this one . . . this was a lesson in seduction.

He wooed her with his lips and enticed her with his tongue, the long, slow strokes licking deep into her mouth, hinting and promising so much more.

He teased, he tempted, he gave her a taste of the carnal pleasures that awaited her if she succumbed before slowly retreating.

It was a masterful dance calculated to drive her mad with wanting.

It worked.

She couldn't get enough of him. His heat. His taste. She wanted to sink into the warmth of his embrace and never let go.

She gripped him harder, sliding her arms around his neck to press her body more fully against his.

She moaned.

He groaned.

The kiss intensified. She could feel his control slipping away. Feel the gentle seduction take on a harder, more purposeful edge.

He cupped her bottom, lifting her against him, and the feel of him big and hard, pounding between her legs and against her stomach, turned her warm and melty and filled her with a wicked craving. A craving for more.

Aye, this is what she wanted. All she wanted.

Whether he would have given her what she desired, she would never know.

The door opened. "MacGowan, I . . . ah, hell, sorry."

They'd jumped apart at the sound of the door, but it was obvious from Lachlan MacRuairi's expression that it had been too late. He'd seen more than enough to know what he'd interrupted.

Thom had instinctively moved around to shield her from the other man's view, but there was no hope of him not recognizing her.

"I'll come back," MacRuairi offered.

"Just give me a few minutes," Thom said.

But the discovery, like a bucket of icy water, had brought Elizabeth harshly back to reality. Perhaps for the first time, she realized exactly what she was risking by being with him.

Everything.

If MacRuairi told anyone . . .

The flames in her cheeks were doused in icy sheets of panic.

"No!" Elizabeth exclaimed, and then less adamantly explained, "I was just leaving. Joanna is waiting for me. I was running an errand for her. It's a secret. From James."

She realized she was babbling and snapped her mouth closed.

"I'm sure it is," MacRuairi said wryly, an amused quirk twisting his lips. When her cheeks flamed again, he added, "Don't worry. Douglas won't hear about your secret from me."

Understanding what he meant, she breathed a sigh of relief. He wouldn't say anything.

Disaster had been averted . . . but for how long? She couldn't keep doing this. Why couldn't she stay away from him? Were her feelings deeper than she realized? Were they making her lose sight of what was important?

She felt the sudden urge to run.

Thom caught her arm before she could flee. "We aren't done here, El."

She looked up at him, feeling her heart squeeze with a fierce jumble of emotions—the biggest of them longing. She longed for him with every fiber of her being. "I know."

He would find her later, and they would settle this. Once and for all.

Apparently satisfied, he dropped her arm and let her go.

Thom muttered a curse as the door closed behind her. That wasn't the way he'd hoped the afternoon would end.

He'd almost had her, damn it. She'd been so close to admitting her feelings for him. Hell, if he'd known all it would take was seeing him with another woman, he would have tried that a long time ago.

He still couldn't believe it: she'd been jealous. Didn't she realize the only woman he'd ever had eyes for was her?

But he hadn't been able to resist teasing her. God knows, she'd been torturing him enough the past week with Randolph, and letting her think he might be considering marrying someone else for a few minutes seemed a pittance by comparison—especially as it forced her to confront her own feelings. They'd been right there on the edge. A little push was all she needed.

Although he had to admit he'd gotten a little off track with that kiss. Maybe he should be glad MacRuairi had interrupted them.

"Sorry about that," MacRuairi said. "But here's a suggestion. Next time you think about putting your life and future on the line by touching Douglas's sister, you might want to latch the door. Christ, anyone could have walked in here."

Thom winced, knowing he was right. "Aye, I'll try to remember that."

MacRuairi gave him a hard look, although with Mac-Ruairi there wasn't really anything else. "I won't ask what the hell you are doing."

"Good."

"It isn't any of my business," he finished as if Thom hadn't spoken. "But I hope you realize what's at stake. You fit in well—and God knows we need that after Seton. But if Douglas or MacLeod finds out . . ."

Thom's jaw hardened. "You don't need to say anything else. I understand."

"Do you? I hope to hell she's worth it."

She was, but that wasn't any concern of MacRuairi's.

He was surprised how much it meant to hear Mac-Ruairi say that he fit in well. He did, he realized. No matter how unlikely that seemed. He was the only lowborn among them, but in the Guard it mattered what you did, not who you were. They were chiefs, chieftains—even an heir to an earldom—but there was no rank among them, no retinues to follow them, and no pretense. If Chief asked one of them to dig in a cesspit, they would without hesitating.

This is what he'd been searching for, Thom realized. Being a part of something that mattered. Something he would achieve on his own merit. Somewhere along the line winning a place in the Guard had become the most important thing to him—even more important than earning his knighthood.

"I assume you are here for a reason?" he asked.

"Two, actually. I wanted to talk to you about a bracelet

Helen mentioned that she'd seen Lady Elizabeth wearing. I believe you made it for her."

Not knowing what he was getting at, Thom nodded. "It was a gift a long time ago."

"Helen said the cuff design was unique, and I was hoping you might be able to make something similar for me."

"For your wife?"

MacRuairi smiled. "Not exactly." When he described what he wanted, Thom had an inkling of who it might be for. He'd both seen the tattoos the Guardsmen had on their arms and heard mention of the Ghost—a spy they had in the English court. But he hadn't realized the spy was a woman.

"Can you do it?" MacRuairi asked.

"As soon as you get me the materials. It shouldn't take me long."

"Good, but take as long as you need. I want this to be . . . it's special."

Thom nodded; he understood. "You said there were two reasons?"

"Aye, it seems we won't have the night off after all. The king has a mission for us."

They'd only just returned from their last mission earlier today, but Thom wasn't complaining. Every mission gave him a chance to prove himself and brought him closer to a place in the Guard. It seemed as if everything he'd ever wanted was in his reach. But at times he felt like he was walking on a razor's edge—one wrong move and everything would come tumbling down. "When do we leave?"

"You have a few hours, but you might want to pack an extra apple or two for whatever horse you end up using— we've a long ride ahead of us."

Thom muttered a foul curse, and MacRuairi shook his

head. "I didn't think anyone was as unnatural as Saint on a horse. But you put him to shame."

Thom told him to bugger off, and then shook his head. "How the hell did an Islander become such a good rider anyway? Aren't you supposed to travel in ships?"

A flash of white suggested MacRuairi was actually grinning. "I'm good with those, too. Just wait until we go out west for your training. I hope you know how to swim."

Thom looked at him, realized he was serious, and cursed again.

MacRuairi wasn't just smiling now, he was laughing. "You are going to have a fun two weeks. MacLeod calls it Perdition, but for you it might be worse than hell."

Thom wasn't even going to ask. He was sure he didn't want to know but would find out soon enough. The Guardsmen seemed to be assuming his place on the team. But until MacLeod came to him, he wasn't going to take anything for granted.

After MacRuairi left, Thom finished working the tang of the sword and cleaned up. He'd hoped to finish his conversation with Elizabeth tonight, but maybe this was better. He'd give her the night to think. But it was time to put this uncertainty between them to rest. For all their sakes, she needed to make a decision.

Elizabeth practically ran back to the abbey—Simon had to hustle to keep up with her—but she couldn't escape the truth. It was the only thing that explained her inability to let Thom go, her seeking him out, her sinful conduct, and the jealousy and panic she'd felt over Lady Marjorie. Her love for Thom wasn't just friendship. Nor was it just lust.

She *loved* him.

But as she had said to Izzie this morning on their way back from the market, what did it matter? Did her grand epiphany really change anything? Was the realization that she loved Thom enough reason for her to refuse Randolph, or did it just make the whole thing more difficult and painful?

Marry me . . . I can make you happy.

Could he? Would it really be so horrible? Was she letting a difficult period in her childhood and what *might* happen influence her decisions too much?

Oh God, what was she going to do? She felt precariously close to tears as she thanked Simon for accompanying her and turned to leave him at the gatehouse.

She needed to find Joanna. At this time of day—close to dusk—her sister-in-law was probably still with some of the other court ladies embroidering in Lady Margaret and Matilda Bruce's solar. The king's young sisters had been given the largest chamber, and that is where they gathered when their duties allowed. The women staying at the abbey were working on a new banner for Bruce that would be carried into battle when the English came in June.

But before she could find her sister-in-law, her brother found her. He was storming out of the guesthouse where they were staying as she was about to go in.

"I was just going to look for you," he said. "Where the hell have you been?"

"Running an errand for Jo."

His face darkened. "That's what she said. Where?"

"I can't tell you," she hedged. Drat, she knew he'd suspected something! "It's a secret."

"That's what she said as well." His eyes narrowed on hers. "But I'd bet my favorite sword that you are both lying."

"It isn't a lie," she said, her mouth setting in a stubborn line. *Technically.*

"You went to go see MacGowan, didn't you?" She didn't say anything but just stared at him mulishly. "Should I go ask Simon?" he threatened.

Elizabeth knew she was caught; she wasn't going to have Jamie intimidating poor Simon because of her. "Leave him out of this. He was only doing his duty."

"I knew it! Damn it, Ella. What are you doing? And why the hell are you involving Jo and having her lie for you?"

"We weren't lying, and I didn't involve her in anything."

He gave her a hard look. "Aye, if I know my wife, it was probably all her idea. She's made no secret of her desire to see you and Thom together. No matter how many times I tell her it's impossible."

"Is it really so impossible?" Elizabeth asked quietly.

Her question seemed to take him aback. By the time he answered, much of his anger had faded. "Do you really need to ask me that? Randolph spoke to me earlier. He has offered for you, and I have given my permission. He will formally ask you tomorrow." He paused. "This is what you wanted, El. I thought you'd be happy."

"It is what I wanted," she said. "At least what I thought I wanted."

"And now you don't?"

She gazed at him pleadingly, the big brother to whom she'd always looked up. "I don't know."

He folded her in his arms and held her, giving her comfort as he had so many times in their tumultuous war-torn youth—especially after the death of their father.

After a moment, he pulled back. "I don't need to tell you how good this match with Randolph is—hell, it's obvious. You'll be wife to one of the wealthiest, most powerful men in Scotland. But that isn't the only reason why I want you to marry him. Randolph is a good man, Ella. One of the best I've ever met—don't tell him I said that," he added as an aside dryly. "I wouldn't see you with someone who I didn't think could make you happy." His ironic choice of words was not lost on her. "Don't you like him?"

She shook her head. "It's not like that. I like him very much." *What's not to like.* "It's just that . . ."

His mouth tightened. "MacGowan."

She nodded.

Something in his expression changed. For a moment she glimpsed the Black Douglas, the man who had struck terror in the heart of the enemy who whispered his name in the same breath as the Devil. "Has he touched you, El? If that bastard has compromised you in any way—"

Knowing there were some things her brother would never understand, she cut him off quickly, "He has not compromised me." That was true. "Or touched me in any way that was improper." That was maybe a little less true. His eyes narrowed, noting her careful language, and she added, "You know him, Jamie. Thom would never treat me dishonorably."

He studied her face before relenting. Sitting back on the bench, he smiled. "Aye, MacGowan has always had a fierce streak of honor and nobility in him. At times when we were young, it was bloody inconvenient. You should have seen him when he found out about Jo." He rubbed his jaw. "Christ, I don't think I've ever been hit that hard."

"Thommy struck you?" she said in an awed tone. Of course they'd been in brawls in their boyhood, but for Thom to hit his lord as a man . . . James could have had him punished severely if he'd wanted to. "Why?"

Suddenly, he looked uncomfortable—as if he regretted speaking so freely. "He thought I'd wronged Jo. He was right."

Elizabeth held his gaze for a moment. She'd always

wondered what had happened between her brother and Jo a few years back—right around the time Thom had left— but from the bits and pieces she'd picked up over the years, she had a fairly good idea.

Perhaps her brother would understand about compromising and touching more than she realized. Not that she'd chance confiding in him. Thom might not have compromised her, but she doubted Jamie would consider the distinction enough to prevent him from killing him.

"I should still kill him," Jamie said, echoing her thoughts. "I told him to stay away from you. He has no business confusing you."

"He has asked me to marry him."

Jamie exploded off the bench beside her. "That overreaching bastard. He had no right! I told him I would never sanction a match between you."

Elizabeth grabbed his wrist, stopping him from probably fetching his sword and going after him. "Even if I loved him?"

He stilled. "It isn't enough, El."

"It was for you and Jo."

"This is nothing like Jo and me. Thom is the son of a smith. No matter how high he climbs in Bruce's army, he can't change that. Nothing will ever make him suitable for you. *Nothing*. Christ, by comparison Jo is a princess, and you've seen how difficult it has been. You've seen the derision, the scorn, and heard the comments. People like us marrying beneath us . . . it offends the community's sense of place. Of right and wrong. Of honor and duty."

"And do you regret it?"

He didn't hesitate an instant. "Not for a minute. But make no mistake: the situations are not the same. Joanna was the daughter of a baron, and I am the Lord of

Douglas—powerful in my own right with the ability to make myself more powerful with my place in the king's army. The match with Thom will not just be seen as 'unfortunate,' it will be seen as an embarrassment—as something shameful. He will never be accepted. Many of the people who welcomed you into their homes will no longer wish to socialize with you." Seeing her expression, he softened his tone. "I'm not saying this to hurt you, I'm trying to protect you. Right or wrong, I want to make sure you know exactly how it would be, what your life would be like if you marry so far beneath you. I cannot in good faith condone such a match. Without a tocher or land of his own, how will you live? I'd wager MacGowan doesn't have more than a few pounds to his name right now. Will you go back and live in Douglas with his father?"

Elizabeth wished she could say she didn't blanch, but she did. She remembered the small, dark house she'd visited all those years ago. The soot-stained wattle-and-daub walls, the rush-covered floors, the clothes strewn all about, the dirty dishes . . .

"I don't need to tell you that there is nothing romantic about poverty—you've experienced it for yourself. How long do you think your love will last when instead of running a castle—a dozen castles—you are cooking, cleaning, and counting every penny?" She thought of the bags of coins she had hidden—counted pennies—and her stomach knotted. "Maybe MacGowan will become a knight, and earn some land along the way, maybe you'll be able to afford a couple of servants in a few years. But it won't be easy."

She knew that. She'd been there before. Poor, shunned, and . . . miserable.

He gathered her hands in his and gave them a squeeze, undaunted by her continued silence. "I know you, El. You

love the excitement of court, being surrounded by edu-
cated, accomplished people, the bustle of the cities and big
castles, and all the luxuries of wealth because you know
what it is like to be without them. Can you see MacGowan
at a salon in Paris or sitting at the king's table during a
feast in one of the royal castles? He doesn't even speak the
same language." French was the language of the nobles.
"Being tucked away in a small village somewhere will kill
you. Is that what you want?" He let the question linger for
a moment. "Randolph will give you everything you've ever
dreamed of. Do you really want to risk that for an uncertain future with MacGowan?"

The picture he painted had tapped into her darkest
fears. Could she be happy like that? Would his love be
enough?

It might . . .

Perhaps sensing her hesitation, Jamie dove in for the
kill. He wielded the one blade that focused everything into
sharp reality. "What about children, El? What kind of life
would you want for them?"

Children? Elizabeth stared at him in horror. She hadn't
thought about children.

Or maybe she hadn't wanted to think about them.

All of a sudden she felt ill. Jamie's question unknow-
ingly evoked painful memories. Memories of those dark
days when no one would help them.

It must have been so difficult for her stepmother, alone
with three children to protect—two of them barely more
than babes—but she'd hid it so well. The formidable
Lady Eleanor, who throughout their difficulties had never
showed a hint of fear or vulnerability, had seemed the
strongest person Elizabeth knew.

But even her seemingly indestructible stepmother had

been broken by Hugh's cries of hunger. Elizabeth would never forget seeing Lady Eleanor's tears and worse, her helplessness and fear in the face of her baby's empty stomach. She'd given up, and were it not for the bag of coins provided by the abbess that took them to her uncle at Bonkyl, they would have ended up in an almshouse.

A baby. Children. How could Elizabeth best protect them? What duty did she have to them?

She looked up at Jamie wordlessly, her heart feeling as if it was being squeezed in a vise. Tears shimmered in her eyes, but there had only ever been one answer.

21

THE NEXT DAY when Randolph came to her with his proposal, Elizabeth accepted. The stark contrast between Thom's heartfelt offer and Randolph's businesslike one perhaps made it easier to bear. There was no confusion; she knew exactly what she was doing. This wasn't romance, this was duty, security, and advancement. The things she'd always wanted.

Jamie had sent for her just before the midday meal. He was in the abbot's private solar with Randolph, but as soon as she arrived, he left.

After offering her a seat on a bench, Randolph began in a formal, no-nonsense tone she'd never heard from him before. "Lady Elizabeth, I am sure it comes as no surprise that your brother and I have been discussing the possibility of an alliance between our families. As you know, my uncle has bestowed many new lands on me of late, and it is well past time that I had a wife to help me run them and to sit beside me at the high table." He gave her a small smile, as if the concession to the impending doom of his bachelorhood should please her. "Your brother assures me that you have been trained well in your duties, and everything that I have seen bears this out. You are undoubtedly the most beautiful woman at court, charming, and will be an asset to my career and future. I can think of no reason why we will not suit." She frowned. Had he been looking for one? "With your brother poised to hold much of southern Scotland, and my holdings in the north and midlands, the connection between our families will create a formidable alliance. Your brother has provided a generous tocher, with which I am very pleased. Indeed, all the important details in the betrothal contract have been worked out."

All the important details but one, she thought wryly. Namely the minor little matter of her agreement. But why shouldn't he take that for granted? Only a fool would refuse him, and he knew it.

"If you are amenable," he continued, "we can sign the betrothal contract tomorrow."

Amenable? For all of the gallantry and emotion in Randolph's proposal, he might have been discussing the sale of cattle at market. Coming from one of Scotland's most renowned knights, a man known for his courtly graces and chivalry, the proposal was almost ridiculously unromantic. Shouldn't he be dropping down on one knee and spouting allusions to the heavens and her beauty?

Unable to resist, she found herself asking, "And what am I to receive in this bargain, my lord?"

She was mostly teasing, but he answered matter-of-factly, clearly appreciating her businesslike attitude. "You will become one of the wealthiest women in the kingdom, and gain a royal connection—as will your children. You will be chatelaine of five castles—at current count—and act in my stead when I am away. You will receive five hundred merks as part of your terce on our marriage, and on my death, you will receive the rest: one-third of our property at that time."

Elizabeth was glad she was sitting or she might have slid to the floor. All thoughts of teasing fled. She stared at Randolph in white-faced shock. Five hundred merks was a small fortune, and one-third of their property? It was the maximum a widow might be provided, and well beyond what she could have anticipated given his vast wealth. Whether Randolph was alive or dead, she would be a very wealthy woman.

She had what she wanted: her future and that of her children's was secure.

Seeing her expression, he gave her a wry smile. "Aye, your brother was a tough negotiator. He made sure you were well provided for—no matter what happens."

"I don't know what to say," she said, still reeling.

"Yes seems somehow fitting," he said with another half smile.

She stared up at him, the simple word sticking in her throat. She thought of Thom as she'd last seen him working at the forge, a little sweaty, face streaked with soot, wearing a simple leather apron and breeches, and more sinfully attractive than any man had a right to be. She thought of his expression as he'd cradled her face in his hand, and the way her chest had swelled until her dress felt too tight. She thought of his mouth on hers as he'd kissed her, and how her body had melted against his as if they belonged together.

I love you. I will always love you.

She pushed the memories away, reminding herself as she'd told Jo not so long ago that she wasn't a romantic. Love alone wasn't reason enough to marry. Duty, security, family, power, and alliances—those were what was important. She'd always seen the bigger picture. People like her just didn't marry whomever they wanted. Her marriage had to have a purpose, and personal happiness wasn't it.

Taking a deep breath, she looked up to face Randolph. "Yes. What else can I say, but yes."

If he noticed the odd wording of her response, he gave no indication. He nodded. "I will inform your brother. He will be pleased. I know he is anxious to have this matter settled."

Elizabeth was sure Jamie was. But what of Randolph, was he pleased?

She couldn't tell from his expression—which seemed unusually unreadable—but she thought he must have something else on his mind. The siege perhaps?

With the matter decided there was nothing left to do but celebrate. The betrothal was announced at the midday meal to a resounding cheer and a steady stream of congratulations from the well-wishers who passed by the high table throughout the meal.

If the mood seemed a little subdued, Elizabeth attributed it to the season. There were only so many toasts that could be raised before the abbot during Lent—not that the king and James were letting it stop them. They, and many of the men from Randolph's retinue, seemed intent on extending the celebration well into the evening.

Sitting at the high table between the king and her soon-to-be husband, Elizabeth plastered a brilliant smile on her face and did her best to appear as she should: happy, excited, and honored by her good fortune.

It was harder than it should have been. It would have been impossible had Thom been there. The thought of him watching her—watching *this*—made her feel like squirming.

But apparently he and the Phantoms were off somewhere again. She'd wanted to find him after she'd accepted Randolph's proposal to tell him her decision in person before he heard it from someone else—no matter how much she dreaded hurting him again, she owed him that—but Jo said he had left the night before.

His wasn't the only absence from the day's festivities. Her cousin had also begged off. Izzie had claimed to be coming down with something and wanted to rest to be ready for tomorrow's betrothal ceremony. Elizabeth hoped she was all right.

At least Joanna was here, seated beside Jamie. But Jo's forced cheer almost made Elizabeth wish she wasn't. Her sister-in-law's reaction upon Elizabeth telling her the news had been a congratulatory hug that was perhaps a tad too tight and a heartfelt wish for happiness. She was clearly disappointed but not surprised. Elizabeth didn't know whether that made her feel better or worse.

Only once had she tried to say something, but Elizabeth had quickly cut her off. "Please, Jo, this isn't easy for me. Don't make it harder to do what I must."

Joanna had looked at her, no doubt read the truth in her eyes, and nodded. But Elizabeth could feel her sadness.

As the meal dragged on, she noticed that Randolph seemed unusually quiet. Their polite small talk had petered out after the third course. He smiled and laughed at the jests directed his way from the men at the table—which grew increasingly bawdy as the afternoon wore on—and raised his glass along with the others, but she couldn't help noticing that he didn't seem to be drinking much.

She'd assumed he wanted this match as much as her brother did. When she'd first arrived in Edinburgh, she was certain he did. But in the past week there had been a subtle shift, and for the first time it occurred to her that she might not be the only one who had needed persuading.

It was a disconcerting thought.

When she finally excused herself, pleading a need to prepare for the betrothal ceremony tomorrow morning, she knew she wasn't imagining his relief. His insistence on walking her to the guesthouse, however, instigated a fair number of ribald remarks, which she pretended not to hear.

But her heart started to beat nervously. Was that what he intended? She thought he was merely looking for a way of escape, too. But they were as good as betrothed now, and there was one thing he'd yet to do.

Why did the thought of kissing him fill her with dread?

Conscious of the eyes upon them as they left the refectory, she couldn't prevent the blush that stained her cheeks.

The blast of cool air upon exiting seemed a welcome relief. The meal had indeed gone long; it was already dusk. Other than a few monks moving about, and a handful of guards patrolling the gate and yard, the abbey was quiet— and peaceful.

They walked in silence to the guesthouse. Elizabeth was beginning to relax, thinking that he truly was just intending to escort her back, when he stopped suddenly. "This is ridiculous."

"It is?" she asked.

"Aye. There is no reason for this awkwardness between us. We are friends, and that does not have to change because we will be married."

Not sure what he was getting at, she said, "My lord?"

He raked his fingers through his hair. "I'm not doing a very good job of this. All I want to say is that I think we understand one another. We know where we stand. This match is a good one for both of us; we do not need to pretend anything else just because we will be sharing a bed."

Her eyes might have rounded at his blunt speech, if it didn't occur to her that he was flustered. There was something oddly charming about one of the most vaunted rogues in Scotland being flustered. And even though it was awkwardly put, she understood what he meant. It actually relieved her to hear him say it—there were no expectations on either side. "I agree, my lord."

"You do?" He immediately brightened and heaved a sigh of relief. "I'm so glad to hear you say that. I worried you might be one of those lasses whose head was filled with romance and faerie tales."

When I get old I'm going to marry you.

She pushed aside the memory—she'd only been six, for goodness' sake. She hadn't known any better. "Far from it," she assured him.

"I knew *you* weren't the type of woman to make unreasonable demands." It almost sounded as if he was referring to someone in particular. He smiled. "Perhaps it is best if we just get it out of the way."

Now her eyes did widen. "My lord?"

He laughed. "I did not mean the bedding, I meant a kiss." He reached down to cup her chin. Every instinct cried out to pull away. To tell him no. To tell him she couldn't do this.

But she had to. She stood there frozen as he lowered his mouth to hers. Just before his lips touched hers, he said, "And don't you think it's time you called me Thomas?"

∞

Light was already falling by the time Thom and the Highland Guard rode into camp. After spending most of the last twenty-four hours in the saddle, all he wanted to do was wash the dirt off him in the river and crawl under his plaid for a few hours of sleep.

"Where is everyone?" MacLeod asked the captain in charge—one of Randolph's lesser household men.

"Still at the abbey celebrating. I imagine they'll be there some time yet."

"Celebrating?"

"Aye. The earl has announced his betrothal."

As Thom was busy trying to avoid his horse's teeth as he dismounted and untied the bag from his saddle, at first he didn't think he'd heard him right. It wasn't until he felt everyone's eyes on him that he realized what had been said.

"Betrothal?" he repeated with surprising evenness for a man who felt like a poleaxe had just clobbered him across the chest. His expression gave no hint to the devastation that was taking place inside him.

"Aye," the young captain said, not picking up on the sudden tension in the air. "To Douglas's sister."

It took everything Thom had not to cross the distance between them, lift the man up by the throat, and call him a liar. Had he truly believed what he'd said, he might have done just that.

But he didn't believe it. Not until he stood at the entry of the refectory, looked over the sea of celebrating occupants, and met Jo's pitying gaze did he know it was true.

He staggered, feeling as if the world had just tilted and everything he knew was sliding away from him.

There had to be some explanation. She wouldn't marry someone else. She loved *him*.

He had to find her. But from the two empty seats beside the king, he realized that both she and Randolph had already left.

It didn't mean anything necessarily, but his heart began to pound like a sword banging on a targe anyway.

He started to leave, but Jo stopped him. "Thom, wait!"

He turned, his spine as rigid as a steel rod, and said through clenched teeth, "Tell me it isn't true. Tell me she hasn't agreed to marry Randolph."

Jo flushed; it was clear she couldn't do that. "She tried to find you, but you were gone."

"Is that supposed to make it all right?"

She bit her lip and shook her head.

"Where is she?"

Jo hesitated. "She was tired and retired a little while ago."

"At her own party?"

"She had some things she wanted to do for tomorrow."

She seemed to be preparing him for something. "Tomorrow?"

"The betrothal ceremony."

For the second time in the space of a few minutes he staggered. Once those vows were uttered she'd be lost to him. He didn't know why he was surprised, but he was. "Your husband isn't wasting any time, is he?"

Joanna winced but didn't bother trying to deny it; they both knew it was true. Now that she'd agreed, James Douglas wasn't going to take any chance of letting his sister change her mind.

Thom swore and turned to leave again.

"Wait, where are you going?"

He looked down at the arm she'd latched onto. "To find Elizabeth so that she can tell me herself."

"I'm not sure that's such a good idea. Why don't you wait a little while—maybe have something to drink?"

He knew why she was stalling him. "She's with Randolph, isn't she?"

She nodded, and he swore again.

Joanna tried to stop him, but he wasn't capable of listening to reason. He left her standing in the entry as he stormed off across the yard toward the abbey guesthouse.

It was nearly dark when he caught sight of the shadowed figures in the garden. He slipped behind the pillar of the arched walkway, watching from the shadows. But hiding wasn't necessary, the fine lord and lady facing each other in the beckoning moonlight seemed to only have eyes for one another.

He stilled, every muscle in his body tensing as if preparing for battle. He sensed what was going to happen even before Randolph's hand moved to her face. Thom's moved to the hilt of the sword at his side. He'd never felt the urge to kill so powerfully.

But something stayed his hand. The need to torture himself? The urge to see if she could go through with it?

Push him away. Tell him no.

She did neither. She let Randolph tilt her face to his and then his mouth touched hers.

Thom flinched, the stab of pain as hot and searing as a blade straight from the forge. But he couldn't turn away. He forced himself to watch even as rage exploded through his body and a red haze dropped like a thick curtain over his vision. But it was the fire in his chest that hurt the most.

It didn't matter that there was not a hint of passion in

the chaste brush of lips, or that it was over as soon as it began. The betrayal cut deep and hard.

She'd let another man touch her—a man she had agreed to marry—and Thom felt like he was being ripped to shreds all over again. He felt like that young boy looking up at what he couldn't have.

He couldn't have let this happen, damn it. Not again. It was different this time. She wasn't blind and unaware of her feelings for him anymore. She wasn't a clueless young girl. She loved *him*—and he would prove it to her.

Elizabeth felt a chill sweep behind her neck right before Randolph kissed her.

Nay, not Randolph, *Thomas*. The horror of his given name hit her for the first time. Dear God, she would be calling her husband by the name of the man she loved. Every time she spoke Randolph's name in intimacy, she would be thinking of another.

If that wasn't enough to cast a pall on the moment, she had the distinct sensation of being watched.

It distracted her enough that she barely noticed the press of Randolph's mouth on hers before it was gone.

"There," he said, as if he'd finally completed an unpleasant task. "Now that wasn't so bad, was it?"

It was . . . nothing. She felt nothing. Had she not known earth-shattering, she might have thought it pleasant enough. But, as there didn't seem to be a really good way of answering what seemed more a rhetorical question, she merely gave him a tentative smile.

Glancing around, she could see that they were alone and the hair at the back of her neck relaxed.

"Now that we have that out of the way, we need not

worry about it tomorrow, and we can get back to being friends. How does that sound?"

A genuine smile turned her lips. "It sounds wonderful."

And it did. It was all so perfectly reasonable and civilized. There was no need for awkwardness, no need for pretense. They didn't love one another, nor did they need to to have a successful marriage. Mutual respect, honesty, and friendship—that was enough to make her happy.

Of course it was. She was doing the right thing. No more than what countless noblewomen had done before her. Why should she be any different?

22

DESPITE HER NEWFOUND clarity, Elizabeth couldn't sleep. Perhaps it was the excitement of tomorrow? If the emotion fluttering wildly in her chest felt more like fear than excitement, she told herself it was only natural. The signing of the betrothal contract and the exchange of vows were nearly as binding as marriage. Breaking it wouldn't be easy, and at the very least would require a hefty payment of recompense.

It was well after midnight when she admitted defeat in finding sleep. Slipping out of her chamber past a sleeping Izzie and the two of the tiring women who'd accompanied them, Elizabeth headed down the single flight of stairs.

Fresh air would help. As a young lass she would have climbed to the roof, but since the simple pitched roof of the guesthouse wasn't accessible, she headed outside. Perhaps a turn about the courtyard would help to settle her?

There would be no stars to look to tonight. The blast of misty cold air hit her as soon as she opened the door, which she did carefully so as not to alert anyone to her nighttime outing.

She was glad for the extra plaid she'd thought to take from her bed to go over her night rail and thick fur-lined dressing robe, but it was still cold enough to almost make her reconsider. The pebbles dug into her feet through the thin soles of her slippers as she walked along the path. A very light dusting of snow had spread over the hard winter ground, as she could feel icy dampness seeping into the soft leather around her toes.

Maybe this wasn't such a good idea. She didn't want to catch a chill.

She started to turn around when someone grabbed her from behind. She was too shocked to scream at first, and by the time she recovered, she recognized who it was.

Strangely she wasn't that surprised that Thom had found her tonight. When they were growing up, he'd always seemed to sense when she needed him. Or rather when she was restless and couldn't sleep. She didn't need him . . . did she?

He'd wrapped his arm around her waist and held her snug against the hard—the very hard—shield of his body. It was the same way he'd held her when he'd talked about doing all those wicked things to her from behind, and she would know the feel of him against her anywhere. Just as she would know the scent of leather and soap and the warmth of his spicy breath against her ear.

"Second thoughts?"

She stilled at the menacing sneer in his tone. "Aye," she said, her breath slightly uneven—from the cold, of course. "It's too cold to be outside tonight."

With a low growl, he pulled her in even tighter. The air in her lungs escaped in a hard gasp.

"That isn't what I meant, and you know it. Did you not wish to tell me something, *my lady*?"

Elizabeth felt her pulse leap as the blood started racing through her veins. *He knows.*

She was almost glad he was holding her from behind, so she didn't have to see the hurt and anger in his eyes as he looked at her.

"Nothing to say?" he demanded.

Elizabeth knew he was angry—and had a right to be—but she wasn't going to let him intimidate her. She twisted out of his arms and turned to face him.

She nearly took a step back. Good gracious, he *was* intimidating. Every muscle in his body seemed drawn up and flared, and his expression was every bit as dark and menacing as his voice, but it was his eyes that jolted her. They pinned her with a fierce intensity she'd never experienced before. She felt like a misbehaving heathen being brought before a panel of inquisitors: guilty, condemned, and about to do penance—or be burned at the stake.

She took a deep breath and forced her gaze to meet his. She hadn't done anything of which to be ashamed. She'd been honest with him about her plans. "What would you like me to say? You obviously know I've agreed to marry the earl. I'm sorry you had to find out like this. I would have told you myself, but Jo said you were away."

"Did you not think you owed me an answer first? Did I not deserve an explanation before you agreed to marry someone else?" The dark expression cracked, revealing a flash of his tormented emotions. "Damn it, El, I saw him kiss you."

The blood slipped from her face, her chest pinched in horror . . . and guilt. "Oh God, Thom, I'm sorry. It . . ."

What could she say? It didn't mean anything? But it did. It meant everything. She was marrying someone else, and they both would have to accept that.

She drew herself up and took a deep breath. "I did try to tell you the other day, but you didn't want to hear it." He'd kissed her before she could finish her refusal.

It was obvious he still didn't want to hear it. "What if I'd come back tomorrow? It could have been too late."

It was already too late.

He must have seen the resolve on her face. "You can't marry him. You don't love him. You love me."

She didn't say anything.

He looked shocked. "You aren't going to deny it?"

She shrugged. "My feelings don't make any difference."

He stared at her in disbelief. "Are you telling me you love me, and it doesn't matter?"

A gust of wind made her shiver. She drew the plaid tighter around her shoulders as she stared up at him, not knowing what to say.

He swore and led her into the closest outbuilding—which happened to be the stables. The pungent scents and sultry air enveloped her. Perhaps the smell would be distracting? Though Lord knew it hadn't been distracting enough last time. *Last time . . .*

Don't think of that.

Sliding the door behind them, he said, "It will be warmer in here. The smell could be better, but at least you will be out of the wind."

"I should go."

"Not until we are finished."

"We are finished. That's what I've been trying to tell you."

"How can you say that?" He reached down and cupped her face in a big, callused hand that seemed to swallow her up. "Christ, sweetheart, you just told me you loved me."

The tenderness and happiness in his gaze made her chest tug hard against her ribs and nearly stole her breath.

She looked away. "It isn't enough."

Even if she yearned for it with every fiber of her being.

The thumb that had been gently stroking her cheek stopped. "You are wrong, it is everything. No wealth or position in the world will ever make up for what is in here." He moved her hand to his heart and covered it with his own. "I know this is difficult for you. I know what I am asking you to give up."

Elizabeth felt a flicker of anger spark inside her. "Do you? I don't think you have any idea." He was living in some kind of romantic fantasy where love was the only thing that mattered. But love wouldn't put food in her belly or a roof over her head. Love wouldn't provide for her children's future. Love wouldn't bridge the gap that separated them in society's eyes and make him an acceptable husband. "My duty to my family—my *only* duty—is to make a good marriage. So in addition to ignoring that, you are asking me to give up wealth, position, and security, for what kind of life? Have you given any thought to how we will live? *Where* we will live? Because I can assure you that without my tocher those bags of coins I saved won't last long."

His mouth fell into a thin white line. "We don't need your brother's damned money—although I'm not surprised the bastard would punish you for marrying me." It wasn't punishment; it was not approving. "I told you I would be able to provide for you. I have some coin saved."

"Coin that you will need if you are to become a knight," she pointed out.

She could see his jaw clamping down harder. The muscle below his cheek started to tic. Obviously he didn't appreciate the dose of reality any more than she had from Jamie. "And enough for a place to live. We may need to live simply for a while, but it will not always be so. I can't see the future and give you all the answers you want, but I can tell you I will do everything in my power to see that you have the life you want. Hell, if that means living in Paris, I'll do my best to get you there."

She couldn't prevent one corner of her mouth from lifting. "You would hate it there. Everyone speaks French."

His mouth quirked at the shared jest. But he sobered quickly. "Don't you see? None of that matters. If you were by my side, I wouldn't care if they were speaking Greek. I would find a way to make it work." He paused. "Do you remember when I asked you to jump to that tree?"

She nodded. How could she ever forget? It was one of the most terrifying things she'd ever done in her life.

"I'm asking you to do that again. I'm asking you to believe in me—to have a little faith. I'm asking you to jump."

She wanted to. God, how she wanted to. Part of her wanted to believe that he would always be there to catch her. That love would be enough. But the bigger part—the more practical part—knew that she needed more. She needed certainty. Thom had said there weren't any guarantees. Maybe not, but Randolph was as close to one as she could hope to find. "I can't."

His face darkened with anger and frustration. "You mean you won't."

She didn't argue.

"I would give up everything for you," he said fiercely.

Elizabeth bristled; that wasn't fair. "Which is easy to say when you are not the one giving up anything."

His face turned white. "I never thought to call you a coward, but if you go through with this—if you agree to marry a man you don't love for the wrong reasons because the thought of marrying me is so terrifying—that is what you will be, and you will get no better than you deserve."

She flushed. "Don't threaten me."

He grabbed her arm and pulled her toward him. "If I thought it would force you to accept the truth, I would do a hell of a lot more than threaten."

"What truth?"

"That if you agree to marry him tomorrow you will regret it for the rest of your life. That every time he takes you in his bed, you will wish it were me. That no other man will ever make you feel the way that I do. That you are mine and have been since the first time you kissed me."

He brought her a little closer, letting her feel the heat and hardness of his body. Letting her feel how perfectly they fused together. How the contact was enough to set off every nerve ending in her body and fill her with a desperate longing.

His eyes darkened as he lowered his mouth to hers. Tantalizingly close. Achingly close. So close that she could taste the spice of his breath on her tongue and feel the warmth of his lips consuming her.

"Should I prove it to you? Should I strip off your clothes, lay you down on that hay over there, and make love to you until the only word you can say is my name over and over as you cry out your release?" He covered her breast with his hand, molding it gently but possessively. As if to prove his point, her nipple peaked at the contact. She arched deeper into his hand and was unable to bite back the little moan of pleasure or the flush of heat that washed over her.

"Would you stop me? Would you tell me no?" He dared her to answer. "And if I took your innocence, what then, Elizabeth? Would Randolph still have you, or would you be forced to marry me?"

She sucked in her breath, staring at him wild-eyed. He wouldn't do that . . . would he? Thom was too noble to seduce her. She didn't need to ask herself if he *could*. She knew the answer. She could no more hold back her desire for him than she could hold back the waves from crashing upon the shore.

He must have seen the fear in her eyes and released her. "Don't worry," he said with a bitter sneer. "I may not have land or a title, but I am not without honor, nor do I share society's view of my worth. Good enough to fuck isn't good enough. I deserve more."

He was right. He did. More than she could give him.

Without another word, he was gone.

"I, Elizabeth, will take thee Thomas to wed . . ."

Thom flinched inwardly at the name—the irony cruel and biting. *It should be me.*

Though his expression betrayed nothing, MacKay knew.

"You don't need to be here," the big Highlander whispered at his side.

The Guard, along with what seemed like half the city, had gathered in the refectory to witness the betrothal ceremony. Although Douglas and Randolph would have signed the contracts this morning in private—probably in the king's presence due to the importance of the alliance— the betrothal ceremony was being held in public before the abbot. It didn't need to be, but it added to the significance and solemnity of the occasion. Douglas wasn't leaving any doubt about the binding nature of the agreement.

"Yes, I do," Thom said.

MacKay gave him a long look and then nodded. "I understand. I've been where you are right now. It won't help. There is only one thing that will, but that will have to wait."

Nothing would help, but Thom nodded anyway and forcibly turned back to the ceremony taking place before him.

Elizabeth had never looked more beautiful, and never had that beauty left him so cold. She looked every inch the regal ice princess in her fine silvery light-blue gown (blue being the traditional color of purity), with her hair covered by a silky veil of the same color and secured by a magnificent circlet encrusted with enormous diamonds. No doubt it was a betrothal gift from Randolph. Every time she moved or a streak of sunlight hit her, she glittered. She was that perfect rare jewel again, and he was the little boy looking up into the blinding magnificence of what would never be his.

What now belonged to the equally blindingly magnificent man at her side. Randolph was also outfitted in his finery—his mail gleaming, his surcoat bright and colorful—every inch the faerie-tale knight of bards' tales. To complete the magnificent picture, the happy couple was flanked by the king on one side and Douglas on the other.

Douglas glanced over his shoulder, his gaze meeting Thom's for a long pause before turning back.

Both Douglas and Jo had been eyeing Thom uncertainly ever since he'd walked into the building, as if expecting him to do something rash. Jo's gaze he couldn't meet—the pity would be too much to bear—but Douglas's . . . Douglas's he met full on. Thom had had years of holding his tongue and perfecting stony indifference, and he used it now to pretend none of this mattered. To pretend that every minute he was forced to stand here didn't feel like his skin was being flayed off and nails were being driven deeper and deeper into his bones.

He'd lost her. He'd fought for her, and it hadn't made a damned bit of difference.

But their fears were for naught. Thom wasn't going to do anything rash. He wasn't going to do a damned thing but sit here and watch.

He'd done everything he could last night.

As hurt and angry as Thom had been after his middle-of-the-night confrontation with Elizabeth, there still had been a part of him that didn't think she'd actually go through with it. A part that thought she would wake up and suddenly realize that she loved him enough to stand down her demons and jump, trusting that he would always catch her. That she could put her faith in him. That no matter how low his birth or the rank that separated them, he would do whatever it took to give her a good life and make her happy.

But standing there, hearing her say the vows that would bind her to another man, seeing her hold out her hand for him to slip on the betrothal ring, Thom knew he was as much a deluded fool as Lady Marjorie had called him. Worse, a deluded *naive* fool.

He'd thought that once she realized she loved him, everything else would fall into place. He'd thought love would be enough. That it would make up for a few castles, fine jewels, and low birth.

But he'd been wrong. Very wrong. With each damning word, with each torturous moment of this farce that passed, she was showing him exactly what was important to her.

And it wasn't him.

He held out a flicker of hope until the last minute. But when Randolph lowered his head and touched his lips to hers in yet the second kiss Thom had been forced to witness, a kiss that sealed the bargain between them, it was the final betrayal—the final act that cut her out of his heart forever.

He *would* have given her everything. Maybe it was easy to say when he didn't have the stake she did, but it didn't make it any less true.

But it hadn't been enough.

The flicker was extinguished for the last time. Inside he went cold, dark, and empty. There was nothing left of the love he'd once felt for her. She was no longer his; she belonged to another man.

He couldn't even hate her. He understood why she'd done what she did. To just about everyone in this room, she had made the right decision. Choosing him was the "wrong" one. But it didn't make it any easier to bear.

He thought she would love him enough to defy society's dictates and her brother's wishes. He thought she would give up the promise of great wealth for a more modest future. He thought she would fight for him as he would have for her. He thought that the strong, spirited girl he'd fallen in love with would face the demons of her past, not hide from them.

But maybe he'd asked for too much. Maybe it had been unrealistic—*naive*—to expect that she'd give everything up when all he had to offer her was himself. He wasn't even a knight yet.

But in the ashes of what remained of his heart, a sense of finality emerged. To hell with her. If she didn't love him enough to fight for him, if she couldn't see that the worth of a man did not lie in bags of gold, castles, or titles, it was her loss.

MacKay and Sutherland tried to make him leave, but he refused. He would do this, damn it. All of it. So when the Guard finally filed before the high table during the long meal to wish the happy couple congratulations, Thom was among them.

He didn't flinch, didn't steel himself, and didn't avoid meeting her gaze. He bowed before her, and with all sincerity wished her happiness. "I hope you find everything you ever wanted."

She gazed up at him, pale and stricken, obviously not knowing what to say or do. Finally she stuttered, "Th-th-thank you."

He would have moved on and left it at that if he hadn't glanced down and seen the thin edge of brass under her sleeve.

His muscles went so rigid they might have turned to ice. For one maddening heartbeat he wanted to reach down, rip it off her wrist, and throw it into the damned fire behind them.

She must have sensed the danger, because she inhaled a gasp and wrapped her hand around her wrist.

But she needn't have been alarmed. As quickly as the flash of rage had appeared, it fled. His expression was perfectly impassive as he looked her in the eye and said, "I think you should probably remove that now."

Before she could respond, MacKay had shuffled him forward.

As soon as they were out of earshot, the big Highlander slapped his hand on Thom's back and said grimly, "I think that's enough of a flogging for tonight. It's time to find that help."

Help turned out to be amber liquid that burned like fire as it went down his throat. For the first time in his life Thom drank himself to oblivion. MacKay and Sutherland—and maybe a few others (his recollections were hazy)—got him good and drunk.

But he did remember one thing. It had been some kind of contest—the Guardsmen were always challenging each other over something. Thom recalled looking up from his flagon of *uisge beatha* to see a blade flying over his head. It stuck in the waddle-and-daub wall of the alehouse the men had taken him to. Another dagger had followed . . . and another. Apparently they were trying to strike a mark and playing a game of who could get closer. But that wasn't what mattered, for an idea had penetrated the drunken haze.

MacKay was right. The drink did help—at least until Thom woke up. But by then, he knew what he had to do.

23

EVERYTHING WAS PERFECT. Elizabeth had to be the most fortunate woman in Christendom. It was the celebration the likes of which she'd always dreamed. She was seated next to the king—who would soon be her uncle by marriage—in a beautiful gown, drinking the finest wine from the royal feasting cup (a jewel-encrusted mazer made of gold!), eating off silver plates, with silver spoons and salt dishes in every direction. Even though it was Lent, her belly would be full. Who in their right mind would refuse a life such as this? Was it so wrong to not want to struggle?

Elizabeth wouldn't admit she'd made a mistake, not even when a cold sweat broke out over her skin and her heart raced so fast she thought she would pass out during the ceremony, or when she couldn't meet Joanna's eyes throughout the feast, or when her nauseous stomach wouldn't let her take more than a few bites of food, or when no amount of wine drunk from the gilded mazer or heat from the fire would warm the chill inside her, and especially not when her heart squeezed through the vise of her throat as Thom came forward to offer his congratulations.

What had she expected? Understanding? Forgiveness? That things would stay the same? Maybe not, but not this either. The look in his eyes had cut her to the quick, and the first vestiges of true panic fluttered in her chest. It was as if she had looked into the cold, emotionless gaze of a stranger. The man who'd held her in his arms and touched her so tenderly and passionately was gone—as was the love she'd always sensed, maybe at times taken for granted, and finally admitted that she returned.

It was at that moment that the full import of what she'd done hit her. What did it matter if the cup she drank from was gold if everything tasted like ash? She'd wanted to call him back. But what could she say? She'd made her decision. *Wrong. Coward.* She wanted to put her hands over her ears to block out the offending voice in her head that wouldn't quiet.

Instead she donned a mask of happiness and slid off the bracelet, tucking it into the purse at her waist. Thom was right: it was time to put the past behind her.

This marriage was what she wanted.

The smile on her face was so brilliant she almost convinced herself that she was happy.

The meal was barely over before she threw herself into the

wedding plans. There was so little time to waste. The wedding was to take place at the abbey in three weeks—a few days after Easter and the end of Lent—and there were many details to which to attend. Every important noble in the country would be there, and Randolph and the king intended to make it the grandest celebration his young reign had yet to see.

Wasn't it wonderful? How fortunate she was! What little girl didn't dream of a faerie-tale wedding fit for a . . .

Princess.

Her chest pinched. She had to stop doing this. She had to stop thinking about him. She knew just what to do to take her mind off it.

Jamie had given her an unlimited budget for purchasing new clothes and shoes—what Jo called his guilt money—and Elizabeth didn't waste any time in spending it. The very next morning she dragged Joanna and her cousin to seemingly every cordwainer, clothier, and haberdasher in Edinburgh. By the time they returned to the abbey they were exhausted, and the merchants on the high street had quite a bit more silver in their purses.

Elizabeth had piles of lace and beaded trim, ribbons of every color, veils, purses, chemises, designs for new slippers to think about, and stacks of colorful fabric for new gowns that were now strewn across her bed.

"What do you think of this?" she asked, holding the long swath of blue to her neck. "Have you ever seen such beautiful silk? The merchant said it was the finest he's ever seen. It's all the way from the Far East, not Spain or Sicily."

"It was certainly priced as if Marco Polo had carried it back along the Silk Road himself," Izzie said dryly. She'd recovered from her illness, although she did seem a bit more wan than usual. "I think cousin James might have a few regrets when he gets back."

Jamie had left this morning on a mission to nearby Stirling to help Edward Bruce with the siege.

"I think it's very beautiful," Joanna said. "The color matches your eyes. And I suspect for once Jamie will have very little to say about your merchants' bills."

Elizabeth ignored the subtle reference to Jamie's supposed guilt—he had nothing to feel guilty about, he had not forced her into this, it had been Elizabeth's decision—but Joanna wouldn't listen. "Do you think it is right for a bridal gown? Perhaps if we have the clothier add some pearls on the bodice and on the part of the underskirt visible beneath the front slit of the surcotte?"

Discussing designs for new gowns was one of their favorite ways of passing the time. Normally, they could spend hours going over just the right placement for a particular piece of trim, embroidery, or beading. That this was for her wedding should make it even more enjoyable.

But no matter how much enthusiasm she tried to muster, it wasn't working. No amount of finery could mask the false happiness and panic churning inside her. The truth that could not stay buried beneath piles of pretty fabrics.

Wrong. Coward.

"God, won't you just shut up?"

Elizabeth didn't realize she'd spoken aloud until both Joanna and her cousin gasped and stared at her in shock.

I must be losing my mind.

Elizabeth quickly apologized. She was so exhausted she was talking to herself, she claimed with a high-pitched laugh.

But she wasn't fooling anyone—least of all herself. The most spectacular wedding, the most gorgeous dress, the most fantastic pair of shoes . . . none of it could change what should be the most important part of the wedding: the groom.

Everything was not perfect after all.

The carefully constructed wall of false bravado crumbled, and Elizabeth could no longer deny what she'd known from the moment she'd stood before the abbot and recited her vows: she'd made a horrible mistake.

And God help her, it was too late to do anything about it.

"Are you sure?" the king asked.

Thom shook his head. "Nay, but it is worth a try."

They were gathered in Randolph's tent—all ten members of the Highland Guard, Thom, Randolph, the king, and the king's closest advisor, Neil Campbell. Douglas probably would have been included had he been there, but Thom knew he wasn't the only one who was glad he was not. If they were successful, Randolph wouldn't want to share the credit with his rival. Was that why he'd been sent to Stirling for a few days?

"If the spikes don't hold, you will fall to your death," MacLeod said.

"They'll hold," Thom said with more certainty than he felt.

"And if they don't?" MacLeod challenged.

Thom didn't say anything. He didn't need to. They all knew the risk involved; risk he was willing to accept. His role in Bruce's army had become his sole focus. He was determined to win his knighthood and a place in the Guard.

It was the game of tossing daggers at the wall that had inspired him, though it wasn't until he'd woken up that next morning with his stomach turning and head splitting apart that he'd figured out how it could be applied to the Rock of Edinburgh Castle.

He'd gone to the forge first thing that morning, and instead of working on Douglas's sword (which was almost done but which he didn't want to look at), he'd modified a few small steel spikes. Each was about six inches in length and tapered from about an inch in diameter below the head to a point. They needed to be strong enough to hold his weight, but thin and sharp enough to be hammered into a small crack in the rock face. A few of them, strategically spaced, should allow Thom to climb the sheer section of wall that he'd been unable to get past before. Once clear of that section, he hoped to be able to drop one of Bruce's ingenious rope scaling ladders fixed with grappling hooks to the rest of the men, enabling them to climb up after him, and—if fortune was with them—surprise and take the castle.

MacRuairi wanted to go up the spikes after him to help with the ladders, but Thom told him it would be an unnecessary risk.

To this, the king agreed. "I have no interest in telling your wife that I let you fall off a cliff."

Bruce shuddered and the rest of the men laughed, though Thom was pretty sure the king wasn't jesting. From what he heard, Bella MacDuff was a formidable opponent. He supposed she had to be to take on Lachlan MacRuairi as a husband.

"Will you be able to secure the spikes without alerting the garrison?" Randolph asked.

It was a good question. No matter what Thom's personal feelings were toward the man, Randolph had not become one of Robert the Bruce's most valued commanders from his familial link alone. He might be an overly arrogant arse at times, but he was a wily one who knew how to wield a sword and wasn't afraid to get a little dirt on all of that shiny armor.

"I will try to muffle most of the sound with a piece of leather or cloth, but preventing the garrison from hearing the hammering will be the trickiest part of the mission,"

Thom answered. Well, except for the possibly falling to his death part. "But I was thinking that maybe you and your men could create some kind of diversion at the gate."

The men discussed it for a while and agreed that it might work.

But there was one part Randolph would not agree to. He insisted on being part of the team that went up the cliff. If this went down in history, he wanted the accolades. That Thom was helping the man who'd won the woman he loved win battle immortality, he tried not to think about. He would win his own, though he did not doubt Randolph would be the man whom history would remember.

They decided to take thirty men. In addition to the Guard, Thom, and Randolph, they added eighteen of Randolph's Highlanders from Moray, all of whom had some climbing experience. Thom had handpicked the best of the lot earlier today.

The king would command the rest of the army responsible for the diversionary attack at the gate. They hoped to draw most of the garrison to the south gate and away from the men trying to climb the north face of the Rock.

Anxious to take the castle and end the nearly two-and-a-half-month-long siege, the king told them to proceed as soon as they were ready. After a reconnaissance mission tonight, they would make their attempt on immortality tomorrow night.

If this worked, Thom knew he would secure his knighthood and his place in the Guard. They were the only things that mattered to him now.

Elizabeth was going out of her mind. Even with all the entertainment and activities that Edinburgh had to offer, she could not relax. All the restlessness that she'd experienced at Blackhouse and attributed to the boredom of the countryside had never come close to what she was experiencing right now.

At least she was not forced to feign happiness with her bridegroom. Randolph and the king had been conspicuously absent from both the evening meal last night and today's midday meal.

Had there finally been some progress with the siege? For Randolph's sake she hoped so, but for her own she wasn't so sure. Without the distraction of the siege, she might see far more of him, and she wondered how long she'd be able to hide her frayed and frazzled emotions.

On Thursday, two days after the betrothal, when Lady Helen mentioned that she was going to camp again to tend to the soldiers, Elizabeth practically jumped at the opportunity to accompany her. It was just what she needed to take her mind off . . . everything.

The thought that she might see Thom only occurred to her afterward. She thought she would be able to handle it.

She was wrong.

No sooner had she and Lady Helen entered camp than she came face-to-face with him. Actually, as fate would have it, she ran right into him as he exited a tent—the king's tent, she realized from the banners outside.

At the slam of contact, Thom instinctively reached for her. But the moment he recognized her, he stiffened and jerked his hand back. She would have stumbled had Lady Helen not been by her side to steady her. For the first time since she'd known him, he would have let her fall.

Startled from the bump—and more startled that it was him—she took one look at his icy expression and felt her emotions shatter. The connection was gone. "I'm sorry," she practically sobbed.

They both knew she wasn't apologizing for knocking into him. But the stony look in his eyes left no doubt that her apology was not welcomed. "The fault was mine," he said blandly. "If you will excuse me. My lady," he said, acknowledging Lady Helen, and then walked away.

The lash of pain was hard and deep, flaying, tearing, ripping her apart in strips. Never had she felt so helpless. She hadn't realized how horrible it would be to not have him. And worse, to have him hate her.

In a state of utter devastation, Elizabeth stared at his back as he disappeared into the maze of tents and trees. Her chest burned. Her throat squeezed. She wanted to crawl into a ball and sob. She would have burst into tears had Randolph not walked out after him. "Lady Elizabeth, what a delightful surprise!"

She turned to him with a watery smile. "My lord."

He frowned, perhaps noticing the shine in her eyes. "Is everything all right?"

She was saved from having to make up an excuse when Lady Helen interceded on her behalf. "I'm afraid I've been making Lady Elizabeth laugh a little too hard with my stories of young William's antics."

It was the truth—at least it had been until she'd slammed headlong into Thom.

The explanation appeared to satisfy Randolph, although he did give Elizabeth a small frown before taking her hand in his. "Was there something you needed? I'm sorry for not sending word today or last night. We've been . . . busy."

"Lady Elizabeth has graciously offered to help me tend the men today," Lady Helen said.

"Ah." Randolph smiled. "Then it is not me you have come to see. I would be disappointed if it were not such an important cause."

Elizabeth finally found her voice. "Is something happening with the siege, my lord?"

Though he smiled, Elizabeth sensed an evasiveness in his manner and expression. "Alas, no. The siege is exactly the same."

She would have questioned him further if Lady Helen had not put a hand on her arm. "We should go," she said meaningfully. "I'm sure the earl is very busy."

Randolph seemed grateful for the interruption—making Elizabeth even more certain that he was up to something.

But for the next few hours, Elizabeth didn't have time to think about Randolph or Thom. She was fully occupied with the steady stream of soldiers who visited the tent. Fortunately, there were no serious injuries. It was a hodgepodge of sore and strained limbs, bruised ribs, a cut that had festered, another that needed stitching, "digestive" problems, and a few fevers only one of which was serious enough for Helen to order him sequestered until it came down. Fever, like the bloody flux, could spread through camp like wildfire. That more men had not come down with sickness in the harsh misery of a winter siege was a blessing.

Elizabeth sensed that something was bothering Helen, but it wasn't until the end of the day when they were alone in the tent that she finally spoke.

"It is probably not my place to say anything—and if I am overstepping my bounds, I apologize—but I can't stand by and watch you make the same mistake I did, indeed if that's what you are doing."

Elizabeth had no idea what she was talking about. "I'm afraid I don't understand."

"That's because I'm doing a horrible job of this. I'm not usually so interfering." The lovely redheaded healer took a deep breath. "I couldn't help but notice how you looked at Thom MacGowan. Not just today, but before at Roxburgh."

Elizabeth's eyes widened in horror. Oh God, was it that obvious?

Lady Helen put her hand on her arm to comfort her—or maybe to steady her, as she suddenly felt wobbly. "Don't worry," she assured her. "I'm sure no one else has noticed. But I guess you could say that I know what to look for. I've been where you are right now."

"But you are married to the man you love." Elizabeth didn't realize how revealing her words were until they were out. A blush heated her cheeks.

"Magnus was not my first husband."

Elizabeth had no idea. "He wasn't?"

Lady Helen shook her head. "I was married to his best friend for a short while—a few days, actually. William left on a mission the night of our wedding and was killed shortly afterward in an explosion."

William . . . like their son?

Helen nodded, hearing the silent question. "Yes, our son is named after him."

Elizabeth's heart immediately went out to her. "I'm so sorry."

"He was a wonderful man, and his passing was a great loss to all who knew him—Magnus and my brother suffered horribly. But I did not love him and never should have married him. It was unfair to him, and nearly cost me the love of the only man I've ever loved. A man whom I've known since I was a girl."

Just like me.

"Why did you marry him?"

Lady Helen shrugged helplessly, as if knowing that the explanation wasn't going to be sufficient after the fact. "There were so many reasons. My family wanted it for one—William and my brother Kenneth were foster brothers." The similarity with James and Randolph's close friendship was not lost on her. "Kenneth and Magnus despised each other."

"But they are such good friends now."

Helen laughed. "Don't let them hear you say that, they'd be horrified. Our families were involved in a long feud. Choosing Magnus would have meant not choosing my family." Perhaps Elizabeth could understand that as well. "When I married William, I thought Magnus was lost to me. I'd hurt his pride in refusing him." She gave her a look as if that might sound familiar, too. "He was stubborn. He told me he didn't love me anymore. It wasn't until after the ceremony that I realized he'd lied. But by then it was too late."

"As it is for me," Elizabeth said, unable to hide her despondence.

Lady Helen shook her head. "It isn't too late. A betrothal can be broken. It will be unpleasant, but trust me, it will be better than the alternative. But . . ." Her voice left off, as if she was struggling with what to say. "You better act quickly."

"The wedding is in three weeks."

Lady Helen didn't say anything, but she bit her lip.

"What is it?"

Lady Helen shook her head. "I've said too much. Magnus will be furious that I've said anything at all. But I'm not breaking any confidences."

She seemed to be trying to justify it to herself.

It took Elizabeth a moment to put it all together, but

when she did, she knew why Lady Helen was being so reticent. "They are planning something, aren't they?" She didn't need an answer. Randolph, the Guard, Thom . . . Oh God, *Thom*. Her eyes widened and she reached for one of the tent poles to steady herself. She recalled her earlier fears of why the Guard might be recruiting him. "He can't . . . he wouldn't," she murmured to herself, and then looked at Helen in horror. "He's going to try to climb Castle Rock, isn't he?"

Lady Helen appeared stunned that she'd guessed. She didn't need to confirm it, Elizabeth already knew.

"It's suicide. I won't let him do it!"

He couldn't die . . . Oh God. Tears choked her throat. She would die without him.

The gaze that met hers was both sympathetic and sad. It was clear the other woman thought it was too late for that. "Just make sure he knows how you feel."

Elizabeth was already halfway through the flap of the tent.

"Wait," Helen said, pulling her back. "You can't just walk across camp and confront him in front of everyone."

Elizabeth was shocked to realize that was exactly what she'd been about to do. Out of her mind with panic, she hadn't been thinking of anything other than the fact that she had to stop him.

"He'll be with the others," the healer said, almost to herself. "We'll need to think of a way to get him alone." She tapped her mouth with her finger. "Give me a few minutes."

Apparently Lady Helen was as good at subterfuge as Elizabeth. In less than that, she'd sent a page with a message that Thom was needed immediately in the "stable" area where the horses were kept. It was located on the far side of camp—due to the stench of the animals—and their conversation would be less likely to be observed.

The boy was instructed not to mention who had given him the message. If questioned he was to say that something was wrong with the horse Thom had been given to ride.

Knowing Thom's affinity for horses, Elizabeth wasn't sure it would be enough. But not long after she was in position—in the tent used to store the hay—she saw him walking toward her.

Heart in her throat, she stepped out to block his path. His expression was so dark with fury she almost lost her courage. But then she remembered why she had to see him. "You can't do it, Thom. I won't let you."

He looked around as if he feared someone was watching them. But they were blocked from sight of the main camp by the tent.

"What the hell kind of game are you playing? You shouldn't be here, and you sure as hell shouldn't be sending me false messages."

"I had to speak with you," she said. "I know what you are planning, and you can't do it—you'll die."

He gave her a hard look—the only way he seemed capable of looking at her now. She chilled from the coldness in his eyes.

"Whatever you think you know, it's none of your concern."

"I know you are going to try to climb Castle Rock tonight and attempt to take the castle. And I know that it's considered an impossible climb, and you'll die if you try. I can't let you do that."

His expression didn't flicker—not once. Her desperate pleas bounced off him like pebbles on steel. "I believe you've made your faith in me perfectly clear. But if you have concerns, they should be for your betrothed."

He started to walk away, but she reached for his arm to stop him. "Wait, Thom, please. You have to listen to me. I made a mistake."

He went completely still. The look he gave her was so scathing it made her wish for the hard and impenetrable expression back. "You what?"

"I made a mistake. You were right. I never should have agreed to marry Randolph. I love you. I'm so sorry."

He stared at her for a moment as if he couldn't believe what he was hearing. She felt like a maggot that had had the gall to crawl across his trencher.

"You are unbelievable. Take your apologies, and whatever else you have to say, somewhere else. I don't want to hear them."

"But—"

The icy composure snapped. He took her by the arm and forced her gaze to his. His voice teemed with animosity and raw fury. "I don't want to fucking hear it, Elizabeth. Whatever you have to say, it's too late. You made your choice, you will have to live with it."

He pushed her away with a sharp shove—as if she were an old poppet he'd grown tired of—and walked away. Had he turned around, he would have seen her crumple to the ground.

But he didn't.

Oh God, what had she done? Whatever they'd once shared, whatever he'd once felt for her, it was gone. And nothing she would say was going to make him listen to her. He wouldn't give her an opportunity.

Worse, she didn't blame him.

All she could do was pray.

24

T HE SPIKES HELD.

Thom dug his fingers into the crevice with his foot balanced on a spike and pulled himself up the last sheer section of rock. Once in position on a narrow plateau, he was able to find a place to secure the rope ladder that he'd slung over his shoulder to drop down to the men below. The sounds of the boards clattering against the rock made him wince, but when he glanced up at the wall, he didn't see any movement in the shadows.

The diversionary attack that the king and the rest of the army were creating at the south gate was working. No one had heard the ping of a spike being forced into a crack in the rock earlier, and now the ladder was down without drawing attention.

Christ, he'd done it.

Thom took a moment to savor the satisfaction of knowing that he'd done something no man had done before. He'd climbed Castle Rock. Well, most of it. There was still another twenty feet or so to go, but the dangerous part of the climb was behind him.

That thought was barely formed before disaster struck—literally.

Randolph, who'd insisted on being the first man up the ladder, had just appeared out of the darkness below when a stone was tossed down from one of the soldiers patrolling the wall above. Had he heard something or seen a movement and was trying to figure out what it was, or was he just passing time? Whatever the cause, the rock slammed into Randolph's blackened helm, and the force and shock of it made him lose his balance. He lost his footing and hold of the ladder and started to fall.

Thom didn't think. If he had, he wasn't sure he would have done what he did. It was pure instinct.

He leapt off the small ledge of grass toward the sheer rock face that he'd just scaled. It was a leap without a landing. Only one small piece of steel would keep him from plummeting into the darkness behind Randolph. With one hand Thom reached for the spike, and with the other the falling man.

"I made a mistake."

Why the hell was he thinking of Elizabeth's too-late plea now? And he certainly shouldn't be thinking about it as he was careening through the air toward a collision with . . .

His body slammed into the rock face, and the edge of the steel from the head of the spike bit into his hand as he held on with everything he had, while the fingers of his other hand snagged just enough of the neck of Randolph's thick leather *cotun* to stop him from falling to his death. Randolph was fortunate that he'd decided to put aside his shiny mail for the lighter armor—a hauberk might not have been as easy to catch.

Thom felt as if his body was being ripped apart. His muscles strained as he fought not to let go of either the spike or the man hanging by his fingertips.

He wasn't even sure Randolph was alive until he muffled a curse.

"Are you all right?" Thom whispered tightly, still not sure whether there was a soldier up there listening for them and his teeth clenched against the strain of the other man's weight.

"My head is ringing but I think so."

"Can you reach for the ladder? It should be just to your right." He didn't know how long the spike would hold with the weight of two men attached.

"Aye."

A few long moments later, Thom felt a surge of relief as the strain was released from his arm and shoulder. Christ, it felt as if it had been yanked out of the socket.

As he was still hanging by the spike with one hand, Thom told Randolph to give him a minute before he started to climb. Thom felt around in the darkness for the ladder with his feet, and after some maneuvering was able to release his hand from the spike and climb up. Randolph appeared beside him a few minutes later.

The wall above them was quiet, the soldier apparently having thrown his rock and moved on, never knowing how close his carelessly but fortuitously aimed rock had come to killing one of Bruce's most important commanders.

Even in the moonless darkness, Thom could see the bloodlessness of the other man's face. He gripped Thom's hand hard. "Thank you. I owe you my life."

Uncomfortable with gratitude from a man he could only resent, Thom shook him off. "It was nothing."

But Randolph wasn't having it. "It was incredible. I'd wager there aren't a handful of men in Christendom who could have done what you just did. You must have hands and fingers of steel. I will see you rewarded for your deed tonight."

"As this night is far from over, you might not be held to that."

Randolph let out a bark of laughter and put his hand on his back. "You are right about that."

Randolph's near plunge off the cliff was the only thing to go wrong that night. The rest of the team made it up the ladder without mishap, and when the warriors dropped over the twelve-foot wall, it was to take the handful of unsuspecting soldiers left to patrol this section of the castle completely by surprise.

The cry of alarm was sounded, but with the noise from Bruce's diversionary attack at the gate, not enough soldiers were able to respond to the real threat: the men who were now inside the castle.

The fighting was fierce and bloody, and more difficult than it might have been for Bruce's men were they not worn from the strenuous, almost three-hundred-foot climb. A few of Randolph's Highlanders from Moray fell alongside the English, and Randolph himself, in his second narrow escape of the night, barely avoided a well-aimed English spear.

But when they reached the south gate to open it for the rest of the army, the battle was won. The English fought with unusual ferocity, but once their commander fell with the initial swarm of men surging into the castle, they quickly surrendered.

The cheer that went up when Bruce's men knew the castle was theirs was something Thom would never forget. The sense of euphoria, accomplishment, and joy was over-whelming.

One of the first men to congratulate him was the king himself. Bruce threw his arms around him and might have spun him around were Thom not so powerfully built. "Your feat of bravery this night will be rewarded! What say you, Sir Thomas?"

Thom stilled. "Sire?"

Bruce smiled and slapped him on the back. "You've earned your knighthood, lad. And"—he paused, with an eye to the man who'd just come up beside them—"I'd wager a place with this bunch."

MacLeod frowned at the king. The formidable leader of the Highland Guard had been in the heat of the battle the entire time, but you would never know it from looking at him. He looked cool, unruffled, and untouched. "I thought asking was my job."

Bruce shrugged unrepentantly. "Royal prerogative."

MacLeod didn't look like he agreed but turned to Thom. "Aye, the king is right. I'd seen enough after what you did at Dunbar, but what you did tonight has only solidified it. You have earned a place with us if you want it." His mouth curved in what was almost a smile. "Assuming you make it through Perdition, that is."

From how MacLeod said it, Thom surmised it was a big assumption. But he had no doubt he would do whatever it took. "I want it."

What a prodigious understatement. He felt a sense of satisfaction that dwarfed even the feeling of climbing Castle Rock. In many ways, it was a higher climb. He'd done it. Actually, he'd done more than he set out to do. Not only would he be a knight, he'd earned his way into the most elite army in Christendom.

All those times someone told him it was impossible, all those knocks, cuts, and bruises, all the hours he'd spent pulling himself out of the dirt, all the digs about his birth, all the times he'd wanted to give up . . .

Christ, it was sweet. Only one thing would have made it sweeter. Fury swept through him for thinking about her at all.

"I only wish that we'd thought of a climber before," the king said with a shake of his head. "It seems so obvious. If we'd had you with us years ago, we would have had a much easier time taking back some of our castles." He laughed. "We can talk about this tomorrow. But now we celebrate!"

The king clapped him on the back again and practically danced him around the yard. It was one of the biggest moments in his kingship, and Bruce was determined to enjoy every minute of it. All but one of Scotland's great castles was now wrested from English hands. When King Edward marched his men to battle in June, they would not have the mighty Edinburgh Castle to protect them. Bruce's chances for victory had just taken a big step forward.

Though it was the middle of the night, from the church tower a bell was rung. What remained of the castle larder was raided and brought to the Great Hall. Casks of ale and wine were carried up from the cellars—more than they expected—and despite the abstinence of the season, the drinking went on well into the wee hours of the morning.

By the time Thom crawled into bed, he wasn't just a soon-to-be knight and member of the Highland Guard, he was also a baron of lands in Roxburghshire. The magnitude of what he'd achieved stunned him.

But he had only a few hours of sleep before he was awakened again.

The fact that it was his new Chief didn't stop him from cursing and rolling over, pulling the wool blanket over his head.

The fierce Islander chuckled—it wasn't a sound Thom had ever heard from MacLeod before and the novelty even broke through his exhausted haze. He pulled back the blanket and cranked open one eye.

"Hail, Caesar. It's time to get up and put on your laurel.

Rome is waiting. You don't want to sleep through your own triumph."

It was far too early for jests. "What the hell are you talking about?"

"You'll have to see for yourself."

A short while later Thom did. The high street from the castle to Holyrood Abbey was lined with a cheering mob—the citizens of Edinburgh had taken to the streets to show their support of the king and celebrate yet another miraculous feat that would perhaps be the crowning achievement in what was to become the almost mythical legend of the Bruce.

Randolph was being hailed as a conquering hero, and Thom, for his part, as the man who had made it all possible. His role as the warrior who'd climbed the unclimbable had been impossible to keep secret. His name was being bandied everywhere, and everyone wanted to see the smith's son from Douglas who'd climbed to the highest peak and set this latest miracle into action.

When he, Randolph, and some of the other men from Moray appeared at the castle portcullis, the cheer was so resounding, so deafening, that Thom indeed knew what Caesar must have felt like when he returned from his victories.

Pretty damned good.

Thom knew the Guard didn't believe in personal accolades or singling out men for accomplishment, but he would fade back into obscurity tomorrow. Today, he was going to bloody well enjoy it.

But if there was one face he wanted to see in the crowd more than any other, he told himself it was to have the satisfaction of knowing that she'd been wrong not to put her faith in him.

Very wrong.

"I made a mistake."

His mouth curled. Damned right, she had.

Elizabeth had returned from camp with Lady Helen in such a state of distress that it was impossible to hide the cause from Jo and Izzie. She'd made a mistake, she told them. She loved Thom, and he was going to die before she could convince him of that fact.

Elizabeth didn't need to swear the two women to secrecy; she knew they would go to their graves before they told anyone what the men had planned. Both women immediately understood the gravity of the situation and the extreme danger.

"No!" Jo said. "Castle Rock? He can't."

"Randolph, too?" Izzie asked.

Elizabeth nodded.

She wasn't surprised when tears filled Jo's eyes, but she was surprised to see Izzie similarly affected. At first Elizabeth didn't understand. But when an explanation finally occurred to her, she knew she had even more reason for doing what she was going to do.

In those long, tortured hours of waiting, of not knowing what was happening, of not knowing whether the man she loved was dead or alive, Elizabeth decided two things: she couldn't marry Randolph (no matter what the consequences of breaking the betrothal), and it wasn't too late for her and Thom. She would do whatever she had to do to prove that to him.

But if she knew Thom, it wasn't going to be easy. She'd failed him, and in the process unintentionally hurt him where he was most vulnerable—his pride. She could see it now, if only she'd seen it before.

She hadn't been strong enough to defy her family and society, or brave enough to face an uncertain future—one without extreme wealth and comfort. She'd let herself be swayed by thoughts of what *could* happen to her children, while losing sight of the fact that the only children she wanted to have were Thom's.

Worse, when she'd refused him, Thom wouldn't have just seen it as a rejection of his offer of marriage for one that was so much obviously "better," he would have also seen it as a rejection of *him*. Of the man he was. She'd made him feel as if he were not good enough—as if he were not worthy of her hand—when nothing could be further from the truth. His crude words of parting came back to her—"*good enough to fuck isn't good enough*"—how horribly he'd misunderstood her motives. To her mind, there was no one better or more worthy. She just hadn't been able to see through the fear.

She had no wish to live in poverty ever again, but Thom was right: there were no guarantees. With him or without him, she did not know what the future held. But she did know that without him she would be miserable, and she trusted him to keep her—and their children—safe.

What he'd accomplished so far should have convinced her. He'd made his way up a ladder that was all but impossible to climb: the smith's son had become a formidable warrior, one skilled enough to be recruited by the greatest team of warriors this country had ever seen. And he'd done so with skill, determination, and hard work. She was so proud of him, but when she'd been given the chance to prove that to him, she'd faltered.

Even if he never achieved more than he had at this moment it didn't matter. Unlike most men of her rank, Thom had skills beyond the battlefield to fall back on. He could be one of the greatest sword makers in Scotland, if he wanted to be.

Of course, it would have been much easier if she could have understood all this *before* she agreed to marry Randolph. But it took making that commitment, Lady Helen's advice, and most of all the fear of losing him to force her to accept the truth. She should have jumped. He was worth the risk. All the gold, land, and security in Christendom wouldn't matter without him. He was all that mattered. And she swore that if Thom gave her another chance, she would do whatever it took to prove to him that she would stand by him come what may.

He just had to survive the night.

The three women huddled together late into the evening. Lady Helen had stayed for a while but needed to return to her son. She was worried, too, but she told Elizabeth to have faith.

She tried.

Finally, they heard the sound of a bell shatter the night. Roused from bed, the occupants of the guesthouse, including Lady Mary, a handful of the other women, and the Bruce sisters, came pouring out into the abbey yard.

"What is it?" Lady Margaret Bruce asked.

"Something is happening at the castle," one of the other women responded.

Elizabeth, Jo, Izzie, and Lady Helen exchanged glances, no one daring to give voice to their hopes.

But the bell was good. Surely it had to be good?

The excitement—the nervousness—was so overwhelming that when news finally arrived in a message from the king himself that the castle had been taken by a group of men who'd climbed the Rock, it was as if a dam had burst.

They laughed, they cried, they hugged, and did all three at once.

Elizabeth couldn't believe it. Thom had done it. Dear God, he'd done it!

Though she had no confirmation that he'd survived the battle, she knew in her heart that he had.

When confirmation did come from Magnus, who'd arrived to fetch Helen to tend the wounded, Elizabeth was overjoyed to hear that not only had Thom survived, he was being hailed as a hero. She wanted to go with Helen, but Joanna held her back.

"Give him time to enjoy his moment with the others," she said. "There will be time enough tomorrow to discuss the future."

Jo was right. Elizabeth didn't want to take this away from him. She would let him have this time with the men, but later she would find him whether he wanted to be found or not.

Besides, she had something to do first. Though unpleasant, it must be done. Before she finally went to bed, she went to the scriptorium to fetch a quill and ink. She had a letter to write.

25

THOM WAS SEATED at the high table. After being roused from bed by MacLeod, he and the others had taken to the streets to join in the celebration, which had eventually wound its way into the Great Hall of Edinburgh Castle. The midday meal was a sea of people, the Hall stuffed to the gills with loyal Scots grateful to the king—and his men—for liberating the castle from the enemy.

And at the center was Thom.

From his position of honor beside the king on the dais, he could take it all in, savoring the moment for all that it meant. This was his moment, damn it. The blacksmith's son had indeed climbed high—high enough to sit next to a princess. Lady Margaret Bruce was seated on his other side. But she wasn't the princess who was bothering him.

Throughout the long meal, Thom was painfully aware of the woman seated on the other side of Randolph, who held the other position of honor beside the king. Fortunately, due to the two men being between them, the only conversation he'd had to endure with Elizabeth was when she and the other women had arrived at the table to take their seats, and she'd offered her heartfelt congratulations and "relief" that he was safe. Ignoring the plea in her eyes the one time they'd met, he'd given her offer more than it deserved: courtesy and nothing more.

But keeping up the wall of steel he'd erected around his heart wasn't easy, especially when he could see how much his remoteness hurt her. But this is what *she'd* wanted, he kept telling himself. Not him. Which didn't explain why he felt like he'd just kicked a kitten.

She'd tried to engage him in conversation a few more times, but the men between them proved a convenient barrier and means of evasion. Not to mention they were also speaking French. Of course they were. All nobles spoke French. Maybe that's why he'd always hated it. It brought home the division between them in a way that could not be denied. He didn't even speak the same bloody language.

It never would have worked out. He could see that now. She had tutors and he had no formal education to speak of; he'd grown up with one pair of boots for the winter, and she had a trunk full of pretty slippers; he melted gold and silver for a living, she wore it decorated with precious jewels in her hair. She was sophisticated and refined, he was provincial and rough.

He could go on and on. But even the fact that he was thinking about *her* made him angry.

He was furious with himself. He'd done what he'd set out to do—hell, far more than he'd ever set out to do— changing his fortune by earning a knighthood, a barony, and a place among the most elite warriors in Christendom. He'd done something no man had ever done before in climbing Castle Rock (solidifying his war name in the Guard as Rock), and in doing so had achieved battle immortality.

He should be basking in the glory, wallowing in the admiration, and delighting in all that he'd achieved. Instead it all rang hollow. None of it could fill the emptiness inside him or dull the ache where his heart used to be. None of it could make up for the one thing that he'd lost.

Damn her.

He made his escape at the earliest opportunity.

"Back to work already, MacGowan?" the king said as they stood to leave.

"Aye, sire. Some of the men have already begun taking down the south gate."

The king nodded. "It is an unfortunate task but necessary. We can't risk letting the English use this as a stronghold against us again, and I do not have the men necessary to defend it *and* meet them on the battlefield." He put his hand on Thom's back. "But at least we will enjoy it for a few days. Tomorrow we will have quite a celebration—I hope you are ready."

Thom nodded. "I am indeed, sire."

Tomorrow Thom would be knighted by the king himself, admitted into the Guard with a private ceremony, and formally be given his barony. A barony that had gotten richer when the king learned of his role in saving his nephew. He was going to be a wealthy man.

By refusing him, she'd given him the means of achieving not only fame but also fortune.

Irony was a cruel bastard.

Elizabeth watched Thom walk away with her heart in her throat. She wanted to go after him, and might have tossed propriety aside and done exactly that, had Randolph not been speaking to her.

Since she'd arrived at the castle with the other women from the abbey, she'd been fighting for a chance to speak to Thom. But he'd been surrounded by hordes of townspeople who all seemed to want to be near him—to touch greatness.

Especially the women. Watching them fawn and flirt had made her heart ache and her stomach turn. What had she expected? That he would become a monk? He was swoon-worthy handsome, tall, with a body that was as hard and impressive as the famous Rock he'd just climbed. Just because she'd been too blind to see it didn't mean others wouldn't.

She'd been unable to approach him until they were seated for the meal, but even then he'd barely spared her a glance and cut off any attempts she made to talk to him.

She'd known it wasn't going to be easy, but it was difficult being patient when every moment felt like his heart was growing harder and harder against her. Soon, nothing would be able to penetrate.

And then there was Randolph. She'd wanted to speak to him as well, but he was so *happy*, she couldn't stand the idea of tarnishing what was sure to be one of the greatest days of his life.

Oblivious to her torment, Randolph had regaled her with a moment-by-moment replay of the battle. Her horror on hearing about his fall—and Thom's crazed rescue—was real. Mistaking the source of her distress, he'd apologized for scaring her, telling her he was perfectly hale. He'd finished the tale—which was a magnificent one indeed—just as Thom was leaving.

Randolph couldn't seem to wipe the grin off his face. "I'd love to see your brother's face when he hears the news. I daresay he won't be happy."

Jamie wouldn't be, but not just because of the castle. Had her note reached him yet? She'd sent it with a messenger this morning.

She smiled. "I fear what he will do next to try to top you."

Randolph laughed. "I'd like to see him try. I think this feat will stand for a while. Your friend MacGowan's idea for those spikes was ingenious. Good thing he wasn't born the son of a baker." He laughed, and then suddenly sobered. "You were right about him; I owe him my life."

It seemed like the perfect opening. Her voice wobbled a little. "My lord, might we speak in private for a moment?"

He took her hand to help lift her from her seat as they stood. "I should like nothing more, but might it wait? My uncle has put me in charge of the destruction of the castle, and the men are waiting for me."

She smiled wanly. "Of course."

"You are a gem. I knew you would understand."

But would *he*? Elizabeth had to admit she was not looking forward to Randolph's reaction on hearing that she wished to break the betrothal. She did not delude herself that he had any real feelings for her, but appearances mattered to him, and his pride would no doubt suffer.

Both Joanna and Izzie looked at her expectantly as she rejoined them for the walk back to the abbey—they'd been seated at a different table.

When Elizabeth shook her head, they couldn't hide their disappointment.

Izzie asked. "What happened?"

"Neither of them would talk to me. Thom barely looked at me, and Randolph was too happy—and too busy. He said we could speak later."

"Perhaps it would be best if you waited for James to speak to Randolph?" Joanna said.

"But you said that you didn't know when Jamie would be back."

"I don't. Although I imagine once he receives your note, it won't take him long. If he wasn't away when it arrived, I'd wager we'll see him sometime around midday tomorrow."

Which was even more reason to have things settled with Thom. The last thing she needed was her brother interfering. When Jamie came back she and Thom needed to be a fait accompli.

But how was she going to manage that when he wouldn't even talk to her?

Her mouth pursed with frustration. He could be so blastedly *stubborn*. Prying him out of one of his dark moods had always been difficult, and this was much worse than a dark mood. She was going to have to come up with something far more than a silly jest or two. She needed a plan. A sure way to get him alone.

She hated to involve her sister-in-law, but there was no other choice. Thom would certainly not answer a plea from her, but he would from Joanna.

When she asked for her help, however, Jo surprised her. "I don't think that will be necessary. I think I know where he will be. I should have realized it right away. He said he would have James's sword ready for me later tonight."

Elizabeth followed the direction of her thoughts. "Which means at some point he will have to go to the forge to finish it."

Joanna nodded excitedly.

Elizabeth smiled. "I will just wait there until he shows up."

"A good Bruce tactic," Izzie said wryly.

Elizabeth grinned. "That it is. So far this war has been won on lying-in-wait ambushes."

It took Elizabeth a moment to realize Joanna wasn't smiling anymore. Indeed, from the way she was biting her lip, she appeared to be having second thoughts.

"What is it, Jo?"

"Thom can be stubborn. What if he won't listen?"

"I will have to make sure he does."

"That's what I'm worried about. You won't do anything . . . *rash*, will you? I don't want you to get hurt."

They both knew what she meant by rash. "I'll be careful, Jo. Besides, you know Thommy."

He was honorable to the core.

Elizabeth, however, wasn't. Douglases did what it took to win. Jo, however, did not need to be reminded of that.

Her sister-in-law immediately brightened. "I do."

Izzie, however, wasn't so easily placated. But surprisingly, her no-nonsense, play-it-straight cousin seemed to be impressed—maybe even admiring of her sinful tactics.

She pulled Elizabeth aside so that Jo couldn't hear. "Don't worry about Randolph. Do what you need to do. Leave him to me."

Elizabeth took note of the determined look on Izzie's face and did not doubt it. She'd been right in her suspicions. She went to the table that still had the quill on it and wrote a quick note of apology. "Give this to him. And thank you."

Something resembling relief flashed in Izzie's eyes. "No, thank you."

Not wanting to take a chance at missing Thom, Elizabeth left for the forge immediately—this time without an escort. She didn't want someone standing outside to alert Thom to her presence, and she certainly didn't want anyone inside with her.

It was late afternoon by the time she arrived. Fortunately, the smithy was already gone for the day, and the young apprentice who let her in was too awed by the lady from the abbey, who knew so much about smithing, to ask too many questions about her waiting for her old "friend."

He was eleven, he informed her, and the smith was his father. She entertained him with stories from her past watching Thom work while he finished up his chores for the day. By the time he left, she was sad to see him go.

With the boy gone and left without distraction, she began to grow nervous. She had not eaten since the midday meal, and her stomach started to grumble as darkness fell outside. She should have grabbed a hunk of bread and cheese. And wine—plenty of fortifying wine. But she hadn't really thought that far ahead.

What was she going to do if Thom wouldn't forgive her? She didn't know anything about seduction—she was a virgin for goodness' sake! She should have asked someone.

Not Joanna, obviously, but maybe Lady Helen? She had the feeling she would have understood. Perhaps she might have offered some tips? Suggestions? Tactics?

Elizabeth took off her heavy fur-lined wool cloak—despite the fire going out some time ago, she was warm—and tossed it on a bench. As it fell, it gave her an idea.

No. She couldn't. She looked down at her remaining clothes—a fairly simple and easy-to-remove surcotte and cotte. Could she?

Elizabeth was pacing anxiously around the room when she finally heard the door open. She froze, glancing over as a man entered. Only when she saw the tall, familiar frame did she heave an inward sigh of relief. He had a sack slung over his shoulder, which from the size and shape she assumed was Jamie's sword.

She was standing to the side, so he shouldn't have noticed her right away. But almost like prey sensing danger, his eyes immediately locked on hers.

His utter lack of reaction sent a pang of foreboding to her heart. He didn't look surprised, he didn't look furious (what she'd expected), and he certainly didn't look happy (had she secretly hoped so?). He didn't look *anything*. There wasn't a flicker of emotion in the cold, blue-eyed gaze that met hers.

Oh God, was it too late? Had she completely destroyed all the feelings he once had for her?

"How did you know—" He stopped, his mouth falling in a grim line. "Joanna."

Elizabeth nodded mutely. He looked so imposing—so distant—so utterly unlike her Thommy that the nervousness she felt earlier returned tenfold. Her confidence wavered and the first icy beads of perspiration dotted her brow. She was so sure she knew him, but what if she didn't? What if nothing she did could make him forgive her? What if all she succeeded in doing was humiliating herself?

It didn't matter. She had to at least try.

"I know I shouldn't be here like this, but I had to talk to you, and you left me little choice."

He crossed into the room, putting the sword down on the table before turning to look at her. "And why should it make any difference what I want?"

"That isn't what I meant—"

He held up his hand to stop her. "Go ahead, say what you have to say, and then leave. I have work to do and people are waiting for me."

Elizabeth felt a flash of temper, but reminded herself that he had every cause to be disagreeable. She'd wronged him. Horribly. But his impatient and indifferent attitude was definitely grating.

"I'm sorry. I made a mistake, Thom. I never should have agreed to marry Randolph."

"So you've said. Why should that make any difference to me?"

Nothing could prevent her temper from flaring at that one. She pressed her lips together, praying for patience. "Because you love me."

"I did. More than anything in the world."

Her heart sank like a stone. Fear gripped her. He still did. *Don't believe him.* She remembered what Lady Helen had said about Magnus telling her he no longer loved her—because he was stubborn. "And I love you," she whispered.

"Not enough apparently."

She took the barb, which although warranted still stung. She lifted her chin and met his gaze. "Enough to break the engagement with Randolph."

The first crack in his steely shield appeared; she'd

surprised him. But then his eyes narrowed. "When did you do that? I was just with your betrothed. He gave no hint that the engagement had ended."

She flushed. "I tried to tell him earlier, but he had to leave. I wrote him a note, though, that my cousin will give him, and sent one to Jamie as well."

"I'm no expert at betrothal agreements, but I believe it takes a little more than a couple of notes to break one."

Condescension *and* sarcasm were definitely not her favorite combination. She glared at him, snapping, "I know that."

Thom merely shrugged. "I still don't understand why any of this should matter to me."

She was fuming and her hands were on her hips. "Because I want to marry *you*. Although right now, I'm trying to remember why."

Her flash of temper did nothing more than elicit a cocked brow from him. "I believe you already refused my proposal, and I don't recall issuing another one."

If he was trying to embarrass her and make her feel foolish, it was working. She looked up at him pleadingly. "I was scared and confused, Thom. Can you not try to understand?"

"I do understand. What I don't understand is what has changed." He paused, as if something had suddenly occurred to him. "Of course I do. My situation has improved enough for you, is that it? Now that I've achieved some renown, that I'm to be knighted and presented with land, I am worth taking a risk on?"

"None of that had anything to do with it."

"So the timing of your 'grand epiphany' is just a coincidence?"

She shouldn't be surprised that he'd question her motives, but it stung. "I knew I'd made a mistake the moment I stood next to Randolph to say those vows, but it wasn't until I learned what you were going to do, and that your life was in danger, that I knew I would do whatever I had to do—no matter what the cost or how unpleasant—to extricate myself from it." Seeing he wasn't convinced, she added, "If you don't believe me, ask Joanna. Ask Lady Helen. Ask my cousin. They'll tell you. I tried to tell you myself, but you wouldn't listen." She took a deep breath that was almost a sob. "God, I could have lost you, Thommy. I was so scared. How could you have put yourself in danger like that?"

The tears in her eyes and obvious despair seemed to mean nothing to him. "You lost me the moment you said those words binding you to another man. Whether you regretted it before or after doesn't matter."

She took a step toward him. "You don't mean that."

But he did. She could see it. *He doesn't want me, he doesn't love me anymore.*

No, he was just being stubborn . . . wasn't he? His feelings couldn't change that fast. She had to find a way to get through to him. "What can I say, but I'm sorry. I made a mistake. It all happened so fast, I couldn't think clearly. I had a plan—I thought I knew what I wanted—and when you came in and tried to change everything at the last minute, I made the wrong decision. I would do anything to take it back, but I can't. All I can do is try to correct it and beg for your forgiveness."

He stared at her emotionlessly. Mulishly. Not giving a blasted inch.

"Is there nothing I can do or say that will make you

forgive me? Is your heart that hard? Will you allow pride and stubbornness to prevent you from taking what I'm offering?"

The hot flare of anger in his eyes was the first sign that he might not be as indifferent as he seemed. "What exactly are you offering, Elizabeth? Somehow I don't see your brother welcoming me into the family. So are we to run off together? You can be damned sure if we do that there won't be a knighthood or a barony—or anything else for that matter."

Was he relenting? From his expression it was questionable, but at least he appeared to be considering it. She felt bold enough to move forward and place a tentative palm on his chest. "That doesn't matter."

His jaw clenched. "It does to me."

Good gracious, the logic of male pride utterly escaped her. First he wanted her to take him with nothing, and now that he had something, he wouldn't take her without it? She prayed for patience. "I will make Jamie understand."

He made a sharp sound of disbelief. "How do you intend to do that?"

"By making sure it's too late for him to do anything about it."

It didn't take him long to realize what she meant. "Hell, no, Elizabeth. I won't do it. Not like that."

She took one look at his expression and knew he meant it. At times, honor and nobility could be decidedly inconvenient.

She sighed, realizing she had no other choice. She winced a little at the thought though. Good gracious, could she really do this? Desperate times . . . desperate measures.

Removing her hand from his chest, she stood back and began to work the ties of her gown.

If her hands weren't shaking, she would have appreciated the nervous way he was eyeing her.

"What are you doing?" he demanded.

She'd never seen him look so shocked; obviously, she'd surprised him. To put it mildly. "Taking off my clothes," she answered matter-of-factly.

"W-why?"

Sputtering was a good thing, wasn't it? "I'd rather hoped that would be obvious, but I'm trying to seduce you. And since you said you wanted to see me standing before you naked, I thought that was a good way to start." She paused for a moment, letting her eyes slide down to the heavy bulge between his legs. "You also said something about having my mouth on you, but I'm afraid I may require some instruction for that."

Holy hell. Whatever else Thom had been about to say flew out of his mind. It was replaced by an image of Lady Elizabeth Douglas on her knees before him—naked—pleasuring him with her mouth. The surge of lust was so hot and heavy, the yearning so intense, it was a hard image to dislodge.

But he did so. Forcibly. And maybe with a little bit of a groan.

She heard it—damn it—and it emboldened her movements, which had been anxious and fumbling, with newfound purpose. Her surcotte dropped into a pool of velvet at her feet before he could get a hand on her wrist.

"Stop it," he demanded angrily. "It won't work. You aren't going to change my mind. I don't want you." She looked down at the proof to the contrary, which was too damned big and hard to hide. His jaw clamped down like a vise. "Not like this."

"You can have it your way next time."

His teeth were literally grinding at all the images that flooded his head. "That is not what I meant, damn it."

"I'm not going to wait for someone else's permission, Thom. Are you going to let my brother decide your future?" He stiffened, as no doubt was her intention. She knew how much the thought of that would grate. *Don't touch. Don't reach too high. Remember your place.* "I want to spend the rest of my life with you, and as this seems to be the best way to guarantee it, I'm not going to let anything stand in the way. Your honor will be intact. You aren't seducing me, I'm seducing you."

"That doesn't make any difference, Ella, and you bloody well know it!"

She tugged her wrist from his hold and resumed her task as if he hadn't spoken.

He should stop her, damn it. He couldn't let her manipulate him like this. He didn't love her anymore. She'd hurt him for the last time. He didn't want—

Ah, hell. Her cotte followed the surcotte to the floor, and his mouth went dry. It felt as if most of the blood in his body had drained to his feet as well.

Want was all he felt.

She bent down to remove her shoes and hose, and then she stood before him in nothing but a chemise. The thin linen left preciously little to the imagination. He could see the high pink tips of her breasts, the heavy roundness of their substantial weight, the slender curve of her waist and hips, the long length of her limbs. With a few tugs at pins in her hair, the luxuriant long blond tresses fell into sensual waves around her shoulders.

She looked like a goddess. Like a creature from his

dreams. Like every sexual fantasy he'd ever had. He wanted to scoop her up in his arms, lay her back against the table, wrap her legs around his waist, and sink into her inch by inch.

He forced his hands to his sides, fighting against the urge to touch her. He was a damned fool. He wasn't going to do this. Not again, damn it. Maybe the first time she'd rejected him he could say that she hadn't been aware of what she was doing, but he couldn't say the same this time.

He tore his eyes away. "Get out of here, Elizabeth. You are only shaming yourself."

For a moment, he thought he'd convinced her. Hell, he almost convinced himself.

She was too quiet. But when he glanced back at her, she shook her head. "No. You still love me, I know you do." She stared at him defiantly—but with enough uncertainty and embarrassment to remind him of her current vulnerability. To remind him that she was an innocent maid who was acting on instinct, not practice, and how hard this must be for her. To remind him that she was doing this for him.

"I made a mistake."

Was she right? Was his heart so hard that he couldn't forgive? Was it pride that was keeping him from pulling her into his arms?

No, damn it. It was the image of her standing before a room of people binding herself to another man.

The fact that she could still get to him, that she thought he could be so easily won over by a naked body and naughty proposition—and that she could make him vacillate, even for an instant—infuriated him. "Think whatever the hell you want. I don't give a shite."

"I don't believe you," she said with an impressive amount of confidence in the face of his rejection. He might have admired her tenacity if it wasn't about to test the very limits of his restraint.

Before he could stop her—he was sure he would have—she crossed her arms, clutched the folds of linen in her fists, and pulled her chemise over her head. An instant later it landed on the floor at her feet.

26

EVERYTHING SEEMED TO stop: his heart, his lungs, movement, time. For a moment Thom forgot the anger, forgot the hurt, forgot the betrayal, forgot that he didn't love her anymore. All he could see, all that mattered, was the beautiful woman standing before him naked. The beautiful woman who'd held his heart since childhood. The beautiful woman he never thought could be his. The beautiful woman who was now offering herself to him like the proverbial virgin to the sacrifice because she wanted to marry him.

Christ, she was gorgeous. His fantasies hadn't done her justice. The dimensions had all been right, but the creamy flawlessness of her skin, the berry pink of her nipples, the height and firmness of her breasts, the dark blond of the triangle between her legs . . . he'd gotten those all wrong. But the details would be etched in his mind forever. Every incredible inch of her.

The pink blush on her cheeks darkened with each

passing moment of silence. She started to shift, and he knew it was taking everything she had not to cover herself as he continued to stare.

But God almighty, he couldn't have turned away if the first Edward of England had risen from the grave and was breaking down the door. And he sure as hell couldn't think of anything to say, not when his mind was filled with erotic images of what he wanted to *do*. And not when his cock was throbbing so hard he had to concentrate on not embarrassing himself.

It was only when he noticed what was on her wrist that he jolted back to reality. She was wearing it again—his bracelet—and somehow the sight of the brass band was like salt being ground into a wound. She wasn't his. She'd never been his. He'd only been fooling himself.

He forced his gaze away from her nakedness and turned away. He wasn't going to let her do this to him. He wasn't going to be manipulated by desire.

He started walking toward the door.

"Thommy . . . ?" He heard the panic in her voice as she rushed toward him. "Wait!" She grabbed hold of his arm to stop him. "You can't go." He couldn't look at her face because he was scared what it would do to him. Scared that her fear would find a way to penetrate the ice around his heart. "Are you going to say anything?"

His fists clenched; the effort not to take what she offered had turned every muscle in his body as rigid as stone. "What do you want me to say? That you are exquisite? That I've never seen anything more beautiful or desirable?"

Her expression fell; apparently compliments weren't what she wanted to hear. "I hoped you might say that you forgive me. That you love me, and still want to marry me."

Hearing the words that he was fighting so hard to

deny slip so easily from her lips snapped the last threads of his control. He hauled her up against him. "What did you think, Elizabeth? That two perfectly formed, lush, and pink-tipped breasts were going to make me forget having my insides torn out as you promised yourself to another man? That a tight, curvy bottom and long sleek legs were going to repair the heart that you shredded apart when I had to watch you kiss him? That taking off your clothes was going to make me love you again?"

Her eyes had widened at his outburst of rage, and her cheeks burned with shame. "No . . . Yes." She looked up at him pleadingly. "I didn't know what else to do. You weren't listening to me, and I wanted to prove how much I loved you. To lay myself bare." She took a deep breath. "I know I hurt you when I rejected your proposal, and I just thought that if somehow . . ."

She looked at him helplessly.

"You put yourself in the same position we would be even?" he finished. "But I bet you never thought I would reject you, did you? You thought I'd be so overcome with wanting you I'd fall to my knees in gratitude."

She appeared genuinely taken aback and hurt by the accusation. "I didn't think that at all. I thought you would see how much you mean to me, and how much I want to be with you."

He ignored her. "Well, sorry to disappoint you. But it's not that easy, Elizabeth. I'm not just going to forget everything that happened because you strip naked and tell me you want to suck my cock."

No matter how incredible that sounded, or how the sight of all that velvety soft nakedness tempted him. But he sure as hell wasn't going to tell her that.

Whether it was his crude words or tone, he didn't know,

but something made her temper flare. She straightened her back, lifted her chin, and met his gaze square on. "Actually, it *is* that easy. Isn't that what you've been telling me the whole time? If I love you nothing else matters, isn't that what you said? I'm sorry my feelings weren't clear enough to do the right thing at the precise moment you wanted me to. But this is new to me. I've never been in love before. You've had years knowing you loved me; I only realized how I felt last week. I was confused. I made a horrible mistake. I let you down. I didn't jump when you asked, but I'm trying to jump now." She took a deep breath. "It *is* simple: either you love me and want a future with me or you don't."

His eyes met hers. "I don't."

His words landed with the sting of a slap. She flinched and sucked in her breath as if the pain was unexpected and sharp. Her hand fell from his arm.

One glance at her face was all he could bear. If he'd wanted to crush her—to hurt her as badly as she'd hurt him—he'd succeeded. She looked . . . heartbroken. Destroyed. *Vulnerable.*

He had to get the hell out of here before he did something stupid and pulled her into his arms and proved himself a liar. Showed her just how much her explanation and last-ditch ploy at seduction had come to breaking him. How much he wanted to forgive her. She'd made a mistake, but maybe under the circumstances it was understandable. She was caught up in the rush of the betrothal and trying to sort out her feelings—feelings that unlike his were new and uncertain.

He made it as far as the door. His hand squeezed the metal of the handle. *Open it,* he told himself. *Walk away.* He wanted to. Just like he wanted to stop loving her.

But wanting, he realized, wasn't the same thing as

actually doing. He could hide his feelings behind anger, but they were still there.

She was right: it was simple. He was furious with her, hurt beyond belief, and his pride was stinging, but the inescapable fact was that he loved her. He would always love her, whether she married someone else or she married him. He had two choices: he could be miserable and self-righteous or he could swallow his pride and maybe—just maybe—find the happiness of which he'd always dreamed.

It wasn't a hard decision. He latched the door.

She couldn't see what he'd done—or realized its import—but she'd recovered enough to call after him. "Go then. Walk away just like you did last time."

He turned around, eyes narrowing. "What?"

She lifted her chin. He tried not to let his eyes drop below it, but it was damned difficult. In her anger she'd forgotten she was naked, and she stood there boldly and unself-consciously, and it was spectacular.

"I didn't react the way you wanted me to on the rooftop three years ago, so you cut me off, refused to let me explain or work out my feelings, left for three years, and told yourself you hated me. And I didn't react the way you wanted me to this time either, so you'll hate me and try to cut me off again. But just like last time, I'll be here waiting. Whether it takes you three years or twenty, I'll be waiting for you to find a way in your stubborn, pigheaded, too-proud mind to forgive me."

Thom frowned, realizing there was more truth in her accusation than he wanted to admit. But they were obviously going to have to work on her apologies.

She wasn't done. "And eventually, you know what? You *will* forgive me, because that's who you are. But by then, God knows, our children will have parents who are old enough to be grandparents." Something in her voice broke and tears started pouring down her cheeks. "So go, but don't blame me when I'm old and wrinkly and you can't bear to bed me, because it will be all your fault!"

He cocked a brow, his eyes scanning over her smooth, creamy, and definitely *not* wrinkled skin. His frown deepened as he looked her over again. "How many years do you think I have?"

She was so busy trying to wipe the tears away it took her a moment to realize what he said. She drew back with a start. "What?"

"Before I can't bear to bed you?"

He wasn't going to tell her he couldn't think of anything more wonderful than growing old with her—and wrinkles sure as hell weren't going to keep him out of her bed.

She blinked, tears clumping on her long lashes like diamonds sparkling in the sun. "That is what you respond to? I splay my heart open for you to see, beg for your forgiveness, humiliate myself with a failed seduction, and you want to know how many years you have before I get a few wrinkles?"

He shrugged. "It might take awhile for me to forgive you, but I can try to speed it up if it means I'm not in bed with a prune."

Her gasp of outrage was followed by a widening of her eyes with understanding.

"And I wouldn't necessarily say it was a failed seduction," he added with a long, heated look down the length of her.

She trembled, and he felt himself thicken.

"You wouldn't?"

He shook his head. "So how long?"

Her gaze met his and the hope he read in her eyes filled his chest with warmth. The ice around his heart that had been cracking since she arrived started to break away in thick sheets.

"I wouldn't wait past tonight," she said with a sad shake of her head. "I fear I'm getting older by the minute. The wrinkles are already starting."

"Well, then I guess we better hurry."

The tentative, carefully restrained hope in her eyes felled him. "Does that mean you forgive me?"

He moved toward her, letting the back of his finger slide down the velvety softness of her bare skin. Her shoulder, her arm, the hard tip of her breast. He let it linger there, rubbing back and forth—in lazy circles—over the delectable pink tip.

He couldn't wait to suck it. To circle his tongue around it. To take it between his teeth and tug until she squirmed and arched into his mouth.

His voice softened as he looked into her eyes. "Aye, it means that I've never wanted anyone so badly in my life. That I have been well and thoroughly seduced. That I couldn't walk away if my life depended on it." And it might. In the back—the very back—of his mind he was aware that it wasn't just honor he was risking. "That I love you and can't wait to make you mine."

The look of joy that broke across her face was not something he would ever forget. It made the euphoria of the past couple of days pale by comparison. "Oh, Thommy."

She threw herself into his open arms and he was kissing her. Hungrily. Passionately. Maybe a little desperately. Now that the last barrier between them had been torn down, the floodgates had opened and everything came rushing out hard and fast.

He'd been good for too damned long. As long as he was

going to ignore his honor, he would bloody well make the most of it.

He kissed her until he couldn't stand it anymore. He broke away as much to catch his breath and try to get a rein on the lust teeming through his body as he did to take off his clothes.

He let her look her fill, which wasn't easy given how easy it was to read her thoughts. He was glad she liked his body, but Christ, those lusty looks weren't helping his restraint any.

"You sure have a lot of muscle."

There wasn't much to say to that. He did.

"I like it."

His mouth twitched. "Good."

All of a sudden she frowned. "Will they go away if you stop using the hammer at the forge? Because if they will, I might have to insist you keep—"

"El." She was killing him. He'd waited long enough.

She looked up from his chest. "Yes."

"Come here."

She did as he asked, and he helped lower her down to where he'd covered the ground with his cloaks. It was hardly a romantic bower, and less than ideal for their first time, but in a way there was something right about it. The forge was where they'd spent so much time together in their youth; it had helped bring them to this moment.

She seemed not to mind the makeshift bed, and when she pulled him down on top of her, he didn't either. The first contact of skin on skin was like a combustion of pleasure, firing everything else in its wake.

∞

Elizabeth's heart was beating so fast she thought it might explode. Her senses already were. The feel of Thommy on top of her, of his hot skin pressed against hers, of his solid weight and rock-hard muscles . . .

She moaned, groaned, and begged for more with her body as his mouth covered hers in a frantic, heady kiss.

It was hard to know where she left off and he began. They seemed fused as one. It was magic. It was perfect. It was meant to be. Never had she been more sure of anything in her life.

She was finding it hard to be patient. She couldn't get enough of his mouth, his hands. They covered her body, skimming, caressing, squeezing. And she wanted it harder, faster, rougher. She gripped the muscles of his shoulders, her fingers digging in to show her need, as she dragged his body against hers—the pressure, the friction, the rubbing, exquisite.

He growled low in his throat, responding to her need. She could feel the scrape of his jaw against her fevered skin as his mouth traveled down her throat, her chest . . .

She cried out as he took her nipple in his mouth, the suction of heat incredible. He sucked her deep and hard, letting his tongue circle the aching tip as his hands slid between her legs.

A rush of heat and dampness followed. She remembered what he'd done. How it felt when he touched her. How much she liked the feel of his finger stroking her, and how it had felt when he'd made her explode.

He did it again. His mouth on her breast, his finger between her legs, she cried out as the spasms of pleasure racked her.

He lifted his head, a pained expression on his handsome

face. God, how had she almost given this up? How could she have been so foolish to think love didn't matter?

"You are so responsive that you are making it difficult to go slow, sweetheart."

"Then don't go slow," she said. "I want you inside me." She put her hand on him to show him what she meant.

She didn't know what she expected, but it wasn't the softness of a thin, silky glove over steel. As it seemed the most natural thing to do, she circled him.

He made a sound of pleasure that was so deep and intense it almost sounded like pain.

"Am I doing it right?"

"God, yes."

"Show me."

"I'm not sure I can."

But he did. He showed her how to stroke him. How to find his rhythm. How to squeeze as she milked him.

And still it wasn't enough.

She stopped. "Show me the rest, Thommy. I want to take you in my mouth."

She's a virgin. You can't. Thom kept telling himself that over and over. But it wasn't working. He wasn't listening. All he could hear was the siren call of her mouth. The soft voice asking him if she could fulfill his most sinful fantasy.

It would take a far stronger man than he to resist that kind of offer.

So he told her—or showed her. He didn't know which. But somehow he was on his back, she was sliding down his body, and her mouth was on his cock. Her soft pink lips were sliding inch by inch down the thick, long length of him, and he damned near shot out of his skin.

He came a little, and when she slid her tongue around to lick it up and made a sound of pleasure low in her throat, he knew he was in danger of letting go.

He held her head against him for one agonizing moment, committing to memory every wicked sensation, the heat, the dampness, the softness of her lips and tongue as she sucked, and then he pulled her off. "Stop."

She looked up at him, shocked. "But I like—"

"And so do I—too much."

She let out a startled gasp when he flipped her on her back, but a moment later she was gasping for another reason when he slid down between her legs, looped her legs over his shoulders, and pressed his mouth against all that honey sweetness.

She bucked at the contact and tried to protest, but he gave no quarter. Cupping her bottom, he lifted her to his hungry mouth.

She came at the first swipe of his tongue, and then he made her come some more. He rubbed and sucked, flicked until she was shaking, and then finally gave her the long, slow drag and pressure that sent her over the edge. When he was done, she was achingly warm and ready.

And so was he. He was on bloody fire and harder than he'd ever been in his life.

He braced his hands on either side of her shoulders and positioned himself between her legs. He would give her one more chance. "Are you sure, sweetheart?"

Her eyes were still soft with pleasure as they met his. "I have never been more certain of anything. I love you."

His heart was damned near bursting. "And I love you."

Slowly he started to enter her. Pushing gently, nudging

with rhythmic circles of his hips. She was soft and warm and ready for him—and tight. Very, very tight. But he tried not to think about that as sweat dripped down the side of his forehead with the effort it was taking for him to go slow when all he wanted to do was go fast. When restraint had turned every muscle in his body to steel. When all he wanted to do was pump in and out of that tight, wet fist and—

She tensed. He stopped.

Her eyes went to his. "I'm not sure this is going to work."

She looked so worried he tried not to laugh. But damn, she was sweet. He dropped a soft kiss on her mouth. "It's already working, sweetheart. Your body just needs time to adjust to me."

Clearly she didn't believe him. "You're too big!" she blurted, her cheeks turning an adorable shade of pink.

He couldn't help grinning at that, but he didn't think she'd believe him if he told her she'd appreciate it later. "Trust me, El, it will be fine." Suddenly he sobered. "It may hurt for a moment—you know that, don't you?"

She nodded.

"Does it hurt now?"

She thought for a second, and then shook her head. "It just feels . . . *full*."

Christ. He groaned and sank in a little deeper, kissing her again. She responded, and slowly he could feel her body opening to him again. But there came the point when it resisted, and he knew he was going to have to hurt her. He hesitated—hating it but telling himself only this once—and thrust.

She cried out, her entire body stiffening with pain.

He forced himself not to move, which wasn't easy when

every inch of his body was screaming with pleasure. She was so hot and tight, gripping him like a fist.

They were joined—connected—in the most primitive way. She was finally his, and he wanted to roar with satisfaction. But, most of all, he wanted to move.

With soothing words and tender kisses, he waited patiently—or not so patiently—for the pain to subside. He met the silent accusation in her eyes with whispered apologies and promises between kisses that it would get better.

She didn't believe him. But she would.

When at last he felt her body relax, he began to move. Slowly at first, with more gentle little thrusts and circles of his hips calculated to tease. To entice. To make her body yearn for more.

He made love to her as he'd never made love to a woman before. Because no one had ever been her. It had always just been her.

It didn't take long before she started to make those half-eager, half-surprised gasps that drove him wild. When she started to lift her hips, her body unconsciously seeking more, he lengthened his strokes. Deeper, harder, faster, until they were both lost in the delirium of pleasure.

Virgin.

It was hard to remember when she met him stroke for stroke. When her body responded to every touch with demands that matched his own.

She liked it hard. Liked it fast. Liked it raw and a little rough.

She felt the same frantic need and wicked desire. He didn't need to hold back. Not anymore. It didn't matter if she was the lord's daughter and he was the smith's son. Passion had stripped away the barriers between them. In bed they were one. He gave her everything. And she gave it back.

Their bodies started to move on their own, control and deliberation giving way to sensation and feeling. He didn't know what he was doing, only that it felt incredible and she liked it. She was telling him so, urging him on with words, moans, and frantic pounding of her hips against his.

"Oh God . . . that feels so good . . . please, Thommy . . ."

It was too much. Too perfect. And he'd been waiting too damned long.

He loved her so much.

The pressure twisting into a tight ball at the base of his spine was too intense, the urge to release almost overwhelming. But he had to hold on. Just a little longer . . .

Her gasps started to quicken; her moans turned more urgent. She couldn't meet his gaze anymore, the pleasure was overtaking her. He watched her face as her head fell back, her eyes closed, her cheeks flushed and lips parted.

Oh God, yes. He thrust hard and deep—as deep as he could go—and it was as if he'd set off an explosion.

The first spasm of her release gripped him hard, snapping whatever threads he had left of his restraint. They came together, their cries of pleasure mingling in the sultry air of the forge as their bodies shuddered with release.

He'd never experienced anything like it. The sensations seemed heightened and more intense—more significant somehow—and the emotions deeper. He felt transcended to a different place—a different level of connection—that he'd never imagined.

They were bound together in a way that could not be undone.

∞

It took Elizabeth a moment to regain consciousness—or rather return to any semblance of her senses. The feelings, sensations, and emotions that had taken hold of her were so overpowering they did not give way easily—or quickly. Only when the last ebb of pleasure had slipped from her body did some level of awareness return.

She felt so deliciously exhausted. Her body was warm and melty; she didn't think she could move if she had to. But it was a different kind of exhaustion—a satisfied kind. A contented kind. Although contentment hardly captured the happiness that glowed inside her and seemed to fill her to bursting.

But it wasn't until Thommy rolled off her—taking his heat and solid weight with him—that her thoughts became cohesive enough to speak.

"Thommy?"

She heard the heavy fall of his breathing before he answered. "Aye, love."

He drew her against him and she snuggled into the warmth of his body as if she'd done so a hundred times. Propping her chin on his chest, she stared up at him. He was so unbelievably handsome sometimes it took her breath away. Like now.

"You were right."

He seemed to be having difficulty regaining his senses as well, but he managed to cock a brow. "About what?"

"It did work."

He gave a sharp laugh, and the smile that turned his mouth was so boyishly charming it wrapped around her heart and squeezed. "I think that's an understatement, El."

Having no previous experience to rely upon, she was enormously pleased to hear it. "It is?"

He tipped her chin to look into her eyes. "That was . . . I don't even know how to describe it."

She grinned back at him. "It was pretty spectacular, wasn't it?"

"*Very* spectacular."

"Does that mean you want to do it again?"

He groaned. "God, sweetheart, are you trying to kill me? I need a little time to recover. And so do you—you will be sore. I should have been . . . easier on you."

Was he blushing? She didn't think she'd ever seen him blush before. It was adorable. If a man as physically imposing as him could be characterized as such. "Don't say that—it was perfect." And worth any soreness she might feel. She started drawing little circles on his chest and stomach, the muscles clenching into tight bands at her touch. "How much time?"

He laughed gruffly. "More than five minutes."

But it turned out not much more. The second time he made love to her was slower and less frenzied, but every bit as powerful. Maybe even more so. There was no pain this time, and when he held her gaze as they broke apart, it made everything seem more significant—deeper somehow. The emotions, the sensations, the force of the spasms racking her body, the intensity of the love she felt for him, and the connection between them . . . everything was stronger.

And so was her exhaustion. This time, she didn't regain much of her consciousness at all before falling into a contented and sated—*extremely* sated—sleep.

She was still smiling when Thom shook her awake. But the smile didn't last long.

He cursed, the word he used conveying the urgency before he spoke. "Hurry"—he jumped to his feet and tossed her her gown even as he began to put on his own clothes— "there's someone at the door."

27

NOT SOMEONE. THE voice that had awakened Thom and thrust him into a nightmare was far too familiar. He swore again, cursing himself for falling asleep even as he hastened to pull on his clothes.

"Open the God damned door now, MacGowan, or I swear I'll—"

"Give me a minute," Thom said, not needing to hear the details. His face was grim as he cast Elizabeth a worried glance.

She paled while hastening to put on her gown. She'd obviously recognized the voice as well.

This wasn't good, damn it. Wasn't good at all. Every foul curse word Thom could think of went through his head.

There was only one way it might have been worse. If he hadn't had the foresight to latch the door, they would have been naked and entwined in each other's arms rather than half-clothed when James Douglas forced his way into the forge.

Still, there was no hiding what they'd been doing. James took one look at them, realized what Thom had done, and gave him a look of such horror, betrayal, scathing condemnation, and hatred that Thom knew there was nothing he could say, no explanation that would right this wrong.

It was at that moment, when Thom saw the scene through Jamie's eyes—the crude forge, the cloaks spread out on the soot-stained stone floor, various pieces of clothing still strewn across the floor, Elizabeth half-dressed with the ties of her gown still loosed, her hair unbound and mussed, her lips swollen, the tender skin of her face and neck still pink from the scrape of his stubbled jaw—that the reality of what he'd done hit him, and he felt every bit as base and dishonorable as his old friend thought him.

Guilt and shame twisted through his gut. He'd ravished her, damn it. Taken her innocence when it was not his right to do so—hell, it was a right that still probably belonged to someone else. The king's nephew, as it happened.

He cursed again.

No matter how right it might have felt, it wasn't. He'd known that, but he'd let himself forget.

Thom steeled himself for what was to come but didn't make any attempt to stop it. He'd been on the other side of one of James Douglas's fists many times before, but still nothing could have prepared him for the force of the blow that landed on his jaw like a war hammer. His head snapped back with a burst of pain that made him see stars.

Elizabeth screamed.

Thom barely lifted his head before another blow followed, this one to the gut, causing him to groan and double over.

"I'm going to fucking kill you!" Douglas jerked him up to hit him again. "She's my sister. How could you . . ."

Thom didn't know what to say—what could he? Nor did he try to defend himself from the pummeling. Maybe part of him felt it was deserved.

"Jamie, no! Stop, you'll kill him."

"Good!"

Elizabeth's attempt to get in front of him roused Thom enough to block the next blow and try to keep her out of the way. "Stay out of this, Ella."

"No!" she shouted furiously, tears streaming down her face. "No!"

She turned on her brother and screamed at him to stop. James was beyond hearing, however, and it wasn't until she threw herself between the two men that Douglas swore and stopped swinging. "Get out of the way, Ella, this is between me and MacGowan."

"No, it's not," she bellowed back at him just as angrily. "This is what *I* wanted. I'm going to marry him."

"The hell you are," Douglas said in a deadly voice that left no room for argument.

To her credit, Elizabeth didn't flinch before the man whose formidable "black" rage inspired epitaphs and nightmares on the other side of the border. "Once you calm down enough to listen to reason, you'll realize that there is no other choice. It's too late."

She didn't need to explain what she meant by that. Douglas's face turned so dark Thom thought he would strike him again and readied himself for the blow.

Douglas's entire body seemed to be shaking and he spoke in chillingly clear words to his sister. "If you think I'll reward him for seducing and dishonoring you, you are out of your damned mind. I don't care what happened here."

Her confidence faltered just a little. She paled slightly before lifting her stubbornly set chin a hair higher. "He didn't seduce me; I seduced him!"

Despite his fury, Douglas took one look at her and laughed. "Which only proves how innocent you are.

MacGowan has been waiting for his chance to take advantage of you since you were sixteen. No matter what he let you think, this has always been his damned plan. He wants you and nothing will stop him. Not even his precious honor."

Thom could stand silent no longer. Douglas had a right to his anger, but Thom wasn't the boy with soot on his face who had to keep his mouth closed and accede to his bidding. He was a skilled warrior—soon to be among the best—with more than enough land to provide for her.

"Whether you believe me or not, I did not intend for this to happen. I made a mistake. I forgot my honor. But perhaps I am not alone in doing so?"

The pointed reminder to a battle between them a few years ago when the situation was reversed—when Thom was defending Joanna's honor—made Douglas flush with anger. "This is not about me, damn it!"

"Isn't it?" The anger and resentment that Thom had buried for years emerged. "Isn't it you who sent her away when she was sixteen to keep us apart? Isn't it you who has never thought I was good enough for her? Isn't it you who betrothed her to another man when you knew she didn't love him?"

Douglas's teeth clenched, his eyes narrowed and feral. "I will not apologize for doing what I think is best to protect my sister."

"Nor should you. But what are you trying to protect her from? I may not have Randolph's wealth, but neither am I just a village lad anymore. I can protect and provide for her. I'll have lands of my own and be fighting with the best warriors—"

Douglas laughed in his face. "Not if I have anything to say about it. When I let it be known what has happened here, you'll be lucky to have a hammer left to take back to the forge. You seduced the woman who is betrothed to the king's nephew."

"Was betrothed," Elizabeth interjected, though they both ignored her.

"How do you think they'll react?" Jamie continued. "You'll be lucky if Bruce doesn't have you strung up and Randolph doesn't challenge you. You are done, MacGowan, done."

Struck cold by the threat that he knew wasn't a threat, Thom felt as if everything he'd worked for over the last three years, and all the happiness, all the hope, all the promise of the past few hours, had just been crushed— flattened—obliterated in one cruel blow.

Thom didn't doubt Douglas would do it; in fact, he knew he would.

In forgetting his honor, in taking her innocence, Thom had handed Douglas the sword to destroy him. One word and everything he'd fought for the past few years, every- thing he'd earned, would be gone. His knighthood, his barony, and most important of all, his place among the best warriors in Christendom.

But it wasn't until Thom glanced at Elizabeth that the full extent of the destruction struck him. In the horror of her expression, in the bloodless pallor of her skin, in the bleakness of her gaze, Thom knew that he'd lost everything. He'd lost her.

She was frantic. Desperate. "No, Jamie! You can't! I won't let you do that. Please, you have to listen . . ."

But Jamie wasn't listening to anything. He was dragging her out the door.

"No, wait. I need—"

Whatever she'd been about to say was cut off when Jamie leaned down and growled something in her ear. She paled and turned to look at Thom helplessly.

"I'm sorry . . ."

The words were punctuated by a slam.

Thom sank to the bench where her cloak was still strewn; Jamie hadn't even bothered to let her finish getting dressed. The hose and surcotte lying in a pool on the floor seemed to taunt him with all that Thom had had—if only for a few hours—and lost.

Head in his hands, he fell into a black hole of despair. The blacksmith's son had reached too high. He'd reached for the stars, and in doing so, he'd lost it all: his fortune, his place in Bruce's secret army, and most important, his heart.

The thing Elizabeth feared most had become a reality. If she married him, she would once again be that little girl left with nothing.

He wouldn't do that to her. Even if she still loved him, he couldn't marry her. Douglas was right. He'd be lucky if Bruce—or Randolph—let him live long enough to return home.

But it was all that was left for him now.

"Unless you want my blade in his gut, you'll leave now, Ella."

Her brother's words had stopped her protests cold. Elizabeth knew it wasn't a threat. Jamie was practically shaking with barely constrained rage. She knew she needed to get him away from Thommy and give him a chance to cool down.

Jamie would have killed Thommy earlier if she hadn't

intervened. Her mouth screwed up into an annoyed purse. And blasted Thommy would have let him. She'd seen the expression on his face when Jamie had burst in on them and knew he was feeling guilty and ashamed for what they'd done. Which was ridiculous. And she would tell him exactly that just as soon as she got her brother under control. Men and their blasted *honor*!

The siblings fumed in silence as they stomped the short distance back to the abbey. She was surprised to see that it was still night—from the number of people, probably around midnight—she and Thommy hadn't slept that long after all. Jamie had just arrived much earlier than they expected. He must have raced back in the darkness as soon as he'd received her note.

They had just about reached the guesthouse when Elizabeth turned on him, unable to hold back her anger any longer. But it wasn't just anger. All she had to do was think of Thommy's expression when Jamie had threatened to ruin him, and her chest squeezed equally with despair.

She knew her brother's heart was in the right place—he thought he was protecting her—but right now it was hard to remember that. "How could you, Jamie? How could you threaten to destroy Thommy like that? You must know how difficult it is to do what he's done to move beyond his birth, how hard he has worked for all he's achieved, and you threatened to take it all away from him out of a misguided sense of vengeance?"

"There's nothing misguided about it at all, and it's no better than he deserves for what he did."

"For what *I* did. This was what *I* wanted, but you seem to not want to hear that. But I swear to you, Jamie, if you say one word against Thommy—tell anyone what happened—I will never forgive you." She gave him a hard look so that he would know she meant it. "I intend to marry him whether you give me permission or not."

Stubbornness was a family trait. He practically growled at her when he said, "The hell you will."

She ignored him. "Thom is the most noble man I know—which you know as well as I do."

He barked out a bitter laugh. "Not so noble after all, as it turns out. When I think of all the times he—" He stopped, his mouth set in a hard line. "It doesn't matter. He's going to pay for this."

"Whatever you do to him you do to me."

"You say that now."

"I will say it forever. No matter what you do. I love him, Jamie. Can't you understand that?" The first crack appeared in his anger, and Elizabeth pressed on. "You are my brother, and I will always love you—and I know you are doing what you think is best—but if you make me choose between you, I will choose Thom."

He paled slightly.

She looked up to see that Joanna had appeared at the door. How much had she heard? From her expression, probably enough.

"I was worried," she said by way of explanation. She came outside, crossing the distance to where they stood in the small courtyard. She took in Elizabeth's disheveled appearance. "I thought you weren't going to do anything rash." Not waiting for an explanation—there wasn't one— she turned to her husband. "What is this really about, James? Why are you so against this? You know that she loves him. Are you trying to rectify your mistake?"

When he realized her meaning, he looked horror-struck—absolutely leveled by the accusation. "How can you think that? You know I have never regretted our marriage for a moment. But you've heard the unkind remarks about your 'scandalous breech of propriety'—probably even more than I have. I know how much it's hurt you, and I hate that I cannot shield you from it, but I can't. I can for Elizabeth. It would be even worse for her. Much worse. Doors will be closed."

"So she will open others," Jo said with her simple logic. "I have been hurt, but I would not change anything for the world, don't you see that? And Elizabeth is stronger in that way than I am." She paused. "I am not minimizing your concerns, but if she understands and is willing to accept it, why aren't you?"

He shifted his gaze first. "I just want to see her happy."

"I will be," Elizabeth said softly.

"And Thom is doing well for himself," Joanna said. "He's a hero. It might not be as bad as you think."

Elizabeth and Jamie exchanged a look, the threat hovering in the air between them. Jamie had the good grace to show a tinge of shame. They both knew how Joanna would react if Elizabeth told her what Jamie had threatened to do. But she didn't. Even if he wouldn't admit so now, she knew Jamie wouldn't say a word about what he'd discovered.

"He has done well," Jamie admitted. "But there will always be some who will see him as unworthy."

"Do you?" Elizabeth asked.

The question hung in the cold night air. Years of friendship, years of anger and hatred, all coalesced in one important pause.

"No," he finally admitted.

"I know you want to protect her, James," Joanna said.

"But doesn't she have just as much right to be happy as we do?"

It was the final blow. They both knew Elizabeth had won. But her brother's pride had taken a beating tonight, and she would not drive in the stake. She didn't need to.

Joanna realized it as well. Always the mediator between the hardheaded siblings, she said, "Come inside. Let's get some rest. We can discuss what is to be done in the morning."

Unfortunately, the morning proved to be too late. When Joanna brought in the linen-covered sword that had been delivered to the abbey shortly before dawn, Elizabeth knew Thom was gone.

28

I**T DIDN'T TAKE** Thom long to realize that he'd made a mistake. His father had summed it up quite succinctly on hearing the story not long after he arrived in Douglas: "Did you give the lass a chance?" Thom's mouth had slammed shut. They both knew he hadn't. "If you love her as much as I think you do, you should have stayed and fought. What the hell are you doing here?"

Was this the same man who'd told him for years that

a future between him and Elizabeth was impossible? "I thought you'd be glad that I was back. I thought you wanted my help at the forge."

"I was wrong," his father had said simply. "You don't belong here any more than Johnny or I belong on the battlefield. You would never be happy here. You were meant for something bigger. Didn't what you did at Edinburgh convince you of that?"

"Aye, well, that's no longer an option. So if you don't want me, I'll have to find another smith who does."

His father had given him a long look, shaken his head as if he couldn't believe a son of his could be so clodheaded, and walked away.

Thom had done what he'd always done when he needed to think. Packed a bag and made the half-day journey to Sandford just outside of Strathaven, where he'd spent two nights climbing the rocks and coming to the realization that his father was right: he was clodheaded. If the king's men weren't waiting to arrest him when he returned home, he was going to hop back on the nag that had brought him here and return to Edinburgh. Even if he couldn't convince MacLeod to let him stay on with the Guard, even if he had to fight Randolph, and the king stripped him of everything, he would find a way to provide for her.

Actually, he already had a way. The sword he'd finished for Douglas and had delivered to Jo the morning he'd left had turned out even better than he'd anticipated. Perhaps more significantly, he'd realized that he'd *liked* working on it. It had relaxed him—the work was strangely comforting—and had given him something to concentrate on in between the intense and high-stress missions of the Highland Guard.

Smithing was a part of him just as much as being a warrior was. It would always be a part of him, and he didn't feel the need to hide from that any longer.

His father and Elizabeth had been right, he could make his fortune as a sword maker if he wanted to. He could provide for her.

If she still wanted him, that is.

Clodheaded.

Damn. His step quickened as he drew near the cottage, so that by the time it at last came into view he was practically running. Then, seeing the smoke pouring out of the window, he *was* running.

Bloody hell, the house had caught fire! He grabbed a bucket, filled it with water from the animal trough outside, and rushed inside.

The bucket dropped at his feet, soaking his boots, but he barely noticed.

His father had his arms around a woman, who was covered in soot. Had she not been wearing a beautiful light-pink gown—reminding him of the first time he'd seen her atop the tower all those years ago—it might have taken him longer to recognize her.

Elizabeth. His chest hitched to somewhere close to his throat. *Here.*

She and his father had both turned at the sound of the door—or maybe the bucket dropping—and Elizabeth's devastated expression (his father had obviously been trying to console her) looked perilously close to tears.

"What's wrong?" he asked, his relief at seeing her outweighed by the fear that she might be hurt.

"The lass is fine," his father said, answering for her. "She was making something to break our fast. The bread just got a little . . . well done."

"I burned it!" Elizabeth said. "I wanted it to be a surprise, and now it's ruined."

Thom had no idea what she was talking about. His father explained. "I mentioned that your mother used to put butter and sugar on the day-old bread and heat it in the bread oven—and that it was your favorite."

Christ, with all the smoke pouring out of the oven, she must have used a pound of sugar!

"And I forgot about it," Elizabeth added, "because the porridge started to stick to the pot."

Thom glanced at the glob of blackened goo in the pot, figured that was the porridge, and didn't need to wonder why.

Disgusting. He might have made a face had his father not shot him a look of warning. With a few more pats on her slender back, his father said to her, "I'm sure it will be delicious."

If his father thought Thom was eating that mess, he was the one who was clodheaded. Hell, Thom wouldn't even give those oats to the nag he'd ridden here that'd snapped at him more than once.

"Why are you here, Elizabeth?"

He meant why was she in his father's cottage cooking—which to his knowledge she'd never done before—but she obviously took it more generally. "Did you think I would let you get away with treating me so dishonorably?" She looked at his father as if to say "see." "You left me. Abandoned me after ruining me"—she turned to his father—"quite thoroughly."

"And more than once, I know," his father added with a chastising look in Thom's direction as he took her in his arms to pat her back again.

Christ, was his father really buying this nonsense?

"Don't worry, lass, I'll see that he does right by you. Even if I have to drag him to the kirk myself."

Apparently so.

Elizabeth ventured a look in Thom's direction, and he could have sworn he saw her smirk.

She *was* smirking, he realized. "She seduced me!"

His father looked appalled at the suggestion. "You shame me, lad. Look at that face." He tilted Elizabeth's soot-stained face to Thom. "A wee innocent lamb like—"

Thom snorted, and they both shot him a look—Elizabeth's was more of a scowl.

"Don't believe that perfect little princess act," Thom said. "She had me fooled for a while. But now I know better. She's isn't perfect at all. Did you see that porridge?"

Elizabeth's gasp of outrage couldn't hide her joy. She understood: he loved *her*—not the pretty little poppet he'd seen at the castle all those years ago.

The look in her eyes . . . It was as if all the love she felt for him was staring back at him. It humbled him.

"I'm afraid he's right," she said with a charmingly repentant glance at his father. "I did seduce him. But it was very un-gallant of him to point that out, don't you think?"

Thom could see his father fighting laughter. His eyes were twinkling as he looked at her. "Very un-gallant, indeed, lass." He kissed her on the head and let her go. "Let me know if you need my help—he's not so big that I can't carry him if I need to—but I don't think you are going to have much trouble in getting him to that kirk."

A moment later his father was gone. Without his presence, she seemed to have lost a lot of her certainty, and the gaze that met Thom's was hesitant and vulnerable. "I like your father."

"I do, too." He'd forgotten how much. The awkwardness that had been between them didn't seem to be there anymore. Maybe they both understood each other a little better now.

"You left," she said softly.

"I was coming back."

"You were?"

He nodded, and she ran into his open arms. A moment later he was kissing her, and a shockingly few moments after that, he was carrying her to his bed. The fear of the past few days in thinking he'd lost her seemed to catch up with him all at once. Clearly he wasn't as honorable as he liked to think, because he didn't even hesitate. They might not be married or even officially betrothed, but she belonged to him in every way that mattered. And he needed the connection, needed to feel himself moving in and out of her body, needed to hear her cries of pleasure mingling with his own as they climbed the greatest peak together and soared.

It was later—much later—when he finally found his voice. She was nestled against him, her soot-stained skirts still tangled around her legs. He'd been in too much of a hurry to even remove their clothes—not that she'd seemed to mind. She'd been in a hurry, too.

"You would really give it all up for me, El? The castles, the fine gowns, the jewels, your position in society, to live in a small cottage like this and learn to cook and clean?"

She stopped doodling with her finger on his chest to look up at him. "I don't think I'd have to learn much in the way of cleaning"—her nose wrinkled in the way he loved as she glanced around at the bed he hadn't bothered to tidy before he left or the clothes he'd left strewn around—"and I'm sure my cooking will improve."

As he doubted it could get much worse, she was probably right. "We'll have to buy you some black gowns," he said wryly, which earned him a surprisingly hard punch in the ribs.

"Ouch," he said, putting a hand over the area.

She rolled her eyes. "Don't be such a bairn. You'll have to be a lot tougher than that if you are going to make it through . . . what do they call it? Hell? Perdition? Something like that."

He frowned. "What are you talking about?"

She bit her lip, which he suspected was more for effect than out of any real contrition. "I might not have been completely forthcoming about our future circumstances."

He quirked a brow. "Is that right?"

She shook her head. "I would give it all up, but it turns out that won't be necessary. Jamie explained everything."

"I'm sure he did," he said bitterly.

She shook her head. "He didn't say anything about what he . . . uh, walked in on. I meant that he explained to the king and Tor MacLeod why you left so suddenly and without word—you can't do that, you know." She gave him a pointed look, and then shrugged. "An emergency at home, I believe." She grinned. "If anyone asks we can say it was a fire."

Thom couldn't believe it. Douglas hadn't said anything? He hadn't destroyed him? He'd *covered* for him?

His gaze leveled on hers. "What did you do?"

She bristled with a dainty huff. "Really, Thom, I'm quite

offended. I didn't do anything other than reason with him."

Douglas didn't reason. Thom studied her a little longer. "You told Jo."

She laughed. "I didn't, but I would have. Nay, truly. I didn't do anything. I just told him I loved you and would marry you whether he destroyed you or not, and that if I had to choose between you, I would choose you." He hadn't thought his heart capable of squeezing that hard. "James is waiting for you at Park Castle right now."

All those good feelings immediately evaporated. "What the hell for?"

"For your formal request to marry me." She held his gaze. "Which I have on very good authority that he means to accept."

"Randolph?"

"Taken care of."

Thom grimaced, not liking the thought of being in-debted to Douglas any more than he already was. Christ, at this rate he'd likely be having to name his firstborn James. "How much?"

She shrugged. "Not as much as you would think. We had help. But we will have to put off the news of the en-gagement for a while. When you are done with your train-ing next month will be soon enough."

"You seem to have it all planned out. Am I to have no say in this?"

"You had your say."

"I did?"

"I told you I was going to marry you when I was six. If you wanted to object you've had eighteen years to do so."

But he had no intention of objecting. He would marry her and cherish her for the rest of his life.

EPILOGUE

Park Castle, one month later

Eᴌɪᴢᴀʙᴇᴛʜ ᴡᴀs sᴛᴀʀɪɴɢ out the tower window again, but this time she knew exactly what she was looking for—or rather *whom*.

She turned to Jo, who was seated by the fire working on a cap for the baby. "Jamie said they would be here by now. Do you think something has happened?"

"You have to calm down, Ella, it's not good for—" She stopped suddenly as if remembering something. "You have to learn patience if you are going to be married to a warrior. These things never go as planned."

Elizabeth plopped down in a chair, not hiding her frustration. "But I'm not patient. I hate waiting and not knowing. I never realized how hard it must be for you. How do you do it?"

"I try not to think about it. I realized it wasn't doing either of us any good for me to worry myself to death. Uilleam helps keep my mind off things."

She looked at Elizabeth meaningfully, as if she should be understanding something. Elizabeth frowned. "Aye, I can see why. He's as much of a handful as Hugh and Archie were." She shuddered. "When I have children, I'm going to be much more firm with them."

Joanna looked like she was choking on something before she managed, "I shall look forward to seeing that."

Elizabeth sighed. "I wish Thom had been able to come back from training on Skye before he'd been called away on a mission with James. He's been gone over three weeks now."

"They'll be back soon enough."

Jo was right. When the call rang out from the yard below a few minutes later, Elizabeth was already halfway down the stairs.

"Careful!" Jo yelled from behind her, but Elizabeth wasn't listening. All she could think about was . . .

The moment she ran into the yard she saw him. The impact of emotion that hit her was like a physical blow. It landed across her chest with the force of a hammer. He was here. Dirty, tired, a little grizzled. His hair was longer than she'd ever seen it and his jaw looked like it hadn't seen a razor in a week, yet he was even more handsome than she remembered. But none of that mattered. The only thing that mattered was that he was safe—and by the looks of it in fine form. *Very* fine form. If possible, he seemed even *more* physically imposing. He looked every inch an elite warrior of the Highland Guard.

The relief was so overwhelming it almost brought her to her knees.

She made a sound, and he looked over from his conversation with Jamie—a surprisingly *un*-tension-ridden conversation, she noticed—to see her standing there. When he grinned, her legs seemed to finally remember how to move. She tore across the yard and threw herself into his arms.

The moment they closed around her the emotion that she'd been trying to control came bursting out in a flood of tears.

He held her for a minute, squeezing her tight and whispering soothing words into her hair as he kissed the top of her head. He smelled of horse, and leather, and wind, and nothing had ever smelled so good. She wanted to hold on to him forever.

It took her a moment, but eventually she felt the shaking in his chest and realized he was laughing.

When she scowled up at him, he took the opportunity to drop a too-quick kiss on her mouth, when all she wanted to do was melt into him (he was no doubt aware of her blasted brother standing right next to him).

"Aren't you happy to see me?" he said, his eyes twinkling.

She felt the strange urge to stomp on his foot. "I am, you wretch!"

"I thought you didn't cry."

"I don't." She wiped her eyes furiously. "I don't know what's wrong with me. I'm crying all the time of late."

"You'll be fine soon enough," Jo said, coming up behind her. "The mission with the Earl of Carrick went well?" she asked her husband.

All the women knew was that it had been a raid in England.

"Well enough," Jamie said with an odd look in Boyd's direction. "We had some help from Randolph and his men."

Elizabeth's gaze shot to Thom's, but he shook his head, telling her it had been fine. Apparently, according to James, there weren't any hard feelings between Randolph and Thom. Randolph apparently considered his graciousness toward the man who was now marrying his former betrothed as recompense for Thom saving his life.

"Now I saved his," Randolph had said.

Thom had disagreed that a battle between them would

be so one-sided, but Elizabeth had just been relieved that Randolph hadn't dropped his gauntlet at Thom's feet and demanded a joust or some other knightly form of satisfaction and forced her to find out.

She suspected she had Izzie to thank for that. If she hadn't wrangled the lauded knight yet, she would soon.

Elizabeth was glad not to have Randolph to worry about; preventing Thom and Jamie from coming to blows had been difficult enough. Although she was relieved to see that no longer seemed the case. Elizabeth didn't fully understand the bond men seemed to form in war, but if it helped restore some measure of the former friendship between them she was grateful for it.

Jo had arranged a feast for the men when they arrived, and Elizabeth stopped crying and let go of Thom long enough to greet some of the others as they walked into the Great Hall. Most of the Guard had already gone on to Dunstaffnage to give their report to the king before returning to their own families for a few days, but Boyd and Lamont had accompanied Thom as far as Douglas and would continue on to their families tomorrow.

Elizabeth was looking forward to meeting them all in a couple of weeks for their wedding, which would take place—fittingly—in Edinburgh at the abbey under the shadow of the great castle Thom had helped restore to Scotland.

Jamie would have put it off for even longer to avoid the taint of scandal after the broken betrothal, but with the English planning to march north in June, he knew the men would be called away at any time. Elizabeth didn't care about what people said. She would have married Thom the day he'd asked for her, if Jamie would have let her.

Once they were seated, she finally had an opportunity

to talk to him. "You are well?" she said, searching for any sign of injury.

"Very well," he said, sweeping a few strands of hair from her cheek to tuck behind her ear. His thumb lingered long enough to caress her cheek. "But I missed you."

Her chest squeezed at the loving look in his eyes. It squeezed with something else as well, but thanks to Jamie that would have to wait. He'd made Thom agree that he wouldn't have cause to walk in on them again before the wedding, and Thom was now honor-bound to keep his word.

Her argument that the horse had already trotted out of the stable was met with extremely chastising frowns from both of them.

The next few weeks were going to be torture.

"I missed you, too. Training was not too difficult?" she asked.

He gave her a wry look that said otherwise. "I survived." Why did she think he left out a "barely" in there? "But it's not anything I'm anxious to repeat."

"The swimming?" She knew he'd been worried about that.

He didn't bother hiding his grimace. "Let's just say I got a lot better—quickly—but I will always prefer mountains to the sea."

Knowing there was only so much he could tell her, she didn't question him any further, but promise or not, she intended to do a very thorough inspection of him later.

She hadn't realized she'd been watching the door until Thom asked, "Are you waiting for someone?"

She shrugged, which only seemed to increase his curiosity.

"I hope I do not have cause to be jealous?" There might

have been a certain sharpness to the question behind the lazy tone.

She had to bite the inside of her mouth to keep from laughing and couldn't resist teasing him. "Well, he is *extremely* handsome and talented and is doing a great favor for me."

Apparently, he wasn't in the mood for teasing. It had been too long for both of them. "Ella . . ." he warned.

"There he is right now."

Thom's eyes moved to the door and a moment later, his gaze turned back to hers. "Which one?"

"Both, but in this case I was referring to the younger of the two."

His father and Johnny had just walked into the room, Johnny carrying the favor. Elizabeth rushed forward to greet them, and a space beside her and Thom on the bench was made for them to sit. If anyone thought it odd that the village smithy and his son were seated at the high table, no one said anything.

"Is it ready?" she asked Johnny.

Thom's younger brother nodded. "Aye."

He handed it to her, and she in turn handed it to Thom.

"What is this?" he asked, eyeing the long, linen-wrapped package.

"A gift. Something to show how proud I am of you."

He took it in his hands. Having made enough of them—including the one that hadn't left Jamie's side since he'd been given it (and had inspired all the envy Elizabeth knew it would)—Thom had to know what it was.

He gave her a questioning look and unbound it. Jamie and Jo knew what she'd done, but the others were watching with interest as he drew out the long sword.

It was nearly the match for the one Thom had made

Jamie in skill and design. The blade was strong and perfectly balanced and weighted, the handle and grip tight and molded for his hand, and the hilt and scabbard were decorated with enough gold and precious stones to be fit for a king. Indeed, she suspected when the king saw this one, he would be demanding that Thom finish the one he'd promised to make for him after he'd seen Jamie's.

One day Johnny might even surpass his brother in sword making. But the design and the scene and words etched on the blade—that was all her. Maybe Thom wouldn't be the only one in the family making swords for kings.

She wasn't sure she'd ever seen Thom speechless before as he took in the picture of the famous castle on the Rock etched on the blade. "You did this?"

She beamed with pleasure. The work on the sword had kept her busy, but she'd also liked it. A lot. Enough to make her hope that it might keep her busy some more in the future. "Johnny and I work well together," she said with a wink in Johnny's direction.

They already had plans for a few more. Thom would be busy in the months ahead readying for war and so would she. She'd found a cure for her restlessness—although she suspected it might have something to do with the man at her side as well.

"I hope I did the words right," Johnny said. "Lady Elizabeth"—she cleared her voice and he smiled sheepishly—"Ella said you had an affinity for French."

Elizabeth was trying not to laugh.

Thommy shot her a look. "She did, did she?"

"It says 'Climb high where honor leads,'" she translated.

Their eyes held. "It's perfect," he said, his voice thick. "Thank you."

She nodded. Seeing how moved he was, her chest swelled to bursting. But then one of the maidservants passed by with a tray of mutton and it was her stomach that swelled—and turned upside down. The wave of nausea hit her so hard she had to grab the edge of the table to steady herself.

Thom reached for her. "What is it? What's wrong?"

"The smell," she said, fighting to keep the contents of her stomach in place.

Thom must have looked so worried that Jo took pity on him—on both of them because Elizabeth was just as unaware of what was going on as Thom.

"I think you might need to move up the wedding a week or two," Jo said to her husband.

"Why?" Jamie asked.

Jo looked around at all of them as if she couldn't believe they could be so dense. Only Thom's father seemed to have guessed, and he was almost as pale as Elizabeth.

"Because as it is, your first nephew or niece is going to be awfully big for eight months."

Elizabeth was stunned, but she recovered quickly. Her future husband, future brother-in-law, future father-in-law, and brother, however, didn't demonstrate such resilience. Good gracious, she had never seen so many big men look close to fainting before!

"Will they be all right?" she asked Jo worriedly.

"In about eight months give or take. Just get ready for the—"

She didn't get a chance to finish before the fussing started. Thom growled for someone to get her a pillow— ten pillows, damn it!—not listening when she said she didn't need one; Jamie called for wine, whether it was for himself or for her, she wasn't sure; and Johnny and Big

Thom took turns asking her if she needed anything and if she felt okay—every five minutes.

It was going to be a long eight months.

But the good news was that a few days later, she found herself standing before a priest with Thom—her brother and sister-in-law at their side just as they'd been all those years ago—repeating the vows that would bind her to the noble man who'd captured her heart when he'd rescued her from a tree.

It had taken her awhile to recognize it, but she would never forget it again. Thom had always been her rock, and she would hold on to him forever.

AUTHOR'S NOTE

T HE TAKING OF Roxburgh Castle on Shrove Tuesday 1314 by Sir James Douglas and—not to be outdone—the taking of Edinburgh Castle three and a half weeks later on March 14, 1314, by Sir Thomas Randolph are two of the most renowned events in the almost unbelievable Bruce journey to kingship.

Douglas's taking of Roxburgh during the Shrove Tuesday celebration happened much as I described it: he and sixty or so of his men took advantage of the garrison's inattention and crawled through the field of livestock on all fours in black cloaks to disguise themselves. Using their ingenious rope scaling ladders, they scrambled over the wall and took the castle. I fictitiously gave credit to my sharpshooter Gregor MacGregor, but the incident with the keeper did happen. Guillemin Fiennes, the Gascon commander, had holed up in a tower but was compelled to surrender after being wounded (mortally it turned out) by an arrow to his face.

Historian David Cornell has posited that Bruce hadn't ordered Douglas to take the castle, but that it was a "rogue operation" by Douglas, who decided to try on his own after watching the castle for a while (David Cornell, *Bannock-burn: The Triumph of Robert the Bruce* [New Haven, CT:

Yale University Press, 2009], 118). Noting the "audacity of the operation," Cornell calls it a "momentous feat of arms" (ibid., 118, 120), which is probably putting it lightly.

There is a great story by Sir Walter Scott surrounding Douglas's capture of Roxburgh. After climbing the wall and dropping down into the castle, Douglas comes upon a woman who is singing to her baby the infamous lullaby about the Black Douglas: "*Hush ye, hush ye, little pet ye, Hush ye, hush ye, do not fret ye, The Black Douglas shall not get ye,*" after which Douglas puts a hand on her shoulder and says, "Do not be so sure of that" (Ronald McNair Scott, *Robert the Bruce King of Scots* [New York: Barnes & Noble, 1982], 139). After presumably scaring the life out of her, he gallantly promises to protect her. Whether there is any truth to it, I have no idea, but as we've seen before, Sir Walter sure knows how to spin a good yarn, and his tales often find their way into the history books as truth.

Edward Bruce, Earl of Carrick, either already entrenched in the siege at Stirling Castle or on his way to start, was indeed ordered to Roxburgh by the king to "receive local submissions" (Michael Brown, *Bannockburn: the Scottish War and the British Isles, 1307–1323* [Edinburgh: Edinburgh University Press, 2008], 107) and oversee the destruction of the castle, which was effected much as I described it, by the digging of "shafts" underneath the walls, and then the "firing" of the "timber supports" with "the tunnels collapsing inwards and bringing the great masonry walls of the magnificent buildings crashing thunderously to the ground" (Cornell, 121).

Randolph, who'd been entrenched in the siege at Edinburgh for well over a month by this point, had to have felt the pressure to do something equally daring and "momentous" after his rival's great triumph at Roxburgh. He proved equal to the task by climbing the never-before-ascended Castle Rock to take the Edinburgh garrison by surprise. ·

Thom MacGowan is my version of the local man who was said to have led Randolph up the rocks: William Francis. The possibly apocryphal story is that as a young man, Francis had a sweetheart who lived in the castle and he'd snuck in to meet her. Whether the romantic part of the story was true or not, Francis was rewarded with lands in Sprouston, Roxburghshire, for his extraordinary efforts (G. W. S. Barrow, *Robert Bruce* [Edinburgh: Edinburgh University Press, 2005], 256).

The castle also was taken much as I described it (with the exception of the makeshift pitons—see below) with a diversion at the south gate, and then the thirty or so rock climbers, "before the art had been invented, inched their way in darkness up the steep and slippery north precipice" (Barrow, 256). This route was "so steep and treacherous that it was considered unscalable" (Cornell, 121). Some of the descriptions of this feat in the accounts are wonderful: "the sharp edges of the rocks cut into their hands" (Cornell, 122) as the Highlanders from Moray ascend the crags "with finger holds and toe holds in the crevices . . . clinging to the rock face" (Scott, 140).

John Barbour in his poetic recounting of the story in *The Brus*, probably written about sixty years later, mentions a stone tossed down by the watch above, but the rescue of Randolph by Thom was my addition.

The momentousness of Randolph's feat is still apparent today. One of the first things visitors see upon arriving at Edinburgh Castle is the plaque dedicated to Randolph commemorating this event on the outer wall by the main gate. If you are surprised by the 1313 date like I was, apparently this is the result of a calendar change to what we now consider 1314.

How big were the English garrisons at the castles? The best guess (Cornell, 114) is about 123 men at Roxburgh and 194 at Edinburgh.

Militarily, the importance of the taking of these two castles was enormously significant—it took away key places of refuge for the English on their march north in the coming summer, as well as eliminated places for resupplying the troops. But I suspect the moral victory of wrenching away these two strongholds in such dramatic fashion so close to battle was just as important. To both friend and enemy, it must have seemed as if God was truly with the Bruce, giving the Scot "Davids" confidence as they neared the battle with the English "Goliath."

Despite his late addition to the Guard, Thom "Rock" MacGowan was one of the first stories I came up with when planning the series. I knew I would need a climber for this part of the story and couldn't help but be inspired by the romantic tale of Francis climbing the rocks to sneak in and see his sweetheart.

Both MacGowan and Elizabeth Douglas are fictional characters. It is possible James Douglas had a sister, but his family tree is particularly sketchy (as noted in *The Knight*), although he does appear to have had two half brothers, Archibald and Hugh.

Douglas was sent to France after his father was killed for his safety, which inspired Elizabeth's later trip. The Douglases—including his English stepmother, Eleanor de Lovaine—were dispossessed of their lands by a virulent Edward. James Douglas's inability to get his lands returned to him eventually set him on a path to join Bruce in 1306.

Eleanor, however, was more successful and was able to get her lands returned about three years after William "the Hardy's" death in about 1298. Wondering what happened to the widow and her two young sons in the interim inspired the difficult period faced by Elizabeth.

Because rank and station were so important in medieval times, I knew from the outset that I had to find a way to write about it. The sister of the powerful Lord of Douglas and the smithy's son seemed like a perfect way to do so. I'd already decided on the clan MacGowan (in Ireland McGowan), which in its Gaelic form (Mac Gobhann) means son of the smith, but in one of those serendipitous research moments that I've had a few times while writing this series, the connection seemed meant to be when I discovered that there was a branch of the clan in Nithsdale in the fourteenth century, which just happens to be the location of an old Douglas castle.

Smiths, sword makers, and armorers were specialized fields at this time, and in the burghs and big cities would have been distinct and likely undertaken by different people. Indeed, most of the different parts of sword making would have had their specialists: from the person who actually smelted the ore, to the swordsmith who shaped the blade, to the cutler who made the hilt, and yet another who might make the scabbard. An important lord might have his own armorer, but in small villages a blacksmith might have been more a jack-of-all-trades—from making everyday items like horseshoes, farm implements, and cooking pots to fixing armor and making swords.

When combining my smith's son with climbing, I couldn't resist having him decide to use a spike to help climb Castle Rock, pre-inventing the first piton, which was reputed to have been used by a climber in France in the next century (in the same year Columbus sailed the ocean blue).

One of the most difficult things in writing this novel was trying to import the rigid social structure and the stigma against marrying down to the modern sensibility. It wasn't just "not done," but it was really looked down upon as offending the social fabric, social order, and to some extent, I think seen as failing the duty (and thus a justification) of being noble. Nobles were "different" from the rest of us, and for their place in society were expected to put aside personal desires for the good of the family dynasty.

Society was clearly stratified, and there was a permanence of where you were in the "estates." The three estates were the clergy, the nobility, and the commoners (later there would be a fourth estate for rich merchants, burghers, and the like). People didn't move around a lot—you were what you were born (except in the church, of course)—and everyone had their place and role. The idea of upward mobility is probably somewhat anachronistic, although you could improve your lot by entering the church, to some extent through marriage, or through warfare.

Whereas today we would just say to marry him if you love him, that clearly wasn't the way people thought seven hundred years ago. In the late Middle Ages there would have been real pressure against a marriage like Elizabeth and Thom's where the difference in rank was so extreme. Blacksmiths in times of war were definitely very important people, but they were of lowly status.

It was very hard to get a sense of how common or uncommon marriages between nobles and people of lower status were, but my sense was that from the few examples I was able to find they were very infrequent. The examples I did come across were more like James and Joanna—the difference in rank more mild. Nowhere did I come across a situation with the disparity of Elizabeth and Thom, which isn't to say that it couldn't have happened.

What is clear is that marriages between unequals were so likely to stir controversy and discord that it was thought they should be hidden and kept private, which flew directly in the face of the medieval belief that marriages should be public affairs, requiring the reading of the banns. Significantly, one ecclesiastical author on the subject at the time—a French priest by the name of Pierre de la Palude—counted as one of the six reasons for dispensation from the reading of banns: "Marriage between a person of noble rank and a non-noble, since these unions excited opposition and scandal" (James A. Brundage, *Law, Society, and Christian Society in Medieval Europe* [Chicago: University of Chicago Press, 1987], 442–43). Another one of the six was, "Marriage of a rich person to a poor one, as these upset the social order" (ibid.).

Historian Alison Weir, in her book *The War of The Roses*, referring to the marriage of Owen Tudor to Queen Kathryn, states, "What is likely is that the wedding had to be kept private because in marrying a man so far below her in rank the Queen had 'followed more her own appetite than her open honor'" (New York: Ballantine Books, 2011, 80). Keep in mind that the "lowly" Owen was the grandson of a Welsh prince.

Elizabeth's fear of poverty would have been a reasonable one; going from rich to poor in medieval society would have been a drastic change in the standard of living. Recent scholarship on the standard of living in England in the late fourteenth century before the outbreak of the plague suggests that peasants were actually a little better off than originally thought, with a per capita income of $1,000 (rather than $400 as was believed). Relative to our poorest nations today, this is similar to Afghanistan ($869) (www2 .warwick.ac.uk/newsandevents/pressreleases/medieval _england_twice).

So if we assume peasants (who might earn up to £2 a year) were living a life similar to today's people in Afghanistan, a blacksmith, who might have earned about £12 a year (Thomas Thomson, *Earliest Times to Death of Robert Bruce 1329* [London: Black & Son, 1896], 201) would have certainly been better off, but nowhere near the barons (£200–£500-plus) and earls (£400–£11,000-plus). (Kenneth Hodges, List of Price of Medieval Items, http:// medieval.ucdavis.edu/120D/Money.html.) Talk about one percenters!

Thom as a man of arms would have made slightly more than as a blacksmith, but as a regular knight would have earned £36 and a knight banneret (one who led men under his own banner) roughly £72 (ibid.). To put this in even more perspective, for Thom to have purchased a warhorse he might have needed as much as £80 (ibid.). Other horses were much cheaper.

I used the term merk or mark, which was a medieval monetary unit (and later a coin); it was valued at about two-thirds of a pound. One pound was 20 shillings, and one mark/merk was 13 shillings, 4 pence (ibid.).

If you've read my books and author's notes before, you know that the complex and complicated subject of medieval marriage has been a recurring thorn in my side. I was very happy to avoid it in this book, but then I realized I had to deal with the betrothal. Ugh. Trying to get a sense of how common it was to break a betrothal was just like many of the marriage issues I've faced: it's hard to say.

Medieval betrothals were quite different from today's

engagements. In addition to being a much more formal, contractual event and undertaken by the *family*, breaking one—particularly a noble betrothal—was a much more serious matter. Although, interestingly, it was more of a secular than ecclesiastical issue—the church was much more worried about consent in marriages (and that they be public). As Genevieve Ribordy notes in *Women and Gender in Medieval Europe: An Encyclopedia* (New York: Routledge, 2006, 72): "In a society where honor and the given word were of the utmost importance, betrothals were instrumental in ensuring that the wedding would take place. Although they were optional according to canon law, in reality a betrothal was an important event that could be revoked only exceptionally and with great difficulty."

A quick—very quick—word on Lent. I usually do my best to ignore what was surely the dominating force in medieval life: the church. I do this mostly because it doesn't lend itself well to a sexy romance (my usually unmarried heroes and heroines would be doing a lot of penance!), but I also think it's very difficult to know exactly how rigorously the strictures were applied in everyday life. For example, married couples were expected to abstain from sex every Sunday, throughout the forty-seven to sixty-two days of Lent, for twenty-two to thirty-five days around Advent, for the period around Pentecost, on some other feast days, during penance, while pregnant, after pregnancy . . . you get the picture (Brundage, 155–59). There were so many days where you had to "abstain" from not only food but other delights, so to speak, you have to think that if everyone was taking this to heart there wouldn't have been very many babies born.

Although Lent certainly sounds like a dreary period—especially for the poor—and most people appeared to have adhered to it strictly with one big meal and perhaps one smaller meal at night, even religious houses seemed to find a work-around: "Lent was kept in the official refectory, but not in the infirmary, where the old and sick needed meat to remain strong. Many monks just went to the infirmary for supper" (Ruth A. Johnston, *All Things Medieval: An Encyclopedia of the Medieval Word* [Santa Barbara, CA: ABC-CLIO, 2011], 232–33). This was pretty much the approach I took to religious matters. People would be very conscious of the rules but didn't always follow them.

Finally, Bruce's location during the taking of the castles is unclear, although he was with Randolph at Edinburgh during the beginning of the siege (probably in January 1314) to negotiate with the keeper, who was later imprisoned by his fellow Englishmen for parleying with the enemy. Where Bruce might have stayed is also conjecture, but there is evidence suggesting that Holyrood was used as a royal residence by 1329 and Bruce held parliament there in 1326 (John Gifford, et al., *Edinburgh* [New York: Penguin Books, 1991], 125).

Would women have been in Edinburgh at the time of the siege? It doesn't seem unlikely. Bruce had his wife, daughter, and sisters with him eight years earlier in much more precarious circumstances after the Battle of Methven. Similarly, during a siege of Stirling Castle ten years before Bannockburn by Edward I, his queen accompanied him from England. Much is made of the entertainment factor in watching Edward's new siege engine "Warwolf" at work. A special window was supposedly constructed so that Queen Margaret and other ladies from court might watch (Cornell, 12).

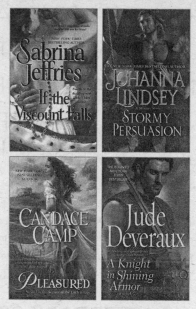